CONVICTED

BOOK #3 OF THE BESTSELLING CONSEQUENCES SERIES

BY:

ALEATHA ROMIG

ALEATHA ROMIG

CONVICTED

You must stick to your conviction,
but be ready to abandon your assumptions.
—Denis Waitley

BY:

ALEATHA ROMIG

-COPYRIGHT AND LICENSE INFORMATION-

Published by Aleatha Romig

2013 Edition

Edited by Lucy D'Andrea and Sherry Weir

Copyright © 2013 Aleatha Romig

ISBN 13: 978-0-9884891-7-2
ISBN 10: 0988489171

-ACKNOWLEDGMENTS-

Thank you to everyone who has made my story *and* Tony and Claire—real!

I couldn't continue to spend untold hours sitting at my computer and interacting with readers if it weren't for the love, devotion, AND patience of my husband and children. Thank you!

Thank you to my fantastic group of betas, affectionately known as *Aleatha's Angels*! Your direction and honesty has helped to create CONVICTED! I couldn't, and wouldn't want to, do it without you! Thank you, Sherry, Val, Angie, Kelli, Heather, and our newest angel Kirsten! Believe me—from time to time—it takes angels to put up with me!

A special thank you to Ilona, a wonderful reader who won a contest and was allowed to name one of the characters in CONVICTED—thank you Ilona—I hope you enjoy your character!

To my agent, Danielle Egan-Miller and my editor, Lucy D'Andrea, thank you! I continue to learn from your wisdom every day!

I absolutely love creating and continuing this saga, but it has been the outpouring of encouragement and support that I've received from the best readers in the world that made this a wonderful journey. I can't thank you *all* enough for the continued love which you have shown to me! Whether it is in person—at an author event or online—I hope you know how much your kind words have meant! Thank you!!

I also, hope that you'll understand how difficult it was for me to end this series. Tony and Claire as well as many of the other characters have become my real life friends and foes...saying goodbye is never easy...but knowing that I'm not doing it alone has given me courage...I hope it will help you too!
Be brave...and learn how with the TRUTH there are
CONSEQUENCES...CONVICTED!

-DISCLAIMER-

This is the third book in the CONSEQUENCES Series. It's recommended to read them in order. The CONSEQUENCES series contains adult dark content. Although excessive use of description and detail are not used, the content contains innuendos of kidnapping, rape, and abuse—physical and mental. If you're unable to read this material—please do not purchase. If can enter this world of fiction—welcome aboard and enjoy the ride!

The evil you create will ultimately destroy you,
you cannot escape the consequences of your actions.
—Leon Brown

CHAPTER 1

-SUMMER 2016-

T he woman stood silently, concealed within the shadows of the tall trees. With the Iowa wind rustling leaves above her head, she watched in fascination as children ran around the well-kept playground. Although many youngsters vied for position on the ladders and ramps, her attention centered on the beautiful, dark-haired little girl and blonde headed little boy playing in the sandbox. She'd seen the children on numerous occasions—always from a distance. She knew the little girl was almost two and a half years old and the little boy was almost two years old. Steeling her shoulders, she decided today was the day she'd finally voice her appeal—face the barrier to her goal—and make her request known.

The children wouldn't know who she was or why she was there. There was no doubt, the woman with the eagle eyes of a mother and aunt—the woman watching the children's every move, wouldn't only know her—she wouldn't hesitate to send her away or call the authorities.

Inhaling deeply, New York Times bestselling author, Meredith Banks, stepped from the shadows into the sunlight. As the proximity of her goal increased, so did her anxiety. This wouldn't be easy. Emily Vandersol had made it crystal clear that she didn't want the children exposed to the media circus. That circus had already exposed too many family secrets—secrets which, for their sake, would've been better left hidden.

As Meredith neared the park bench, Emily's ever present scan of the crowd zeroed in on her, and their eyes met. Before Emily could protest, Meredith rushed to the park bench and touched Emily's sleeve. "Emily, please let me speak. Please...let me finish their story."

Momentarily looking away from the children, Emily stared toward Meredith, her green eyes burned with emotion. Her back straightened as her hushed words overflowed with intended harshness. "You're *not* allowed to be this close to me or to her. I have a restraining order against *all* members of the press."

"I know, but I'm not just the press—I'm Claire's friend—I was"—Meredith added thoughtfully—"Please—I want the world to know the rest of their story."

Emily leaned closer as her perturbed tone hardened. "Don't you think *you've* told enough? One day, I'm going to have to explain your book to her. Don't you think you've done enough damage? Or maybe it's just the money you want. I'm sure revealing more private information will sell more books."

Meredith didn't like Emily's tone. Although she knew she deserved it; she wouldn't let it stop her quest. After all, engaging Claire's sister in any conversation was more than she'd accomplished in the past. "I hope you know this isn't about selling books. Claire approached *me* with her story. We had an agreement, and I followed through. I'm not denying that her story's made me a fortune. What do you want me to say? I'll donate all proceeds from the rest of their story to Nichol? I'd gladly do that, but we both know she isn't lacking for money."

Emily looked up as the dark-haired little girl came running toward them. Undaunted by the visitor, Nichol spoke loud and clear, "Momma"—shaking her little head, she corrected—"I mean, Aunt Em, Mikey's not sharing. I want my..."

Meredith stared, mesmerized by the young girl's features. Her long, dark hair was pulled into two pigtails which swung side to side as she ran. Her light complexion emphasized her pink sun-kissed cheeks, and her deep brown eyes shimmered in the sunlight. Meredith recognized the intensity of the young girl's stare, the perfect combination of her parents; however, the determination and diction in the small voice unquestionably came from her father.

This was the closest Meredith had been to Anthony and Claire's child. With all of her heart, Meredith wanted to pull the little girl into her arms and hug her tight—anything to help make Claire's daughter's world a better place.

While Emily rectified the situation between the children, Meredith pondered the events that brought them all here today—the events that changed Nichol's life forever. Meredith remembered the Claire Nichols of the past—the carefree young woman who skipped class at Valparaiso to spend the day at Wrigley Field. She recalled the woman who recounted horrific details of a life she never wanted or deserved, and she recollected the last time they met— almost three years ago.

Claire had arranged their meeting. She wanted to discuss Meredith's first book *My Life As It Didn't Appear*. Claire desired to stop the publication.

Momentarily, Meredith recalled Claire's countenance—finally happy and obviously in love. While they ate lunch in Chicago, Claire opened up, talking about her change of heart, and confessing her pregnancy. It was a step of faith on Claire's part. Her pregnancy hadn't been publicly announced, yet during that luncheon, Claire entrusted her long-time friend with her special news. Undoubtedly, it could've been a great coup, but Meredith wouldn't leak the news. She'd done that to her friend once before, and the repercussions of that deception would haunt Meredith forever.

Unfortunately, the book was beyond Meredith's influence; it was in the hands of a publisher with specific instructions. Claire offered any amount of money to hide the story—forever. She worried that someday her child would learn the truth behind her parents' meeting, and Claire didn't want that to happen.

Meredith promised Claire she'd try—and she did.

Then, less than a month later, Claire disappeared—the disclosure clause of their contract went into motion. Publication was imminent. Meredith's efforts, along with a multitude of Rawlings' attorneys, were unable to keep the book from being published. Upon publication, *My Life As it Didn't Appear* entered the bestseller list and has broken records ever since.

Meredith hoped that by continuing their story—telling the world the rest of their saga, maybe—just maybe—someday Nichol would understand.

Emily's voice brought Meredith back to present. "The answer is *no*, and if you release any information about Nichol, I'll have you fined, and with my husband's help—arrested."

"I'm not here to expose Nichol," Meredith continued. "I'm here because I want to talk to Claire. The people at the Everwood facility said all visitors must be approved by you; therefore, I'm asking for your permission."

Emily sat taller. "Ms. Banks, I'm not sure what part of this conversation you're not hearing or comprehending, but the answer is *no*." Before Meredith could respond, Emily continued, "Besides, it wouldn't do you any good. Claire can't tell you her story—she can't answer your questions."

"Then let me just talk with her."

"Don't you understand? She can't *talk* to anyone."

"The staff didn't say visitors were restricted due to her condition. They said they're restricted due to your insistence."

"Ms. Banks—so help me God—if I read about this in a news release, I'll come after you myself. Do you understand?"

Meredith nodded and replied, "I want to help Claire—I truly do. I want to expose the truth so the world will know what happened."

Emily continued, "I'm only telling you this because my sister considered you a friend. Some of the doctors call it a psychotic break brought on by physical and mental stress. Others have said it's the result of multiple head injuries." Shaking her head, she added, "Claire hasn't spoken to *anyone* in over two years!"

Meredith's mind swirled. She'd read about the insanity plea. She knew the history and read about the incident. Truly, if anyone had reason to be insane, it was Claire, yet Meredith hadn't considered the severity of the situation. "What do you mean?" She lowered her voice. "Claire *can't talk?*"

"No—not exactly, she speaks. Sometimes she carries on conversations—just not with anyone present. She doesn't know where she is or even that she has a child. Sometimes she's a child—other times she's with *him*. Honestly, out of context, it's difficult to tell what she's thinking at any given time."

"So, when Nichol just called you Momm—"

Emily interrupted, "Nichol knows I'm her aunt, but sometimes, with Michael calling me Mom—she forgets."

"Maybe I could help? I could talk with Claire and help bring her back?"

A tear slid down Emily's cheek as she watched the children's interaction. "If I thought there was a chance, I'd allow you access immediately, but honestly, if those of us who do visit can't reach her—if Nichol couldn't reach her"—Emily sat taller as her tone hardened—"No. Please don't come around or ask again."

"Emily, what about Mr. Rawlings?"

Emily abruptly turned toward Meredith, her tone now a resonating growl of a mother bear. "*He's* gone, and I will *not* allow anyone to mention his name around Claire or Nichol. His reign of terror over my family is done!"

"But one day—"

Emily abruptly stood, dismissing Meredith. "Goodbye, Ms. Banks. I'm taking *my* children home. If I *ever* see your face again or read any of this conversation—anywhere—I won't only press charges, but I'll make it my goal to see you behind bars. Good day."

Meredith nodded in understanding, remained upon the bench, and watched as Emily lifted Michael into her arms and reached for Nichol's hand. Without turning around or acknowledging their conversation, Emily held tightly to the children and walked away.

It was obvious Emily loved and cared for both children; nevertheless, Meredith questioned the fairness of Nichol's situation. If things stayed status quo, Meredith feared Nichol would never know the truth about both of her parents.

The sounds of the busy park were lost to the gentle whisper of the breeze as Meredith contemplated her own children; she couldn't imagine her life without them. She wondered about Claire, unable to imagine the emptiness and sense of loss her sorority sister must be enduring. Everything and everyone she'd ever held dear was gone. Before Meredith realized, the park blurred and tears coated her cheeks.

She'd read the news reports and knew in her heart that there was a story in need of telling. Truly, she didn't care about the money or the fame. Her memory went to a pledge—one made a lifetime ago. She and Claire pledged sisterhood. It wasn't a blood bond like the one Claire shared with Emily—it was more—it was a commitment. Meredith refused to allow her *sister* to be lost forever—somehow she'd learn the truth.

She remembered the day—years ago—when she met Claire in San Diego. During their discussion, Meredith told her friend about a desire to tell the world the *truth* no matter the *consequences*. Perhaps Emily would choose to prosecute; however, as Meredith watched the small family disappear over the hill toward the parking lot, her mind was set. If Claire's mental health and Nichol's solace resulted in arrest—so be it. She'd rather be *convicted* for being a true sister than live her life free and allow that beautiful little girl to live uninformed.

The private mental health facility, Everwood, was as beautiful as the website boasted. It was an upscale residential mental treatment center exclusively for women located in the countryside near Cedar Rapids. On forty-eight beautiful acres it had walking paths and nature trails—perfect for Claire.

Meredith knew Claire's initial institutionalization was the result of a legal plea. At the time of the plea, Claire had been placed in a state operated facility. That placement was short-lived, and she was moved to this esteemed private facility with top-notched security, confidential care, and a respected staff.

As next of kin and power of attorney, Emily Vandersol had complete jurisdiction over Claire's treatment. Without Emily's permission, Meredith couldn't approach Claire in the facility's guest accessible areas, much less Claire's private room; therefore, in order to access her sorority sister, Meredith had to devise a plan. She'd always dreamt of being an investigative journalist—now was her time.

The money she'd made from the sales of her book afforded her children the best education. Currently, that was at a respected boarding school on the East Coast. Although she hated having them so far away, that distance permitted Meredith the time and freedom she needed to learn Claire's story.

Her plan wasn't complicated—if she couldn't visit Claire as a guest—Meredith decided she'd frequent the facility as an employee. She didn't have the credentials to impersonate a therapist or doctor, but fortunately, the center was in need of kitchen staff.

A small investment to a questionable source provided Meredith with a falsified identification complete with a verifiable past work history. She wasn't sure she could remember to answer to a different name; therefore, Meredith chose to use her husband's last name—one she rarely used. An interview and sob-story later, Meredith Russel was hired by Everwood Behavioral Center. As Meredith looked in the mirror, smoothing the white cafeteria uniform, she smirked—a bit sarcastically and thought, *my life's ambition is now complete—I have a minimum wage position.*

The first few days of her new job were merely research. She needed to learn the lay of the land and the ins and outs of Everwood. Almost immediately, she learned Claire was listed as *Nichols*. Claire didn't participate in group activities, group counseling sessions, or eat in the common dining room. Meals were taken to her room, and the note on the computer indicated that on occasion, feeding assistance was required.

Apparently, Ms. Nichols sometimes went outdoors accompanied by her therapist, facility staff, or limited visitors. The first time Meredith saw Claire, her long ago sorority sister was returning from such a walk...

∞∞∞∞∞∞

Claire knew she loved the outdoors. She always had—the wind in her face—the smell of fresh cut grass or newly fallen leaves—kindled warm feelings. She knew it somehow connected to her past—she didn't know how—or remember a name or a face—but something about nature brought a feeling of security. When she was led outside, she'd close her eyes, wanting to see the world as a new place. Often times, flashes of a man in uniform came and went. Claire assumed these feelings and sense of safety also came from her past. Assumptions were much easier than questions.

She didn't question—anything. Claire understood her only access to the fresh breeze or the sun on her skin was when she was accompanied by another person. She didn't always know the person beside her, but she did know accessing the refreshing outside without someone else was against the rules. She knew all about rules and how to follow them. Oh, it was true that, in the past, she'd made mistakes—used poor judgment—or made poor decisions— decisions that resulted in unfavorable consequences. That's what Tony taught her—behaviors had consequences.

Claire preferred positive consequences. Yes, more than once she'd disappointed him. With each passing day, she vowed not to let him down— again. After what she'd done—she wasn't sure it mattered; nonetheless, since it was all she had left—she wouldn't let go—she wouldn't disappoint.

During her days, people with different faces and different voices came and went. Their words weren't real, and sometimes the food they delivered wasn't either. Oh, it looked real. She could even smell the aroma as they entered her room, but if it were real, she'd be hungry. Most of the time, she wasn't.

There were people who helped her shower, dress, and fix her hair. At first, she fought their assistance and intrusion; then with time, she chose to accept their help. In a way, it was comforting. She'd been taught the importance of maintaining appearances, and since day-to-day activities were too overwhelming, the assistance of these faceless hands helped her fulfill her responsibility.

Under no circumstance did she want to disappoint Tony. Sometimes the tears overwhelmed her. After all, she had to live with the reality—she surely disappointed him. *Why else would he not make his presence known to everyone?* Occasionally, people would tell her he was *gone*. Claire knew better.

She knew he was there. Even if the faceless people couldn't see or hear him—he was there. When he came to her she could truly sleep and dream. She lived for his touch—it took away the suffocating ache that filled her otherwise empty life. Yes, there had been times when they were together that there was pain; however, it was nothing like the pain of not knowing when he'd return; therefore, when they were together, she'd compartmentalize that pain away. While he was there, she'd refuse to show her misery. It would remain her private agony—after what she'd done—she deserved it.

Claire remembered every word—every syllable he'd ever said. He told her the offer of a psychiatric facility was to protect her. Now, whether she deserved to be or not—she was protected.

Sometimes people asked her questions. With each inquiry, she'd hear his voice, "*Divulging private information is still forbidden...*"

She no longer questioned what constituted *private information*. Whether it was her memories, their history, or what she wanted to eat, she wouldn't divulge. In an effort to refrain from revealing anything she shouldn't, Claire chose to not speak. With time, that decision became easier and easier—the faceless people's words rarely penetrated her bubble.

Then without warning, the people before her would morph into other faces, and she'd forget her vow of silence and speak. After all, it was so exciting to see long-lost friends and faces, yet as fast as they'd appear—they'd fade away. Most of the time, it didn't matter—whether real or imagined—the people with her rarely understood her conversation. Whenever this occurred, she'd remember her disobedience. The overwhelming sense of shame instigated an internal turmoil that according to the voices *threatened her well-being*.

That internal turmoil would manifest in ways Claire couldn't control. She wanted to stop—to behave—but sometimes she couldn't make her body do what she wanted it to do, and then the faceless people would restrain her. So many images would race through her mind—she hated restraints. The faceless voices would tell her the restraints were for her own protection—so she wouldn't hurt herself. Claire would still fight—after all, she'd never hurt anyone—but wait—she had.

Her history of violence had been well documented, and since she had the capability, it was better to be safe. Then when things seemed lost—when she least expected it—relief would come.

Claire would hear his voice.

She couldn't predict when it would come; she couldn't encourage it, or even beg for it. No, Tony appeared on his own schedule and of his own volition. His voice would come in—a word, a whisper, or a long rambling speech. The deep baritone melody could soothe her like no drug.

When Claire first arrived at Everwood, the faces and hands that took her outside encouraged her to garden. They'd put tools in her hands, but she wouldn't grip—she couldn't. It was too painful. It reminded Claire of the gardens on the estate or those in paradise. In time, the faces gave up. That was Claire's assumption—she didn't ask. No matter the why, they no longer asked her to comply.

On the occasions, when she tried to remember her life—she couldn't. It all blended into the same grayness—the place where dark became light and light became dark—the place between places. There was before—earlier—long ago—once upon a time—when life had color, and there was *then*—the time when all life disappeared—when the grayness won—the time after the dark.

Her efforts to contain the grayness were useless, and with time, she no longer tried. It seeped from every compartment, leaked into her thoughts, and filled every void. Her world—her reality—was gray—colorless.

Then, unexpectedly, like his voice and without reason, hues of color would infiltrate her world. It was the color of unsolicited memories. She was powerless to stop them. Usually, they'd begin well enough with greens of spring and the blues of waves upon a lake. Without warning, an overwhelming pain—a demobilizing sense of loss would stop her. Worse than the gray, this was nothing—not white—not black—NOTHING!

This void wasn't only brought on by the loss of Tony. Oh, Claire knew his ways; he'd return long enough to rekindle the passion, ignite her need, and disappear again. This nothingness was something else—an emptiness she couldn't identify—one that even the gray couldn't penetrate—one that clawed at her heart. If she allowed her thoughts to linger in the nothingness for too long, it tore her soul to shreds, and she felt every slash—fleeting memories of a baby and a fire. It was the most agonizing pain she'd ever experienced, and without a doubt, Claire was a veteran of pain. She'd endured loss, undergone tragedy, and withstood physical suffering—hell, she'd braved death itself.

Without warning, this emptiness would approach—rattle her soul—and bring her to her knees. When it did, her body would collapse. She'd hear a primal plea escape her lips—not a cry—not simple tears on her pillow. She'd hear a wail of torment that no one but she could understand. When this happened—the people would come. They'd speak words she couldn't comprehend and a new pain would come to her arm.

Sometimes she'd scream just to feel the bliss of the sharp prick. The faces and voices didn't understand...she couldn't ask—that would constitute as divulging information; nonetheless, the sharp sensation led to sleep—a reprieve from the conscious grayness and suffocating nothingness. Life was no longer real. Perhaps it never had been and it never would be...

Sometimes Claire remembered black voids. Those thoughts didn't frighten her; on the contrary, the black overpowered the gray—consumed the nothingness and filled her with the promise of intense emotion. Nothing about Tony had ever been gray. There were always colors...blues, greens, reds, and browns. So much could be assessed by the shade of brown. The memory of that brown becoming black made her heart beat faster, pulse rage uncontrollably, and body hunger for the passion only he could provide.

At times, Claire fantasized about Tony's eyes—starring endlessly at anything, remembering his ability to communicate with a simple glance. The sight of something dark brown or black electrified every nerve within her body, but when she saw chocolate brown, it sent her entire being into spasms.

Claire stopped caring, months or years ago. Time was no longer relevant. She had a new goal. It was to wait until he returned, held her, caressed her, and loved her. Until his gaze filled her being, until he consumed the nothingness and made the grayness go away—until he brought the color back to her bleak world.

Claire had been walking outside with a faceless voice. The voice had been talking, and she'd been walking. The air was warm and the sky was clear. Claire assumed it was blue, although she only saw gray—the way things appeared on black and white television. The woman beside her seemed familiar—yet not—as she spoke on and on.

Claire didn't try to listen; instead, she concentrated on walking with the talking woman. This obedience earned her temporary exodus from her desolate room. It was a compromise she could sometimes stand. As they entered the building and walked through the cafeteria, Claire peered beyond her bubble, long enough to see someone familiar. The realization sent her back—immobilized her—memories sped by—colors flooded her gray. She couldn't compartmentalize fast enough.

Before Claire knew what happened, she was on the floor. Shoes and voices were all she saw and heard....

∞∞∞∞∞∞

Meredith couldn't react fast enough. She knew the woman across the room was Claire. Despite her dull, brown hair pulled back into a ponytail and her too pale complexion, Meredith recognized her sorority sister. It was her eyes. Yes, they lacked the luster of their youth, but Meredith had no doubt—the too thin woman with emerald eyes was definitely Claire.

Meredith wanted to call out, but if she did, she'd blow her cover. Briefly, their eyes met, bringing a momentary spark of recognition. Before Meredith could move, comment, or anything—Claire fell to the floor as if she'd been struck. Suddenly, she was lying in a fetal position, shaking her head, and mumbling incoherently.

The woman who'd been walking with her calmly knelt beside Claire and made a call. Within seconds, they were surrounded by other members of the facility's staff. Meredith moved forward in seemingly slow motion as they scooped Claire onto a gurney and slid an IV into her arm.

Meredith's ragged breath pulled at her chest as the needle entered Claire's skin. She quietly eased herself closer to the woman she once knew. By the time she was beside the gurney, Claire's emerald eyes held little sign of recognition. Under the guise of the commotion, Meredith gently touched Claire's forearm and moved her lips near Claire's ear. "Claire, it's me, Meredith. Please help me tell your story."

The trembling woman before her slipped away. Her last gaze toward Meredith was one of relief as the peaceful calm of medication overtook her body. Helplessly, Meredith watched the gurney being wheeled away.

∞∞∞∞∞∞

The pain in her arm was back, but so was the calm. Before the dreams began, Claire tried to process the identity of that woman. She felt an undeniable belief that she should know her, but it wasn't right. The woman didn't belong here, not in her safe haven. Claire's thoughts were scattered...*her* story. No, the story wasn't just hers.

The story belonged to so many others, so many others, who like her, would never be able to tell the world what happened; so many others, who were now silenced—now and forever, yet Claire knew every word—she'd lived it.

Tell her story? No...some things were better left unknown!

People are stupid; given proper motivation,
almost anyone will believe almost anything.
—Terry Goodkind

♠ ◇
♡ ♣

CHAPTER 2

-SEPTEMBER 2013-

Sighing, Claire fastened the final clasp on her luggage and turned toward Phil. "I'm glad you didn't need to fly back to Iowa, to meet with the Iowa City Police Department."

Golden flecks shimmered in Phil's hazel eyes as he responded, "Well, *Mrs. Alexander*, it wouldn't be very *husbandly* of me to let you travel to Venice all by yourself." Nodding toward her midsection, he continued, "Especially, not in your condition."

Claire's hand instinctively moved to her growing baby. With a small smile, she replied, "Mr. Alexander, I certainly appreciate that."

While Phil spoke, Claire made the final adjustments on her dark wig. She'd gotten good at making the fake hair look real. That didn't mean it didn't itch. She was beyond ready to forgo the disguises.

Phil continued, "It seems the ICPD no longer needs my information. The prosecutor's office said they had *new evidence* to investigate and asked that I keep in touch."

"Hmm," Claire hummed in agreement as she placed a few more hairpins. When her lips were clear, she asked, "I wonder what new evidence came their way?"

Stepping behind her, he gazed into their reflection. When their eyes met, he grinned and answered, "Since I heard your end of the conversation, I'd say they were informed of a very—"

A loud knock interrupted Phil's words. The straightening of his stance told Claire he saw the concern in her eyes. Every contact was suspicious and required scrutiny. Phil nodded silently, stood taller, and walked toward the door.

Claire didn't realize she'd been holding her breath until she released it, hearing her husband announce, "It's the bellhop. Are you ready to leave?"

Allowing her shoulders to relax, Claire took one last look around the suite. The luxurious furnishings paled in comparison to the lovely view beyond the balcony. As the sun rose in the East, hues of blue and sparkling waves danced across the water of Lake Geneva. The unseasonably warm breeze bathed her cheeks as she paused and gazed at the sight for one last time. She knew it was time to go; their things were packed and ready. Exhaling, she replied, "Yes, I'm ready to move on."

Phil nodded as he opened the door and allowed the hotel employee to enter.

"*Signore, Signora,*" Although the predominant language of Geneva was French, the *Alexanders* were thought to be Italian, as such, even the staff addressed them in their *native* language. Truthfully, most residents of the metropolitan city spoke fluent French, Italian, or German, or a combination.

Claire silently reached for her purse as her husband instructed the staff regarding their luggage. Standing patiently, Phil placed his arm casually around his wife's waist and led her toward the elevator. Their performance remained flawless as they sat within the confines of the taxi.

The streets filled with people blurred as Claire contemplated her future. "Are our reservations set?" Claire asked in a whisper.

Phil leaned closer. "Yes, *my dear*, let's discuss it further in private."

Claire sat straight, gazed toward the driver, and nodded. No one could be trusted. She reminded herself to be mindful of listening ears. Disappearing into the night was Phil's specialty. Doing that with a pregnant wife and multiple pieces of luggage was a new test of his clandestine skills.

As the early morning streets of Geneva passed by the windows, Claire reflected on her last piece of business. She'd made one last visit to the financial institution, the one that only a few days ago made her an incredibly wealthy woman. If the bank employees were surprised to have *Marie Rawls* visit for a second time, they didn't show it; instead, they willingly took her to the safety deposit box where she completed her business. Claire couldn't be one hundred percent certain, but her intuition told her that—when push came to shove— Tony would make his way to this hidden fortune. She decided his pot-of-gold shouldn't be totally empty. She also knew the contents she left wouldn't make him happy; nevertheless, this time, it was *her* game—she was the one holding the cards. He'd follow her rules, or he wouldn't. She had no intentions of trapping him. No, she knew what that was like. In their figurative game of chess, she had him in check. If she'd taken the conversation with Marcus Evergreen another direction then it could have been check-mate. Watching the sidewalks fill with people, Claire wondered if Tony deserved the opportunity she was providing.

Truthfully, she couldn't answer that question. She could only say that she *wanted* him to have the opportunity. With that said, what he did with the opportunity was his choice.

Phil gently squeezed her hand. "You seem far away. Are you going to be all right?"

Claire shrugged. "I don't know. I guess time will tell." She wondered how she and Phil had come this far, how their interaction had become so casual. Given their initial meeting in San Antonio, it seemed unlikely. Sighing, Claire turned back toward the window as the car slowed. It seemed very few of the relationships in her life could boast normal beginnings. Placing her hand gingerly over her midsection, she prayed for a normal ending.

Their reservations on *Air France* had them leaving Geneva early in the afternoon and flying directly to Rome. They both knew they'd miss their flight. Phil had a private plane waiting to whisk them away from Switzerland and take them directly to Venice. Claire's new-found wealth allowed him the luxury of creating a rather tangled web of trails. She wasn't sure if anyone would seriously try to unravel their trail, but if they did, she agreed Phil was making it difficult.

Once they arrived in Venice, their identities would again change. Sometimes Claire felt as though she needed a name tag to help her answer to the correct name. She really didn't care what name she used as long as she could forgo the wigs and colored contacts.

Unfortunately, her sister, Emily, was working overtime to keep Claire's name and face in the news. The last information Claire read online said she was still missing and speculations were centered on Anthony Rawlings. It reassured Claire to know that her call to Evergreen cleared Tony's name.

If Claire could make one more call, it would be to Emily. As she and Phil rode toward the airport, she remembered how it felt to have her communication restricted by Tony. Ironically, she recognized she was once again in the same situation. This time, Claire didn't know who to blame. *Was it Catherine's fault?* After all, she was the reason Claire fled. *Or was it Tony's?* If he'd never taken her—Claire couldn't even imagine that scenario. Her life was so different than anything she'd foreseen in her youth; nevertheless, she reminded herself if Tony had never taken her then she wouldn't be having his child. Tears threatened to permeate her colored contacts as Claire accepted the truth. Her current state, current deception of friends and family was self-imposed. She couldn't place blame anywhere but on the woman in the mirror, no matter who she looked like at any given moment. Once again, her impulsivity played into her opponent's hand. When the cards were dealt, Claire should've demanded a re-deal. She should've stayed true to the agreement she'd made with Tony, and she should've trusted him; instead, she wagered with fear and went full in.

The payoff, the safety of her child, was too important. Claire needed to see the game through until the end—folding wasn't an option.

Mr. Evergreen explained that the FBI would soon be involved and instructed Claire to check in periodically. Evergreen warned that the FBI would more than likely want direct contact; however, Claire wasn't willing to give the prosecutor anything more than Geneva as her current location. She'd lived through too many lies to trust anyone.

Claire agreed to Evergreen's terms in that she'd remain hidden and safe. During her conversation with Marcus, she didn't mention she had assistance. The information didn't seem relevant. In this high stakes poker game, Phil was her ace in the hole.

Claire appreciated Phil's concern. His desires toward her had been acknowledged. She knew that she was more than a job to him. If circumstances were different, she might entertain the idea of reciprocation; however, he understood her stance. Her acceptance of his platonic affection was purely for her and her child's safety. She'd promised Marcus Evergreen she'd remain temporarily under the radar, and in return, he'd keep Tony safe. Phil helped her fulfill her side of that agreement.

∞∞∞∞∞∞∞

-TEN DAYS LATER-

Harry looked at the screen of his phone and his eyes grew wide. Glancing around the room, he saw Amber's expression. No doubt, by his sudden change in demeanor, she knew something was up. He steadied his expression and nodded.

"Who is it?" Amber asked in a hushed tone as the rest of the room continued chatting.

Harry didn't respond; instead, he stepped quickly from Amber's kitchen and the collective ears present. Before he knew it, Harry was standing in Claire's old bedroom and answering his phone, "Hello, this is Agent Baldwin."

The call was not only a surprise, but an overwhelming relief. He listened carefully as Agent Williams, Special Agent in Charge of San Francisco FBI, explained the new turn of events: Claire Nichols was alive, safe, and hiding overseas. She'd personally contacted the Iowa City prosecutor who immediately informed the FBI. Even more interesting was the tale of deception Ms. Nichols spun to Mr. Evergreen. She claimed that though she'd left town because she feared for her safety, she now had reason to fear for the safety of Anthony Rawlings, and she emphasized—under no circumstances was she implicating her ex-husband of any wrongdoing.

With each word, the muscles in Harry's shoulders relaxed. Up until that moment, he'd fooled himself into believing he wasn't worried about Claire.

From the second Harry hung up the telephone after the bizarre call from Anthony Rawlings, asking him if he knew where Claire had gone, he told himself, *Claire made her own decisions.* She'd put herself willingly in Rawlings' sphere of influence and deserved to reap the consequences. Rawlings was responsible for her disappearance, either from his own doing or as a by-product of his wealth. Either way, it was no longer Harry's concern. Besides, she was pregnant with Rawlings' child.

Then, without warning, he'd remember her voice. For a split second, that time when the conscious mind wasn't fast enough to stop the unconscious thoughts, he'd wonder what would've happened if the child was his. He'd see Claire's picture flash across the television screen or hear Emily's worried voice and the concern, he'd told himself Claire didn't deserve, would flood his chest.

Listening to his supervisor, that concern now seeped out. Standing in Claire's room, hearing that she was indeed safe and alive gave birth to tears of relief which trickled down his cheeks. Of course, Harry couldn't let that emotion infiltrate his voice—hell, his attachment to his assignment was part of the reason he'd been relieved of his duties: their connection truly severed.

It was after Patrick Chester's attack and after the news of possible fatherhood that SAC Williams personally placed Agent Harrison Baldwin on temporary leave. Williams claimed the publicity over Chester's attack threatened to expose their long time operation. Permanent termination from the bureau was threatened during more than one conversation.

None of that mattered anymore, as Harry listened and the SAC briefed him on the new developments. When Williams emphasized Rawlings' innocence, Harry could no longer hold his tongue. "I know what that bastard did to her in the past. Maybe she's speaking under duress?"

SAC Williams replied, "I haven't spoken to her directly, but Evergreen believes her."

"Sure he does. This time, her testimony helps Rawlings. Evergreen's a Rawlings pawn. When she had something to say against him, the damn prosecutor wouldn't listen and spun everything against her."

"Listen Baldwin, if the Deputy Director hadn't specifically asked for you to be back on this case, it wouldn't be happening. If you're going to make this work, then you need to get your head straight."

Harry nodded. Williams was right. If he were to help again and learn more about the secrets involving the Rawls' vendetta, then he needed to think like an agent—not a boyfriend. "Yes, sir, I understand. I'm grateful to be allowed back on this case."

"Be at our office tomorrow at 9:00 AM. You're taking a trip."

His chest burst with excitement. This was an opportunity he couldn't afford to miss. "Sir, what about Rawlings? Where's he?"

"He's currently in FBI custody; although, I don't anticipate that being the situation for long. We'll discuss this more when you arrive."

"I understand." Harry continued, "Special Agent, if there is questioning of Rawlings to be done, I request to be involved."

"I believe you were told Ms. Nichols cleared Mr. Rawlings of anything to do with her disappearance."

Harry leaned against the wall and took in the empty room. Claire hadn't lived there in almost three months. Her things had been packed and shipped, yet if he closed his eyes, he could see her face and hear her laugh. The scent of her favorite perfume lingered in the recesses of the room and lofted into his senses. He shook his head and tried to focus. "Yes, of course. I'll be there tomorrow."

"Agent, this goes without saying; however, I realize you've became close to Ms. Nichols' family. This information is classified—no one else can know."

Harry thought about the people in the kitchen: *Amber, Keaton, John, Emily, and Liz. How could he possibly walk out there and not tell Claire's sister that Claire was alive?*

Harry swallowed hard. "Yes, sir, I understand. Thank you, Special Agent, for this opportunity."

"Don't blow it, Agent Baldwin. It may be your last chance."

"I won't, sir."

After Harry disconnected the call, he walked into the attached bathroom. Looking at his reflection, he worked to subdue the smile that begged to fill his face. Finally, he gave in to the relief. Tears flooded his eyes, and his grin emerged as he whispered, "Thank you God. Thank you for keeping her safe. Just help me nail that son-of-a-bitch once and for all!"

I regret those times when I've chosen the dark side.
I've wasted enough time not being happy.

—Jessica Lange

CHAPTER 3

Tony made no attempt to subdue his glare. This ridiculous mockery had gone on for far too long. The walls of the small interrogation room were beginning to close in around him. He didn't try to keep his volume in check as he addressed the FBI agent across the table, "Agent Jackson, I've been listening to you for hours and I've—"

Brent interrupted, "What my client is trying to say is—if you don't plan on charging him with a crime, we're leaving."

Agent Jackson pulled out a binder of papers. It was surprising he could locate anything within the clutter of jumbled stacks upon the table. While Brent had more recently arrived, Tony had been sitting there for hours, listening as the FBI agents tag-teamed his interrogation. One would ask questions and then disappear. Moments later, another agent would enter the room and resume the inquisition. The barrage was taking its toll; between the throbbing in his head and the ache in his back, Tony was ready to leave the small room. He didn't care how—he just wanted out.

Agent Jackson leaned forward. "I'll tell you what; I'm tired—you're tired, and I don't anticipate this ending anytime soon. The Bureau has kindly arranged for you, Mr. Rawlings, to spend the night. Mr. Simmons, by signing the gag order and release forms, you too will be provided accommodations until this situation is resolved."

Brent stood. "This is Anthony Rawlings, CEO of Rawlings Industries. You cannot hold him without probable cause."

Agent Jackson stood to meet Brent's gaze. "Despite your client's recent loss of memory, I guarantee we have probable cause; however, if you gentleman aren't ready to call it a night"—he handed Brent the binder—"Then I suggest you and your client review this testimony. We can continue this discussion in a few hours."

Tony's blood boiled. He'd spent hours being questioned about Claire, their relationship, and her disappearance. Not once had anyone from the FBI volunteered information regarding her safety or whereabouts. Getting angry hadn't produced any results; he decided to try cooperation. Slapping his hand on the table, he exhaled. "If this will help you find Claire, I'll stay, but once again, I'm telling you, I had nothing to do with her disappearance. I want her found—safe and sound. If you have information regarding her whereabouts, I deserve to know."

Agent Jackson looked at his watch. "Mr. Rawlings, what you *deserve*, has yet to be determined. Gentlemen, I'll have food delivered. I suggest you utilize this time as a meeting of the minds. This case has taken unexpected twists and turns, and I want answers when I return."

Tony looked down at his hands. This man and the whole damn FBI were holding him essentially against his will. He hadn't had this kind of restriction placed on his comings and goings since childhood—it was absurd. As Agent Jackson left the room, Tony didn't bother to stand; being polite to the man holding him hostage wasn't high on Tony's priority list.

His mind spun trying to decipher meaning from the agent's questions. Agent Jackson asked Tony when he last saw Claire. He asked if he'd spoken to her while he was in Europe. Why he cut his European trip short? Why he hired a bodyguard for Claire? What happened in California that led to Claire's hospitalization? After showing pictures of Claire with Harrison Baldwin, the agent asked if Tony was sure he was the father of Claire's unborn child.

Yes, that innuendo could have landed Tony in custody for assault, if Brent hadn't been quick enough to separate the two.

Looking around at the drably painted walls, he rolled his head upon his shoulders and looked toward his friend and attorney. It was their first opportunity to speak *alone* since Brent's arrival. Tony cleared his throat. "Thanks for getting out here to Boston so fast."

Brent's stance softened. "You know it's true; they can hold you up to forty-eight hours without charges."

"Why won't they give us any information on Claire?"

"I'd assume they want to learn what you know first." As Brent spoke, he opened the binder. Tony watched Brent's face blanch as he scanned the pages. For minutes, Tony sat and studied his friend's expression. With each passing second Brent's expression became harder and grimmer.

As the tension grew, Tony asked, "What is that?"

Brent didn't answer; instead, he walked to a chair in the corner of the room, turned on another light, and continued reading.

"I'm getting fuck'n sick of no one answering my questions," Tony muttered as he paced about the room. The day had been too long.

Tony thought pensively about Sophia and wondered if she'd shown up for dinner at the Inn at Crown Pointe, only to be stood up. Glancing at Brent engrossed in his reading, Tony collapsed once again in the metal chair, placed his elbows on the table and supported his head. In desperate need of a reprieve, Tony closed his eyes and tried to push his concerns for Claire away.

What did unexpected twists and turns mean? Could Claire be—dead? No! Tony refused to believe that.

Behind his closed lids, he didn't see the darkness of escape; instead, emerald green filled his imagination. *When was the last time he saw her?* They asked him that over and over. He'd seen her image on his video surveillance getting in the car, but in person—he remembered it vividly:

It was early—very early—the morning he left for Europe—much earlier than Claire liked to wake. As the first rays of sunlight emerged from behind the heavy drapes, Tony was ready to leave. Claire wasn't stirring, yet he didn't want to leave without talking to her. Actually, she'd asked him to wake her; however, as he stood watching, she looked so peaceful and content. He hated disturbing her slumber.

Her rhythmic breathing moved pieces of her hair as they hung over her beautiful face. Before he could stop himself, Tony brushed the strands away from her cheek. Beneath the disheveled brown hair he found pink, slightly parted lips. Without hesitation he bent down and touched his lips to hers. The warmth of his kiss stirred her, causing her face to incline toward his. Though her eyes were still closed, her lips engaged as she reached for his neck.

Her sleepy voice questioned, "You woke me up before you left?"

"You told me to."

Her eyes opened, revealing a bewildered expression.

"Why are you looking at me that way? You said you wanted me to wake you."

"I know." She sat up, their gaze unbroken. "I'm just not used to you listening to me, or doing what I say."

He pressed closer, feeling the sensation of her breasts against his chest. "Well, we could go back to—"

Claire shook her head as she, once again, surrounded his neck with her arms. "No, I like this better."

His devilish grin couldn't be contained. "Well, last night you didn't seem to mind a few directions or should I say suggestions?"

Her cheeks reddened as she hid her face in his shoulder. "Yeah, well, I like that too."

Taking her chin in his gentle grasp, Tony searched her eyes. He could get lost in the depths of the green—emerald green—so deep and rich. "I was hoping I could change your mind about joining me on this trip."

Their noses nearly touched as her lids fluttered and her expression softened. "When do you need to leave?"

It wasn't the response he wanted; he wanted her to say she'd come to Europe with him. "The plane's ready. Eric's waiting in the car."

Claire's expression beckoned, her fingers found the buttons of his shirt, and her words came between butterfly kisses to his neck, "I don't think"—"Eric would mind"—"waiting a little longer"—"Besides"—"you're going to be gone"—"for almost two weeks"

As Claire's fingers moved toward his belt and her lips touched his newly exposed chest, Tony's travel plans seemed suddenly insignificant. Then, before Tony could take this moment any farther, Claire kissed him, smiled, and said, "Give me a minute."

"Seriously, you're going to do this to me and walk away?"

Claire didn't look back as she walked toward the bathroom, giggled, and mumbled something about 'it' being his fault. She was right. The pregnancy was his fault; nonetheless, watching her in nothing but her long silk nightgown, he couldn't help grinning. Her normal clothes didn't accentuate their growing baby, but in that nightgown, he could see her growing midsection plain as day. When she returned, he was back in bed. His travel clothes neatly piled on a nearby chair.

As Claire started to climb in bed, their eyes met and Tony shook his head.

"What?" she asked, as her smile melted his soul.

He tried for his most formidable voice. "Ms. Nichols, you started this. I believe you are excessively overdressed."

Her demeanor looked anything but intimidated. She barely hesitated as she ignored his comment, climbed onto the bed, and pushed Tony back onto his pillow. Hovering above him, he inhaled the scent of toothpaste as Claire's freshly brushed hair swept across his face. With a sexy smile she challenged his demand, "Then, Mr. Rawlings, I suggest you do something about that." Within seconds, their worlds reversed. Claire was pinned to her pillow, her nightgown gone and her hands secured above her head. Her giggle quickly became a moan as her eyes closed indicating her approval of his actions.

It wasn't just the moan that indicated her approval—no, her entire body approved, as did his. For the next forty minutes they were lost within one another. Tony couldn't help caressing and kissing her midsection as he moved up and down her sensual body. Her soft skin and amazing scent dominated his thoughts. Any concerns of his impending departure disappeared.

When he finally redressed and started to leave, her aura pulled him back for one last kiss. "I love you and I'll be back as soon as I can. I wish you were coming."

Her eyelids fought an unseen weight. "Travel safely. I love you, too."

As he pulled the covers over her soft exposed skin, he asked, "Are you going back to sleep?"

She nodded. "Yes, I think after that strenuous morning workout, I need a nap."

Grinning, he kissed the top of her head and watched as her smile faded, her eyes closed, and she appeared blissfully serene. It was then Tony remembered something he wanted to say. With more authority in his tone, he added, "Claire."

Her eyes immediately opened. His tenor wasn't playful. Although Claire didn't speak, she obviously recognized his change in meaning. Perched on the edge of the bed, Tony reminded her, "If you leave the estate—"

She stilled his words with the touch of her hand. The large diamond on her left hand glistened, as she responded appropriately, "I promise, I'll take Clay."

"This isn't debatable."

"Tony, I'm not debating — I'm trying to sleep."

He kissed her lips. "I'll call when I touch down in London."

She nodded. "Be safe. I think Eric's waiting."

Tony hadn't relived that memory in over a week. All the questioning from the FBI brought it back along with so many others. They seemed so real, he wanted to reach out and touch her. For just a moment, Tony believed he could actually smell her perfume.

The slap of the binder hitting the aluminum table pulled Tony from his fantasy and back to reality. He must have fallen asleep. "What the hell?"

"Food's here." Brent's voice sounded strained.

"What were you reading?"

"I gave it to you, but you might want to eat first. It sure as hell ruined my appetite."

Tony looked suspiciously at the binder as Brent continued, "Since I'm your personal counsel, we need to talk about it. As your friend, I don't want to." Brent grabbed a Styrofoam box and leaned against the wall.

With an overwhelming feeling of doom, Tony pushed the food aside and picked up the binder. Instantly, the words on the page assaulted him. They weren't new—they weren't a revelation—they were, however, supposed to be gone.

Three years ago, Marcus Evergreen informed him of Claire's testimony. At that time he made deals and greased palms. This documentation was supposed to disappear. He paid quite a bit of money to get it lost in the shuffle. His pulse raced as he thought about promises he'd heard. *Now—now not only was it present—it was in the hands of the FBI! Brent had just read it!* Tony's heart sank. Brent was right, his appetite was gone. He paced the confines of the small room and began to read:

January 26, 2012: Claire Nichols Rawlings:

I swear my recounting to be true, to the best of my knowledge. I met Anthony Rawlings March 15, 2010 in Atlanta, Georgia at a restaurant named the Red Wing. I was tending bar and he was a customer. That night I agreed to meet him at the bar for a drink. We had wine and talked for about an hour or so. I left the bar alone. The next day, he called the bar and asked me out on a date. Initially, I declined his offer. He was persistent and I agreed to a date the next night. I knew his name, but didn't know who he was. I really didn't.

On the 17ᵗʰ of March, he picked me up at the Red Wing after my shift. Earlier that day, I went grocery shopping. I think that's significant. It proves I had no intentions of walking away from my life. I had milk in the refrigerator! After dinner, I agreed to go to his hotel room for dessert and some more wine. He was friendly and sensual. I do admit that I slept with him that night.

The next time I woke, I was in his home in Iowa. I didn't know where I was. I remember very little about how I got to Iowa. There are flashes of memories—none of them are good. I remember crying and banging on the door. I remember begging for someone to let me out of that room. I remember being restrained.

Oh God, I remember him...

Tony's vision blurred. He didn't want to relive these memories. The ones of her smiling and happy, those he wanted. Not this. His stomach churned. *Had that really been him? Had he truly done those awful things?* Closing his eyes, he saw beyond the words. He remembered what Claire's account never would—he recalled the hours the drugs took away from her:

Claire dozed peacefully on the king-sized bed, in the Presidential suite of the Ritz Carlton as Tony eased himself out of bed. Watching her closely, he emptied one vial of GHB liquid into her wine glass. He'd been told combining it with alcohol would accelerate his desired response. He poured more wine and sniffed. It didn't smell different than normal wine.

Easing himself back into bed, he moved toward her radiating warmth. This was really it! He'd wanted this for so long and it was finally here. When Claire accepted this dinner invitation, she'd secured her fate. Truthfully, that future had been secured years ago, her acceptance of dinner only made it easier. Watching her sleep, he thought about the sex. Yes, that would be a great bonus. She could pay the Nichols' debt and he could keep her busy. Running the tips of his fingers over her collarbone he sighed. This was so much better than he'd imagined.

Now, he needed to get her to Iowa.

She turned toward him and smiled a sleepy smile. "I really need to get back to my place. I don't want to disrupt your schedule." Claire started to move away as she added, "I'm sure you're busy."

Tony reached for her arm. Her soft skin and toned bicep flexed slightly at his touch. She was everything a twenty-six year old woman should be and more. He wanted to explore every inch of her, but first he had a mission to accomplish.

Despite his efforts to the contrary, his sexual desires were making themselves known.

Trying for his most sensual tone, he said, "I promise this isn't a disruption, and maybe after some more dessert, we could have another glass of wine? There's still some in the bottle from room service." The dessert he had in mind wasn't the remnants of Crème Brulée on the nearby table.

He waited for an answer. Though it wasn't verbal, Claire laid her head back on the pillow and looked into his eyes. Tony didn't want to see the trust in those eyes. They were too innocent and pure. In all his research, he'd never gazed into the depth of her emerald soul, and he didn't want to do it now. He lowered his lips to her collarbone and tasted her skin, moist from earlier "dessert". Her body arched as he tantalized the tips of her firm breasts. The knowledge that she'd soon be his for the taking—whenever and wherever he desired—threatened to push him to the brink too soon.

Would she always be this accommodating? How would she handle her new reality? As he nibbled at the now hard nubs, he didn't care—it didn't matter. What mattered was how he'd handle it. She would be as accommodating as he wanted... her penance for the sins of her forefathers.

Supporting himself above her petite frame, he lingered in the aftershocks of their merger, contemplating his acquisition. Each time his hips moved, her body responded in sync. He could stay like this for hours, but that would need to wait, for another day. Smiling, he considered all the "another days" they had in their future. Not wanting to move away, Tony peered down to see her eyes part in that not quite open, not quite shut, satisfied gaze. He offered, "Can I get you a drink or something to eat?"

"I really don't think I want you to move."

"Oh?" he cooed, as he teased her with each gyration. "Are you sure? Maybe some more wine."

"Now, Anthony, I think it's pretty obvious, you don't need to get me drunk."

"Who said anything about drunk? I just don't want you to dehydrate."

Claire smiled as he slowly eased himself from the bed. Reaching for the glass, he added, "I mean—if you're willing to stay, I'd like to make a toast."

When he turned back around she was sitting up against the head board with the sheet wrapped tightly around her breasts. Her modesty intrigued him. Most of the women he dated were the type to flaunt their assets—not cover them. Smiling a shy smile, she reached for the glass. "By all means, I'd hate to ruin your toast."

The drug took effect faster than Tony planned. The cooperative, pleasant woman he'd spent the night with suddenly became agitated and combative. This new behavior didn't last long. When it ended, her entire body relaxed and her head bobbled upon her neck. For a moment, Tony feared they'd need to carry her from the hotel. Despite her appearance, Claire wasn't unconscious, only detached. The green eyes no longer held the window to her soul; instead, they were clouded with a veil of confusion and separation, as if Claire's body was there, but her mind was somewhere else. She followed every command. In many ways, it was like dressing a child. He told her to stand—she stood. He told her to lift her arms—she did.

Once he had her dressed, he called for Eric. As they rode the elevator down to the lobby, Claire leaned into his chest. He hoped to interested bystanders, she merely looked tired. Although she didn't answer, he spoke softly in her ear. Tony reasoned it would appear more natural on hotel surveillance. Next, he walked her to the car, kissed her goodbye and let Eric drive away. It was all part of the plan.

A few hours later, Tony met Eric at a side door and entered the back seat of his car. Sleeping soundly on the seat, covered with a thin blanket was his acquisition. The room at the Ritz was Tony's for a few more days. After he had Claire in Iowa, he'd return to Atlanta and attend more meetings. More of the plan, his leaving town couldn't coincide with her departure.

Walking from the car to the plane, she stumbled with unsteady footing. Once aboard, she paced, unwilling to sit. Each time Tony got near her, she pulled away and walked toward the door. Using more physical persuasion, he steered her toward the seat. When her knees bent, she spoke for the first time since the GHB took effect, "I donnnnn't feeel well."

He didn't comment as he secured her seat belt. At first, she stared at the restraint. When the plane lifted off the ground, her head fell to her chest. Tony wondered if she comprehended any of what was happening.

Suddenly, her limp head sprung upward and her slurred words filled the otherwise empty cabin, "I'mmm gonna be siccccccccccccccccc."

Losing patience, Tony noticed Claire's sudden pallor. He unstrapped himself and walked toward her. He saw fear within her eyes as she frantically fought her seat belt.

"Stop it," he commanded. "You're on an airplane. You're not going anywhere."

She turned away, tears streaming down her cheeks, unable to move against the latched belt. He reached for her chin and turned her toward him; before he could reprimand her on the importance of maintaining eye contact, she wrenched and vomited. It covered her dress and his slacks.

"Shit!" he barked. It was disgusting!

"I told you...I was sick!" she cried.

He looked at the mess and then at Claire as she sunk against the chair.

"Don't get the damn chair dirty, too."

His words only increased her tears. As he reached for the seat belt and unbuckled, revulsion at the mess was somehow interspersed with sympathy.

"Come here," he said as he held out his hand.

Retracting further against the seat, she asked, "Why am I here? What are you doing?"

Tony tried once again for compassion, "Claire, you aren't feeling well; let me get you some water and clean you up."

Hesitantly, she stood, allowing him to walk her to the bathroom at the back of the plane. With each command, her compliance decreased while her defiance increased. He suspected she needed more of the drug.

"I shouldn't be here. Where are we going?"

"You'll feel better if you have some water."

Apprehensively, she took the cup laced with the second vial of GHB. He watched the liquid slosh within the confines of the glass as her hands trembled. Finally, afraid she'd spill it, he helped her get the glass to her lips where she took a drink.

She spit it in the sink. "It tastes funny."

"That's because you were sick, you need to rinse your mouth." He filled another cup with water and she rinsed. Next, he handed her the first cup. "Now drink."

Claire nodded and did as he said.

"We need to get you out of these filthy clothes."

As he tugged at her dress, she reacted violently, trying with all of her might to get away from him and out of the bathroom. Her screams echoed above the hum of the engines. It was like in the hotel when the drug first entered her system; however, this time, Tony didn't need to worry about anyone else hearing.

Blocking the door, he let her have her tantrum. Her fight intrigued him. The blows to his chest with her tiny fists were almost comical, but when she tried to scratch, he had to make it stop. He had meetings and work. Scratches would be questioned. "That's enough!" She didn't stop. Her nails contacted his arm and blood trickled from their trail. Seizing her hand, he slapped her. "Stop it!"

The shock showed behind her clouded eyes as she covered her face, allowing one hand to linger on her now red cheek. In a way, it was humorous; she was naked, hysterical, and attacking him—and she seemed surprised he'd retaliate.

He leaned over her quaking body. "Get in the shower—now." When she didn't move, he reached for her arm and pulled her under the water. Although fully clothed, he joined her in the small cubicle and held her under the streaming water until the fighting stopped.

Within minutes, the drug was once again in control, and Tony was directing her movements. With trembling hands, she obeyed, removing his wet clothes and following each command. Her fight was gone. The fire he'd momentarily seen in her eyes was now detached terror.

When he turned off the water, they were both clean. As Claire huddled against the shower wall, Tony contemplated his next move. There were so many possibilities; he told himself to take it slow. His plan had been in place for too long; he wanted to savor every moment.

Stepping into the small bathroom, he added his wet clothes to the pile containing her ruined dress and handed her a towel. Apprehensively, she took his offer and wrapped it around herself. Her long, dark hair dripped down her back as the water puddled on the floor.

Without looking up, she asked, "Are you going to hurt me?"

He'd read about the GHB. He knew these scenes would be forever erased from her memory. He could do whatever he wanted, and she'd never remember.

The sensual tone of seduction was gone; in its place was the authoritative tone of someone with an agenda. Tony refused to allow her fear or emotions to alter his plans. "That isn't my plan. We'll see how well you can follow directions."

Tony pulled on the edge of Claire's towel as she stepped back against the wall. Her clouded eyes opened wide and quickly looked away. He wondered if she could subconsciously fight the effects of the drug. He watched as she worked to form the right words. Finally, she mumbled, "Please."

He stepped closer, his nude body still wet and his desire visible. "Please, what?"

"Please, don't hurt me."

"I have rules, Claire." He gently pushed her wet hair away from her face. "Can you follow my rules?"

Avoiding eye contact, she nodded.

Abruptly, he raised her chin. "Don't look away. I asked you a question. I expect an answer."

"Yes, I can follow your rules."

"Rule number one is to do as I say. I suggest you learn to follow that rule, if you want to make the best of this."

Keeping her eyes downcast, her shoulders quaked as she silently sobbed. Once again, his hand struck her cheek.

"I told you not to look away."

Her eyes immediately flashed toward his. Instantaneously, the clouds returned as pools of tears spilled onto her cheeks. "I'll do as you say; please stop hitting me."

The memories made Tony's stomach turn. Of course, none of that was in Claire's testimony. The GHB hid those memories from her, as well as other memories of the things he did during that flight and once they returned to Iowa.

Her testimony picked up the next day, when the drug was fully out of her system. It wasn't until then that she started to understand the magnitude of her situation; nevertheless, the truth hit Tony between the eyes. Perspiration drenched his face and the illness he'd felt in the pit of his empty stomach erupted into full blown nausea. No matter what he did to make Claire's life better or show her he'd changed, these memories would always linger in the recesses of his mind. For the rest of his life, he'd know what he'd done.

Tony hated himself for all of it—hell, he always had *the end justifies the means* argument, but even *he* didn't believe that anymore. Not now. Not now that he *knew* Claire and *loved* Claire. The thought of someone doing to her what he'd done filled him with rage. If it were another person whom she described, Tony would want him dead. He'd leave no stone unturned to make him pay for his sins.

Tears coated his cheeks before he realized Brent was standing right in front of him.

"I take it you've read Claire's testimony?"

Tony nodded. He didn't want Brent knowing about this. Now Courtney would know. He should deny it and argue—but the image of Claire—not from her testimony—but from his memory—on his plane, wrapped in that towel, trembling and scared—wouldn't let him lie.

"If the shit in that binder's true, you're one sick bastard"—Brent turned a circle—"I'm your personal attorney and friend. Tell me what we're up against."

Tony remained silent, his eyes so clouded with memories he could barely see the room around him.

"Damn it, Tony!" The table vibrated with the slap of Brent's hand as his fury and anger filled the air. "Tell me the truth!"

The ferocity within the room grew as Tony's anguish also began to build. Springing from the chair, he pushed past Brent and paced. "Where the hell did they get this? What the fuck does it mean? Is Claire alive? Do they know where she is? Did she press charges? Is that what this whole damn day is about?"

Brent seized Tony's shoulders, as he demanded. "Fuck'n tell me if it's true."

Never had Brent spoken to Tony with that tone. Tony couldn't help but retaliate, "Let go of me, or I swear to God I'll punch you in the face!"

"Do it! Do it! Go ahead. Then maybe I'll understand more of what Claire endured."

Tony staggered backward. Brent's words cut deeper than any knife and were more painful than a fist to the jaw. "It was before"—Tony's fight evaporated as his knees buckled against the chair—"It was a *long time* ago. Things are, or were, different—this time. I didn't have anything to do with her recent disappearance."

Brent fell into a chair and fought to control his words. Finally, he asked, "So, you're telling me this is true? You did this shit to a woman you claimed to love—a woman you married—a woman you charged with attempted murder and later wanted to reconcile with? You did this sick-ass-shit to *the mother of your child*?"

"No!" Tony stared at Brent. He felt the black fill his eyes as red filled his vision. "I'm not saying that. I'd never do that to the *mother of my child* or the *woman I was reconciling with*. Like I said—it was different." He rubbed the stubble on his cheeks. Suddenly, his face weighed too much for his neck. Tony collapsed against the back of the chair allowing his head to rest against the cinderblock wall. "The only person, who understands—me—or any of this—is Claire." Indignation returned and his neck strengthened. "Tell me this isn't relevant. Tell me you can suppress this evidence"—Tony stood as the volume of his voice rose—"I paid a lot of money to have this disappear!"

Brent shook his head. "Shit! Did you just tell me, an attorney, that you paid to have evidence suppressed? Jesus, tell me you didn't just say that!"

Tony felt the blood drain from his face as his limbs suddenly felt heavy. "I—I"—Perspiration appeared on his brow as he contemplated his answer and sunk back against the cool cement wall—"What I meant to say is that this evidence is old—things change, people change. Please..." It may have been the first time he'd ever used that word with Brent, but that didn't make it any less heartfelt. "Please, tell me you can convince them I didn't hurt her."

Brent stared.

"This time"—Tony's tone hardened as he pushed back the emotions he refused to reveal. His words slowed—"I didn't hurt her *this time*"—he paused momentarily and gathered his thoughts—"This time she came to Iowa of her own free will. We were having a baby"—shaking his head he corrected himself—"No, we *are* having a baby. She accepted her engagement ring"—He held Brent's gaze—"You *are* my friend as well as my personal attorney; tell me you believe me."

Brent's shoulders relaxed and he said, "We should eat."

"No! Food doesn't matter."

Leaning forward, Brent steadied his tone. "Tony, listen to me—I know that's not your forte, but shut-up and let me help you."

The air left Tony's lungs. "You're still willing to help me?"

"I'll be honest with you. We *have been* friends and maybe we still are, but right now I'm pissed as hell and friendship isn't why I'm willing to do this for you." He sat straighter while maintaining eye contact. "When this is all done, you can fire me, but going in, you should know, I'm not doing this for you—I'm doing this for Claire. If she trusted you again—after all this shit"—he pointed to the binder—"I will too."

Tony's neck gave way as his face fell forward. Rubbing his hand through his hair, he exhaled. "You're not fired. What can you do?"

"I'll make some calls. If the FBI isn't pressing charges, I think I can get you released, at least momentarily. When we're back in Iowa, we're gonna talk about this..."

Only those you trust can betray you.

—Nathan Rahl

CHAPTER 4

"M r. Simmons, we believe it's in the best interest of your client to keep him here for at least forty-eight hours."

Brent tried to clarify an earlier statement, "You're saying you believe Mr. Rawlings is in danger? Yet you won't tell us what threats or evidence you have to support this claim."

"I'm not at liberty to divulge that information." Hearing the mechanisms of the door, everyone turned to see another agent enter. Agent Jackson introduced the newest member of their conversation, "This is Special Agent in Charge, Easton."

SAC Easton stepped toward the table. Tony searched his expression; deep lines embedded in his forehead displaying years of concentration and stress. Though Tony looked for some sign of accommodation, Easton's grimace, instead, warned of impending doom.

Clearing his throat, Easton began, "Agent Jackson, thank you for your diligence. Mr. Rawlings, it's come to our attention that you're to be released." He straightened his stance, and added, "At this time we're not prepared to formally charge you with any crimes."

Tony exhaled. His gratitude quickly evaporated as irritation prevailed. Incredulously, he stood and glared at the federal officials. Before he could speak, SAC Easton continued, "Nevertheless, your safety *is* a concern and we want to again—"

Tony interrupted, "My safety? What about Claire? What about her safety?"

"Sir"—Easton shifted uncomfortably from foot to foot—"Your ex-wife is the informant who alerted us to this danger."

Tony's lungs deflated as he turned his gaze toward Brent. Sinking back into the chair, he whispered, "She's alive. Thank God, she's alive." As quickly as the oxygen left, it returned, with a rush of blood to his cheeks making his face a bright shade of crimson in the poorly lit room. With each word, his volume increased and his stance straightened, "She's alive. My fiancée, the mother of my child, is alive and you've had me here for hours playing some sick mind games!"

Brent silenced Tony with a touch of Tony's sleeve. "Special Agent Easton, Agent Jackson, I believe you just said my client is free to go?"

"Yes, counselor; however, it is the recommendation of the—"

Brent continued, "Thank you, we'll be spending the night here in Boston. You have my number. If we don't hear from you by tomorrow morning at 9:00 AM, we plan to return to Iowa. If you need to speak with my client again, you may do so, through me."

There was so much Tony wanted to say, so much he wanted to know, yet Brent's slight pressure on his arm told him to leave the room—escape now before the FBI changed its mind. Momentarily, Tony's body refused to move. *What else did these men know?* Trying with all his might, he swallowed his words and walked toward the door; nevertheless, before he reached the point of exodus, he turned back around. "Where is she? Is she in danger?"

SAC Easton met his eyes. "Mr. Rawlings, she's the one who made contact with authorities. It's our understanding that she left the country—your home— of her own free will."

"Country? Did you say she left the *country*? Where is she?"

"Of—Her—Own—Free—Will, Mr. Rawlings. She doesn't wish her whereabouts to be disclosed. The danger she's alerting you to is still present."

The agent's words reverberated through Tony's thoughts—*Out of the county—own free will. Did Claire leave him? Did she leave in a way to purposely create a public scandal? Had she been playing him—some kind of sick revenge—was it all a charade to get back at him? No!* Tony *knew* that wasn't the case. He refused to spend another second entertaining that notion.

Brent's tug brought Tony back to present, as his counsel addressed the assembly, "Thank you agents, we'll collect Mr. Rawlings' things."

Tony glared one last time, momentarily speechless.

At a front desk, Tony signed for his belongings, which included his brief case and cell phone. He could almost taste the blood as he bit his lip, holding back the words he couldn't bear to think much less say. When they stepped from the building, the fresh air filled his lungs as the late hour registered. The FBI had come to Tony's hotel room almost twelve hours earlier. Turning on his phone, he managed, "I'll call Eric and get us to a hotel."

Brent shook his head. "No, I sent Eric back to Iowa. I didn't know how long this would last. I'll call for a taxi."

Tony nodded as he saw the number of messages and missed calls mount on his screen. He tried to remember a time when he'd been unwillingly inaccessible to the world for twelve hours. While it was incomprehensible to think the FBI had removed him from his life, with total disregard for his personal or public obligations, he couldn't shake the agent's words. *Of her own free will.*

During the taxi ride to the hotel, neither man uttered more than a word or two as they both busily returned emails and text messages. The emotion of the day was finally gone—swallowed back into an unyielding hole. Unconsciously, Tony contemplated the possibility he'd been played. *Of her own free will?* The hairs prickled on the back of his neck.

∞∞∞∞∞∞

It wasn't until they were checked into a two bedroom suite that they began talking. "I don't believe them." Conviction came through Tony's voice stronger with each word.

"You don't believe the FBI?"

"If Claire left willingly, she was coerced."

"Why would the FBI insinuate otherwise?"

"Why would they keep me for the entire damn day and then drop that bomb at the end?"

Brent shrugged, so many thoughts bombarding his head.

The strength and concern in Tony's voice morphed into his familiar dominating tone. "I don't want you to tell Courtney about what you learned today."

Brent considered his words. *Was this the time to tell Tony he'd known for years?* He straightened his neck and stood taller than he had in his friend's presence in many years. "I told you, I helped you because of Claire. She's alive and safe. That's what matters."

"Apparently she is, and apparently we aren't privy to know anything more."

"No, we aren't, but at least we know she isn't in prison on trumped up charges."

Tony spun and met Brent's gaze. "What did you just say?"

"I said—we don't know where she is"—Brent continued his stare—"We know where she isn't."

"I'm going to assume that offer to fire you is still on the table."

Scanning the mini bar, Brent chose a bottle of whiskey, unscrewed the small lid and drank from the spout. Shaking his head, he laughed. "Sure, why not? I'm considering an early retirement anyway."

Even with his back toward Tony, Brent could sense the darkening of Tony's eyes and imagine his expression as Tony repeated, "Don't say anything to Courtney."

Brent turned back around. He was done being bullied. "Tony, I'm not promising that. I don't keep secrets from *my* wife."

"This isn't debatable." Tony grabbed a similar bottle from the bar. As he unscrewed the lid, Brent saw his shoulders slump. His tone was no longer full of domination; Brent heard something new as Tony said, "I care what Courtney thinks"—he kept his gaze away, as if looking out the large window and the lights of Boston—"And you."

Brent reeled. All the accusations and declarations he'd practiced in his head were suddenly gone. Brotherly love wasn't a comfortable gesture between the two of them. Clearing his throat, Brent managed, "You and Claire made it through this. Do you swear you never treated her like her testimony states, since her release from prison?"

Tony nodded. "I swear."

"Courtney is pretty perceptive; I don't think she'd be too surprised." When Tony didn't answer, Brent continued, "Do you want to call for a jet to come and get us in the morning, or should I?"

"I already have. It'll be waiting by 10:00 AM." Throwing back the rest of the small bottle, Tony said, "She can be as perceptive as she wants. I don't want you confirming anything. Confidentiality—hell, I pay you enough to at least expect that."

Brent's shoulders fell—so much for *brotherly love.* "Yeah, Tony, you pay me. Without a doubt, within the last twelve hours—hell, twenty years, I've fuck'n earned it!"

Tony threw the empty bottle on the bar. "I'm going to try to get some sleep."

"Wait!"—Brent faced his *best friend's* dark eyes—it was now or never— "That early retirement—firing—whatever you want to call it—it's still on the table, and you should know, I'm seriously considering it. I know too much shit to keep saving your ass."

"You know too much *shit* to ever consider walking away. It's not an option." Tony turned toward one of the bedrooms. Before he shut the door he added, "I'm not accepting your offer. Good night."

It was after midnight when the knock came to the door. It took multiple raps before anyone from within the suite budged. Brent was the first to make it to the door. He'd spent most of the day with federal officers. It didn't take a genius to figure that the two men in dark suits were among those ranks.

"We're looking for Anthony Rawlings."

Before Brent could answer, Tony came up behind him. "I'm Anthony Rawlings. What the hell do you want at this time of night?"

The two officers displayed their badges and credentials. "Mr. Rawlings, may we enter?"

The last thing Tony wanted was a discussion with the FBI held in the hotel's hallway. He and Brent took a step back allowing the agents to enter the suite.

Tony's anger temporarily faded into concern. "Is this regarding Claire? Do you have new information?"

"There's *more* information." The men in dark suits went on to explain the threats upon Tony's life have been verified and confirmed. The information Ms. Nichols disclosed was only the beginning. The Bureau believes it's in everyone's best interest to get Tony home, safe and sound, where his security team can keep him from harm.

They also explained that Tony's activity could be currently monitored by the perpetrator and insisted Brent remain in Boston. They emphasized that in the morning Brent needed to go to the FBI office and complete legal documents regarding this transfer. Of course, then Brent and Tony would be able to meet up in Iowa tomorrow after Brent finished all the legalities.

Tony considered their concerns. Looking toward Brent, he shrugged. Honestly, he wanted to be home. It made more sense than sleeping in a hotel room. "Give me a minute to gather my things."

As he left with the agents, Tony told Brent, "I'll talk with you more when you get back to Iowa. Come straight to the house once you land."

∞∞∞∞∞∞

Brent agreed and watched as Tony left with the two plain-clothed agents. The feeling of foreboding lingered in Brent's mind. He considered calling Courtney, but it was nearly 2:00 AM. She didn't need to lose sleep just because his mind was racing. Finally, Brent fell into a restless sleep.

A mere four hours later, Brent rolled toward the vibrating phone echoing on the hard surface of the night stand. Before he could answer the call, his attention went to the loud pounding on the suite door.

Pulling on his slacks, he read the unknown number, rejected the call and pushed the phone into his pocket. In a still sleep deprived haze, Brent made his way toward the loud banging. This time, when he opened the door, Brent recognized at least one of the agents. "Agent Jackson, couldn't you wait until I came to the office this morning?"

"So, Mr. Simmons, you were planning on coming to the FBI office today?"

"Yes, that's what I was told."

"And, what about Mr. Rawlings? Was he planning on coming too?"

Brent stepped back and allowed the two men entry. "He would, but now—"

"Now"—Agent Jackson completed Brent's sentence—"Now your client is gone, disappearing in the middle of the night?"

"No." Brent shut the door. "Well, yes—because he left with your agents." When the FBI remained silent and exchanged quizzical looks, Brent added, "The men from your office who came here last night. He left with them."

"I assure you, we didn't send agents here last night."

"What?" Brent ran his hands through his bed-messed hair, struggling with the new information. *Could Claire's threat have been real? Did someone take Tony?*

"Mr. Simmons"—Brent focused as he attempted to subdue his impending fear—"A plane left Boston airspace, a private plane, contracted by one Anthony Rawlings. That same plane made an emergency landing in the Appalachian Mountains approximately an hour ago. No survivors were found."

Brent collapsed onto the sofa. "As in *dead*?" The words hurt exiting his lips. Yes, there were times he hated Tony for what he'd done or said—that didn't change the fact—the controlling asshole was his best friend.

"No, sir, as in *missing*. The plane was empty. A FBI forensics' team is investigating. So far, no signs of struggle or injury have been found and"— Agent Jackson emphasized—"no signs of *anyone*."

"But...the FBI took him. I saw their credentials and badges."

"Do you remember the names of these agents?"

Brent shook his head. "No, it was late. Jesus... I didn't really look. I assumed it was legitimate. I don't remember."

"Mr. Simmons, the FBI didn't come here last night."

"What does this mean?"

"For right now, it means you're coming back with us to the Bureau. We're going to review hotel footage and discuss your late night visitors."

∞∞∞∞∞∞

Sitting in the familiar office of SAC of the San Francisco FBI, Agent Baldwin listened attentively to his supervisor. "Anthony Rawlings was in FBI custody. Now he isn't."

"I'm sorry...what do you mean *he isn't*?"

"Due to persuasion from unnamed political sources, Agent Easton, SAC in Boston, was unable to keep him detained."

Harry's blood boiled. "So, sir..." Although, well engrained, the title left a bad taste on his tongue. "You're saying—*he* did it again? Anthony Rawlings played his political cards, flashed a little money, and got himself out of FBI custody?"

"Agent, despite the Deputy Director's request, you clearly aren't interested in pursuing your career in the service of—"

"I apologize. Sir, please go on. Claire Nichols. Where is she?"

"The last direct communication was from Geneva, Switzerland. That was over a week ago. We have local field agents who've confirmed her departure from Switzerland."

"She left..? Where did she go?"

"This is a briefing son—I inform; you listen. Agent Baldwin, you seem to have forgotten the protocol. If you choose to honor the Deputy Director's request and assist in this ongoing investigation—your duty is to say, *Yes, sir. Thank you, sir.* If that duty is too difficult for you to fulfill, I'll gladly inform our director, and your duties can be reassigned."

Harry bit his tongue. Working undercover had a way of removing the bureau formalities from an agent's vocabulary. Harry had enough problems with his future in the service of the FBI; he didn't need to add insubordination to the list. Sitting taller, Harry said, "Yes, sir. Thank you, sir. I'll do whatever the bureau wants me to do."

"The bureau wants you to travel to Italy. We have two possible sightings of Ms. Nichols—one in Venice—the other in Rome. We have pictures of the woman suspected of being Ms. Nichols. You'll see she's always in disguise." SAC Williams pointed toward a large screen on the wall of his office. Still pictures projected. Some were grainy, as if taken from a distance and enlarged. Others were much more clear and detailed. Harry studied the woman in each photograph. The last time he'd seen Claire, in person, was in June. That was four months ago. The woman in question could be pregnant, or just heavy. Her hair color and length varied from photo to photo, yet there was something about her—in a few of the photos—when she smiled—Harry's chest tightened.

"Sir, I believe that *is* Ms. Nichols."

"This man has been seen with her on numerous occasions. Can you identify him?"

Repeated pictures projected, again with varied quality. "Most of these pictures don't show his face. It's like he knows to keep it away from cameras." The man's hair color varied, and he often wore a hat. "I'm sure it isn't Anthony Rawlings, sir"—Harry studied the pictures closer—"He's familiar. Are they believed to be *together*?" The way he emphasized the last word made his meaning clear.

SAC Williams' eyes narrowed. "It appears so. Ms. Nichols told the Iowa City prosecutor that she left the home of Mr. Rawlings of her own free will, and that she feared for the safety of her and her unborn child. She emphasized that the threat wasn't from Mr. Rawlings. Although you are aware, their relationship has had its perilous moments."

"Yes, sir. Ms. Nichols told me about that herself."

"She also informed Evergreen that she believed Mr. Rawlings is still in danger."

Harry shifted his footing ever so slightly.

"I'll ask this one more time, can you reenter this case with a sense of impartiality? Our assignment is multifaceted. Agent Nichols was one of us. Though not publicly disclosed—his death is still an open case. The ME found traces of a rare toxin in his blood, actaea pachypoda, more commonly referred to as doll's eyes. This plant toxin has a sedative effect on the cardiac muscle tissue and can cause cardiac arrest. That same toxin has been identified in very few other deaths. A reoccurring denominator seems to be Mr. Rawlings or should I say *Rawls*. After years of nothing, it was Ms. Nichols's research and persistence that pulled these cases together. Upon further investigation, actaea pachypoda was also found in Mr. Rawlings' blood when he was poisoned in 2012. Interestingly, it was the first time it has been identified in a nonlethal dose."

Harry wanted to say, "That's too bad"—however, he wisely chose to remain silent.

SAC Williams continued, "Honestly, it doesn't come up in a normal toxicology screen and could easily be missed. Not all cases lead to Mr. Rawlings directly. Since other drugs indicating poisoning were found in Mr. Rawlings' 2012 toxicology report, this toxin wasn't initially discovered. Thankfully, in criminal cases such as Mr. Rawlings' attempted murder, trace evidence is retained. When his blood was retested, the toxin was discovered. If it were left up to those idiots in Iowa, it would've never been found. We have no way of knowing how many other cases have been missed."

"May I see the other names and case files which have been identified?"

"Yes, agent, you'll be leaving today for Venice. A debriefing file will accompany you on that trip. Familiarize yourself with it."

"If I locate Ms. Nichols, am I to maintain the ex-boyfriend from SiJo persona?"

"For the time being, yes. She trusted you. That's your role again, to regain her trust. As I said, this case is multifaceted. Ms. Nichols believes a significant threat exists—a threat which was severe enough to cause her to leave the country. Although she remains unaware, Ms. Nichols is our informant. We need her safe. Mr. Rawlings is an influential man with many connections. For the time being, it's in the best interest of many people for him to remain hidden and safe. With the political and financial climate as it is, the collapse of Rawlings Industries could have global financial repercussions. That's not something the prominent U.S. government officials want to see at this time. After his location is confirmed, it's been determined to allow him to stay hidden. Actually, that was the bureau's plan. I can't say I agree with the Boston office's tactics. I think they should've been straight with him all along, but it wasn't my call. Now, we have to clean up their mess."

"What if the evidence points back to Mr. Rawlings?"

"If it does, we bring him in."

Externally, Harry maintained his neutral expression; internally he smiled from ear to ear. *Bring him in*—yes, Harry liked the way that sounded. He wanted to be the person placing Rawlings' wrists in cuffs—and he didn't mean the thousand dollar, diamond studded kind. Harry's need for retaliation wasn't solely based on what he did to Claire, although admittedly it was a predominating factor. No, Harry's incentive stemmed from the implication of so many other criminal activities. Rawlings hadn't only taken Claire's life, but he'd also, potentially—theoretically, hurt countless others—taking and destroying lives at will. Yes, Harry wanted to see Anthony Rawlings behind bars more than he wanted anything else. Maybe, just maybe, when Rawlings' crimes were brought to light Claire would see the truth. Oh, there was no doubt that when Claire learned that Harry's presence in Palo Alto was *not* coincidental—that he also lied to her, she'd be upset, but lying for good was much better than killing, beating, raping...it twisted Harry's stomach to think how long the list of Rawlings' sins could possibly be.

Snapping back to reality, the photo of the man on the wall screen registered, and Harry said, "Phillip Roach."

"Excuse me?" SAC Williams asked.

"The man in those photos with Claire Nichols, his name is Phillip Roach. He's a private investigator. I ran preliminary background checks on him. He has a military background and on multiple occasions he's fallen off the grid. He did work for Rawlings. I don't know why he'd be with Ms. Nichols now."

"Well then, that's on your list of things to learn."

"Sir, why am I suddenly in Europe?"

SAC Williams smiled. "Welcome back, Agent."

Doubt separates people. It is a poison that disintegrates friendships and breaks up pleasant relations. It is a thorn that irritates and hurts; it is a sword that kills.

——Buddha

CHAPTER 5

Brent tipped the Styrofoam cup upward attempting to garnish the last drops of caffeine, praying for a jumpstart to his exhausted body and mind. He'd been sitting and watching the feed from the hotel's surveillance cameras for hours. Agent Jackson remained with him, but the second agent occasionally changed. The one who accompanied Jackson to the hotel was back; however, he'd left for a while and been replaced with another man, wearing the same customary black suit.

Regardless of who was within their room, they sat and watched the same loop over and over. It consisted of a hallway view of Tony and the two agents leaving the suite—the three men alone in the elevator—their walk through the lobby—and all of them entering a waiting black SUV. Brent wondered if Agent Jackson expected something to change, some new information. He wasn't seeing it; at this point, he was pretty sure he'd see the same video in his dreams—if he ever had a full night's sleep.

Without a doubt, Tony walked away willingly. There seemed to be little communication occurring between Tony and the agents; however, without audio, that couldn't be confirmed. Watching his friend disappear from the camera's view, Brent wondered, *was Tony being taken by the person Claire feared?* The FBI insinuated otherwise. Without coming out and saying it, Brent sensed that they thought Tony's departure—like Claire's—was *of his own free will.* Regardless of the reason, Brent saw no advantage to watching the same footage a thousand times. *Shouldn't they be tracking down the SUV or something?* Suddenly, Agent Jackson's voice refocused Brent's thoughts. "There it is! That's what I've been trying to see. I knew something seemed odd." The other agent hit pause and backed up the video; soon they were all watching the footage again.

Finally, Brent asked the question he could no longer contain, "What do you see? All I see is the man on the left sending a text."

Agent number two replied. Brent gave up trying to learn all the different names of the different agents. Most of them looked alike. That's what made last night's charade so believable. He didn't really look at the men. He momentarily thought of the movie *Men in Black;* they had it right by naming their agents with letters. *J* and *K* were much easier to remember.

Number Two replied, "Look at that phone. What's the time on the feed?"

Jackson read the bottom of the screen, "01:36:58"

Suddenly, Number Two was typing feverishly on a nearby keyboard.

"Is someone going to tell me what you're thinking? Will this help find Tony?"

Exasperation showed in Jackson's expression; he exhaled and said, "See his phone. That isn't an FBI issued phone. It isn't even a smart phone."

Immediately, Brent recognized what Jackson was seeing. Looking at the phone in the agent's hand upon the stilled image, he saw the same kind of phone Courtney used to use to communicate with Claire. Brent nodded, "Yes! It's one of those throw away phones. Why would an agent have one of those? Or why would he use it?"

"Exactly—why indeed? While we may not be able to answer *why* with 100% certainty, but I can, with 100% certainty, say he isn't texting the bureau."

"Here it is!"

Brent and Jackson turned toward Number Two, who exclaimed, "At exactly 01:36:59 the nearest tower received and forwarded a text message!" He continued to type, then he added, "It originated from a disposable phone, purchased at a convenience store on the east side of Boston, from the coordinates of the hotel."

"And it went to..?" Jackson asked.

Number Two exhaled. "Another disposable phone, purchased at the same store, same time, with cash."

"Can you see the text receiver's location?"

"Give me a minute."

Brent sat back and lifted his cup again, trying to locate any remnants of coffee lingering in the depths of Styrofoam. He marveled at the FBI's resources. Their impressive and intrusive technology gave him confidence they'd soon learn more about these fake agents. That both soothed and worried Brent. Despite the fact, he repeatedly told the story of the late night visit, each time emphasizing Tony's surprise and agitation, they actually alluded to the possibility Tony arranged for the fake visit and his own disappearance.

As the two agents talked, Number Two typed and typed, and Brent's thoughts went back to last night in the suite. He recalled Tony's declaration, saying that he didn't believe the FBI and feared Claire had been coerced to leave the country. Brent wanted to believe his friend. He wanted to believe that the Tony of 2010 was gone; nevertheless, the fact he once existed, lingered in Brent's thoughts.

He knew Claire's theory on why Tony chose her all those years ago—a lifelong vendetta having to do with their grandfathers. Regardless of the reason, in 2010 Tony risked everything—money, appearance, *everything*, to kidnap and have Claire Nichols. To the outsider, it didn't make sense. Anthony Rawlings was incredibly wealthy and not bad looking. No one would believe he'd jeopardize all he'd worked to accomplish, to kidnap a woman from Atlanta, Georgia. As Brent's thoughts came together, he felt the rush of understanding. Suddenly, the picture made sense. It was like watching cards fall just right to close an inside straight. If Tony had been willing to bet everything to take Claire—then surely he'd be willing to gamble it all—again, if he believed she needed rescued.

Closing his eyes and rubbing his temples, Brent allowed his thoughts to volley. One minute, he worried someone dangerous had taken Tony—the *someone* Claire told the FBI about. The next minute, he believed Tony arranged the escape, in an effort to find Claire on his own. If that were the case, his friend and his boss—Anthony Rawlings—was now a fugitive. If that were the case, Brent couldn't have been prouder!

With the sleep deprived pounding behind Brent's closed eyes, he made a decision. He wouldn't quit, and he hadn't been fired; however, *without a doubt—he wasn't getting paid enough to put up with this shit! He deserved a raise, and if Tony weren't around, then damn, that was something Brent could facilitate on his own! This shit deserved more money!*

∞∞∞∞∞∞∞

Catherine answered the door to the estate, knowing who'd be on the other side. Large iron gates greatly reduced the odds of surprise visitors. When Marcus Evergreen checked in, security informed him that Mr. Rawlings wasn't home. He asked to come up to the estate anyway. Without Anton home, Catherine reasoned, she was the one to handle whatever the prosecutor wanted to discuss.

"Hello, Mr. Evergreen, please come in."

"Ms. London, I wanted to come out here personally. I hope you don't mind the intrusion?"

Leading him into the sitting room, Catherine answered, "I don't mind; however, I'm not sure what you want. Mr. Rawlings is still out of town. I haven't heard from him since he left Friday."

"Yes, that's what I'm here to discuss."

They sat, facing one another as Catherine replied, "Mr. Evergreen, perhaps you should talk to Mr. Rawlings' assistant, Patricia. She's usually much more abreast of his schedule than I. I'm sure if he's supposed to meet with you, he will. There's no reason he wouldn't." Catherine's words flowed faster as she spoke.

"Mr. Rawlings has no family, does he?"

"No, sir. Why are you asking?"

"You've worked for him for a long time, isn't that true?"

"Yes, I've known Mr. Rawlings for a long time. I'm sorry, but I don't understand where you're going with this."

"Ms. London, I received a call from the Boston bureau of the FBI yesterday. They instructed me to not release any information until everything was confirmed. This morning, they called and informed me that the news media would soon be reporting the incident."

Catherine's anxiety grew with each passing second. She didn't know what was about to be said, and the uncertainty made her inhale deeply. "Mr. Evergreen, what are you trying to say?"

"Mr. Rawlings chartered a private plane during the early hours of the morning, Sunday. That plane made an emergency landing in the Appalachian Mountains." He quickly added, "It didn't crash—it landed, and no one has been found."

Unexpectedly, tears formed in Catherine's gray eyes. Stoically, she pushed forward. "Why? How? That doesn't make sense. He has his own plane and access to many more. Why would he charter a plane?"

"All I know is that the FBI had reason to believe Mr. Rawlings' life was in danger."

Catherine's hand quickly moved to her throat. "In danger? By whom?"

"They haven't revealed that information to me. They said they're not making any declarations. Your employer is neither considered dead nor missing. They hope to locate him. Ms. London, if you hear from him, I'm imploring you, please contact my office immediately."

Catherine nodded. "Yes, Mr. Evergreen, of course. So, they think he's alive?"

"The FBI isn't being very forthcoming. I'm sure this'll result in all kinds of speculations." The prosecutor stood. "I need to get back to the office. I wanted to do something and informing you seemed like the best option. I realize he was your employer; however, after so many years of devoted service, I felt you deserved to hear the information first hand."

"Mr. Evergreen—the FBI? Does this also involve Ms. Nichols?"

"I wish I could tell you more. I wish I knew more. As of now, both Ms. Nichols and Mr. Rawlings are both officially—considered missing."

Keeping her eyes downcast, Catherine led her visitor back toward the door. "Thank you, Mr. Evergreen. I appreciate the personal message. I'll contact your office if I hear anything."

"One more thing, Mr. Rawlings' driver, Eric Hensley?"

"Yes, that's his name."

"Is he here?"

"Yes," Catherine replied. "He left with Mr. Rawlings Friday evening, but returned on Saturday alone. We haven't spoken; I'm not sure why he came home alone."

"You haven't spoken?"

"Mr. Evergreen, this is a large home and estate. We all have our duties and when we have the chance for some uninterrupted time, we take it."

Marcus nodded.

It was true the prosecutor made a decent salary, but the way of life in the world of the extremely wealthy was a mystery to those who didn't live it. Catherine believed her answer made sense, and Mr. Evergreen had no reason to doubt her.

He added, "Thank you, Ms. London. I, too, will let you know of any new developments which I am privy to share. Would you like me to be the one to inform Mr. Hensley?"

"If you feel the need to speak to him personally—by all means."

"No, if you want to break the news to him, I won't intrude. Once again, I'm sorry to be the one to inform you of this disturbing news."

"Thank you, for taking the time." Catherine closed the door and leaned against it. Taking in the grand stairs and large glistening foyer, a smile crept upon her face. She'd give this some time. Although, she wasn't sure what that amount of time should be; nevertheless, when that acceptable mourning time was over, she'd meet with Mr. Simmons or Mr. Miller. Catherine remembered the legal documents she'd signed years ago naming her the executor of Anton's estate. They would have been null-and-void if Anton had family—a wife or children, but he didn't. He was divorced, and Claire was also missing, as was the child she claimed was his. That all worked together to make those documents now valid.

Catherine's smile grew as she made her way to his office. It was so nice of Marcus Evergreen to come all the way out to the estate to speak with her personally. She couldn't have planned this better herself!

∞∞∞∞∞∞

The café was outside. After almost two weeks in Venice, Claire couldn't stand to be held up inside their hotel suite another minute. Yes, the Hotel Danieli was stunning; nevertheless, Claire had experience at being held prisoner in beautiful places, and she needed air. If that meant more of the disguises, she'd do it. Sipping her warm tea, Claire leafed through the pictures one more time. The blue water and white sand reminded her of her honeymoon. *The private island was amazing, but could it be home?* She knew she needed to make a decision. Phil had been patient, but this was taking too long; even the two of them, being out in public made him uneasy. Claire knew he wanted an answer.

"I'm not sure. I mean it reminds me of Fiji, but what about my baby? Is there medical care"—she added with emphasis—"*real medical care* nearby?"

"Yes, we discussed this. There's a town a mere boat ride away. In that town there's a UK educated doctor. If more extensive medical care is necessary, the town has an air field. You can afford the necessary flight. In less than two hours you can be at a state of the art facility with specialists."

Claire looked down. Maybe she wasn't ready to make this move. She hadn't checked the American news feed in a few days, honestly, she hadn't checked anything. As the adrenaline from her escape waned, the hidden fortune and impending move seemed burdensome. Claire was tired of making wrong decisions.

Phil leaned across the small table and covered her hand with his. The care and compassion she'd seen in his eyes was slowly turning to irritation. His voice was but a whisper in the din of conversation occurring on all sides of them. "Listen, it's your choice and your money, but if you don't make a decision soon, at the *very least* we need to leave Venice. I realize traveling is difficult for you; however, this is my job, to keep you safe—whether you accept it willingly or not." His last phrase held a bit more determination than Claire appreciated.

With the hairs on the back of her neck springing to attention, Claire's lingering sadness at what she'd lost gave way to her new independence. Sitting straight, she removed her hand from his and said, "You're doing your job because I'm paying you—very well—I might add. It *is* my decision and I'm sick and tired of making the wrong ones."

"Yes, you're paying me and I've earned less for more. The fact remains, my job is to keep you safe"—his voice lowered again—"all the damn disguises in the world won't keep you outside the radar on a public street in Venice. Despite the fact the FBI is probably looking for you, your ex-husband's reward makes everyone a possible threat."

As Claire moved to stand, so did Phil.

"Stop," she declared.

He lifted a brow.

In a hushed but determined tone, she said, "I'm going for a walk. I don't need a babysitter. I have my phone and I need to think. I'll be back when I get back." This time, she leaned toward him. "If you don't respect my privacy, I'll find another babysitter. I need a break."

She saw the turmoil in his eyes. She wasn't just a job to him, he genuinely cared about her. Claire knew that; nevertheless, she needed to think. Walking helped her do that. When he didn't respond, Claire nodded and turned away. Though the sky was clear, the temperature was brisk, especially with the breeze blowing between the buildings. Claire reasoned it had to do with impending autumn and all the water.

With the tirade of thoughts swirling through Claire's mind, the world around her was a blur. Unconsciously, her feet moved toward St. Mark's Square, and her eyes watched the pigeons while directing her body to avoid other pedestrians. Though surrounded in all directions, none of the historical beauty registered. Her mind was busy searching for answers. She thought about Tony. They hadn't seen one another for almost a month. Momentarily, memories of their last encounter filled her vision. She remembered him asking her *again* to go to Europe. The irony of the fact that she was now where he'd wanted her—wasn't lost. If only she'd gone with him, perhaps she'd be enjoying the sightseeing, instead of hiding for her life. Berating herself, Claire recognized—*another bad decision*.

She didn't want her move to be impulsive. *Did she even want to move away—forever?* Claire questioned: *was Catherine truly that much of a threat?* Then she remembered Tony's parents and her parents. *Could Catherine have been responsible for her parents' accident as well? What about Simon? No— that didn't make sense. Why would Catherine care about Simon Johnson?* Claire knew in her heart, if Simon's death wasn't a real accident, the guilt belonged with Tony. *If Tony was responsible for Simon, was he also responsible for her parents?*

Her entire body ached with indecision. *How could the woman she'd grown to love as a mother be responsible for so much? How could the man she loved also be guilty?* Claire shuddered against the cool breeze as she remembered scenes she'd compartmentalized away. The images from 2010 streamed through her memories. They weren't as vivid as they used to be— time does that. It takes away the color and dims the sound, yet as she wrapped her arms around herself and felt the tears fill her eyes, she knew, in early 2010, color hadn't been necessary. The only thing that mattered was black.

This unwanted realization struck hard. No matter how much she wanted to love and trust Tony, that black veil of fear would always be nearby. She'd suppressed it and compartmentalized it away; however, its presence was what Catherine used to her advantage. Conceding to this revelation momentarily immobilized her. She sat upon a concrete bench facing the lagoon and watched the number of pigeons multiply at her feet. She didn't see the other people, although they were all around. It wasn't until she heard *his* voice that she even knew he was present.

Of course, she recognized it. Looking up, she saw his blue eyes penetrating her black veil. Her world was no longer concealed, yet it didn't make sense. *How could Harry be there in Venice? Why was he there? Was he really there?* New questions flooded her already saturated mind.

Listen to your intuition.
It will tell you everything you need to know.
—Anthony J. D'Angelo

CHAPTER 6

The familiar ring beckoned Sophia to the kitchen of their Provincetown home. She recognized the melody, telling her of her husband's waiting call. Hurriedly, clicking the *ANSWER* button, Sophia allowed her smile to radiate through the screen. They hadn't spoken in almost a week and her excitement at the handsome profile picture was hard to contain. Waiting for their conversation to connect, Sophia stared at his smiling face knowing that soon she'd see him, as if he were right there with her.

"Hi, honey," she answered as the video feed fought to catch up to the audio. Her thoughts and concerns from earlier in the day disappeared as her husband's soft brown eyes transcended miles, continents, and oceans.

"Hey, beautiful." After almost a week apart, merely the sound of his voice made Sophia melt into her chair. "Tell me you've heard the news."

Sophia's mind searched for recent information. She'd been so busy with her parents' affairs, art studio, old friends, and preparations to return to the West Coast, she hadn't looked at a newspaper or even her homepage in a couple of days. That was part of the charm of living on the Cape—it was a world of its own. Grinning at her husband's image, Sophia answered, "Oh, you know me—always up on the latest headlines!"

Derek grinned and shook his head.

Sophia continued, "I don't think I have. Whatever it is, it must be pretty big if it got to you in Beijing."

"Yeah, I'd say it's big. It's big enough that I'm heading back to Santa Clara tomorrow."

"I'm getting there tomorrow too! I already have my flight booked." Excitement about their reunion dimmed as Sophia pondered the possibilities of Derek's agenda change. "I'm thrilled, but why? You aren't scheduled to come home for another week. What happened? Does it have something to do with travel—has there been a safety alert, are you all right?"

"No, travel is fine. I'm fine, but Anthony Rawlings is missing!"

Sophia stared incredulously at the screen, trying desperately to put her husband's words into a frame of time and space. She hadn't spoken to Derek since her strange encounter in her studio with Mr. Rawlings. Wrangling her thoughts into a manageable quorum, she asked, "When? What do you mean he's *missing*?"

Derek shrugged. "I'm not sure of all the details. A mandatory webinar just concluded. Roger gave everyone from Shedis-tics the basic information. I don't think he wanted any of us to learn it from the news or internet. I haven't had a chance to look, but Roger said it'll be everywhere soon. The entire Rawlings Industries Empire is in defense mode. You know—circle the wagons—stand tall—and get ready for whatever happens."

Sophia shifted in her chair. "Honey, remember we were supposed to talk last Saturday?"

Derek's attention was suddenly diverted to something at the side of his screen. "Ah, sorry, babe, I couldn't get to Skype. Things were crazy. You know, being back in the states for your parents'..." His voice trailed off as he looked back to the camera, concern filled the blue eyes peering only at Sophia. "I'm sorry. Don't get me wrong. I didn't want to be anywhere else, but with you"—the lines in his forehead disappeared as tiny creases formed around his eyes and a loving grin emerged—"That's where I want to be now, too."

Sophia smiled and shook her head; strands of long, blonde hair moved gently across her face. "I know that. Don't worry, but Derek, I need to tell you something that happened on Saturday. First, tell me, when did Mr. Rawlings disappear? And what do you mean *disappeared*?" With each word, her volume increased, exposing her growing concern.

"I think it was last weekend, sometime—something to do with the FBI and the disappearance of his ex-wife." The sound of an incoming call echoed behind Derek's voice. "I really need to go. I'll see you at home tomorrow. Things are insane! I love you!"

"Derek!"—she yelled toward the small monitor—"Derek!" Making her words move fast, Sophia added, "He was here last Saturday! He was in my art studio!"

Her speed of speech was inconsequential. Her husband's image was gone—their connection severed. Sophia stared at the screen for a minute. In place of her husband's moving, talking image, she once again saw his profile picture and name. It went without saying; things must be wild at Shedis-tics and all the other Rawlings' subsidiaries. No matter, Sophia wanted to know when Mr. Rawlings went missing, and when did his ex-wife go missing? She did remember Mr. Rawlings saying he was *off his game*. It was *all* so strange.

Sophia had thought it was odd having him at the studio, asking her to dinner, offering to buy a painting, and then not showing to dinner. She remembered waiting at the restaurant for an hour before she left. Of course, she was perturbed and wondered why he'd invite her, just to stand her up. Then, as she sat alone at the table, Sophia recalled Mrs. Cunningham's remark during the gala, last spring. She said Mr. Rawlings was well-known for his inclination for punctuality.

This new information added to the peculiarity of his visit.

Trying to make sense of everything, Sophia walked back to the bedroom to finish packing. Going home to California held much more promise now that Derek would be there too.

∞∞∞∞∞∞

Claire looked up to see Harry's customary blonde hair blowing in the brisk wind off the lagoon, while his blue eyes stared steadfast in her direction. The black veil covering her world ripped open, exposing her sudden vulnerability. Shaken by this new paradigm, she was unable to speak. Everything was out of context. She had a wig which made her hair black, and contacts that made her eyes a dark brown. She wasn't *Claire Nichols*, yet she was. Phil was the only familiar person who belonged in her new parallel universe. He was the only one she could trust. *How many times had they both discussed that? How many times had they practiced what should happen if their bubble was indeed penetrated?*

Words didn't form as she continued to gape. *Her instinct told her to turn, run, and pretend she didn't know the man now close enough to touch. She could respond in Italian and act offended by his proximity. If she did, would Harry understand? He'd never mentioned his ability to speak other languages—nor had she.* While her internal debate raged, Claire stood and faced the man she hadn't seen since the hospital in Palo Alto—the man who saved her and her baby's life—the man who, for a brief moment in time, thought he was the father of her child. Claire's hand fought the urge to flutter above her growing midsection.

Oh, she knew Phil would tell her to turn away. They were supposed to leave soon. If only she'd made her decision about their hidden location. If only she hadn't gone out alone. If only her life wasn't such a mess—alas, she hadn't—she did—and it was.

As Harry's gaze intensified and his hand reached toward her arm, better judgment prevailed and in near perfect Italian, Claire responded, "Excuse me, sir. I'm afraid you have mistaken me for someone else." Immediately, hurt registered on Harry's face. It wasn't confusion brought on by a language barrier—no, she saw anguish caused by her deception.

He gripped her arm. With emotion filled Italian rolling off his tongue, he asked, "Why Claire? Why are you hiding? You have so many people worried. Why, after *everything* would you lie to *me*?"

Claire nervously glanced from side to side. The people in St. Mark's Square came into focus. Not one of them looked in their direction or cared what was happening. *She didn't know if this was what she wanted to see. Did she want to find Phil lurking nearby? Did she want him to save her and stop her from revealing any of her secrets? Or, was she confirming his absence— verifying her momentary freedom and ability to be honest with an old friend?*

Looking down, away from his icy blue gaze, Claire whispered, "It isn't safe. I can't talk to you." There was no reason to speak in Italian.

When she looked back up, Harry wasn't looking down at her; he was scanning the terrain, perhaps assessing her concern for danger. In the next few transpiring seconds, his grasp of her arm controlled her movement and her, at first, unwilling feet. With quick uninterrupted steps he directed Claire away from the open square, through a large stone archway, down a narrow path, and into a quiet dark tavern. By the time they entered, Claire was no longer resisting. Appearances were too engrained in her behavior. She couldn't make a scene even if she wanted. Besides, it wasn't like he'd kidnap her—Harry wouldn't do that. He was just an old friend, concerned about her safety. That's what she told herself as they passed the small group of customers near the bar. No one seemed interested as they pressed into a booth. Claire sat first while Harry eased in next to her. After so many months apart and the circumstances of their *break-up*, Claire found his approach and proximity unnerving. The warmth of the tavern combined with the touch of his knee against hers, felt suffocating. The man beside her held an air of control she'd never witnessed in him before. Though she hadn't experienced it with Harry, Claire recognized the suffocating sensation. Her face flushed with a consciousness of captivity, as Phil's words: *no one can be trusted*, dominated her thoughts.

Keeping her well-used mask intact, Claire harshly whispered, "What's going on? What do you think you're doing?"

Before her eyes, the look of determination, which had overshadowed Harry's expression, melted away. She watched as the kind, hurt man from Palo Alto emerged. It was as if he were two completely different people. The familiar one looked down at the table and gently shook his head. His voice brimmed with emotion, as he asked, "Do you have any idea how worried your sister is? How worried we all have been?"

Claire wanted to trust him, she did. There was just something wrong with the whole scenario. "How did you find me? Why are you looking?"

The pain in his eyes, the same eyes that had said goodbye to her at the hospital, mellowed Claire's concerns. At the same time, they increased her sense of unease. After all, months ago, she'd been the cause of that pain. Seeing it right in front of her brought back her sense of guilt at the way things had transpired.

"Emily."

More guilt flooded Claire's overflowing emotions. "What about Emily?"

"She asked me to use my resources and try to find you."

Claire looked down at the table as she weighed her words. With hormones raging and emotions swirling, the internal cyclone was difficult to maneuver.

Harry's hand reached for hers. When his warm fingers contacted her skin, the cyclone stilled. She wasn't seeing Emily or John; she wasn't worried about Phil's reaction to this encounter. Immediately, Claire retracted her hand as Tony dominated her thoughts. No matter what she'd done to him in the past, despite the fact she'd left him without a word, her heart was his. Yes, she'd been debating her memories, worried about their future, but none of that mattered. She told Marcus Evergreen Tony was in danger. She hadn't told him the cause, but she would—when the time was right. She'd asked Marcus to secure his safety. Once she was sure that Tony was no longer in danger, her accusations could be told. First, she needed to see Tony—her ex-husband—her fiancé—perhaps her ex-fiancé.

"I'm sorry, Harry. We're friends, I hope"—looking down at their hands—"but not that close of friends—anymore."

"I assumed since you left him—"

"You assumed wrong"—Claire inhaled and softened her tone—"I know it looks that way. I left Iowa for my safety and the safety of"—she almost said *our,* thinking of Tony, but changed it to *my,* since she didn't want to rehash old injuries—"my child. I didn't leave Tony. I know it doesn't make any sense, but it will someday."

The man with determination in his eyes returned. "Safety? If it wasn't Mr. Rawlings you feared, then who?"

"Please don't say anything to Emily. I'm not trying to hurt her; I'm trying to protect her. There's a danger that can hopefully be stopped." Looking directly into Harry's eyes, she added, "And it isn't Tony."

"Claire, none of it makes sense. Does this have anything to do with Chester? Was he working with someone? Does Rawlings know where you are?" Sitting straighter, he asked, "Is he with you, here in Venice?"

Without thinking, Claire answered, "Of course not, he's still in Iowa."

"No, no he's not. Haven't you heard?"

Claire's heartbeat quickened; her arm protectively covering her midsection, Claire asked, "Heard what?"

"A few days ago, a plane Rawlings chartered made an emergency landing in the Appalachian Mountains."

Claire's mind went to Simon; his plane crashed in the mountains. Tears materialized as terror filled her chest. She opened her mouth to speak, but nothing came out.

Harry continued, "They didn't find anyone. The officials aren't claiming anyone died. They also aren't saying anyone survived. At first, I thought about Simon." He reached for Claire's hand. This time, their common bond united them, and the warmth of his skin fused their brief past. She didn't pull her hand away. "But then..." he continued. "I thought maybe it was a ruse for him to disappear and get to you. Emily was so frightened. At first, she assumed he was responsible for your disappearance, then she thought if you did leave, on your own, and not tell anyone, it was because you were scared"—He squeezed her hand—"I believe she's right about that. Of course, she assumed it was Rawlings you were frightened of; then when he disappeared, she was overwrought with worry. She was sure that he'd track you down. She asked me to do it first."

Claire felt the heat of his hand and heard the concern in his voice; however, something didn't feel right. She didn't know what it was. Maybe it was that the whole picture didn't fit together. It was like trying to squeeze the wrong puzzle piece into the opening. The shapes were similar, but when you stood back and looked, the picture was wrong. Sitting with her hand in Harry's wasn't the right picture. She eased her fingers away.

"It's amazing that you were able to track me down. I mean, I've tried very hard to stay hidden."

Harry grinned and nodded. "I didn't say it was easy."

"Yes, but according to that scenario, you were able to accomplish it, in what, in just a few days? SiJo must have resources I never knew."

The casual poise faded. "Well, I called some of my old law enforcement buddies."

Smiling, Claire's expression softened. "I guess it's good you did. Otherwise, I'd never have had the chance to tell you how sorry I am about how everything ended."

Shrugging, he started to answer when a dark-haired waitress came to their table. In Italian, she apologized for the delay and asked if they'd like drinks. Replying appropriately, also in Italian, Claire asked for warm tea while Harry ordered a beer. Before the waitress left, Claire spoke to Harry, still in Italian, "If you'd please excuse me, I need to use the restroom."

She saw the indecision sweep across his face. *If he didn't allow her to get up, it would look suspicious to the waitress. If he did, could he trust her?* Claire spoke first to the server, "You know how it is when you're pregnant. I know every restroom in Venice!" The young woman smiled as Claire turned to Harry and said, "When I get back, I want to hear what you were about to say."

His expression eased as he stepped from the booth. The waitress pointed toward the hall near the rear of the tavern. Claire's eyes scanned from side to side as her feet eased down the back hall. Seeing the exit, she glanced back toward Harry smiling down at the screen of his phone, and she prayed the door wasn't locked. One last glance over her shoulder to see him still looking down, and Claire was again out in the cool autumn air. Reaching for her phone, she dialed. Keeping her face hidden from the wind, she hurried toward Hotel Danieli and listened for a response.

Phil answered on the first ring, "Are you all right?"

"I don't think so. Something's weird. Where are you?"

To be trusted is a greater compliment than being loved.

—George MacDonald

CHAPTER 7

Each step down the west corridor seemed like a hundred. The call requesting his presence in Mr. Rawlings' office was more than strange. First, the news hit the wires over twenty-four hours ago; Mr. Rawlings' plane made an emergency landing. Eric wondered with each step who wanted to see him and what they wanted. If it were the police, he'd been advised to *play dumb*. After all, he'd used alternative identification to fly back East. That same identification was used to rent the vehicle he drove across the Canadian border. Yes, Mr. Rawlings also had alternative identification which no one else knew anything about. They'd had them for years and had used them on occasion. Through the years, Eric never asked questions. Yes, he was paid exceptionally well for his service and discretion; nevertheless, he knew too much, they'd been through too much together.

From the time they were both young, back when Mr. Rawlings was a budding entrepreneur—Mr. Rawlings asked—and Eric did. Maybe he didn't *ask. Was it really a request, if denying wasn't an option?* No matter—neither party ever questioned. It was the perfect working relationship.

Truly, Eric had planned on sleeping for the next few days. Meeting Mr. Rawlings, driving to Canada, seeing him make his way down the concourse on his way to Europe, and driving back to the United States, only to fly back to Iowa all within a forty-eight hour period wiped him out. No one at the estate should've monitored his activity, but if they did, Eric had a story for his recent absence.

During his long trip back to Iowa, Eric contemplated the activities he'd done, over the years, to help Mr. Rawlings. There'd been more than a few happenings which encroached upon the limits of the law. Abducting Ms. Nichols was, without a doubt, the most damning; however, Mr. Rawlings said he saw her statement to the police and there was no recollection of her travel to Iowa. Eric's assistance was only known by his employer.

Since he hadn't officially been informed of Mr. Rawlings' disappearance, Eric planned to enter the office as he would on any given day. Unless he was told others were present, Eric usually opened the door without hesitation. He assumed Mr. Rawlings allowed this because there wasn't much that Eric didn't know. Years of overheard conversations and encounters gave Eric a database of information. Rarely had he opened any door to find something of surprise. On those numbered occasions, when the scene caught him off guard, staying true to form, Eric neither reacted nor later mentioned the incident. In Eric's line of work, secrecy was a valued and essential commodity.

Standing before the grand double doors, he remembered the last time he'd been in the office. It was to retrieve the small key from the top right drawer. That, some cash from the safe, and the alternative identifications, including the *Anton Rawls* identification were Mr. Rawlings' only requests. Eric never said *no*; therefore, when the call came in the middle of the night from a non-traceable phone, those requests—just like all before them—were carried out exactly as instructed. The last thing Mr. Rawlings told Eric, before he walked through security was to go back home and act like nothing happened. He instructed Eric to act like the last time they were together was in Provincetown. Eric didn't question; instead he said, "Yes, sir. Stay safe." Mr. Rawlings nodded in return. It was as close as they would get to an emotional good bye.

Opening the door and stepping inside the regal office, Eric caught the hard gray stare as Catherine rose from the leather chair and said, "In the future, I'd appreciate you knocking before you enter this office, just as you would for Mr. Rawlings."

Although he had years of practice at maintaining a stoic expression, the scene before him incited a combination of shock and rage. His mind swirled with possibilities for Catherine to be behind Mr. Rawlings' desk. None of them made sense.

Reigning in the emotion which threatened his impenetrable veneer, Eric stood before the grand desk and asked, "Catherine, where is Mr. Rawlings?"

"First, I'd like to know where you've been. I needed you two days ago and you were gone."

"I talked to Mr. Rawlings about my aunt a week ago. He gave me a few days to visit her."

Catherine sat again and nodded. "I see, an aunt. Have you mentioned her before?"

"I've mentioned her many times. I don't recall you being present during those conversations. Where is Mr. Rawlings? Mr. Simmons said they'd be back."

Catherine leaned back against the soft leather chair as her cheeks rose in a smile. In Eric's opinion, it was neither warm nor comforting. She began, "That's why I was looking for you. Haven't you listened to the news?"

Eric relaxed his stance. "Why so many questions about my personal habits? No, I usually avoid anything that isn't music or silence." He went on, "Before you ask, there's no real reason, I like quiet."

She motioned toward the chairs near the desk. "Have a seat; we need to discuss a few things."

Suspiciously, Eric eyed the chairs. "Before I sit, tell me what's going on Catherine."

Sitting straighter and squaring her shoulders, Catherine exhaled, "From now on, you and anyone else who wishes to maintain their position here on the estate will address me as Ms. London." When Eric didn't speak, Catherine's eyebrow raised. "Tell me, do you wish to maintain your position?"

Honestly, he had enough money to walk away and live contently for the rest of his life. He'd invested well and had little to no living expense; however, Mr. Rawlings told him to go back to Iowa and act normal. Maintaining his current position would be *normal*. "Yes, Ms. London"—the title only hurt the first time. Eric Hensley was a man of service; as such, he'd accommodate whomever necessary—"I would like to retain my position." With that, he made his way to the chair and listened as Ms. London informed him of Mr. Rawlings' disappearance.

While she spoke about the plane and the emergency landing, he did his best to maintain his facade, while showing the appropriate amount of concern and shock. The best part of being a man of service was that silence was considered accommodating. He didn't need to agree or disagree with Catherine. He only needed to maintain eye contact, nod occasionally and say, "Yes, Ms. London." He had years of practice.

∞∞∞∞∞∞

The text Harry received was exactly what he'd wanted. He looked up and glanced toward the young waitress. With a sly grin, he nodded. Oh, he'd already paid her for her photography skills, and now he had his proof. On his phone were two pictures of him with Claire. There was one of the two of them in the booth talking, and there was the one of them in the same booth with, her hand in his. She was in disguise, but to the knowing eye, it was Claire Nichols. Within seconds, Harry forwarded the non-contact picture to his superiors in the FBI with a text message:

"*CLAIRE NICHOLS FOUND AND SAFE.*" After he hit *SEND*, he saved both photos to his card. He didn't know if they would be useful.

His confident grin began to fade as he realized Claire hadn't returned. It was true, a woman in her condition needed to use the restroom, frequently, but looking at his watch, he thought it seemed odd she hadn't returned. It wasn't until the waitress returned with his beer and no tea that Harry questioned her absence. "Where is my friend's tea?"

"Oh, I'm sorry, Signore. I assumed, since she left..."

He didn't wait for the rest of the story. Harry pulled a few euros from his pocket, placed them on the table, and hurried towards the restrooms. Seeing the rear exit, he quickly reached the door. Harry couldn't believe she'd left. He never assumed she'd slip away that fast. As the cool autumn air filled his lungs, Harry scanned the crowds. Since she'd left the booth over five minutes ago, he truly didn't expect to see her.

After a brisk walk through the Piazza, Harry leaned against a pillar and pulled out his phone. Hitting a few buttons, he found the beacon. According to the locating device he'd successfully dropped in the pocket of her jacket, Claire wasn't far away or moving. Following the pulsating dot, Harry headed toward what he assumed to be Claire's hotel.

∞∞∞∞∞∞

Phil helped Claire with her coat and led her to the sofa. He must have felt her trembling as he said, "Calm down and tell me everything."

Claire stared into his eyes. She'd expected him to be upset. Obviously, he was unhappy when she left him at the cafe; however, instead of anger, she saw concern as golden flecks shone from the depths of his green eyes. Taking unexpected solace in his calming presence, Claire began, "I was sitting on a concrete bench, in St. Mark's Square, looking out at the water..." As she told Phil about her unlikely encounter with Harry, he remained quiet and supportive. She also told him about Tony's plane. When she finally finished, she said, "I'm so sorry. All this work you've done to keep me and my baby safe and in one afternoon I throw it all away."

Phil stood, leaving Claire alone on the sofa, and paced the width of their suite. Claire watched as he contemplated her story. Finally, he answered, "First, you didn't throw it all away. You and your baby are still safe. Also"—he turned towards her and smiled—"your instincts are getting better, I'm glad you're learning to listen to them."

Claire opened her eyes in question.

"Claire, you've been far *too* trusting of *too* many people for way *too* long."

She nodded. "I realize that. I suppose it's the way I was raised. I never expected my life to be like this. Truthfully, I can't even remember what I expected"—she shrugged—"Something like my parents, I guess. Isn't that the basis of everyone's expectations? You either want the same as them or better. My parents were married twenty-six years when they died—together. I never once dreamt that I'd be twenty-nine, divorced and pregnant with my ex-husband's/fiancé's/ex-fiancé's child, nor did I imagine that I'd be hiding from some crazy woman who's a threat to me and my child—or that I'd be filthy rich, because I stole my child's father's secret money." Claire shook her head and grinned. "I don't think I could've even made-up that scenario!"

Phil sat back down. Claire marveled at the emotions she saw in his expression. It wasn't that long ago that he was her shadow, her voyeur; now she considered him a trusted friend. Phil's voice reflected his earlier concern. "No one signs up for this. It is what it is, and life goes on—or it doesn't. I've made choices I regret. I'd assume everyone has. I also made the decision that life would go on. Perhaps some of the things I've done are less than scrupulous; however, my more recent endeavor, despite the legalities, could be considered one of my most honorable. I will *not* fail. You and your child will be safe. I realize you're paying me, well, as you stated, but even you should understand this is about more to me than money."

Claire fought the urge to look away. She knew what he meant. Claire knew she meant more to Phil than anyone ever had. Over the weeks, they'd been together, she learned a lot about Phil. She knew about his military background and some of his special ops. She knew he had no family and no connections. From the time he was very young, he succeeded in his assignments and moved on. This was the first—the only—time he'd made personal contact with anyone. Claire also knew he respected her enough to keep their friendly relationship professional—*or was it, their professional relationship friendly?* Either way, it was more than he'd ever had, and she was grateful for his commitment.

"I don't know what it was about this afternoon," Claire said. "Something didn't feel right. I have no reason to be suspicious of Harry. He's never been anything but nice to me. It's just...I mean, I know how hard you've worked to keep our location secret, and with the help of some *California policemen*, he tracked me down?"

"See, that's the kind of intuition that'll keep you and that baby safe"—Phil sat straighter—"I should also tell you, I've known about Mr. Rawlings' plane since it happened, or since they released the information. I thought you knew and weren't saying anything."

"No, I've been avoiding news from the states lately. I'm so tired of hearing about Emily's quest to find me. It makes me feel guilty"—she looked back to Phil—"If we're confessing, I should tell you, I left something for Tony in the safety deposit box in Geneva."

Phil's brows creased.

"It wasn't like I told him where we're going. I hoped that after Marcus Evergreen, or the FBI, contacted him, he'd know to get away from Catherine. I assumed he'd eventually get to Geneva, to the safety deposit box. I figured after he opened it, he'd want to contact me"—she snickered—"He won't be happy to find his money is mostly gone."

Incredulous, Phil asked, "You left something in the box that allows him to contact you?"

"I promise—he's the only one who'll know. I have a back-up plan if someone else gets in the box."

"Is that why you've been so hesitant to leave Europe?"

She shrugged. "It was; however, after this afternoon, I'm ready."

Phil patted her hand as it rested upon her knee. "Good, we'll leave soon." Standing once again, he asked, "And where, Ms. Nichols, are we going?"

Claire smiled, and this time, despite the colored contacts, even her eyes joined the celebration. "You swear it's a real medical facility?" Phil nodded. "Then, Mr. Roach, I trust you, and we"—she paused and widened her grin—"the Alexanders, are going to paradise!"

I cannot say whether things will get better if we change;

what I can say is they must change if they are to get better.

—Georg C. Lichtenberg

CHAPTER 8

Derek listened as Sophia talked about her unusual encounter with Mr. Rawlings. Although she held all the information, her expression was that of a doe in headlights, wide-eyed with wonder. He couldn't understand why the CEO of his parent company would travel all the way to Provincetown and visit Sophia's small studio.

"I agreed to meet him for dinner, but he never showed. I guess that's when he went missing. I've thought about calling the authorities and letting them know he was in my studio that Saturday morning..."

"I don't know if that's necessary. I asked Roger a few more questions and did a few online searches. Apparently, prior to his disappearance, he was in FBI custody. All I've been able to figure is that it has something to do with Claire Nichols."

Sophia took a sip of her wine as they watched the waves of the Pacific Ocean crest and crash along the strip of shoreline. It was one of their favorite places to visit. Sophia would bring a blanket, and Derek would bring the picnic basket with wine and food. On this autumn day, the beach was virtually empty with the exception of a few dog owners allowing their pets the rare opportunity to exert energy. Sophia assumed the weather was too cool for the Californians. For a woman from the East Coast, the warm sunshine and brisk wind were perfect; sharing it with her husband made it heavenly.

Thoughtfully, she asked, "Didn't you tell me she's missing too? When did she disappear? Don't you think it's strange that they're both missing?"

"She disappeared a little over two weeks before him, and her family thinks he's
responsible. They're making all sorts of noise to anyone who'll listen. Stocks in all of Rawlings holdings are dropping fast now that the news has gone viral."

Snuggling against her husband's shoulder, Sophia sighed. "I'm sure this will be huge for you and everyone employed by one of his companies, but I'm tired of talking about it." Turning her face toward his, their noses touched. She smiled and whispered, "I've missed you so much."

Derek may have answered verbally, but with the sound of the waves and the wind combined with the pressure of his body laying her back on the blanket, she didn't hear him. Concerns for Ms. Nichols, for Mr. Rawlings, and for anyone or anything outside the two of them were forgotten. Yes, Sophia loved her studio in Provincetown; nevertheless, home was definitely wherever she could be with her husband.

∞∞∞∞∞∞

For the second day in a row, Harry followed his electronic bread crumbs along Venice's characteristic slab streets to the Hotel Danieli. The luxurious hotel was made up of three beautiful Venetian palazzi. Staring at the magnificent historic structure, he wondered how Claire could afford her accommodations. All of the information he'd read regarding her disappearance claimed she left without accessing any of her available funds. She didn't take her credit cards or any known cash. As Harry read that information, he remembered thinking, *well, at least this time Rawlings gave her access to funds, or so it appeared;* then Harry reminded himself, *appearances have been known to be deceiving.*

Harry knew the beacon on his phone wasn't deceiving or misleading as it had led him to the same structure two days in a row. Claire Nichols was within the walls of this well-known, beautiful hotel. Yesterday, with help from the bureau, he learned she wasn't registered—at least, not under her name. The hotel had 225 guest rooms and suites; 72 rooms were registered under only a man's name, 23 were registered under a woman's name, and the rest had *Mr. and Mrs.* in the registration. The rooms and suites registered to residents of the United States were immediately eliminated for one reason or the other. That left only 174 rooms/suites as possibilities. When he remembered Claire's near perfect Italian retort in St. Mark's Square, Harry asked for a search of either single women or couples from Italy. Once again, the results were excessive.

Entering the very impressive lobby filled with glass chandeliers, pink marble columns, antique carpets, and gilded ceilings, Harry knew the hotel was too large to hope for another *chance* meeting. He also suspected that after yesterday afternoon, Claire would remain within the confines of her room. Taking in the opulence of his surroundings, Harry decided to go another direction. Obviously, Claire had funds. Once again, he called the bureau. This time, he asked for information on the suites at the Hotel

Danieli, particularly the *executive suites*. If Claire were staying in one of the top hotels, Harry reasoned she was also staying in one of the best rooms. Within seconds, he learned all were occupied by couples; however, there was only one that caught the attention of the agent on the other end of the line. It had been retained by a couple, Mr. and Mrs. Alexander of Paderno del Grappa, Italy, for the last ten nights. There was a note on the registry indicating that Signore Alexander had recently informed the front desk that they'd be leaving first thing in the morning.

Writing down the suite number, Harry grinned. His instincts told him that he'd found her; then, without warning, his satisfaction waned. *If she were registered as Signora Alexander, and Signore Alexander called the front desk, who was Signore Alexander?* She acted genuinely surprised by the news of Rawlings' emergency landing. Her reaction caused Agent Baldwin to assume she wasn't here with Rawlings, but then he remembered the pictures at the San Francisco Bureau and wondered, *could the person in question be Roach, and if it was—was their cohabitation all an act? Or could it be real?*

∞∞∞∞∞∞

Claire packed her luggage while trying to convince herself that leaving civilization, for a while, was the best move. Although Phil asked her to limit her baggage, she wondered how she'd get the things she needed in paradise. It wasn't like she imagined paradise with a drugstore on the corner or a boutique just a boat ride away.

Her thoughts went back to Fiji. Claire remembered the suitcases of clothes she took with her on her honeymoon and how very few of them were ever worn. The memories warmed her and—despite her sweater and slacks—left her chilled at the same time. Sadly, Claire's anticipation for this trip, to paradise, was significantly different; instead of love and romance, she sought peace and tranquility. It wasn't the allure of moonlit strolls on the beach or the stone shower reprieves from the sultry humidity that Claire envisioned. It was the calmness that came with knowing you can go inside or outside without fear of danger. It was the knowledge that she had done everything—sacrificed everything—to ensure the child growing within her would be able to live in peace.

Grasping the long, gold chain that hung from her neck, Claire's knees buckled as she sat on the edge of the king-sized bed and shed a tear—or two. With all her heart, she wanted to hear from Tony. She wanted to tell him that she hadn't left him—she'd left because of Catherine. Claire longed to explain—to have him acknowledge her fear as real; however, part of her, a part that grew every day, also feared him. It wasn't the fear of physical retaliation, right or wrong, she'd compartmentalized that away. No, it was the fear that he wouldn't accept her reasoning, wouldn't acknowledge Catherine as a threat, and wouldn't forgive her for wavering in the trust she promised to give to him. After all, her leaving was the first flake resulting in an avalanche of problems.

Sobbing quietly behind her closed door, Claire decided, *no.* Catherine was the one who covered their world with the deadly depths of snow. Claire's leaving was only the final flake to start the tumble—a simple flake, that became a small snowball, and lead to the avalanche which threatened to cover them all—forever. The last time Claire looked, stocks in Rawlings holdings were still falling, the publisher was threatening to publish her book, and Emily and John were stirring up noise and doubt at every turn. Placing her hand over her midsection, Claire felt the fluttering of butterfly wings.

Did her child understand what she was doing? Did her little one know that this was all for him or her? Claire vowed that she'd do anything and everything to keep this baby safe. By the time Phil knocked on Claire's door, she had two suitcases filled. The rest of her things would remain in the suite. After all, the difference in climate alone didn't necessitate much of her attire. Claire knew she'd be glad to be rid of jackets and coats!

Acknowledging Claire's puffy eyes, Phil asked, "Do you want to go down to one of the restaurants, one last time?"

Claire looked toward the dinner dresses she'd left hanging in the closet. "Thanks, but no. I'm still freaked out about yesterday. Would you please call, and have dinner brought up here?"

Phil nodded. "You know, I'm pretty sure you're going to like it."

"I'm sure I will. How long will you be able to stay?"

Phil shrugged. "Long enough to be sure you're all right with it. I won't leave you, if you don't want to be there."

The fluttering in her midsection suddenly felt like her baby was doing flips. Her hand went to her belly as her eyes opened wide. Oh, she'd felt movement before, but this was different—her entire stomach moved. Claire believed it was probably even visible. More than anything, she longed for Tony. She wanted to share these moments with him; instead, she saw Phil's concerned expression. When he asked if she was feeling all right, tears filled her eyes. "Yes, I'm feeling fine." The baby moved again. With more vulnerability than she intended to show, Claire asked, "Would you like to feel my baby? He's really moving around."

∞∞∞∞∞∞

Phil had never imagined placing his hand on a pregnant woman's stomach, but there was something in Claire's voice—a need he wanted to fill. He knew she didn't want him the way he wanted her; however, at that moment, she needed someone—someone to share in this experience. Being her second choice was more than he'd ever been before—to anyone.

Tentatively, he stepped toward her. When he hesitated, Claire reached for his hand and placed it on top of her stomach. He was afraid to press, but her petite hand pressed his down. Without warning, from under his hand, her stomach moved. *He felt it!* When his gaze met hers, he saw the excitement in her beautiful eyes. "I felt that," he whispered.

Claire nodded, her smile breaking some personal sadness. "Isn't it amazing?"

Phil nodded. "It is." Although he was apprehensive to allow his hand to rest too long, Claire kept her hand pressed against his, taking away his choice. Once the movement slowed, her pressure released. Never in his life had he experienced such an amazing sensation as that of a new life moving beneath his touch. Smiling down at her, he said, "Claire, thank you. That was unbelievable."

Blushing, Claire replied, "It is, maybe my little one is excited about a place to call home—even for a little while."

Phil couldn't help but respect the woman he'd come to know. "It'll take some travel time, but we'll be there soon." Looking down at her packed luggage, he asked, "Do you need anything before we leave? I can go to a shop before we call for dinner, or we can go out together."

Focusing once again on the world around them, Claire shook her head. "I do need a few things, but first I'll need to sit down and make you a list. If we're traveling early, I'd like to get some sleep; maybe you can go after we eat?"

A few hours later, Phil left the suite in search of the items on his list. With each step and the turn around each corner, his clandestine skills worked overtime. Claire's story about Harrison Baldwin didn't make sense. He didn't want to upset her any more than she already was, but the entire encounter worried him. He'd worked too hard to create an untraceable trail, and it wasn't like he was new at this. Claire was right; contacting some California cops would *not* suddenly unlock the secret to their location.

Walking along the slab streets illuminated by lamp light, Phil's thoughts continually looped back to Claire's child. He wanted Claire safe. Now, after the experience of feeling the baby move, he was suddenly concerned about the kid as well. Phil knew that he wouldn't hesitate to assure that both Claire and her child made it to paradise unharmed. Knowing his own history, nothing was beyond the realm of possibilities—Phil would willingly lie, steal, cheat, or kill to fulfill his quest.

Scanning each new location for Harrison Baldwin, he wondered, *would one of those actions be necessary when it came to him?* Claire assessed Catherine London to be her main threat. Phil contemplated, *could it be more involved?* He'd done a background check on Harrison and Amber for Mr. Rawlings; however, he had to admit, he took the preliminary information at face value. Phil ascertained, he'd get Claire settled; then he'd look further into the backgrounds of the *nice siblings* who took Claire under their wings.

    Phil's pocket vibrated.   ∞∞∞∞∞∞

Claire was nearly ready for bed when she heard the knock on the door to the suite. Reaching for her phone, she sent a text:

    "IS THAT YOU? WHY ARE YOU KNOCKING?"

Before she received a response, the second round of knocks echoed through the suite. Cautiously, Claire moved to the peep hole. The lump in her throat grew as she saw Harry with flowers and a sign that read:

    CAN WE PLEASE TALK?

She debated her movements when the phone within her hand vibrated. Looking down, she read:

    "IS WHAT ME? NO! DON'T OPEN THE DOOR. I DON'T CARE WHO IT IS! I'M ON MY WAY."

The next time she peered through the hole, Harry's sign had changed:

    I HAVE SOMETHING I NEED TO TELL YOU—PLEASE?

Wondering how he'd located her again didn't pass through her mind, and what he wanted to tell her didn't seem as important as the look on his face. It was the sadness. She'd left him in Palo Alto. They'd said goodbye at the hospital, but she left without seeing him again. Then yesterday, she'd allowed the stress of her escape to overpower her feelings of friendship—he was her friend—*wasn't he?* They'd been together, he helped her start a new life, and he'd been encouraging and supportive—up until Tony came back in the picture.

Claire placed her hand on her stomach. Their baby wasn't moving. *What was her little one trying to say? Should Claire take the advice of her child and be calm? After all, tomorrow she and Phil were leaving. If she didn't talk to Harry tonight, would she ever again have another chance?*

Let us not be content to wait and see what will happen,

but give us the determination to make the right things happen.

—Horace Mann

CHAPTER 9

P hil wasn't far from the hotel, and his list from Claire wasn't complete. Without a doubt—none of that mattered. Getting back to Claire was his only thought as he pushed through the crowded streets. His stomach clenched with an overwhelming sense of déjà vu. All at once, he was back in Palo Alto outside of her condominium—

Phil knew Claire was with Baldwin. He'd followed them from the airport, and then, he read his computer—telling him about the sensors. He ran as fast as he could. It didn't matter; he couldn't get to her—to her condominium—in time. When he reached her—it was too late...

With blatant disregard for anyone else on the streets of Venice, Phil's adrenaline-filled veins helped him maintain a full-out run. Some people cursed as he pushed past them, while others sent him hateful looks. None of it registered. The only image in his mind was that of Claire laying on the floor, and Chester reaching in the pocket of his jacket...

Phil didn't stop to ride the elevator; instead, he took the stairs two and three at a time. By the time he reached the door of their suite, no one was outside. The hallway was empty and calm. Instinctively, he leaned his head against the door and listened. No sounds were registering from inside the room. All he could hear reverberating in his ears was his own heavy breathing and the sound of his pounding heartbeat. Slipping his key into the lock, he opened the door.

It took only a second for Phil to assess the scene. Claire was sitting on the sofa, her expression neither happy nor sad. It was a look he recognized—the one she wore when she was suppressing her feelings. From the doorway, Phil saw the back of a man's head. Even before the blonde-headed man turned toward the sound of the opening door, Phil knew it was Harrison Baldwin. Phil wasn't thinking about his movements; it wasn't planned; nonetheless, as Baldwin stood, Phil found himself suddenly across the room and chest to chest with the younger man. The fear Phil felt for Claire and her child over the last few minutes came bubbling out. "Tell us what you want! How *in the hell* did you find her?"

"Hey, man"—Harry's open hands came up in a commonly accepted sign of surrender—"I'm not the bad guy here. Claire's in no danger from me."

Phil's volume decreased, yet his tone remained hard. "Then why are you here?"

Claire interjected, "Phil, Harry was just telling me an interesting story. Please"—she looked toward Phil—"please, let's hear him out." Then she added, "Together."

∞∞∞∞∞∞

She'd never seen such rage in Phil's eyes. He'd told her of jobs he'd done, never with too much detail; however, at that moment, when he entered their suite, she saw military—special ops—private detective—and bodyguard—all rolled into one. It wasn't that she'd ever questioned his ability to protect her, but at that moment, there was no room for doubt. Phil's eyes stayed fixed on Harry as he stepped backwards toward Claire.

Despite Phil's obvious displeasure, Claire believed he'd be as surprised as she at Harry's news. Yes, Claire had the monopoly on *hurt;* that went without saying. Even so, Phil would definitely be surprised. Both men stared at one another. Finally, Claire broke the lingering silence, "Harry, why don't you show Phil what you showed me? Show him the reason I finally opened the door." She wanted Phil to know she hadn't acted impulsively.

When Harry reached for his pocket, Claire felt Phil flinch. Reflexively, she placed her hand on his arm and whispered, "It's all right. It's not what you think." The calmness of Claire's voice released some of the tension from the suite; nevertheless, Claire sensed that if it was necessary, Phil was ready to pounce.

Harry opened his wallet and offered the contents for view. Phil stared for a moment, processing the sight before him. Inside the confines of the leather billfold was a badge. Phil turned questioningly to Claire and then back at the badge. Reaching for the wallet, he looked closer. The golden eagle, the woman with the scales of justice, and the words: *Federal Bureau of Investigation.* Next to the badge, in its own compartment, was a card which read: in bold letters—FBI with Harry's picture and the name—Agent Harrison Baldwin.

Clearing his throat, Harry began again, "Mr. Roach, Claire's been telling me what a wonderful job you've been doing keeping her safe. I'll add that it's taken a lot of time and manpower to locate the two of you. I applaud your abilities."

Phil looked once again at Claire. His displeasure at this turn of events was evident in his voice. "Mr., or Agent, or whoever the hell you are—what do you want with her? Why are you utilizing federal manpower to locate her?"

"I can't exactly divulge that information at this time." Shifting slightly in his chair, Harry added, "To be honest, I shouldn't even be divulging my position. It's that we, the FBI, learned of your plans to check-out of Hotel Danieli tomorrow. After locating Claire, we don't want to lose her again."

Phil sat straighter. "I don't believe that's your choice. We're leaving."

"All I'm asking is that you"—his blue eyes softened with his plea—"Claire, remain in contact with me. I'd like to know your location and that you're safe."

Phil interjected, "She has been and will continue to be *safe*. Maybe the FBI should worry about things like terrorists and leave private citizens like Ms. Nichols alone."

Ignoring Phil, Harry urged, "Please listen"—he leaned forward—"You and I—we—Claire—I'm worried about you. There's reason to believe"—Harry shifted in his chair—"*We* have reason to believe that Rawlings will be looking for you. Currently, his resources are limited. We know that; however, there are rumors that Rawlings has funds outside the United States. If he accesses those funds, we can assume"—his icy blue eyes turned to Phil—"despite *your* best efforts, Mr. Roach, that Rawlings will locate Claire."

Claire concentrated on her hands laying calmly in her lap. She didn't want to make eye contact with either man; both knew her too well. When the silence became palpable, Claire took a deep breath, looked up, and green met blue. "So, Harry, did my sister send you?"

"No," he answered truthfully. "She *is* worried and rightfully so. Claire, I wish you acted more concerned about Rawlings."

"Did you receive help from your law enforcement friends?"

"Yes, but they are FBI, not California—"

"Were you ever employed by the California Bureau of Investigation?"

Harry looked down. "At one time."

"SiJo—were you ever employed by SiJo?"

Harry's eyes met hers. "Yes, and I knew Simon; he wasn't only my sister's fiancé, he was my friend. This case has meaning to me!"

Claire's jumble of emotions steadied. She knew Phil's presence helped; nevertheless, she also realized she was once again facing someone who had lied to her on more than one occasion—someone she'd trusted. With her voice rising an octave, Claire asked, "Tell us, what else have you lied to me about in the past seven or eight months? I'm very curious. What about *us*? Was that a lie too? Was there any meaning there?"

Harry looked from Claire to Phil and back. "Claire"—Harry's voice calmed—"perhaps this is something we could discuss in private?"

Placing her hand again on Phil's arm, she replied, "I don't intend to have that, or any other discussion with you in private. Please leave."

"You're in danger. You know that. The FBI wants to help you. Don't be stupid and trust the wrong people."

Claire stood. "Hmm"—straightening her shoulders and feeling the fire flash in her eyes, she replied—"Yes, I've definitely been *stupid*"—emphasizing his word—"in the past. I believe I'm finally learning from my mistakes. Goodbye, *Agent* Baldwin."

Harry took a step toward her. "Claire."

Phil quickly moved between them.

Harry continued speaking, "Listen to me—I didn't call *you* stupid. It's just that you have a blind spot when it comes to Rawlings. Even after everything he's done." Harry spoke quickly, "What I mean is that you never would have left, like you did, if there wasn't some part of you who still feared him." When Claire started to turn away, Harry reached for her hand. "Just give it some thought. Seriously, I don't blame you for being upset with me, but I never kidnapped you, raped you, hurt—"

Claire interrupted and pulled her hand free, "No, you didn't, but you weren't honest with me either! You misled me into believing you were someone you're not. At least Tony was honest with who he was."

"Really? Was he honest when he said his name was Anthony Rawlings or Anton Rawls?"

The intensity of Claire's eyes grew with each word. "*Anthony Rawlings is* his legal name. That isn't, nor was it, a lie; however, I have yet to be assured of *your* legal name." When Agent Baldwin failed to respond, Claire continued, "I will repeat—Tony *has* changed, and *he* isn't the person who I'm running from."

"Then tell me, who *are* you running from? Who scared you enough to leave him, let your family and friends think you're possibly dead, and hide out in another country?"

"You're the FBI—figure it out."

Phil's deep voice entered the conversation. His steadfast tone didn't invite debate. "I believe Claire asked you to leave."

Once again, disregarding Phil, Harry continued, "Claire, how about if you don't leave?" His tone mellowed. "Stay here a day or two longer and think about what I said. Tell me who you're running from. Let me tell you what we know about Rawlings and his connections to other open cases."

Claire stepped past Phil and walked toward the door to the bedroom. "Phil, please show *Agent Baldwin* out." With that, she disappeared through the threshold, shut the door, and left the two men alone. If she tried, she could hear their words, but Claire didn't want to try. She didn't want to think about how yet another person, someone she'd trusted, had lied to her. Tears formed as she remembered late nights with Harry, sitting with him on the sofa of Amber's condominium and recanting details of her private life. During those times, she'd felt safe and supported as she recounted things she never thought she could share with another man. Today, she felt used.

Harry's words from only a few minutes earlier came back to her: *I never kidnapped you, raped you, hurt...*Before she walked into the bathroom to get ready for bed, Claire whispered, speaking aloud, yet not for anyone to hear—more as a validation to herself, "You're wrong, Harry. Now you've hurt me."

When she returned to her room, Phil was standing in the open doorway. His presence surprised her. He usually knocked before he entered her room. "What are you..?"

"Are you all right?"

The concern in his voice wouldn't allow Claire to be upset by his invasion of her private space. She swallowed and nodded.

Phil grinned. "You see, your instincts were right."

A renegade tear slid down Claire's freshly washed cheek. She didn't want to be sad. After all, she'd left Harry for Tony. She wanted to compartmentalize Harry away; however, from the moment she watched Harry walk out of that hospital room, she'd thought she was the monster, the one who took advantage of his feelings and crushed them. During those months in Palo Alto, she considered Amber and Harry her reinforcements, her chess pieces fortifying her with the strength to face Tony. She wondered, *was she just a pawn in a much bigger game? Was anything real?*

With a lump in her throat, Claire answered, "Why doesn't that make me feel better?"

"It will, one day. Just keep listening to them. What are they saying right now?"

Claire shrugged. "That I need to push this away, get some sleep, and concentrate on getting to paradise."

"Are we still leaving?"

"Oh, yes." Her eyes brightened. "Can you get us away from Catherine *and* the FBI?"

Phil smirked. "I've always done better under pressure, and just in case my recent *babysitting* assignment has in anyway caused you to doubt my abilities, you should know—I love a challenge! Tell me, how attached are you to the things in those two suitcases?"

Claire smiled. "I've started over from nothing before. I could care less about the contents of those suitcases, and for the record, I think you've done an amazing job with your babysitting assignment. If I didn't, then I wouldn't continue to trust you with me and my baby's lives."

"Good." Phil casually leaned against the door jam. "We'll keep our reservations for 10:00 AM. There's a taxi scheduled to pick us up; however, we'll leave earlier. There's a seldom used private water entrance to the hotel. We'll be going by motorboat. It'll be cooler, so you might want..." Phil grabbed Claire's jacket, the one that had been lying on the chair since Claire's afternoon outing, and flung it toward her. When he did, something dropped from the pocket.

His casual demeanor evaporated. Putting his finger to his lips, he picked the object up and turned the small device all different directions. Claire watched as his eyes shone and his lips turned upward. With new excitement to his voice, Phil said, "You get some rest. I have a little work to do. This just got easier."

Claire nodded.

As he started to walk away, Phil added, "Oh, and Claire, no matter what sort of ID someone shows you, please don't..."

She grinned. "I won't open the door. I'm going to sleep."

Phil closed the door to her bedroom. Seconds later, she heard the door to the suite open, close, and lock.

∞∞∞∞∞∞

By the time they reached the plane, Claire wasn't sure where they were, or *who* they were. The *Alexanders* were gone—forever. At Phil's urging, she agreed to keep Harry's card with a phone number tucked inside her carry-on bag. Phil said it was *just in case*. Prior to their departure, he examined everything—her purse and clothing—everything, to be sure there were no more tracking devices. The best part of his plan, in Claire's opinion, was when he found another couple scheduled to leave Venice the same time as their reservations. Ingeniously, Phil planted the tracking device in their luggage. Eventually, the FBI would learn it wasn't Phil and Claire; in the meantime, his diversion bought them some additional time.

It wasn't that Claire wasn't willing to work with the FBI or any other branch of law enforcement to bring Catherine down. It was—well—she was hurt. Yes, it may be petty in the grand scheme of her troubles;

nonetheless, she needed time to process the new notion of who Harry was and who he wasn't.

He was an FBI agent.

He wasn't her friend—or at least—he wasn't the friend she thought he was.

∞∞∞∞∞∞

The haze of sleep faded slowly as the harshness of Tony's new reality filled his consciousness. Fighting the need to wake, he heard the sound of another person breathing. Instinctively, he reached for the source. As his hand brushed the rough surface of the cheap sheet covering the twin-sized mattress, he pushed away the disappointment and contemplated the turns in his life. Forcing his eyes to open, he faced the drab, dimly lit interior of the hostel.

The room where he'd slept held ten twin beds—all occupied. As he looked about the room, Tony even noticed that one bed contained two people. Laying his head back on the pillow, he exhaled and questioned this reality. Venice, Italy had always been the lap of luxury. From the first time he visited with his grandfather, it was a milieu of opulence. Looking up at the cracked plaster and listening to the sounds of multiple sleeping people, Tony knew the customary five star suites and gourmet meals were nearby; nevertheless, until he reached Geneva and accessed the safety deposit box, they might as well be a million miles away.

Rubbing his face, the softness of his recent beard growth continued to catch him by surprise. It was part of his new persona. The proprietors of the hostel didn't know him as Anthony Rawlings or even as Anton Rawls. No, the identification he carried, as well as the passport he held, contained a different name.

His departure from the United States had been well planned, well executed, and

well—sudden. After the FBI agents removed him from his hotel suite, Tony was given two options: be retained on charges stemming from harming Claire Nichols or disappear and allow the FBI to continue an ongoing investigation. The Federal Bureau of Investigation guaranteed the charges would eventually be confirmed, amended, or dropped—though their disclosure was less than full. The fact the FBI offered an *out*—a plan B—seemed preposterous. Tony knew something wasn't as it appeared. After all, when it came to deceptive appearances—he was the master.

It was, without a doubt, the card game of Tony's life. As he listened to the potential choices, he maintained his *poker* face and kept his cards close to his chest.

The FBI made it perfectly clear; he was going to be protected from the undisclosed threat. How he chose to accept that protection was up to him: incarceration or temporary vanishment. Although the agents offered a minimum security prison with many liberties, incarceration didn't sound appealing, even if it was, as they said, *for his own good*.

Tony chose option number two.

Of course, Anthony Rawlings wouldn't take their offer at face value. Being the true businessman, Tony negotiated the terms of his disappearance. During those negotiations, he failed to mention the hundreds of millions of dollars he had socked away in Swiss bank accounts. The FBI made demands: all contact with *anyone* from his past was *forbidden*. No one could know about his current situation, with the exception of Brent, since the bureau had a gag order signed by him. Tony agreed to the loss of contact and offered anonymity; in return, he was free to travel. Tony told them it was his opportunity to see the world without the responsibilities of his empire—a rather transparent lie—if he had time to work on it, Tony knew he could've come up with something better. Not buying their story about Claire leaving on her own, he needed the ability to search.

Agreeing to his proposal, the FBI provided Tony with a new identity. With that, they even provided limited funds, including credit cards; however, they too had stipulations for their negotiations. They wanted to be able to reach Tony at all times. When he countered their demand, they remained adamant—determined that they needed a way to contact him in the event of new information regarding Claire. It was clearly an attempt at manipulation—move; countermove.

Honestly, in Tony's opinion, the FBI had been less than forthcoming. *Why would he all of a sudden believe that they needed to contact him to reveal deep secrets?* There was no reason to believe that the distance between he and them would suddenly make them forthcoming. On the other hand, Tony couldn't take the chance of missing information—if they were willing to share.

After their negotiations, the agents gave Tony his new identity and a cell phone. The final words from Agent Jackson still infiltrated Tony's consciousness from time to time, *Mr. Rawlings, this phone must be with you at all times. You're not to re-enter the United States or contact anyone. If you fail in these directives, option two is gone, and you are suddenly a fugitive on the run from the federal government. Be confident—we will find you.*

Tony stood straighter. Although his mind was dominated by thoughts and concerns about Claire, the agent's words registered. He considered retorting: *perhaps like you've been able to find my ex-wife?* In a brief moment of decorum, he chose to remain silent. Maintaining his look of indifference, he replied, "I find this extremely unusual—all this deception and secrecy over a possible charge of domestic violence."

"Oh, Mr. Rawlings, we both know it's more than that, and when the evidence presents itself, I know of more than one agent who's looking forward to contacting you, via your phone."

Tony tried to make sense of the agent's innuendos; his mind swirled with possibilities. While he debated his response, Agent Jackson added, "Rest assured, when it comes to our own—we never forget, and we never stop. No case is ever too old or trail too cold."

"Agent Jackson, I seriously have no idea what you're trying to say."

"Of course not, Mr. Rawlings. That seems to be a reoccurring theme with you. Perhaps, while abroad, you should look into treatment for your memory issues."

Tony's jaw clenched. Fighting with the man who was presenting him with temporary freedom would be counterproductive; nevertheless, the displeasure rang clear in his voice. "I *don't* have *memory issues*, Agent. I'm sure we'll be talking again."

"Yes, I'm sure we will—soon."

Tony knew that his current paradigm was his own doing. He could've taken the bureau's credit cards and identity and maintained a better standard of living than he was currently enduring, but he wasn't willing to play by their rules—he had his own rules.

Before Tony left the clandestine meeting with Agent Jackson, he made one request. Tony asked that Brent *not* be informed of this new reality. It was one of the few unselfish moves Tony had ever made for Brent. It was strange how, when faced with the possibility of never seeing him again, Tony finally saw the friend Brent had been. This non-disclosure was a gift. If things turned out badly, and if undisclosed truths became evident, then Tony didn't want Brent suffering the consequences. Agent Jackson promised to continue the ruse.

With his newly-issued government identity, Tony made it to the airport with a ticket in hand. After passing security, he slipped from the terminal, and with a newly purchased phone, he contacted the only man Tony knew, without a doubt, would respond. He didn't consider it breaking the FBI's rules—Tony considered it playing by his own rules—the way he'd always lived his life.

Tony's requests to Eric were simple: money from the safe—not enough to raise suspicion—the key to the safety deposit box, and his alternative identifications. In case Eric was being tracked, Tony told him to also use alternative identification. As Tony predicted, Eric didn't question Tony's directives or motives—he never had.

Tony did keep the FBI issued phone—for a little while. After purchasing an international disposable phone—with the government given credit card—he texted the new number to the only contact listed within the FBI phone. Tony knew too well that phones could be tracked, and he was pretty confident the phone he'd been given was a constant beep on someone's radar. Leaving the phone in a bathroom in New York State, that beep would now remain stagnant. As Eric drove him across the U.S. border into Canada, Tony received a text:

"WE'LL ASSUME THIS IS OUR NEW CONTACT NUMBER?"

Tony grinned—they'd given him an offer he couldn't refuse. He'd replied with a statement of non-compliance. Their cooperation within his parameters wasn't a win, but it was something. Right now, Tony would take that. With a grin, he replied:

"YES" and hit *SEND*

The cover story—the small plane's emergency landing in the mountains—was completely fabricated by the authorities. Tony didn't even know he'd supposedly chartered a plane, or that it landed unexpectedly until he heard the news. The length the FBI was willing to go for this case proved to him that it was something much bigger than it appeared. Like an iceberg, Tony believed he'd only been allowed to see a small portion. As far as he was concerned, that was fine. They'd created a cover story, which allowed him to do the one thing he wanted to do. He was now free to assess the table, determine the odds, and decide—for himself—what cards he should play. He was free to search for Claire.

Flying from Montreal to Brnik, Slovenia, Tony then took buses and trains in a non-direct route toward Geneva. Before he could start his full-out search for his ex-wife, Tony needed money. The days ran together as they were filled with cheap transportation and accommodations. Every nonstrategic thought was dominated by Claire and their child. During the course of his exodus, Tony concluded her disappearance was somehow related to the gifts and letters they'd received on the estate. Although the thought hadn't occurred to him before, Tony found it interesting that the mailings stopped after her disappearance. Tony hoped and prayed that if Claire were truly running *of her own free will,* that she was ahead of—not with—the asshole who'd sent the threatening packages and tried to run her and Clay off the road. As his thoughts ran together, Tony also worried about her finances. He didn't want Claire and his child living in conditions like he was enduring. Hundreds of times a day, he'd question why. *Did she plan to leave and if she did, why would she do so without money?* As much as he wanted her safe, Tony couldn't wrap his mind around her being alive and talking to the FBI. None of it made sense.

As he planned his return to financial freedom, Tony felt a trace of guilt. It was true, he'd always been the one to move and invest the money, but truthfully, half of it belonged to Catherine. Tony knew Nathaniel entrusted him to take care of her. Taking this money without disclosure seemed wrong; nevertheless, he reminded himself, half did belong to him. Catherine was safe in Iowa, sleeping in *his* house with access to more of *his* money. Honestly, the feeling of guilt didn't last long.

His indirect trail to Geneva was planned and plotted. He had enough cash to lay low and watch things unfold. He wasn't using the federal credit card; it was too obviously a means to track him. Tony was listening to his instincts—they'd served him well in the past. Throughout his life, he'd accomplished many goals. Those goals took time and patience, and without exception, they were all done *his* way. His extremely high rate of success was proof of his own abilities. Tony didn't see a reason to change his strategy. Despite the FBI's directives, this endeavor would be on his terms, and his terms alone.

The financial institution in Geneva was his ace-in-the-hole, one of the cards he didn't reveal. With his current plan, the institution wouldn't be reached for at least another week. He'd love to move faster; however, perseverance was essential to his plan. His profile was low; he maintained anonymity, even if it was with his own false identity and not the one provided for him. He was also doing what he said—traveling. After his financial reserves were accessed, he'd continue to travel; however, at that time, his goal would be to find Claire. The money would make all of it more tolerable.

With Agent Jackson's words replaying in his mind, Tony vowed that after he had his money and located his family, he'd learn more about Agent Jackson's innuendos. *What did the FBI know or think they knew? What was meant by 'one of our own?'* Though he was a master at multitasking, his current situation required his full attention. Tony pushed the agent's words away—he had more pressing matters consuming his thoughts.

Learn from yesterday, live for today, hope for tomorrow.

The important thing is not to stop questioning.

—Albert Einstein

CHAPTER 10

-JUNE 2016-

Meredith's Journal:

June 24, 2016

Finally! It's been almost two weeks since Claire collapsed in the cafeteria. Since I don't have clearance to go anywhere except the cafeteria and kitchen, I haven't been able to learn anything about her progress. That was until today; it was after the lunch, before dinner that a few patients and visitors were sitting in the dining room, talking when I noticed Claire and Emily enter the dining room. They were traveling that same path from the outside toward the residential wing.

I only glanced momentarily; Emily was scanning the room with her eagle eyes! Damn, that woman is suspicious of her own shadow! I turned away just as she looked in my direction. Good thing! If she'd recognized me, then it would have made the last three weeks a complete waste of time.

It was after I turned away that I received my first tidbit of information. At the time, I was delivering coffee to Ms. Juewelz and her visitor who'd left the room for a few minutes. Ms. Juewelz has been at Everwood on and off for years. I'm not sure of her exact diagnosis, but if gossiping were a possibility, I'd put my money on that! Even in my short time getting to know some of the residents, I've realized that Ms. Juewelz seems to have her finger on the pulse of Everwood.

"Can I get you any cream or sweetener?" Meredith asked, as she placed the ceramic mugs on the table.

Ms. Juewelz spoke, her voice barely a whisper, "You're smart to turn away from that woman. She'd probably have you fired if she thought you were looking at them." At first, Meredith wasn't registering Ms. Juewelz' words; it wasn't uncommon for some of the residents to speak about something completely off base from what was said to them.

Keeping her eyes diverted, Meredith watched Emily lead Claire hurriedly along the edge of the dining room. Neither woman seemed to be talking. She tried to read Claire's expression; however, all she noticed were Claire's eyes remaining downcast, avoiding everything as she walked with her arm linked in the crook of her sister's elbow. Refocusing on Ms. Juewelz, Meredith asked, "Why, who is she?"

"She was the wife of that rich guy—but no one can say his name. That woman with her is her sister. She's super protective, but it's a pain in the ass! I mean, everyone here deserves confidentiality, but that woman has that poor lady so isolated she'll never see the outside again."

It was then Ms. Juewelz' guest returned to the table. "Aunt Juewelz, you aren't talk'n about people you're not supposed to, are you?"

Looking her niece straight in the eye, Ms. Juewelz replied, "Who me? Can't believe a word I say. I'm crazy, you know!"

Her niece reached over and covered Ms. Juewelz' hand with hers. Looking straight into her eyes, she said, "I think you're the sanest person I know, Aunt Juewelz."

Ms. Juewelz laughed. "Honey, you need to meet more people!"

Meredith walked away, contemplating Ms. Juewelz' information. Her words broke Meredith's heart and hardened her resolve at the same time. One way or the other, Meredith was going to get herself to Claire!

July 7, 2016

I can't believe how tired I am at the end of my days at Everwood. It isn't mentally tiring; it's physically draining. I've never cleaned so many tables or picked up so many dishes in my life, but I think it's about to pay off! After almost a month, I believe that I'll finally be allowed to deliver meals to patients' rooms. Tomorrow, I have a meeting with Ms. Bali, my supervisor. She said we need to discuss the "parameters of increasing my job duties". I have to give the whole facility credit; they don't allow just anyone to interact with the patients. Considering the amount of money these people spend for their treatment, I guess it's a good thing Everwood makes sure that everyone's following their rules. I'd write more, but honestly, I'm exhausted. I'll write more tomorrow.

July 8, 2016

I did it! I've been "promoted"! I'm calling it that, but there's no increase in pay, only an increase in clearance. I think the stories I've recently been telling about caring for my ill grandmother helped me get this additional duty.

Starting next week, I'll be part of the residential room rotation. There are six women who eat all their meals in their rooms. Ms. Bali took me around to each of their rooms today, and I met three of them. The other three, including Claire, weren't in their rooms. Before we went from room to room, I was shown how to review the ICP on each patient. That's their "Individualized Care Plan". I hadn't been able to access more than the generic information before, but now I have a code where I can see specifics. Most ICPs include food allergies, likes, and dislikes.

Claire's Food ICP was very specific, with certain rules spelled out:

Ms. Nichols will have three meals delivered each day. Upon delivery, attendants will assess Ms. Nichols' ability to eat unassisted. If she engages, leave food and return to remove tray in thirty minutes. If she doesn't engage, direct her to her table and explain your actions as you assist in feeding her.

Talking is recommended by Ms. Nichols' doctors; however, Mrs. Vandersol will not allow any conversation regarding Ms. Nichols' previous life. Under no circumstance can the name Anthony/Tony Rawlings be mentioned. IF Ms. Nichols brings up this name, staff is to change the subject immediately and notify a supervisor.

Failure to adhere to the set rules will result in immediate dismissal.

I was surprised to see her room. Unlike the other rooms we visited, Claire's looked generic and sterile. The colors were all pale. She didn't have any pictures or personal items, other than her clothes and hygiene items. Even the bedspread and window treatments were neutral; there were no bold colors. Since Ms. Bali was with me, I couldn't look around too much, but I mentioned the starkness in passing.

"Is this patient new?" Meredith knew the answer; nonetheless, she was fishing.

"No, this is Ms. Nichols, the patient you read about with the specific rules regarding discussion. She's been here for over two years."

"Her room isn't as personalized as the other ones we've been in."

Ms. Bali dismissed Meredith's observation. "That's none of our concern. It's Mrs. Vandersol's doing, and I do believe it goes along with the conversation rules."

I wanted to ask more, but was afraid I'd raise suspicion. As we walked toward the kitchen, Claire passed us with a tall, pretty blonde woman. She looked our direction momentarily, but didn't seem to recognize me. I don't know if that's good or bad, but I guess in a way it's good. I've been concerned that she'd react as she did in the cafeteria the first time we saw one another. If she did that again when I entered her room, I surely wouldn't be able to continue doing it.

After they passed, Ms. Bali whispered, "That was Ms. Nichols with Dr. Brown. It's sad, you'll see when you start visiting her, but she's lost all sense of reality. You may have read the book about her, but she's had a pretty rough life for someone so young. I keep hoping that one day she'll snap out of it."

Meredith paused for a moment before asking, "Is that possible? Can people really *snap out* of it?"

"I've been here for over twenty years, so I've seen a few cases; however, we shouldn't keep our hopes up. Cases like that are extremely rare..."

I'm going to do some research and see if I can find out how you can facilitate that "snapping". Oh, I told her I hadn't read the book, but I'd look it up. Then she told me not to, that she probably shouldn't have told me, and it would probably bias my opinion.

She has no idea how biased I already am!

∞∞∞∞∞∞

Emily entered the waiting room of Everwood's counseling center. She knew the facility backwards and forwards, and this was her favorite area—that is, if she had one at all. It was airy and open, with plenty of sunlight. They'd paid extra to get Claire a window that faced East. Emily knew her sister loved sun and hoped that the sunrises would help her; however, according to the reports, each morning when the staff entered her room they found her draperies still closed. At first, Emily had been more willing to entertain suggestions for Claire's recovery, but with each passing day, week, and month, Emily's optimism waned.

This was Emily's bi-monthly meeting with Claire's doctors, where she'd listen to their theories and suggestions. Once a month, she met with the administrators and discussed confidentiality. At those meetings, she emphasized the importance of maintaining her rules. With these obligations, as well as visiting Claire at least three times a week, Emily's schedule was very full. She also had a family at home that needed her attention. That family was larger than it would have been without Claire, and for that reason, Emily swore she'd never be regretful. Nichol was a joy, whom she and John were honored to raise. Of course, sometimes she wondered if Michael suffered because of loss of attention, but then she'd see the two cousins interacting like siblings and realize, Nichol was a blessing—despite her parentage.

"Mrs. Vandersol," the receptionist's voice brought Emily back to present. "Dr. Brown is ready; may I take you back to her office?"

"No, Sherry, I know the way."

Sherry smiled. "I'm sure you do, please help yourself."

As Emily walked the corridor toward the doctor's office, she thought about Claire's various doctors and therapists. At Everwood, every employee was female. Since a number of the residents were victims of domestic violence, the belief was that decreased male interaction helped to facilitate their recovery. Even male visitors were restricted to special rooms, away from the general population of patients. Emily had visited those rooms too, the first few times John visited. Now, at least once a month, he'd come visit Claire. The moment he laid eyes on Nichol, he abandoned his anger regarding Claire and Anthony's reconciliation. John not only stepped up as an uncle and a father-figure, but also as a brother-in-law.

After everything happened—the incident—John needed to return to California. After all, he worked for SiJo and had obligations. Of course, Emily stayed in Iowa with Claire. At first, Claire was too frail and Nichol needed care, then there was the trial. With time and Emily's pregnancy, traveling became difficult. Staying in Iowa was convenient; nonetheless, she never assumed they'd make it home. Truthfully, they didn't consider it—until Timothy Bronson approached John.

Tim was named acting CEO of Rawlings Industries, by the board of directors, when Anthony initially disappeared. Although he was young, he'd proven himself to both the board and investors. Considering all she and John had done to harm Rawlings Industries, it seemed unbelievable that Tim would ask John to help rebuild the empire, or that the board of directors would approve his request. Tim did—and so did the board. Emily recalled the lengthy discussions by both John and Tim and her and John. The final deciding factor was the court's decision allowing Claire to enter a private mental treatment facility. The court had one stipulation—Claire couldn't leave Iowa. Prior to that, Claire had been in a state run facility. It wasn't awful, but Emily hated it. She visited almost every day to assure Claire's well-being. Of course, back then, Emily's hopes for her sister's recovery were much higher.

There was no question—Everwood was a much better facility; nevertheless, Emily didn't feel right leaving Claire and living across the country. In the beginning, Emily believed having Nichol near her mother would be beneficial. Unfortunately, those visits proved to be another failed attempt to facilitate Claire's recovery. Once Nichol was old enough to understand the situation, Emily believed her niece's best interest needed to be considered—Nichol hadn't been to Everwood in over a year.

The court no longer dictated Claire's treatment; as next of kin with power of attorney, Emily had complete control. Iowa was now their home, and John was gainfully employed by a recovering Rawlings Industries. Meredith Banks was right when she said Nichol didn't lack for money, and neither did Claire. That was John's incentive. This time, when he considered the offer to work for Rawlings, he wasn't accepting charity from a family member. No, this time, he was providing help to his family. Claire and Nichol couldn't manage or grow their fortune. Since Anthony was gone, John did what he'd done years earlier when Emily and Claire's parents died; he stepped up.

Emily squared her shoulders and knocked on Dr. Brown's open door. The pretty blonde psychiatrist stood and welcomed her, "Emily, please come in. I hope you don't mind, but I've invited Dr. Fairfield to join us today."

It was then that Emily noticed the older gentleman sitting off to the side of the room. The fact he was male caught Emily by surprise. "Hello"—she extended her hand as Dr. Fairfield stood and shook it.

Before Emily could say more, Dr. Brown began, "I've asked Dr. Fairfield to join us today because he's a research professor at Princeton, specializing in traumatic brain injuries. I heard him speak a few weeks ago at a conference and believe he could give us a fresh perspective on Claire."

Emily sat taller. "Research? I'm sorry, Doctor, but I don't want anyone *experimenting* on my sister. She's been through enough already."

Dr. Fairfield spoke—with a thick English accent, "Mrs. Vandersol, I assure you, I'm only here to offer my opinion. I won't use any of the data regarding Mrs. Rawlings without your permission."

"Ms. Nichols, Doctor, I need you to understand that the name *Rawlings* may *never* be used in the presence of my sister—No exceptions."

Dr. Fairfield looked toward Dr. Brown. Dr. Brown smiled and spoke, "Emily, I've only shared the medical information with Dr. Fairfield—nothing personal. I promise we'll review all of that before he examines Claire. Currently, he's only seen her CT scans and read my notes. I believe there's something I'm missing. I don't know what it is; however, Dr. Fairfield has documented cases of spontaneous recovery—"

Emily interrupted, "I've done my research. Most recoveries occur within the first year. After that, the likelihood is greatly diminished. Isn't that right?"

Dr. Fairfield replied, "That's correct; however, the cases to which Dr. Brown is referring were significantly outside the normal time period for recovery." Emily contemplated his words as he added, "One case was four years out."

Four years! Emily thought about that. It'd already been over two. She'd come to terms with the idea that Claire would never recover, *but was that a life?* "What does this mean? What will you do to Claire?"

Dr. Brown replied, "We need your permission for Dr. Fairfield to examine Claire and possibly perform more tests."

"More tests? What other tests could you possibly perform which other doctors haven't already done?"

The doctors spent the next forty minutes explaining Dr. Fairfield's research. The tests weren't invasive, and Emily's rules would be maintained. They may introduce some medications or combination of medications that have been previously untried. First, Dr. Fairfield wanted to determine if the cause of her psychosis was indeed head injury, or if it could be something else.

Emily reluctantly shared Claire's history. She didn't like the idea of more treatment. After all, Claire was content. *Why make her uncomfortable or uneasy?* Then again, if there was even a remote possibility—Emily couldn't say no.

That night, at home with John and the kids, she watched as Michael and Nichol played. When she looked at her niece, she saw Claire and the same carefree ambition her sister once possessed. She also saw the dark eyes of Anthony Rawlings. There were times she detested those eyes. When that negativity crept in, Emily reminded herself—nurture verses nature. Nichol wouldn't know the life of revenge that her father had allowed to destroy him and anyone else unfortunate enough to be within his sphere of influence. Her eyes would see the world as a place of endless possibilities where love and forgiveness prevail. Emily vowed that with her and John's help Nichol would see the world as her mother once had—before—

∞∞∞∞∞∞

July 15, 2016

I finally did it, but I don't know if I'm happy or not....I delivered Claire's lunch and was able to talk to her. When I entered her room, she was sitting at the window, looking out at the bright skies. Although I spoke and made noise, she didn't acknowledge my entrance. At first, I hesitated to make eye contact.

What I didn't realize was that I couldn't. I stepped in front of Claire, but her expression didn't change. She continued her gaze, exactly as it had been, as if I weren't there at all. I tried speaking, quietly at first;

then louder. Although she didn't speak or look at me, she eventually got up and walked to the table where she allowed me to feed her.

After Claire ate about half of the lunch, she abruptly stood and walked back to the chair by the window.

Truthfully, I'd been so emotional while she ate that I'd forgotten to speak. When I looked at my watch, I realized I still had ten minutes before I was expected back to the kitchen, so I went back to her. Kneeling in front of her, I touched her knee...

"Claire, can you hear me?" Meredith desperately tried to keep emotion out of her voice; however, with the tears sliding down her cheeks, she wasn't sure it was possible. Intellectually, Meredith knew the rules regarding Ms. Nichols. Truthfully, she wasn't thinking. Her heart was breaking at the sight of her friend, now a shell of the vivacious woman she'd once been. "Claire, it's me, Meredith. Don't you remember me? We went to Valparaiso together..." Meredith was careful not to mention Anthony, Nichol, or anything else from the last six years. She did, however, ramble on for ten minutes about life as it had been when they were college students.

Never once did Claire's expression change; although, at some point, she began humming. Undeterred, Meredith rambled about their sorority house and Chicago. It wasn't until Meredith was out of Claire's room, nearing the kitchen, that Claire's tune resonated in her mind. Meredith recognized the song: *Take Me Out To The Ball Game*—the seventh inning stretch at Wrigley.

July 15th, 2016 continued:

I want to believe she heard and understood. I don't know; maybe I'm grasping at straws. After all, most of what I've read says that if recovery isn't made in the first year, it rarely happens—but that song! I was talking about Chicago and baseball games. I don't think I even mentioned the Cubs or Wrigley, but I know I mentioned baseball...

Without a doubt, I know she was humming "Take Me Out To The Ball Game!"

Contentment consists not in adding more fuel,

but in taking away some fire.

—Baldwin Fuller

♠ ◇
♡ ♣

CHAPTER 11

Claire marveled at the shades of blue as the small plane circled over the island, completing the final leg of their journey. Although her mind constantly went back to her honeymoon, Claire reminded herself this was another place and another time. On her honeymoon in Fiji, Tony was with her, and he was in control.

Here, instead of Tony, she had Phil by her side. With each passing day, Claire appreciated his devotion and presence more and more. His honesty exposed her true threat, and his skills freed her from Catherine *and* the FBI, keeping her and her baby safe. She knew, without a doubt, she wouldn't be where she was without him, yet despite all they'd experienced, their roles were so different than anything she'd ever known with Tony. In every matter of importance, Claire had control. After all, her money purchased this paradise retreat. Phil presented her with choices, but every decision was hers. At times, that power was intoxicating; at other times, it was daunting. After years of submission, it was a whole new way to live. Surprisingly, there were times she found herself missing the sense of security that accompanies that loss of responsibility.

As the scenes below her—those of a tropical paradise—bright blues, greens, and whites faded from her consciousness, Claire recalled memories of her recent life in Iowa—the one she left, walked away from, or more accurately, the one from which she ran. In the depths of her heart, she knew, for a short time, she had everything she wanted and more. She and Tony had an understanding; he had the control he needed, but so did she. She came and went as she pleased. Yes, she informed him first, but that was it. Claire *informed* Tony—she didn't ask permission—nor did she seek his approval. He allowed it because they *trusted* one another. In the pit of her stomach, Claire knew she'd been the one to break that trust—to break the promise they'd made in their meadow of confessions. Perhaps that was Catherine's plan; by convincing Claire to flee, Catherine successfully broke the trust she and Tony had built. Even if Tony contacted her, Claire wondered, *could it be rebuilt?*

What they had, before Catherine took it all away, was the perfect blend. Claire knew her sister, Emily, would never understand, and with the recent news of Meredith's book's pending publication, the rest of the world would probably never understand. Claire wished she could explain. Thankfully, she didn't need to. It was one of Phil's most endearing qualities—he didn't pry.

Understandably, she never gave Phil the word for word, action for consequence, reminiscence of her life with Tony—At least, not like she'd done with Harry; nevertheless, Phil's job involved knowing. If he hadn't been good at his job, then he'd never sent the note in San Diego. Phil knew her past and never once had he questioned Claire about it; instead, Phil encouraged. He encouraged her to stay strong, protect her child, and trust her instincts. Right now, although she longed to hear from Tony, her instincts told her that she was finally safe. They reassured her that the trust she'd bestowed on Phil wasn't misplaced. For once, she'd made a right decision.

As the plane's pontoons touched the surface of the shimmering water, Claire pushed her memories and desires away. This was her experience, her new life, and the future she was choosing to have with her child. The sound from the plane wouldn't allow them to converse; therefore, Claire straightened her neck and squared her shoulders as she touched Phil's leg. When he turned to acknowledge her, Claire smiled.

She wanted him to know that she enjoyed the view outside of the plane—she was content. Phil probably realized her expression was forced; nevertheless, as far as Claire was concerned, it was real. She was tired of compartmentalizing—her new theme was *fake it until you make it.* Maybe in reality it was a bluff, but she had a lot riding on this bet—she'd secure her poker face and see it through.

As Phil helped Claire out of the plane, she held onto his hand for stability, and looked all around. Below their shoes was a white, sand lined beach, and behind them was the shimmering lagoon which opened to an endless horizon of blue sea. Waiting patiently on the shore were two people.

Phil's research of possible destinations included staff members' biographies as well as complete histories of the locations themselves. On this island, the main house was built in the late 1970's by a wealthy Englishman who arrived with his staff of two. Francis and Madeline were married in Haiti prior to traveling to this destination. When the

Englishman died, they stayed, and over the past thirty plus years, they've maintained the estate and cared for multiple families. Claire's new house had many bedrooms and would have more than enough room for her and her child. Apparently, some of the previous owners had multiple children and grandchildren.

The isolation of this retreat was one of its most appealing aspects. There was a time when Claire didn't like being alone; however, she was tired of unknown threats. This retreat would provide her child with the security that only comes from seclusion. For her child, Claire was more than willing to accept the loneliness that came with an island that was only accessible by boat or plane. Civilization—or something close—could be reached by a thirty minute boat ride; weather provided. This region boasted 363 days of sunshine a year; however, the lush vegetation required rain. Though usually short in duration, Phil's research reported storms which could be intense. Deluges of rain followed by powerful sun created the perfect combination for a sultry, humid climate. After nearly a month in cloudy, cool Italy, Claire was ready for the warmth.

As they stepped toward the warm smiles of the caretakers, Madeline, a large woman with dark skin and a deep, rich voice, was the first to speak, "Welcome Madame el and Monsieur Nichols! I am Madeline and this is my husband, Francis."

Claire looked at Phil and grinned. She liked the sound of Madeline's voice; it added to the warmth in the air. Offering her hand in greeting, Claire said, "Hello, thank you. I'm Ms. Nichols, but please call me Claire, and this"—she looked to Phil. *How could she possibly explain who he was?* His definition had changed so drastically over the last year—"This is my *friend*, Phillip Roach. He helped me find your wonderful island."

Francis shook Phil's hand. "Madame el, but this is *your* island, and we are so very happy to help you with anything you need."

Placing her hand over her midsection, Claire sighed. "I'd love to see the house."

Madeline nodded and led Claire toward a path. Her smile shone brightly as she said, "Why of course, let me show you your home, and I'll get you something to drink. We cannot let you dehydrate. The sun here, it is very strong; even now, before noon." After a few steps, Madeline asked, "Your baby, Madame el, when is she due to join us?"

She? Claire didn't know the sex of her child, but she'd always referred to it as *he*—the dark-haired, dark-eyed little boy who would look like his father; however, the little boy in her dreams would never know the sadness his father did. Her little boy would grow up with love and support; then, one day, he'd become the man his father finally became. "Oh, I don't know if I'm having a girl or boy." Madeline didn't speak, but her deep brown eyes sparkled knowingly. Claire continued, "And my little one is due the middle of January; a New Year's baby."

"We love babies. Francis and I—we were never blessed with children of our own; however, we've shared our hearts with babies who now live all over the world. Thank you for bringing us another baby to love."

Although Claire hesitated to trust anyone ever again, she instinctively liked this woman. It wasn't just what Madeline said, but it was her whole aura that pulled Claire near and filled her with promise. When they passed the threshold to her new home, Claire exhaled. For the first time in ages—she was home. Her home was beautiful, light, and open—everything she'd always desired. Claire walked to the open doors, inhaled the sea breeze, and listened to the sound of the surf. Madeline's voice refocused Claire's thoughts. "We like to have everything open; there's usually a refreshing breeze, but if it's too hot for you Madame el, we do have air conditioning."

Although the perspiration dripped between Claire's breasts, and she needed to lift her hair off her neck, she grinned. "It'll take me a while to get used to it, but I will"—Adapting was one of her specialties—"Please don't use the air conditioning. I love the fresh air and the heat."

Her heels clicked on the shiny bamboo flooring as they entered the master bedroom suite. "This is your"—Madeline hesitated—"and Monsieur Roach's room?"

Claire placed her hand on Madeline's arm. "No, Madeline, Phil is my *friend*. He and I are *not*—together. He isn't the father of my child."

"He loves you. I see that in his eyes."

Claire stared. They were friends—but *love?* She'd have to think about that another time. "He's helped me a lot."

"It's not my business. I simply work for you."

Claire wanted to explain that her baby's father would hopefully be coming to the island; however, she didn't know if that were true. Besides, her story was so complicated that she didn't have the energy to share; instead, Claire nodded and walked beside Madeline as she learned more of the amenities of her new home. The master bedroom also had a wide, closable opening to the lanai. When they stepped back outside and peered around the drape of flowered vegetation, the view took Claire's breath away. The sea below was multiple shades of blue. Staring at the water, Claire wondered if depth influenced the hues. As she scanned toward the horizon, the waves blended seamlessly into the crystal blue sky. Walking further out into the sunlight, Claire realized the lanai wrapped around the house. It was the same porch she'd seen from the living room, the one with the large infinity pool, umbrella covered tables, lounge chairs, and groupings of chairs all perfectly arranged.

When Claire entered the kitchen, she couldn't contain her grin. They were in the middle of paradise, not even a dot on most maps, yet she was in the middle of a high tech, state-of-the-art kitchen. "Wow!" was all she could say.

"Oui, the last family loved cooking. The previous owner, she had the kitchen rebuilt, making it even bigger than the original."

"I love it! She did a great job, and so have you. Everything's amazing!"

Madeline's eyes brimmed with pride. "There is so much more. Francis and I have a home too. You may see it, and there are gardens, paths, orchards, and so much more."

"I want to see it all; however..."

Madeline nodded. "Oui, Madame el, you've had a long trip and need to rest. Let me bring you some water and maybe some fruit?"

"Thank you, that sounds wonderful." Turning to return to her suite, Claire said, "I'm not sure where Phil is."

"He is with Francis, Madame el."

"When he returns, can you please show him to one of the other bedrooms?"

Madeline agreed and promised to bring Claire some water and a snack soon. Once Claire was back in her private suite, she decided to investigate her surroundings a little further. The attached bathroom was modern and bright with a skylight above a large, sunken tub. There were two other doors she hadn't yet opened. The first one led to a small, private office. Nodding approvingly, Claire knew it would make a perfect little nursery. Fleetingly, thoughts of the nursery in Iowa came to mind; instead of compartmentalizing them away, she stared at the office and imagined it filled with a crib and changing table—the new thoughts overpowered the old. Her cheeks rose as she focused on her future.

The next door led to a closet, only slightly smaller than the office/nursery. The clothes she'd ordered filled the drawers and hung from the racks. Slipping off her heels, Claire fingered the soft fabric of the sundresses and contemplated changing out of her traveling clothes. She also considered a relaxing soak in the big tub when she smiled. The realization gave her a sense of peace she'd been missing for too long. She was doing it—she was adapting to this new normal.

Her epiphany, Madeline and Francis's friendly greeting, and Phil's unrelenting support, all worked together to bring happiness back to her life. When the knock came on her door, Claire called, "Come in, Madeline."

The door opened, and Phil answered, "I'm not Madeline."

Seeing the golden flecks in his green eyes, Claire thought about Madeline's assessment. She didn't know if it were true; she didn't see love in Phil's eyes—

she saw concern. Wanting him to know how delighted she was about the island and all he'd done, her voice brimmed with excitement. "You're right! I love everything about it!"

Phil exhaled. "I'm glad to hear that. What do you think about Francis and Madeline?"

"I don't know for sure, but I think I like them."

"Good, so do you think you can stay here?"

Claire grinned. "I do. What were you doing with Francis?"

Phil explained that Francis showed him around the outside of the estate. There's a boat at Claire's disposal—any time she wants to travel into town, Francis will accompany her. There's also access to a helicopter or plane in case of emergencies.

Claire sat on the edge of her bed. "Well, I hope they won't be necessary; however, I want to schedule a doctor's appointment for a check-up."

"Talk to Madeline; she can help with that. Remember, there's a real doctor in town."

"I think this'll work. Thank you so much—for everything."

Phil nodded. "You're welcome, Claire. It seems my job is done here..."

Her new-found contentment evaporated with his declaration. Suddenly, the remoteness of the island filled her with angst. "You're leaving?" she asked. "But—I—I just asked Madeline to show you to one of the other rooms."

"She did, and it's great, but if you're happy and safe, I don't think I should—"

Tears teetered on the edge of Claire's eyes as she stood and asked, "Will I be able to contact you?"

"Is that what you want?"

What did she want? Claire knew she didn't want what Phil wanted, or at least what Madeline said he wanted; nevertheless, she didn't want him to go. The way she'd introduced him to Madeline and Francis was accurate; Phil was her *friend*. She trusted him, and she wanted him around. For most of the last year, he had been. Even before she really knew him, he was there—watching—protecting—a constant in her world of change. Claire blinked her eyes, and the teetering tears slid down her cheeks. "I want to have people around me that I can trust. I don't know Madeline or Francis—not yet."

"I did a thorough background check. They're very transparent, so what you see is what you have."

Claire nodded.

"I have another job waiting."

Claire's neck stiffened. "I understand; you're tired of babysitting."

"Claire, I asked the pilot to wait. I think this is best."

"Thank you. Thank you for protecting me, getting me here—for everything." She wanted to reach out and hug him; however, she couldn't bear to hurt anyone else. If Madeline's assessment was true then Phil was right—his leaving was best. "Maybe someday—"

He interrupted, "I'll leave you my number, but remember—only make emergency calls—and also—for you and your baby's safety—don't contact anyone but me or the FBI."

Claire swallowed and nodded.

Before she could think of anything else, Phil was gone. An overwhelming sense of seclusion engulfed the room as she watched the door shut. Inhaling deeply, Claire fought the feeling of suffocation, suddenly threatening her ability to breathe. When the air finally filled her lungs, a sob erupted from the depth of her chest. The trip from Venice had taken days. They'd created an intricately woven web designed to detour anyone's efforts in finding them. Suddenly, the trip and Phil's departure were too much. Claire collapsed on her big, lonely bed.

The ceiling fan that moved the hot, sticky, midmorning air did nothing to cool the room. Despite the oppressing heat, Claire wrapped herself in the soft comforter and cried herself to sleep.

When she woke, her eyelids felt swollen. Claire wasn't sure how long she'd slept. The clock near the bed read 3:18, and the sun on the horizon told her it was afternoon—not morning. Rubbing her temples, Claire realized she needed food to help her aching head and settle her nerves.

As she neared the table by her door, she knew Madeline had been in her room. There was a pitcher of water and a covered bowl within a bowl of ice. Lifting the lid, Claire's stomach growled as she saw the luscious fruit. She tried not to think about Phil or being alone; instead, she ate the fruit, drank the water, and talked out loud to her baby. *Perhaps if she explained how everything would work out, in a calm, reassuring voice, then she'd believe it too?*

Within days, the customary staff/lady of the house, protocol was forgotten. Claire spent hours with Madeline in the state-of-the-art kitchen, learning to cook foods she'd never previously tried. She also spent time with Francis, caring for the tropical gardens and fruit trees.

Madeline arranged for Claire to visit the doctor, and Francis accompanied her. Traveling by boat was something that would take time to get used to. Once on the mainland, Claire loved how Francis helped her feel welcome and secure.

She was both relieved and happy to learn that the doctor Phil promised truly did exist. He was educated in the UK and spoke English as well as many of the native languages. His clinic was modern and even had an ultrasound. Claire was now twenty-six weeks into her pregnancy. Since it had been over a month since her last visit, the doctor recommended an ultrasound. The image amazed Claire—so unlike the original peanut-shaped picture she'd shown to Tony. This time, she saw her baby's profile, as well as, little hands and little feet. When he asked if she knew the sex of her child, Claire remembered the conversation she'd never had with Tony; the one asking him to go with her to her next appointment. With tears in her eyes, Claire replied, "No, doctor, I don't, and I don't want to know—not yet." He willingly kept the information hidden.

Every midday and evening, Claire would sit down to eat with Madeline and Francis. The idea of eating each meal alone was too daunting. Within no time at all, meals became Claire's favorite time of day. She loved to watch the two of them interact, as Madeline's expression absolutely glowed when she was near Francis. They had so many stories to share; Claire could sit and listen for hours. To Madeline's insistence, each meal began with a prayer. It was a ritual Claire hadn't practiced since she was young, and after so much change and discord in her life, she found it comforting. It wasn't what Claire imagined her life would be, but at least she felt safe and accepted. Considering everything she'd endured—that was a lot—more than she could ever ask for...

Those who have trusted where they ought not,

will surely mistrust where they ought not.

——Marie von Ebner-Eschenbach

CHAPTER 12

A
lthough it was only a little over two weeks since Tony was with the FBI in Boston, it seemed like a lifetime had passed. Even he didn't recognize his reflection in the mirror. His beard growth and unkempt hair, along with his uncustomary clothes, created a person Tony was tired of being. As he lay within the hostel in Geneva, he knew his first goal was in sight. He'd sacrificed comfort to maintain the cash necessary to, once again, become Anton Rawls. That wasn't who he planned to be forever; nevertheless, *Anton* was a necessary step to accessing his hidden treasure.

The new suit hanging near his bed took more of his cash reserve than he'd used on living expenses for the entire two weeks. That, plus the razor he'd just bought, was waiting to reveal the man beneath. Tony tried unsuccessfully to sleep as thoughts of his morning filled his mind. In the morning, he'd finally access the financial institution and resume a more accustomed lifestyle.

During the past seventeen days, Tony had done more than travel. He'd spent time at internet cafés, learning what he could. At first, he followed the developments of Rawlings Industries. The Vandersols were continuing to taunt the press with accusations. With each statement or news release, the price of stock in Rawlings and it's many subsidiaries took another hit. One article said the board of directors named Timothy Bronson temporary CEO, *in the absence of CEO Anthony Rawlings.*

Tony wasn't sure how he felt about their decision. *Did they truly feel he was that easily replaced?* Then, as the days passed, Tony came to the realization that he supported Tim's new role. After all, over the past few years, he'd been grooming him for just such a move. It wasn't like Tony planned to disappear, but Tim had shown promise from the beginning. It was good to know he was the man in charge.

Once that realization struck, Tony experienced an unexpected release from his business obligations. He could spend his time watching his empire struggle to survive and still do nothing, or he could spend his time learning more about Agent Jackson's odd remarks and tracking down his family. For the first time in his life—Rawlings Industries paled in importance.

Whenever he could, Tony researched rabbit trails of information. Nothing came together. He knew he was missing too many pieces of the puzzle.

He'd also taken two short calls from Agent Jackson. He read somewhere that fifty-six seconds of connection was necessary to track a call. He wasn't sure if that were true, but to be safe, he kept their conversations under that mark. Understandably, the FBI wanted more; nevertheless, Tony divulged just enough to keep them pacified.

"Yes, I'm in Europe"—"No, I haven't been in contact with anyone in the States"—"Yes. If I didn't have the damn phone, then you wouldn't be talking to me now"—"Goodbye." Although he hated the monitoring, thinking about the calls made Tony grin. Each time he kept the information limited and heard the distain in Agent Jackson's voice, Tony felt like he'd accomplished a small victory. Maybe it was only one hand in an all-night card game; nonetheless, each winning hand adds to the final jackpot.

The razor pulled at his facial hair as Tony worked to, once again, become Anton Rawls. The financial institution was a mere drive from the hostel where he'd slept. Although his body ached from the too soft bed, it was nothing compared to the mayhem cursing through his mind. After all these days, his goal was so close.

During the last few weeks, he'd learned to utilize public transportation, but Tony knew that wouldn't do for the bank; therefore, dressed in his new, finest suit, Tony entered the lobby of one of the nearby five star hotels and casually ate breakfast in one of its finer restaurants. No one questioned his presence—he obviously belonged. Tony wanted to enjoy the fine cuisine. Undoubtedly, it was the best he'd eaten in a while, but his thoughts of the safety deposit box wouldn't allow the aroma or taste of Eggs Benedict to register. When he was done, he exited the front door, told the bellman to flag him a cab, and rode to the bank. On any other day, it would have been a customary thing for him to do, but today it was revolutionary.

No one within the financial institution questioned his identity. Even if they'd seen him before, he was the same Anton Rawls who always visited the institution—the only one to access the safety deposit box in the last twenty-five years.

When presented with the customary ledgers, Tony stared at the list of signatures. There were his own—or more accurately—Anton Rawls written repeatedly; however, that wasn't what caught Tony's attention. *That* wasn't what caused his neck to straighten and his jaw to clench. The last two signatures—directly above where he was about to sign—were from *Marie*

Rawls. The first signature was dated: 11-09-13. It always took a minute to remember that not everyone dated as Americans did. The numbers he saw meant: eleventh day, ninth month of the thirteenth year. The second signature was signed two days later.

Speaking perfect French, Anton inquired, "Who is this? Did someone else access my box?"

The employee looked puzzled, read the signature, and then referred to some documents. When he was done, he sheepishly replied, "Yes, sir, your safety deposit box can be accessed by two individuals—you and a Marie Rawls. It appears that the woman who was here presented the clerk with appropriate identification." Then he asked, "Mr. Rawls, is there a problem?"

Tony could barely see. He didn't know what this meant—except that he needed to see inside his safety deposit box and verify his accounts. His short, curt words revealed his obvious displeasure, "There better not be. I want to see my box immediately."

"Yes, sir, I need your key, please."

Tony handed him the key and followed the nervous man into the vault. The process of inserting both keys took longer than Tony ever remembered. He knew it was his impatience; however, he swore the whole thing was happening in slow motion. Once the box was removed, Tony followed the employee into a private room.

"Sir, do you want me to stay?"

"No, leave." His directive was more of a growl as his dark gaze assaulted the bank's employee. Tony didn't care; he wanted the man gone. He needed to see what was inside the box—or more accurately—what may be missing, in private.

The employee stepped quietly from the room and Tony opened the box. In all the years he'd transferred and reinvested Nathaniel's funds, never had the contents of this box taken him by surprise—until now.

Instead of the customary documents, Tony reached into the depths of the steel container and removed a disposable international cell phone. It was very similar to the one he had for the FBI. Along with the phone, there was also a charger and an envelope.

He wasn't sure if his shaking hands were from rage or fear. His entire plan rested on the collection of these funds. *If his money wasn't here, where was it?* Tony thought back to the dates on the signatures: September 9 and 11. During those days, Catherine *was* in Iowa—with him. *Who else could know about this?*

Tony opened the envelope to a letter that was very short—and unsigned:

Congratulations, you've found your way to this clue.
I can't be sure who'll be reading this note, so I can only say that you've passed
your first test. Congratulations—I believe that deserves a positive Consequence.

I realize you're not accustomed to being the student, but please know that I
sincerely hope your educational experience is glitch-free.
If you are who I believe you are—it will all make sense.
I didn't leave you without resources—I wouldn't do that. I've heard it's a
difficult experience to be removed from your life and left at the complete disposal
of another; therefore, as your positive consequence, I've created one account which
is available to you. It can be accessed through the information below.
To continue your education, I've provided you with a cell phone. I assume a lecture
in general operating instructions won't be necessary; however, choose wisely—
remember all actions have consequences.

The temperature of the small room increased with each word. *The weeks of worry about Claire and—and—it was all some kind of ruse—some kind of game—a way to steal his money! But why? He had money in the States—more money than she accessed in these accounts. She could've had anything she wanted.* Thoughts came too fast. *Was it about the money, or was it to bring him down publicly—public failure—public humiliation—appearances.* Red infiltrated the room. Perhaps it came through the low buzz of the florescent lights. He tried to stop it—tried to maintain control. After all, there was an explanation; Tony knew there was. *How? How did Claire even know about this account? How could she access it? He had the key!*

Inhaling deeply, Tony closed his eyes. *Glitch-free? Consequences? Was that some kind of sick joke? Maybe it wasn't Claire; after all, she told her story to Meredith.* Tony didn't know how much she'd said—hell, she told her story to the attorneys in Iowa. The FBI had that account—he'd read the opening sentences. Suddenly, he wished he'd read more when he was with the FBI. *Maybe, just maybe, this was some FBI set-up?*

Tony had no choice—he had to take the bait and turn on the phone. He couldn't remember ever feeling so trapped. In their game of chess, he was in figurative check; however, he didn't know for sure who'd put him there. Tony looked around the room for an outlet. Finding one, he plugged in the phone. While the small gadget came to life, he worked to still the mayhem in his head.

What about the account? The last time he checked, he and Catherine had over 200 million dollars invested. *What stipend had he been allowed to keep?* Red seeped into his thoughts as he considered the possibilities. *If the fuck'n FBI thought they could take away his life and his money, then they were sadly mistaken. He was going to get to the end of this, come hell or high water, and damnit, the last seventeen days had been hell!*

When the screen finally lit, Tony accessed the contacts. There were three. The first *programmed* number wasn't associated with a name—it was an asterisk (*). The second was the name: *Claire*. The third was his name: *Anthony.* He felt the muscles of his neck tighten. *Was the information about Claire's cell phone in that FBI report? The shit about the asterisks? Or was* *this Claire's way of saying it was her? Claire's way of saying, now I've done it to you, and didn't he deserve it? Tony knew he did; nonetheless, he wouldn't accept it willingly or play her damn games!*

The signal within the room was too poor to assure a connection. He refused to live in fear. *If there was fuck'n teaching to do—he'd be the teacher.* Slipping the phone into the pocket of his jacket, Tony collected the charger and the note. Channeling his *business-self*, he made his way to the front of the bank to learn the contents of *his* account.

∞∞∞∞∞∞

Claire thought daily about the items she'd left in the safety deposit box. Tony's plane reportedly went down over two weeks ago. She never considered the possibility that he was truly injured; nevertheless, with each passing day, she felt the need to entertain the possibility. *After all, if he were able, wouldn't he be in Geneva accessing his fortune?*

There were times she worried that he had accessed the box and had chosen not to call. In her mind, she created all different scenarios for his decision. Claire knew, no matter what he decided—whether to call or not to call—his decision wouldn't be based off his understanding or misunderstanding of her clues. She knew beyond a doubt—Anthony Rawlings was the only man who'd know what she was saying.

He would know the correct number to call; however, she needed to entertain the possibility that he wasn't the person who accessed the box. If that were the case, Claire had a back-up plan. She had cell phones associated with each number. The only phone she'd answer was the one identified by the asterisk. During their marriage, when Tony finally allowed her to own a cellular telephone, he programmed her contacts—the only calls she was permitted to answer—were those programmed with an asterisk preceding the name. No one else knew this part of their history; she hadn't shared it with anyone—not even in her memoirs.

If someone else discovered the safety deposit box, then they would more than likely call one of the numbers associated with a name. If that happened, if one of the other two phones rang, Claire decided she wouldn't answer; instead, she'd destroy all three international disposable phones and focus on *her* future.

She'd spent the morning in the gardens with Francis. The fertility of the soil, combined with the sun and rain, produced yields Claire could never have imagined in Iowa or Indiana. After a cooling swim in the pool, a shower, and lunch, Claire was spending her afternoon relaxing on her bed and reading a book. The tranquility of the sea breeze and the sound of the surf had her in a near hypnotic state. An afternoon nap was growing nearer as the words of her book lost focus and her eyelids fought to remain open.

The ring to her untraceable international phone made her jump, evaporating the tropical serenity. It was the correct phone—the one linked to the asterisk. Although she was apprehensive about his initial reaction, she had no option. Claire wanted to answer—it was now or never. *Ring...ring....*

Steadying her voice, despite her trembling hands, Claire hit the *RECEIVE* button and spoke, "Hello, Tony."

"My God, it *is* you!" As his volume increased, she imagined his dark eyes and the vein in his neck pulsating. She recognized the change in his tone as his words came in a low growl from behind gritted teeth, "What have you done?"

Staying steadfast, Claire spoke with confidence, "If I hang up, then you'll never be able to contact me again. The choice is yours."

Closing her eyes, Claire listened as he struggled for composure. It took a few minutes until he finally sighed and said, "I'm glad you're alive. Do you have any idea the hell we've been going through? What about...our...baby?"

A smile broke through her concerned expression. With relief, she replied, "Our baby is well."

Finally, he spoke coherently, "Thank God"—She didn't know if it was anger or pain; either way, his words were laced with emotion—"How in the hell did you do this? Where are you? And where is my money?"

"It's nice to hear from you, too. I'm sure you're confused, but"—her tone mellowed—"I've missed you, and I'm glad the reports of your untimely demise were also exaggerated."

"Claire, what the hell is happening?" He repeated, "Where are you? And where is my money?"

"I'm here, and your money is nicely invested. You'll be happy to know it's made some unexpected positive returns—of late. You know, with the recent increase in oil options."

"I'm thrilled." He exhaled. "Where is *here*?"

"Of course, I'm considering a heavier investment in logistics. I've read that it's the wave of the future. Manufacturing has so many variables."

"Could we forgo the discussion on investment options? I want to know what you've done."

"And I want my life—the one we just had. Can we both get what we want?"

His voice reminded her of the business Anthony Rawlings; assessing the climate and gathering the facts. "Were you taken? Or did you leave me?"

"Tony, do you trust me?"

"What?"

"Do you trust me?"

"I want to, but you left me—*again*. You took my money"—His volume, once again, increased—"How? How did you even know about it?"

Her resolve was fading. If he hung up, then it was over. She didn't want that. "Tony, I made a mistake—many mistakes. I believed someone else—

instead of trusting you—and living up to our promise. I've learned the truth, and I want you to know that I trust you, and I'm so sorry."

Tony struggled for words. "Someone else? W—what are you talking about?"

"We're *both* children of children...and so is our child..."

Initially, he remained silent. Claire wondered if he was truly processing her meaning. Finally, he asked, "How did you pull this off?"

"Trust me, and we'll see it through together."

"I don't seem to have any other choice."

"Actually, you do," Claire said as she looked at the large diamond engagement ring hanging from the gold chain around her neck. Although she hadn't been wearing it on her finger, she never gave it away, sold it, or let it be far from her. She'd followed his rules; nevertheless, she needed to give him an out. If she didn't then she'd always wonder if he wanted her or the money.

"Claire, don't play games. You're not making any sense."

"I can assure you, this isn't a game. I gave you an out, similar to the one you presented to me years ago. You may leave, with your freedom and a new identity. Being the generous person I am, I left you one million dollars—of your money—which is more than you gave me when you divorced me." Claire heard an exasperated *humph* on the other end of the line. She waited, but when Tony didn't speak, she continued, "That's enough to support you for the rest of your life. You may need to cut a few coupons, but I believe you'll eat regularly, otherwise, you may agree to be with me, on my terms, and we'll work together to right some wrongs. The choice is yours."

"Are you serious?"

"Am I serious? Well, I realize you've been removed from your life. I realize your reputation has taken a hit. I also realize your company is suffering. I can't and won't take responsibility for most of that, but believe me, I know what it's like to have your entire world turned upside down." She waited; he didn't respond. "I also know who's done this to both of us. I know that disappearing for a while is our best option, and most importantly, I want to spend my disappearance with you. Do you want to spend yours with me?"

He exhaled. "Claire, I'd give up everything in the world to be with you and our child."

"Tony, that's not enough for me. I want you—I want our baby—and I want our life back. Will you help me?"

When he didn't immediately respond, Claire's heart dropped. Would he take the out? "Tony?"

"I want it all too. What do you mean, *your terms*? *Who* did *what* to us? And who told you about the money?"

"Really, Tony? How many people knew about it? How many people would consider us both children of children?"

Claire waited as tears, once again, coated her cheeks. He was supposed to understand, forgive and trust—that's the scenario she'd imagined. *That* was what she planned. Unable to contain the sound of her cries, Claire took a ragged breath and lay back on the bed. While she waited for Tony to respond, she felt their child moving within her.

When she, once again, heard his voice, she immediately knew it wasn't the tone she'd hoped for. "Are you and our baby safe?"

She managed to say, "Yes."

"Claire, if I call this number again, will you answer?"

Her head nodded, but her lips wouldn't communicate the same message. *Damn him! Didn't he understand she'd been through hell too?* "Are you saying you don't want to be with us?"

"No"—he lowered his voice—"You don't understand what I've been through."

She clenched the ring on the golden chain. "Tony, it hasn't been easy for me either. I need you—*we* need you." It was more of an admission than she wanted to make, but somehow she wanted to make him understand.

He repeated, "Will you answer?"

Claire knew he didn't like to repeat himself. Wiping her eyes with the back of her hand, she said, "All I wanted from you was a simple *yes*. Was that so difficult?"

"Will you answer?"

She couldn't lie; then again, she couldn't be truthful. At that moment, Claire wasn't sure of what she'd do. "I don't know, Tony. Will you call?"

"I don't know."

The line went dead...

For every good reason there is to lie,

there is a better reason to tell the truth.

——Bo Bennett

♠ ◇
♡ ♣

CHAPTER 13

Agent Harrison Baldwin settled into his hotel room in Zurich, Switzerland. It had been two weeks since Claire and Phillip Roach left Venice. Baldwin wasn't making points with the bureau. They definitely weren't happy with his unnecessary trail of the Italian couple from the Hotel Danieli. Although it thankfully went unnoticed by the Italian embassy, SAC Williams didn't hesitate to lecture Baldwin—at length—on his failed attempt. Maybe Baldwin had been undercover for too long. Without sounding conceited, Baldwin truly believed his tracking device would lead him to Claire's next destination. Honestly, he'd underestimated Phillip Roach.

The bureau had agents throughout Europe looking for Rawlings. Baldwin truly didn't know where he'd be. Each time Rawlings answered a call from the bureau, he hung up before his location could be confirmed. The only reason Baldwin was sitting in Switzerland was because of *rumors*. It wasn't high tech FBI probing. No, it was hours of research, drinking untold amounts of coffee, and reading article after article. The gossip that brought him to Zurich was actually from Claire's research. There were rumors that Nathaniel Rawls hid money overseas. Although discounted by people who knew him and never confirmed, Harry reasoned that Rawlings wouldn't have willingly walked away from his life and agreed to exist on the measly compensation from the FBI if he didn't have more money to access. Common sense told him that Switzerland was where one would hide money. Of course, there were other options. Currently, more Americans probably used the Cayman Islands or Bahamas; however, Baldwin reminded himself that these funds were originally hidden by Rawls in the 1980's.

Harry wanted—and needed—to prove to the FBI that Rawlings was ultimately responsible for multiple unsolved crimes. In effect, not only were they concentrating on the murder of an FBI agent, but more than likely a string of murders. Baldwin ran his fingers through his blonde, unruly hair. *Why couldn't Claire understand that Rawlings wasn't just a monster who abused her, the man was essentially a serial killer?* He tried to think about the case and not remember her green eyes. He knew he blew it at their last meeting. Truthfully, he didn't mean to call her stupid—she was just too willing to trust Rawlings. Baldwin vowed that he'd stop Rawlings—before he could hurt Claire—again.

Harry decided to start at the beginning. Utilizing the bureau's databases, he worked to identify a list of individuals who died with the confirmation of actaea pachypoda in their system. Not all of the individuals on the generated list could be connected to Rawlings or Rawls; however, the number that could be connected—even with a *possible* connection—was too high to allow for coincidence. The first documented case—the cause of this entire investigation—was Agent Sherman Nichols. His cause of death in 1997 was publicly declared as *natural causes*. Agent Nichols was seventy-three with a history of high blood pressure; nevertheless, as a retired federal agent, a full autopsy was required. The toxicology workups took time. When unidentified markers were found, it took more time. To Agent Nichols' family and the public, the original cause of death was confirmed. To the bureau, the case remained open.

Actaea pachypoda was next identified during an autopsy in 1989, by the minimum security federal correctional facility, Camp Gabriels, in upstate New York. The inmate's name: Nathaniel Rawls; again, blood workups took time. The simple answer was heart failure. That's what SAC Williams said; *actaea pachypoda had a sedative effect on the cardiac muscle tissue causing cardiac arrest.* Baldwin wondered why Rawlings would want to kill his own grandfather. Jotting down a note, he wanted to research the record of visitors at Camp Gabriels Correctional Institution. Being a minimum security prison, visitors came and went with regularity.

The biggest problem with Harry's search, even with the help of the federal database, was that *actaea pachypoda* wasn't commonly sought in toxicology screenings. Truthfully, a search of all cardiac-related deaths should be done; however, that would produce an overwhelming list of possible victims. Even Harry had to admit that Rawlings was probably not responsible for every person who died of cardiac-related problems; nevertheless, if Baldwin included Rawlings' parents, his grandfather, and Agent Nichols, that was four deaths in a relatively short period of time. From Forensics 101, that fit the definition of a serial killer, and then add Simon Johnson, and the killing spree had not stopped.

Harry had compiled health history workups on his entire list of potential victims. Not all fit the possible profile for heart disease as well as Agent Nichols and Nathaniel Rawls. Simon, for example, was very healthy. The only indications found in health records were allergies: sulfa drugs and penicillin as well as sensitivity to H1 antihistamines. If his death had been ruled to have been due to natural causes, then red flags would have finally flown. Luckily for Rawlings, Simon's body was too badly burnt in the crash. Harry had requested a new toxicology screening from tissue samples recovered at the time of Simon's accident—but that would take time.

Harry was about to start a state-by-state search of medical examiners' records—searching specifically for *actaea pachypoda*—when his phone rang.

He answered, "Hello?"

The voice on the other end expected action. "Agent Baldwin, Rawlings has been spotted leaving a well-known bank in Geneva. According to the agent, he's not trying to disguise himself."

Baldwin wanted to say, *"What an arrogant son-of-a-bitch"*—instead, he said—"I can be there in less than an hour, sir."

"The bureau has a plane ready. Be on it, ten minutes ago."

"Yes, sir."

"Agent, while you're flying to Geneva, you can review your assignment. I'd like to assume you won't fail again; however, we both know what happens when we assume."

"Yes, sir. I won't fail."

His research needed to wait.

∞∞∞∞∞∞

Settling into a suite at the Grand Hotel Kempinski, Tony sucked back the best two fingers of Glen Garioch Bourbon he'd ever tasted. There were too many thoughts swirling through his mind to think about one in particular. One thing he knew for sure, he'd had enough of the common life. One million dollars wasn't much, but it would sustain him until the FBI came for him. He didn't care anymore—*what the hell?* Agent Jackson's cryptic threats needed to be supported. The way Tony saw it, *the fuck'n bureau needed to ante up or get out of the damn game!*

Tony had stayed at the Kempinski before, and decided that due to its size and reputation for excellence, he'd stay there again. He reasoned that a businessman spending money—enjoying what life could offer—would get lost in the crowd. Anonymity, plus the modern, clean line decor and opulence were exactly what Tony wanted and needed at the moment. He could spend a few days in his suite, soaking the stench of hostels and common living from his skin, while he drank the thoughts of Claire leaving him and stealing his money from his head. It seemed like the perfect combination.

Another two fingers of bourbon and he might just go down to one of the clubs—hell, he hadn't been with another woman since before he and Claire married—not even when she was in prison. He went out on dates and made

107

appearances; *that's* who Anthony Rawlings was; nevertheless, his heart wasn't in it. He was always polite and gentlemanly, even when advances were made on him. It wasn't that he didn't have needs. It was that during the instances when his lips touched another woman's and he closed his eyes, all he saw was the sparkling emerald he wanted to have in his arms. When he opened his eyes and the sight before him wasn't what he truly desired—the rest of his body wasn't interested in proceeding. Although there were many women willing to help the situation, Tony wasn't interested.

Of course, that didn't mean Claire had afforded him the same exclusivity. In Tony's current condition, that was somewhere he shouldn't go. One thought opened the floodgate to many more—*had she left him to be with someone else? Was she with someone now? There was always that thought that periodically infiltrated his thoughts: what if the baby wasn't his? Refocusing on their conversation—where the hell was here? What kind of an answer was that?*

Tony snickered as he poured his third glass. Damn, if he weren't so refined, then he'd drink the shit from the bottle. He may still be using the same name as the man at the hostels, but he wasn't that man. He'd drink like culturally duped men do—out of a glass.

He definitely had more questions swirling through his head than answers. Tony thought back to the research he tried to do. There were too many pieces of this puzzle still missing.

Slumping back into a plush chair and gazing out to the twilight sky above Lake Geneva, Tony acknowledged the FBI was right. *Claire left him—of—her—own—free—will!*

Slightly dimmed by the onslaught of ninety-six proof liquor, Tony's thoughts were forming slower; nevertheless, Claire's words were coming back, *Really, Tony? How many people knew about it? How many people would consider us both children of children?* He knew that answer in the pit of his stomach. With each second, the truth burnt within him—Catherine knew—she knew they were both children of children. Catherine knew about Nathaniel's money. Catherine knew how to access Nathaniel's money. *Catherine knew!*

Reaching for his nearest phone, Tony almost spilled his drink. As he steadied himself, he thought about Catherine's number—not hers—no *his*! The idea that he could call *his* house and she'd be there—fueled the rage coursing through him. Just as he considered entering the number—with the phone in the palm of his hand—it rang.

He almost dropped it!

With a slight slur to his speech, Tony answered, "Hello, Agent Jackson, how are you this fine evening?" The momentary silence made Tony laugh. "What's the matter, Agent? Cat's got your tongue?"

"Mr. Rawlings, we have word that you're making yourself visible."

"Oh, you see, that's not true. No—no one can see me, right now"—Tony scanned the corners of the room for signs of cameras—"or, can you?"—he lifted his free hand to wave—"Can you see me?"

"No, Mr. Rawlings, I can't see you; however, you've been spotted."

"Well, is that so? I'm not using my real name."

"Mr. Rawlings, we'd like you to meet with a field agent. He'll instruct you on better ways to stay hidden."

"I don't think I'm up for more learning today. You see, I've already had a lesson or two, so I'm really over the entire educational system at this moment."

"That wasn't a request. You're staying at the Kempinski; our agent will meet you in fifteen minutes at Mulligan's near the train station."

Tony looked at his watch. "I'm gonna have to pass. You see, I had room service in mind."

"Mulligan's—fifteen minutes." The line went dead. On the corner of the screen, the time said 02:24, so—they were finally able to trace a call—it didn't matter. They already knew where he was staying.

Tony made his way to the bathroom, splashed water on his face, and straightened his tie. If he were expected to meet with some FBI asshole, then he'd at least do it with dignity.

∞∞∞∞∞∞

Phil watched Tony leave the Kempinski. If Rawlings was supposed to be in hiding, Phil didn't think he was doing a very good job. His demeanor, swanker, and aura all screamed *Anthony Rawlings*. It truly didn't matter what name he chose to use, no one who knew him would mistake him for someone else—hell, Phil was good, but anyone could've found him.

From the time Phil left Claire on the island, he'd been staking out the bank. She'd told him the name of the institution where she'd secured her new fortune. It only made sense that sooner or later, Rawlings would show up at the same place. Claire never told him what she'd left for Rawlings in the safety deposit box, but whatever it was, Rawlings didn't appear happy about it when he left the bank. He hardly looked like a man who'd just accessed his hidden millions.

Flagging down a cab, Phil instructed the driver to follow the cab up ahead. It may not have been the best detective work he'd ever done, but this wasn't about learning. Phil didn't want to know any more about Anthony Rawlings than he already did. In all honesty, he knew more than he wanted to know. Phil had something he wanted to *tell* Rawlings.

The cab with Rawlings pulled up to a small tavern, Mulligan's, not far from the train station. Again, Phil wondered what Rawlings was thinking. This was way too public for someone who was supposedly missing. When Phil entered the tavern, it took all his self-control not to stand and gape at the scene unfolding in front of him. Even Rawlings seemed bewildered as he tried to comprehend the reality. Harrison Baldwin was meeting Rawlings mid-room. Yes, there were other patrons, sounds—talking, music, chairs moving, yet as Phil slipped into a dark corner, none of that registered. It was like a movie where the rest of the room turns to fuzz. All Phil could watch were the two men standing chest to chest. If it were a western, then their hands would be on their revolvers.

When Rawlings left the hotel, he didn't look happy. Unhappy was an understatement to describe his current demeanor. Phil couldn't hear their conversation, but he could feel the waves of tension radiating from their encounter. For a second, when Baldwin took out his badge, Phil was afraid Rawlings would deck him. It wasn't true fear—actually, Phil would've enjoyed the show; however, for Claire's sake, it was something that shouldn't happen— at least, not in public.

Phil wanted to hear what they were saying; however, slipping into the neighboring booth wouldn't add to the warmth of their reunion. If Phil were to trust his own intuition, this meeting had blindsided Rawlings. Phil wondered who Rawlings thought he was meeting. Shaking his head, he assessed—*if this was set up by the FBI, it seemed pretty shitty.*

Phil ordered a beer and continued to watch. Neither man in the booth across the room ordered when the waitress approached. Although they sat calmly, an aura of discontent fell like a cloud all around them. Phil didn't think it was his imagination or the fact he knew their background. Even strangers were steering clear of that corner of the bar. Despite their too low voices, their body language suggested a heated discussion. Baldwin was talking, and Rawlings wasn't interested; however, when Baldwin pulled out his phone and showed something to Rawlings, Phil thought he saw virtual sparks fly. Rawlings' finger pointed at Baldwin and moved to emphasize every word of his retort. Without warning, Rawlings stood and headed toward the door.

Phil watched to see if Baldwin would go after him. When he didn't, Phil laid a few Euros on the tabletop and slid out after Rawlings. As he watched the cab stop and Rawlings begin to enter, Phil let out a breath and told himself, *this is for Claire.*

The next second, Phil reached for the handle of the cab's door. When it opened, he eased onto the seat next to Rawlings.

"Excuse me, this cab is—" Tony's words, in French, stopped when their eyes met. It's understandable that he didn't recognize Phil right away; after all, they'd only met a few times in person. Most of their correspondence had been via email and text message, but when Rawlings realized who'd just entered his cab, his eyes darkened and he growled, "What the hell?"

Also in French, Phil replied, "I'd address you by name"—Phil moved his eyes to the driver—"however, I'm not sure what that is."

"Collins," Rawlings said, as he exhaled and laid his head against the seat.

"Monsieur Collins, I'm sure you'll want to hear me out."

"This fuck'n day won't ever end, will it?"

The cab driver looked back at Tony and asked if everything was all right. Tony nodded and replied, "Oui, to my hotel." Then under his breath, he continued the conversation, "Monsieur, I assume you'll be joining me?"

Phil nodded. "Bien sûr."

A little more persistence, a little more effort,
and what seemed hopeless failure may turn to glorious success.
—Elbert Hubbard

CHAPTER 14

E ach day was a little better than the last. Claire only allowed herself to cry or acknowledge her loneliness when she was alone in her suite. It wasn't compartmentalization—she'd accepted her fate. These weren't the cards she'd been dealt; no, they were the ones *she'd* drawn.

She reasoned that Madeline and Francis didn't need to be burdened by her sadness, and her child didn't need to experience the anguish coming from its mother—all of the time. Claire kept the sadness defined, and the rest of the time, she bluffed her way through. *Fake it until she made it—her new mantra.*

The odd thing—the thing that surprised Claire—was as she *bluffed* and feigned happiness, the real pleasures of day-to-day activities seeped into her life. One afternoon, while in the kitchen with Madeline and without pretending, Claire heard her own laughter. The light, foreign, and whimsical sound surprised her more than anyone else. It had been so long since she'd truly laughed that she almost didn't recognize it.

On the afternoon after she and Tony spoke, she lay on her bed, phone in hand, for what seemed like hours. Her plan was well thought out and well designed; nevertheless, he hung up. The pain from his decision and her situation was physical. She'd experienced physical pain before, and this was equally as immobilizing. Had it not been for the child inside of her, Claire might have chosen to remain forever on that big bed; however, as the life within her moved and grew, she knew that she too, must go on.

The tides still rose and the sun still set. Madeline and Francis still did what they did. Claire had a decision to make; she either centered her life on waiting for his call or moved on. It wasn't a desire—it was a need. Claire needed closure. With strength she didn't know she possessed, she turned off the phone Tony called, gathered the cords, and placed all of the phones associated with the safety deposit box in a container. She wouldn't trap him, and she couldn't persuade him—all Claire could do was move on.

When her reality finally hit, Claire realized she was facing her greatest fear—Catherine had won. It didn't matter that Claire knew the truth, or that she told Tony. All that mattered were the consequences of her betrayal. On a warm night in June, she and Tony stood in an open field and promised to trust one another. Even at the time, Claire knew it was a difficult promise for Tony; nevertheless, they made a vow. It wasn't said in front of family and friends, but it was an oath. Although some of Tony's promises over the years were made for the wrong reasons, he showed Claire more than once that he was a man of his word.

On that same night, Tony asked Claire if she was afraid of him. Claire replied: *Of you—personally—not anymore. There was a time, but I've changed, and you've changed. No, I'm not.* If only she'd focused on that—on her promises.

All vows endure tests. These tests were rarely planned—but they happened. Catherine planned Claire's test, deceptively using Claire's experience, her fear, and her maternal instinct against her. By failing that test, Claire was hurt—Tony was hurt—and ultimately, their child was hurt—all the children of children. Truly, it was an impressive win on Catherine's part. She could live on that jackpot for a long time.

It was a few days after their conversation, when Claire saw the irony. In this strange world of vengeance, Claire did what Tony said Nathaniel had done—Claire had trusted the wrong people. She couldn't take it back. Not only had she trusted the wrong people, she'd pushed away the ones who truly cared. Whether it was Emily, John, or Phil, they were all gone, and Claire knew it was her doing.

When she sat down to eat and Francis held one of her hands and Madeline the other, Francis' words spoke to an entity who Claire remembered from childhood. It wasn't that she didn't believe—she did. It was that she wasn't sure she deserved the blessings Francis described. One day, in the gardens, Francis told Claire about his personal journey. He wasn't only a believer, but ordained.

Each day and each meal opened Claire's mind a little more. Before she knew it, Claire was talking to God too. No, it wasn't audible, yet it was comforting. She didn't ask for anything. There was nothing more she wanted. She made promises, promises to focus on her new friends, her child, and her well-being. The more she talked, the more she listened. The replies weren't words, they were peace. Claire didn't know how it would work, but somehow, she believed it would. In a way, it was like being with Tony; she willingly gave over control of her life.

∞∞∞∞∞∞

Tony took a deep breath. Although the multi-colored sea below him reminded him of his honeymoon, the tension in his neck and shoulders was something completely different. It was no secret; Anthony Rawlings didn't like or want to be indebted to anyone. Truly, he could count the number of people, on one hand, besides himself, who deserved credit for anything in his life. Unfortunately, that short list went all the way back to his childhood; nevertheless, someone who was no longer obligated to him in any way may have changed his life forever. The jury was still out. As the small plane continued toward some mysterious island, Tony closed his eyes and remembered the happenings of the other night.

He'd bet everything on the money in his accounts. Hovering somewhere around 200 million, the possibilities for that money were limitless. His world began to crack and cave in when he signed the ledger. Tony knew, without a doubt, Catherine hadn't traveled to Switzerland and accessed their accounts. She hadn't stolen Tony's money out from under him; nevertheless, on the ledger, and on two separate occasions, he saw the signature—*C. Marie Rawls*.

When he first heard Claire's voice, Tony's world exploded—the relief was instantaneous. *Claire was alive! Their child was safe! He almost* experienced a giddiness he'd never known; then all at once, the sensation evaporated and crimson saturated his happiness. No longer did he think about Claire's safety—that was apparently assured. Now, the obvious dominated his thoughts—Claire willingly left him and stole his money.

As she spoke, he heard memories of her proclamations. Over the years, Claire had repeatedly told him that his money didn't matter, yet somehow, he was standing on the street in Geneva, Switzerland, minus almost 199 million dollars. Claire quipped something about growing his investment. *The only damn investment she needed to grow was inside of her. No! He reminded himself, she'd stolen that too.*

Claire's accusation made no sense. *Who would know they were both children of children?* The only person was Catherine, and Tony and Catherine had been together—forever. It wasn't like they were *together;* however, they'd *always* been there for one another. He recalled catching her when she fell down the stairs, helping her after the incident—or rather *accident*—with his parents, and securing her freedom with annual payments to Patrick Chester.

It hadn't all been one-sided. Catherine had helped Tony too. After Claire's accident, Catherine was the one who convinced him not to call the police. She contrived the story that later became their statement. She helped with Claire, especially when he first brought her to the estate. Catherine taught her lessons that Claire needed to know. Tony knew he loved Claire, but he also knew he couldn't abandon Catherine—not after everything they'd been through.

Anthony Rawlings was a businessman. He looked objectively at information and analyzed the ledgers. When he compared the two columns—he, unfortunately, saw more cons on Claire's side. Catherine had been his rock, and more importantly—Tony's connection to Nathaniel for as long as he could remember.

Then, there was the arranged meeting! Agent Jackson wanted Tony at Mulligan's. From Tony's perspective, it was ridiculous. *If the FBI knew where he was then why not come to him? No, the directive was to meet at a public place.*

Even days removed, the memories fueled Tony's rage. Agent Baldwin—*Agent! Harrison Baldwin was an FBI agent?! Why? And how? And when? Was it before or after he was with Claire?*

After the initial shock, Baldwin convinced Tony to sit. It was then that Baldwin began some tirade about plants. Baldwin asked about Tony's knowledge regarding plants. Although a few smart-ass answers came to mind, Tony honestly replied, "Nothing. I don't know shit about plants; well, other than what I've learned from Claire."

It was after the mentioning of Claire's name that Baldwin got some sick smile on his face and smirked. "So, Rawlings, how is Claire?"

"I haven't seen her in a while. You know that. I called you when she first went missing."

"Missing? I guess she is...depending on whom you ask."

Tony's patience was spent on the call with Claire—no more remained. "What the hell do you mean?"

"Well, as a matter of fact, just the other day"—Baldwin offered his phone, turning the screen toward Tony—"I was in Venice, and she was in Venice...you can see—she's well. Oh, she's staying in disguise"—he lowered his voice—"I believe that's because she's hiding from some threat, someone possibly, but if you look closely, I'm sure you can tell it's her."

Tony stared at the picture—Claire and Baldwin with their hands entwined. Tony didn't know what else was said. The rest of their conversation vanished behind a rush of rage. In hindsight, it was a good thing Baldwin made his federal status known. If he hadn't, Tony might have been able to add *bodily harm of a federal agent* to his resume. Before Tony left the pub, he turned back to Baldwin and asked, "One question, asshole, was Claire some kind of informant—an assignment?"

It was the first sign of true emotion Tony saw on Baldwin's face as he replied, "At first, she was, but it became more."

Walking away, Tony contemplated his question and Baldwin's answer. Although Tony wanted to lay him out and wondered if Claire knew she started out as some FBI project, as he settled into the cab, Tony realized, he was no better than Baldwin. The relationship he started with Claire wasn't meant to be personal either; then, in the midst of his epiphany, the door to the cab opened.

Tony started to speak, to ask the man to leave, when suddenly, Tony recognized him—Phillip Roach, the private detective he'd fired; the one who failed to protect Claire.

Education had always been important to Tony. He finished his bachelor's and master's with honors. Whenever possible, he read, researched, and acquired knowledge; however, in the past twelve hours, he'd been told by three different people that they possessed information he *needed to learn.* By the time Roach entered his cab, Tony's receptiveness to tutelage ceased to exist.

After they entered Tony's suite, Roach told him a story. If Tony hadn't been one of the major players, then he would've thought the man was crazy, yet every date—every instance—and every detail—was verifiable in Tony's mind. Tony had an uncanny ability to remember dates, names, and conversations. Somehow, through Roach's story, everything he knew and believed took on new meaning.

Roach explained that he was the one to mail the gifts and cards to the *Rawls—Nichols* baby. He was the one who purposely breached the estate's security and tried to run Clay off the road. He emphasized that on no occasion was Claire *ever* in danger. It was all a ploy to create fear and suspicion.

When Tony asked *why,* Roach's answer was simple. "It was a job—Ms. London hired me." The story of the laptop made Tony's stomach turn. He couldn't believe it had been in his own closet.

Yes, Claire should've waited and talked to him, but hearing it from Roach, seeing this new perspective, Tony's heart broke for the woman he loved. He understood—Claire was too frightened to wait. It pained him that at that moment—she was frightened of him; however, that's how it was meant to be— how Catherine planned it. Roach also explained that Claire defended Tony to Evergreen and Baldwin. He also mentioned how Baldwin caught her off guard.

Taking the time to listen and consider the timeline, Tony understood Claire's reasoning and justified her fear. It was then that he remembered the phone call and reevaluated her words: *Tony, I made a mistake—many mistakes. I believed someone else—instead of trusting you—and living up to our promise. I've learned the truth, and I want you to know that I trust you and that I'm so sorry.* After everything—she still wanted him—and he'd hung up on her.

Now, as he and Phil approached her hiding place, he knew that the two of them had much to discuss, so much to say. He could've tried to call; however, he didn't want to give her the opportunity to tell him to stay away. Honestly, he feared she would—the possibility still existed. Technically, he could argue that it was *his* money that bought the island, but he wouldn't. Tony wanted to see Claire—to look into her eyes and tell her the truth. If she wouldn't listen, then he'd leave.

Above all, Tony wanted to hold Claire in his arms, tell her how sorry he was, and how much he loved her. As the plane neared the water, Anthony Rawlings hoped she would give him that opportunity.

∞∞∞∞∞∞

After an afternoon in the orchards, Claire took a leisurely swim, sunbathed by the pool, read, and napped. When Madeline woke her, she showered and readied for dinner. It was a variation on her normal routine, and with everything considered, Claire didn't think it was too bad.

Running her fingers down the fabric of her pink sundress, Claire pondered her dinner companions. It wasn't like she needed to look good for Madeline and Francis. It was an ingrained behavior—dinner meant formal. Truly, Claire enjoyed that. It was the climax to her day. Securing the shell necklace, she observed her hair—pulled up with ringlets of blonde and brown hanging down over her neck. In only a few weeks, the sun had successfully lightened her hair. Claire smirked, *of course, what did she expect by living this close to the equator?*

As they were about to sit down to eat, the sound of an airplane filled their ears. Where only moments earlier the sound of birds and surf dominated, now the roar of propellers amplified over the island. Claire's first thought was Phil. *Who else would know their way to her island?*

When she stood, Francis placed his hand on her arm. Claire stopped as he warned, "Madame el, it is better if you wait to see."

Instinctively, she hugged her midsection and nodded. Standing on the lanai, she looked down at the lagoon. As she watched the small plane land on the sparkling water, she felt her heartbeat in her throat. The landing and stopping of the propeller seemed to take hours rather than minutes. Perhaps it was the anticipation of greeting the first plane to land in the lagoon since Claire arrived, or more likely, her excitement at again seeing a familiar face. Regardless of the reason, Claire stood on the lanai with baited breath. It wasn't until she saw Phil emerge from the small vessel, that she allowed herself to smile.

Losing her heeled shoes, Claire ran down the path, toward the shore. The green vegetation, colorful flowers, and lush trees hid her view of the beach. She was just about to call out—to shout to Phil—when she emerged from the foliage. As her bare feet hit the beach, they stopped and slowly sank into the soft sand.

Stalling under an arch of flowers and vines, Claire experienced one of those moments where time stood still—the sun and moon forgot their roles—the earth no longer turned—and the tides no longer ebbed or flowed. She stood speechless as a second passenger emerged from the plane and stepped toward the path. When he looked up, he stopped mid-step. Claire bravely met his gaze, taking in the darkest, most intense eyes she'd ever known.

Claire knew she'd seen every emotion in those eyes—from anger to adoration. Currently, she saw a mixture of apprehension and desire. With each second, desire overpowered apprehension—desire overpowered—everything—everything else—everywhere.

Perhaps there were stars falling, volcanoes erupting, or epic winds blowing. Truthfully, at that moment, the entire world could've been lost and neither one would have known. Later, when she reflected, Claire believed Phil had been speaking. He was giving reason or explanations—at the time, all Claire heard was the beating of her heart—maybe, just maybe, it was their baby's heart. No matter, the *whoosh—whoosh* was what filled her ears and her consciousness. Unable to move, Claire stood, waiting for Tony to make his way to her.

Tears filled her eyes and spontaneously escaped her lids as she watched each elegant step. *How could a world as perfect as the paradise, where she'd been living, have been lacking?* In the last moments, seeing Tony gracefully move toward her, Claire knew her sphere was now whole.

When he was within reach, Claire remembered all she wanted to say—all the questions she'd compiled in her thoughts. Though the questions came to mind, with increased vigor, no words materialized on her lips. Standing tall and proud, Claire remained silent. She couldn't calm the mayhem long enough to decipher her words. The best plan was silence until...

Without warning, one of Tony's arms surrounded her growing waist and the other captured her neck. The sound escaping her lips couldn't be classified as words. On the contrary, it was more involuntary as her body submitted to his. Every touch, every move, and every angle was determined by him. Claire's body no longer waited for internal instruction. It was programmed to respond to the contact of the man towering above her, inhaling her aroma, and caressing her body.

His hands held her tightly within his grasp. She didn't fight. *Why would anyone fight their rightful place?* Instead, the sounds from her mouth—the moans from her chest—were a plea, a request for more. Truthfully, Claire wasn't even aware she was making the noises, yet she heard them. Within seconds, his fingers were intertwined in her hair. It wasn't much, but Claire suddenly felt the need to apologize. "I'm so sorry."

The strong, determined mission of his lips quieted further commentary, until he came up for air and said, "No, *I'm* sorry."

Could six words mend an insurmountable gorge? At first, Claire wasn't sure—until they did. As the words left their lips—the gap disappeared. They were together, and nothing could separate them. Claire was in Tony's arms, tasting his kiss, and inhaling his amazing scent. The world beyond their bubble was suddenly insignificant. She wasn't sure how long they stayed like that, on the beach, holding one another.

His eyes held the key to her heart and soul. Peering into Tony's dark gaze of desire, her world lightened into the place she wanted to be. Claire knew she could remain there for a lifetime. Then, slowly, the world around them infiltrated her senses—soft sand materialized beneath her toes—a gentle, salt scented breeze moved strands of her hair—the orange glow of the setting sun created an orange hue—and sound of propellers told them that the plane was leaving.

Unable to contain her sudden panic, Claire held tight to Tony's hand and looked beyond their bubble. Heading back toward the plane was the man who'd made their world right. Claire gasped and looked up to Tony with her head shaking. "We can't let him leave." Then louder, she yelled toward the plane, "Phil!"

He looked their direction.

"Stay," Tony commanded.

Phil's progress stalled. He turned back as they walked toward him.

When they were all together, Tony held out his hand. While the two men shook, Tony said, "Thank you. We can never thank you enough."

The glowing sun reflected in the golden flecks of his eyes. Phil looked to Claire and then to Tony. "You already have."

Tony said, "I was wrong to fire you. You've kept Claire safe and brought us back together. I want you to work for us. Stay."

"With all due respect, Mr. Rawlings, my bank account is quite healthy. There's only one person for whom I'd be willing to postpone my early retirement."

The rush of panic that moments earlier had filled Claire's chest, as she saw Phil leaving, subsided. Smiling, she released Tony's hand and took a step toward her babysitter—her bodyguard—her *friend*. When she was but inches away, she lifted her arms. "*Please* stay. You've given me back *everything*. I know I can never repay you...but I hope you know—I want you to be part of our lives."

∞∞∞∞∞∞

Their hug wasn't intimate. It was nothing like the display he'd witnessed moments earlier; nevertheless, it was a connection—a bond he'd never before experienced. As Claire's arms encircled Phil's neck and her petite frame leaned against his chest, Phil knew that he'd stop at nothing to protect her, to protect her baby, and to facilitate her happiness.

He spoke softly, "Do you want me to stay?"

Her green eyes spoke volumes, but it was her words that secured his future, "Oh yes, more than I can say, but the decision is yours."

"I have one stipulation."

Tony stepped forward, protectively placing his arm around Claire's shoulders. "And that would be?"

"I don't do diapers."

The lingering sound of the plane faded into the twilight sky as Tony, Claire, and Phil made their way up the path toward the house.

Do what you feel in your heart to be right—
for you'll be criticized anyway. You'll be damned if you do,
and damned if you don't.
—Eleanor Roosevelt

♠ ◇
♡ ♣

CHAPTER 15

-JULY 2016-

Stepping through the doorway into a sea of familiar faces, Emily held tight to John's hand. Everwood's conference room bustled with counselors, therapists (speech, occupational, and physical), doctors (primary care, neurology, and psychiatry), rehabilitation nurses, and administration representatives—all with one patient in mind—Claire Nichols Rawlings. Various members of Claire's care team greeted the Vandersols as they made their way to some empty seats at the table.

When it came to planning and treatment, Everwood was well known for their excellence. This was true with all their patients, but some patients received extra attention. It was no secret—Claire Nichols Rawlings wasn't the average patient. First of all, she was incredibly wealthy. Second, her sister, next of kin and power of attorney, was excessively demanding, as well as incredibly involved, and lastly, Claire's brother-in-law was an attorney, well versed in medical law. If pertinent revelations regarding her case were to be discussed, it required the presence of all members of her care team.

Today's meeting was in regard to the information in Dr. Fairfield's report. Dr. Carly Brown eased herself into the chair beside Emily. Squeezing Emily's free hand, she whispered, "Don't worry. Dr. Fairfield wouldn't be addressing this entire crowd if he didn't have some valuable theories."

Tired of theories, Emily feigned a smile. Fighting the emotion building in her chest, she managed, "Thanks, Carly, I'm just afraid to get my hopes up."

Dr. Brown smiled. "Hope is all we have. Don't give up on your sister."

Breathing deeply, Emily blinked back the tears. "It's one thing for me to be disappointed—I'm used to it, but I keep thinking about Nichol having to deal with this one day."

John leaned over, keeping his voice low as the rest of the room continued to murmur, "Let's concentrate on Claire. Nichol's young; we can keep her uninformed as long as possible."

Emily nodded as she swallowed her tears. Everyone was taking a seat— some around the table and many in chairs at the perimeter. The overflowing room quieted as Dr. Fairfield began his presentation.

"Thank you all for joining me here today. I've spoken to many of you in the last few weeks; many over the phone. It's nice to meet you in person. Let me begin by explaining my role as a neuropsychologist..."

Emily listened as Dr. Fairfield reviewed Claire's condition. At first, it wasn't anything she hadn't heard before—

"It's well documented that psychosis like what Ms. Nichols is experiencing can be the result of traumatic brain injury. Recent studies have supported the theory of delayed psychosis. This has been well documented in veterans as well as NFL players. It's characterized by slowly developing psychosis or delayed rapid onset. There are case studies which have documented rapid onset occurring as long as fifty-four months post injury."

Emily liked to think that Claire's psychosis was *slowly developing*. Although previously undiagnosed, that theory justified Claire's decisions over the last years. As Claire's sister, it made it easier for Emily to accept some of Claire's actions and decisions—especially regarding Anthony Rawlings. Emily mentally reviewed the timeline: Claire's initial concussion resulting in prolonged unconsciousness—hell, a coma—although, when she was capable, Claire refused to use that word—was in September of 2010. Though not a concussion, her second brain injury was in June of 2013, when she was attacked by Patrick Chester. Claire's break with reality occurred in March of 2014...

"There have even been suggestions that a hormonal imbalance as well as weight gain, like that associated with pregnancy, could have exacerbated previous injuries..."

To Emily, it seemed very cut and dry—and the timeline worked.

Dr. Fairfield continued, "...Although Ms. Nichols' brain scans support a history of traumatic brain injury, I do not share the theory that this has led to her psychosis..."

Emily's neck straightened, and she turned to her husband. *What was he saying? Of course TBI was the cause of Claire's psychosis! It was all Anthony's fault! He injured her. If it weren't for him, she never would have been Patrick Chester's target.* Emily's internal monologue drowned out the doctor's words. She needed to listen.

"...The studies are less conclusive on the rate of recovery, from non-TBI induced psychosis. It's true; this patient's current scans indicate previous damage to the right hemisphere of her brain." He projected various scanned images on the screen and utilized a small blue arrow to point to Doppler generated specifics. "You'll note, as is consistent with TBI, the damage is most pronounced in the temporal and parietal lobes. What's of specific significance with Ms. Nichols is the reduction in gray matter. As that reduction occurs, patients tend to feel pain. Ms. Nichols' history does suggest problems with headaches. Now, if we compare the MRI of 2013 with the one taken two weeks ago, you can see..."

Emily listened, trying to remember the previous evidence. Everyone had said it was the TBI which indeed had caused Claire's psychotic break. She recalled discussion of injury—evidence of concussion, yet as she tried to focus, Emily realized, Dr. Fairfield wasn't nullifying that evidence. He had acknowledged that the injuries occurred, but he was also stating that he didn't feel that the injuries were the cause of her psychosis.

Turning to Dr. Brown, Emily whispered, "Is he saying the head injuries aren't the cause of her psychosis?"

Dr. Brown's eyes opened wide as she turned to Emily, nodded, and shrugged.

Dr. Fairfield continued, "If the injuries prove to be the cause of the patient's current state of mind, then in that case I'd have to agree with the conclusion of others that no further recovery will occur."

Emily's mind spun. *Who said that? No one had voiced that opinion to her.*

Dr. Fairfield went on, "I have based my current prognosis on the patient's most recent DTI, or Diffusion Tensor Imaging. This is relatively new imaging and wasn't commonly available at the time of Ms. Nichols' break. As many of you know, I've worked with the NFL on this subject and have been personally involved with many of the more public cases. Accurately monitoring and measuring brain activity is essential in any prognosis. Let me show you this segment of consecutive DTI." Again, everyone's attention was brought to the screen. The image before them moved, or—more accurately—it pulsated. The defined areas of color moved, reminding Emily of an intense area of thunderstorm activity on a weather map. "Note the increased activity in this area of gray matter. What's significant is that this image was recorded during one of the patient's hallucinatory episodes. Let me also show you the increased stimulation in this patient's auditory cortex. For those of you less versed in the medical terminology"—Emily knew he was specifically rephrasing for her benefit—"I'm saying that even though we may not hear what Ms. Nichols hears, or sense what she senses, she *is* indeed hearing and sensing. More importantly, her brain is active. Yes, there are areas of damage, but the human brain is very powerful and is quite capable of regeneration and compensation. I conclude that with the right antipsychotics and a significant change in therapy, progress can be made to bring Ms. Nichols back from her current state."

As everyone discussed this new prognosis, the room buzzed with whispers. John leaned over Emily in an attempt to speak with Dr. Brown. Emily remained silent, contemplating the possibility that Dr. Fairfield's assessment could possibly be true. Her mind fluctuated between hopeful optimism at the possibility of recovery and less than guarded indignation at the possibility that Anthony's guilt could be more indirect than direct.

When the room began to quiet, Emily stood. Slowly, silence prevailed. Clearing her throat, she utilized the voice she'd reserved years ago for addressing students. "Dr. Fairfield, if brain injury wasn't the cause of my sister's condition, please enlighten us on what was the cause?"

Everyone turned toward the good doctor, watching as he shifted his footing. "Mrs. Vandersol, psychotic breaks can occur for a number of reasons. Let me emphasize that I'm not insinuating that your sister isn't truly in the throes of such a break."

Defensively, Emily stood taller. Pressing her lips together, she refrained from speaking as she waited for the doctor to continue.

"The most common causes of psychotic breaks include brain injury and drug use; however, it's also well documented that a significant life event can precipitate such a break." For all of his large words and doctor attitude, Emily saw a sudden shift in countenance as he asked, "Your sister had a significant life experience, wouldn't you agree, Mrs. Vandersol?"

"Yes, Doctor, I do; however, the length of my sister's break has—in the past—been reason to believe that there was more than a significant life experience to blame."

It was as if they were the only two in the room. No one else dared breathe, much less speak. Dr. Fairfield continued, "As I stated earlier, the human brain is a truly amazing organ—one that's essential for each of us to continue living. Without it, we would be incapable of simple involuntary behaviors such as breathing or the beating of our heart. That same amazing brain can also protect us"—he paused and waited; silence prevailed—"It's my opinion that this patient's break may have been initially associated with previous injury. It's also possible that the swelling of blood vessels during pregnancy, her difficult child birth, and even the hormones associated with breast feeding could have contributed." Dr. Fairfield cleared his throat and pushed on, "After observing more than one of your sister's hallucinatory episodes, I believe your sister is where she wants to be."

Momentarily, Emily was at a loss for words. She stuttered as she looked to both Dr. Brown and John. "Ex—excuse me, do—"

John's voice prevailed. "So, am I correct to understand—you believe Claire is willfully keeping herself in this state? Are you saying she's faking?"

"N—no, Mr. Vandersol, I believe she's in a true psychotic state. She's obviously delusional, blissfully unaware of her surroundings or the burden her behavior has had on others. I also believe she doesn't know she's a mother nor of the fate of her husband." When Emily shifted, Dr. Fairfield added, "I didn't ask her those questions specifically. Mrs. Vandersol, your directives were maintained; however, in an effort to assess Mrs. Rawlin—Ms. Nichols, I breached some subjects that had no effect on her. Which I may add, I feel is a shame—"

John interrupted, "Dr. Fairfield, could my wife and I continue this conversation with you in private?"

"Yes, I under—"

Emily stopped his response. "No! I want answers, and I'm sure the others here will need to know. First, is Claire uncomfortable or in pain?"

"Mrs. Vandersol, the patient has been maintained in a static state of comfort—which I believe is the problem."

Everyone in the room turned toward Emily. To the observers, it was like watching a tennis match: all heads turned one way and then they turned the other.

∞∞∞∞∞∞

July 26, 2016

Today, Ms. Bali called and asked me to come in early. Since Claire has been doing well with me bringing her meals—she asked if I'd take her on a walk. Apparently, there was some big meeting regarding her diagnosis, prognosis, and treatment. Everyone associated with her care had to attend. I wish I'd been at the meeting, but Emily was probably there, so it was better I wasn't.

I know I should write about the walk. That's the whole point, right? Record my thoughts and comments so that I can later come back and see if any progress was made—have a basis for writing the follow-up to my book. Well, here's the thing; I don't want to. Oh, I want to stay with Claire. I want to help her—but for a journalist who's supposed to be indifferent—I picked the wrong project.

Just in case I don't remember when I come back to read—on the way home from Everwood, I stopped at the store and bought a bottle of wine. No— it isn't the normal size—it's the big one!

I hated it today! I went to her room—and surprise—Claire was sitting in the chair by the window. When she saw me and heard my voice, she went to the table to eat. Keep in mind, she'd just eaten! I explained that I was taking her on her walk. At first, she didn't budge. I just kept talking about the outside. Finally, she stood. I stepped closer, like I'd seen the other woman do and Emily do. Claire didn't move. I had to reach for her hand and place it on my arm.

After that, she stayed in step as we walked through the facility. The part that broke my heart was that when we went outside she didn't look up. She kept her eyes downcast and walked wherever I led. I remember her stories, the ones of her at her lake on the Rawlings Estate. She'd talk about her love of the outside, the breeze in her hair, and the sun on her skin. I think I was expecting to see some sort of recognition or excitement; instead, there was nothing.

I hated that she had to be subdued when our eyes first met in the cafeteria a month ago, but honestly, I'd rather have a negative reaction than none! I think I'm done writing for tonight. I have more wine to drink!

∞∞∞∞∞∞

Michael, Nichol, and John finished their dinners while Emily continued to pick at the food on her plate. She heard the chatter, but her mind kept replaying Dr. Fairfield's words, *No, the patient has been maintained in a static state of comfort—which I believe is the problem.*

Indignantly, she listened as Dr. Fairfield hypothesized that Claire's current provisions were *too good.* In essence, he blamed Emily's directives on Claire's compliance. He went on to discuss Claire's history of compliance and adaptability.

Emily argued internally, *too good?! Her sister was detached from the world, living in a place that wasn't real. How could he possibly think that was too good? Besides, Dr. Fairfield's resources weren't primary! Wasn't that an essential element of research—primary resources? The only way he could've learned about Claire's past, from those who knew first hand, those who were there, would be to interview Claire or Anthony. Obviously, that hadn't happened. He had to have researched not only Emily's accounts, which she confessed were second hand, or read Meredith's book. Yes, the book was relatively accurate, but even that had an element of fiction. The blatant truth would be too difficult for the world to read.*

So what? So Claire had survived her ordeal by complying and adapting. That was because if she didn't, then Anthony would punish her. Claire's current situation wasn't even remotely similar. *How could he suggest it was?*

That was what he'd said—he said, *the accommodating surroundings worked to mold Claire's behavior.* By not requiring her to face the consequences of her past, they were allowing Claire to live in her make-believe world.

The way Emily saw it, she was affording her sister the safe haven she'd been denied.

The sound of laughter returned Emily's thoughts to present. Focusing on the table, she watched Michael giggle as Nichol blew bubbles in her milk.

"Nichol! What are you doing? Don't teach your cousin those things!" Emily's unusually harsh tone surprised everyone. She saw the shock in her husband's eyes.

Nichol's brown eyes, that only seconds ago glistened with laughter, were suddenly brimming with tears and looking down. "I'm sorry, Aunt Em."

John stood and reached for the children's plates. Keeping his voice steady, he reassured, "It's all right, honey. Aunt Emily's tired. You're fine; no mess. How about you two go upstairs and let Becca help you get your pajamas on, and we'll make some popcorn."

Peeking her eyes upward, Nichol asked, "Can we watch a movie?"

"Sure we can," Emily's voice softened. "I *am* tired; I'm sorry that I snapped. If you two hurry then we can all cuddle in our bed." As small feet rushed out of the dining room with their nanny, Emily's head dropped and her tears flowed. It wasn't until John's hands massaged her shoulders that she found the courage to speak. "Do you think he's right?"

"I don't know, but I do know that we haven't seen much progress in the last year. I think it's worth a try."

"I don't want her to have to face—I don't want her to have to deal with—"

John helped Emily stand. "I know what you want. You want Claire well, and her past gone. That's not going to happen."

Emily's cheek settled against John's chest. She listened as he repeated everything Dr. Fairfield said earlier. It may have been the quiet setting of their dining room, his tender embrace, or the relief from allowing the tears to finally surface—no matter the reason, John's words made sense. Nodding her head, Emily replied, "I guess I get it, but I still don't want her to have to deal with memories of *him*."

Pulling her close, John whispered, "She's survived more than most. Maybe these past few years have been a well-deserved break. As much as you want to, you can't keep the truth from her forever. When she's stronger, she'll be able to face it, and perhaps this new protocol will help her get stronger."

Emily conceded, "I'll call Dr. Brown tomorrow and give my okay."

Darkness restores what light cannot repair.

—Joseph Brodsky

CHAPTER 16

Madeline and Francis met Claire and her guests on the lanai. Francis shook Phil's hand as the two men exchanged familiar greetings. Still holding Tony's hand, Claire introduced him, "Madeline and Francis, let me introduce Anthony Rawlings."

Madeline's smile lit the room. "Monsieur, we're so happy to have you with us before your fille arrives."

Claire smiled. She'd never mentioned Tony to Madeline; she wondered how she knew he was the father of her baby. Looking up at Tony's expression, Claire realized what Madeline had just said and squeezed his hand. "No, I haven't learned our baby's sex; however, Madeline seems to believe we're having a girl."

Tony bowed his head. "Madeline, Francis, I too am happy to be here before the arrival of our bébé—fille or fils; either is fine with me."

The smiles coming from Madeline and Francis warmed Claire's heart and continued her inner peace. She hadn't considered that they might not be receptive to him. After all, they weren't married. They had been, but Madeline and Francis didn't know that.

Claire said, "I know dinner's ready and I'm sorry, but first, I'm going to show Tony to our room. Could you please show Phil to the room he didn't take before?" Her eyes sparkled teasingly toward Phil.

Phil replied, "That won't be necessary; I remember."

Madeline announced, "I'll have dinner ready for you. After you're done, Francis and I will eat at our house."

Although Claire and Tony had started to walk toward their room, Claire turned back. "Oh no, I don't want you to do that. We'll all eat together—all of us. I'm so happy to have everyone here, and I want everyone to get to know one other. Please, give us a little time. We'll be back in fifteen minutes."

No one argued with *the lady of the house* as Claire led Tony down the hallway. When they reached their suite, Claire entered, expecting to show him around. The sound of the closing door surprised her. When she glanced back toward Tony and saw his expression, the deep yearning she thought was forever gone—ignited. The heat immobilized her; she couldn't move toward him or away. Her only option was to stare into the dark, velvety depth of his gaze. For seconds or days, Claire was lost in his eyes. The black penetrating stare no longer filled her with fear; instead, it was a beckoning, a desire that only she could fill—truly an overwhelming and exhilarating responsibility. Within seconds, his strong arms surrounded her and their lips united.

Once again, her world was no longer her own. He didn't take it—on the contrary, Claire relinquished it willingly. Not the control of the island or the money—those were truly insignificant. What belonged to Tony, probably before she ever knew him, was her heart and soul. As their bodies touched, her growing breasts pressed against his chest and his hands caressed her skin; Claire was totally and completely lost. Any thought of life outside their suite disappeared as the scent of his cologne and the taste of his kiss took on life giving power. Eventually, his deep, baritone voice penetrated their world while each word, each syllable dripped with desire. "God, I've missed you. I thought I'd never hold you like this again."

Claire couldn't respond verbally. Not only because her mouth was preoccupied—which it was—no, she couldn't respond because the overwhelming sense of relief that was washing over her had removed her ability. It drained her and set her hormone-filled emotions into a new and terrifying cyclone. Tears fell from her eyes as she broke away from his kiss and buried her face in his wide chest. When her shoulders began to shudder from the sobs she couldn't contain, Tony led her to the sofa. His sultry expression turned questioning. "Do you want me to leave? Isn't this what you wanted?"

Claire shook her head and wiped her eyes. "No! I don't want you to leave. This is *exactly* what I want"—she sniffled—"I can't believe you're really here. When you hung up—"

Tony knelt before her, his sad eyes a stark contradiction to the passion she saw moments earlier. "I was wrong. Everything was overwhelming." She heard the restraint in his voice as he tried to subdue his shock and anger. "I had everything planned; how I was going to get the money and look for you." His volume rose with each phrase. He shook his head. "I've told you before that you're the only person in this world, who can keep me on my toes. I *never* imagined you'd access the accounts before me. I was totally blindsided! When I saw the signature of Marie Rawls, my gut told me that something was wrong! I still wasn't sure until I called the number..." He exhaled and waited. Finally, he took her petite hands, surrounded them with his own, and reigned in his tone. "I wasn't even sure it was you. I couldn't fathom how you could possibly gain access—and then, when I heard your voice—"

The hint of anger faded into a sadness Claire couldn't identify. She'd never heard so much pain in his voice. With all her heart, she wanted to make his world better; however, she couldn't take away his sense of betrayal—initially from her and then from Catherine. He needed to say what he was thinking. While tears silently overflowed her eyes, Claire kept her gaze locked with his. Even with his visible pain, his dark eyes completed her world.

He continued, "It wasn't that I didn't want to believe you, but to believe you meant admitting that Catherine deceived..." His head bowed to Claire's lap.

When he didn't speak, Claire ran her fingers through his hair and waited.

Swallowing his emotions, Tony looked back up to her eyes. Dark windows of remorse matched the anguish she heard in his tone.

"I put you in harm's way," Tony said. "Since Roach explained everything, that's all I've thought about. I took you away from California and put you in the worse place possible. Tell me—tell me—you know—I didn't know. I never would've—never thought—she was capable—of hurting *you* or *me* or"—he touched Claire's stomach and rubbed, causing Claire to smile—"*our* child."

The baby kicked Tony's hand, and Tony's eyes opened wide. "Did I just feel that?"

Claire nodded.

"That was amazing!" For a moment, their excitement and joy overpowered the shadow brought on by Catherine's name.

Despite her moist eyes and tear-covered cheeks, Claire giggled, "I've been praying for you to feel our little one move and kick. I think we have a soccer player on our hands."

Tony sat straighter and tipped his head. When their noses touched, he said, "Mighty fine!" Tenderly wiping her cheeks with the back of his hand, Tony brushed his lips over hers. "We've both made mistakes, too many to count, but this little life inside of you isn't a mistake. He or she isn't a Rawls or a Nichols. It's a Rawlings! I've had many accomplishments in my life, and in comparison to this little life, they all pale. Beyond a doubt, this child is my—no, *our*—greatest achievement.

I don't deserve you or an innocent child in my life. Thank you for keeping both of you safe. Roach explained how scared you were. If only I'd been home—"

Claire interrupted, "No, Tony. Don't you see? It was all planned to happen with you away. Neither one of us is to blame for what happened."

The nodding of his head moved hers. His words were barely a whisper, "For this one—"

Claire's fingers touched his lips. "Stop—please. I know we have a lot to talk about. We both have questions, and hopefully we both have answers, but right now and tonight, can we please just have us?"

Tony kissed the tips of her fingers, which only moments earlier stopped his words. "You're right. Besides, Madeline and Francis are waiting." Claire stood, yet Tony refused to relinquish her hand. Standing close, he looked down and said, "I need to know one thing."

Tipping her eyes up, Claire saw need in the depth of his dark eyes and her heartbeat accelerated. "What? What do you need to know?"

"Has all of this changed our relationship? I mean—are we still engaged?"

Claire smirked. "We definitely have a lot to talk about; however, if this little one is to be a *Rawlings* and not a *Nichols*"—her eyes twinkled—"I believe we only have a few more months to move our status to *married*." She paused. "If that's what you still want?"

"So, me being an ass and hanging up on you didn't change your mind?"

"Well, you see—I'm used to you being an ass. It's the part where you recognize it—that's new, and that's the reason my mind hasn't changed."

Tony pulled Claire closer and encircled her with his arms. "Well, how about I work on *not being such an ass*, and you work on restraining that smart mouth of yours?"

Claire pushed up to her tip-toes and kissed his neck. The familiar growl rang like music in her ears. "I was under the impression you liked my mouth."

His lips seized hers. Without hesitation, she met him with equal ferocity. When their force eased, their eyes met,
and his sparkled as he replied, "Oh, I do. I love your mouth, your eyes, your neck, and every other part of your amazing body; however, some of the things you do with that amazing mouth I like better than others."

"Really?" she bantered, as she purposely suckled his neck.

Tony seized her shoulders. "Do you plan on going back out there for dinner? I'm asking, because if you don't stop, it isn't happening."

Claire smiled. It was true; they had a lot to discuss, and a lot to work out; nevertheless, she felt empowered. She knew at that moment dinner could be a memory. If she continued her persuasion, then they could be naked and in bed in seconds; however, she needed food. Somewhere in her memory, she heard his advice, *I suggest you eat. You'll need your strength.* Grinning, she replied, "I do, and they're probably waiting." Pointing toward one of the other doors, Claire said, "The bathroom is over there. I'm going to freshen up. I'm afraid with my crying I look like hell."

"You, my dear, could never look like *hell*. You're radiant!"

"Oh, really?" Claire smiled knowingly at Tony. "Give me a minute"—she kissed his cheek—"After dinner, when we get back here, you can remind me what it was you liked my mouth to do."

Again, he pulled her close for one last embrace. "It's a date. I certainly hope Madeline doesn't cook twelve course meals."

Once Claire was ready, Tony disappeared into the bathroom, and Claire went into the closet. She found the box from the other day, the one with the cell phones and sat it on the floor. Kneeling, she looked into the depth of the container. At the bottom was her long gold chain with her engagement ring. Until a few days ago, she'd kept it close to her heart. After her conversation with Tony, she'd decided that there was no longer a reason to wear it. Begrudgingly, she tucked it away in the container.

Now, things were different. Claire removed the ring from the chain and placed it on the fourth finger of her left hand. Feeling his presence, Claire sighed and looked up. Tony was standing in the doorway, his dark eyes watching. By the erratic beating of her heart, she knew he saw everything.

"I took it off the other day," she confessed.

Taking her left hand in his, Tony helped her stand. Though his eyes hadn't softened, his words were more of a plea, "I hope you never feel the need to take it off again." Peering into the box, Tony added, "It seems as though it would've been difficult to hear that phone ring, tucked away, in a box, in the closet."

Claire smiled and pushed herself against his chest. "Since I don't believe it ever would have, we've someone to thank. My guess is—he's waiting for us for dinner too."

They left their suite hand in hand. While they'd been alone, the sun had fully set. In the middle of nowhere, the beautiful blue that filled the daytime view was now hidden behind shades of black. A star-filled sky sparkled above a dark sea, and the gentle rush of the waves filled the air as a soft breeze blew through the open doors of the dining room. Before they reached the others, Tony squeezed Claire's hand. "This place is amazing. Now that I look around, it's beyond words."

Claire agreed. "Now, it's truly paradise."

The evil that is in the world almost always comes of ignorance,
and good intentions may do as much harm as malevolence
if they lack understanding.
—Albert Camus

CHAPTER 17

Catherine sat at Tony's grand desk. She didn't consider it *his* any longer—it was hers, like so many other things. Besides, from all the reports she'd heard, he wouldn't be sitting there anytime soon. Though the FBI wouldn't confirm or deny, Catherine was under the impression Tony was either in custody or on the run. All she knew for sure was that he wasn't in Iowa. After meeting with Tom and Brent, the provisions of Anthony Rawlings' trust went into effect. Catherine Marie London was officially the executor of the Rawlings' estate and anything related to it. The title came with a nice trust fund. That money, plus the large sum she'd accumulated over the years, left Catherine more than financially solvent.

Once in a while, she thought about the money she'd given to Claire. Catherine wasn't sure exactly how much it was; however, whenever she started to regret giving it all away, her mind would go to the possibility of Tony on the run. If he were out there, she knew, without a doubt, he'd go for that money. Imagining him finding an empty box brought a smile to her face.

For almost twenty-five years, Anton had been in control, or so he thought. It was true; right after Samuel and Amanda's *accident*, Marie had offered to work for Anton. After all, she was alone, and he was all she had left of Nathaniel. The arrangement wasn't meant to last a lifetime. Nathaniel told Marie multiple times how he wanted her to live; never once did he say he wanted her to work as Anton's housekeeper.

It wasn't that Anton had ever been unkind. On the contrary, if anything, he'd been indifferent. Perhaps that was worse. He seemed to take Catherine for granted—she just was. It never appeared as though he worried if she would or wouldn't be there, if she would or wouldn't carry out his objectives—he never *asked*. Smirking to herself, she admitted that his complacency worked to her advantage on more than one occasion.

Maybe her name wasn't Rawls, but what did a name matter? Now that she had the legal documents confirming her title as executor, Anton's office was gone. It was hers—as was the house, the grounds, and the estate. Catherine Marie leaned back against the plush leather chair and scanned the room. The regal decor was very similar to Nathaniel's office from a quarter century ago. She'd always liked that. Smiling, Catherine decided the view from her current side of the desk was definitely the more appealing perspective. She also decided the room could use a feminine touch.

Catherine opened the drawer on the lower right to inspect Anton's private files. She fingered the tabs; in this paperless world, it surprised her he'd kept so many printed documents. Thankfully, the Iowa City Police hadn't felt the need to confiscate everything as evidence.

They did take all of Claire's documents. That didn't matter to Catherine; she'd already gone through everything on Claire's laptop and was honestly impressed with the amount of research Claire had accomplished during her short time in California. Catherine never imagined Claire would uncover Patrick Chester. The entire turn of events was far better than Catherine could ever have imagined or planned. The only possible better scenario would have included Chester actually killing Claire. If he had then Catherine would have been able to watch Anton's anguish first hand.

Reminiscing, Catherine admitted she did get the pleasure of witnessing some of it right after Claire's disappearance; however, to see Anton's face in Geneva when he realized Claire wasn't taken, but instead, she'd left him again, and disappeared with his money and his bastard child—*oh, that would have been priceless!* Well, not priceless—it cost Catherine whatever amount of money had been in those accounts.

It wasn't that Catherine originally planned on extending Nathaniel's decree to his grandson. Anton was safe as long as he stayed focused and on task. All the time and effort planting seeds, watering them, and watching them grow, paid off on more than one occasion. Everything was going the right way until—until his damn obsession with Claire Nichols.

Catherine knew something had changed after the Nichols' funeral. At first, she feared Anton had discovered her undertakings, or the true extent of them. That wasn't it. He'd been watching the Nichols family for a while; however, Catherine misinterpreted the depth of his fixation. *How unrealistic of her to think Anton's actual desire was to honor Nathaniel.* Although Anton claimed that was his goal, his actions proved otherwise. Bringing Claire to the estate was even acceptable—at first. It was when he began to take her out into public that Catherine knew his motivations were changing.

That was all right. Catherine could adapt too. As long as Catherine was covertly in control, she was able to keep her goals in sight. Besides, Claire and Anton were both so easily read and played. Even though it appeared to be a high stakes game of poker, it was more like *Old Maid*. The trick for success was in knowing the opponents. The fact that they didn't know they were opponents also aided her effort.

Catherine knew Anton better than he knew himself. She knew his limits and his needs—not sexually, of course. No, Catherine understood Anton's craving for control. It was his unspoken aspiration to be like Nathaniel. The grandfather he knew dominated everyone and everything. Some might say it was a disservice that Nathaniel showed so few people his gentler side. In hindsight, that omission proved very useful to Catherine. She could fuel Anton's need and depend upon his impulsiveness. Truly, it was a comical contradiction. For a man who prided himself on control, with the right triggers, he could lose it all. Anton didn't hold the monopoly on impulsivity. Catherine could also continually depend upon Claire's impulsiveness.

To be good—very good at manipulation, a person must understand their opponents' motivation. Anton possessed a lifelong yearning to please Nathaniel. Claire was much simpler. She craved interaction and affection. The smartest move Catherine ever made was sending only Carlos into that suite while Anton was away. Looking back on it, the move had been pure genius. In a way, Catherine hoped it paralleled Claire's current situation. *Oh well, perhaps Claire could learn the language of wherever she was?*

Claire's impulsiveness turned the key on each car that drove her off the estate. That same impulsiveness led her to burn the documents in her prison delivery. At least she read them before she destroyed them. That information was the seed that later grew to her impressive research and blossomed into the police department's evidence.

Besides impulsivity, Claire proved exceptionally obedient. The note in the box told her to read the entire contents—of course—she read it all. Catherine admitted the manipulation of Claire was amusing. After she was gone and in prison, Catherine even missed it. Claire and Anton's obliviousness throughout the whole game was the best part. This was especially true in the beginning, when he thought Claire knew him well enough to behave accordingly, and Claire feared his reaction if she misbehaved. Neither one realized Catherine was the one setting the rules—it was perfect.

If Governor Bosley hadn't pardoned Claire, Catherine believed Claire would've used that information in the box to expose Anton's secrets. The knowledge combined with the isolation would've energized Claire's retaliation. *After all, who wouldn't want vengeance after what Claire experienced?*

That was as far into the past that Catherine would allow her mind to wonder, because it was during that time that her plan took an unexpected turn. Anton was upset; his anger was peaked. Claire *should* have been angry. They *should* have worked to bring each other down. That wasn't what happened. Not only were they not adversaries, their behavior with one another changed to a more even playing field.

Catherine encouraged Claire's return to the estate for one reason—to intercede—to put things back on track; however, mild, meek Claire didn't return. Oh, she wasn't suddenly loud and boisterous. She also wasn't obedient and accommodating. What she was—made Catherine's blood boil. *Claire was a Nichols who had the audacity to think she was the lady of the house! She was a Nichols who was pregnant—with a Rawls baby!*

In 1985, that had been Catherine. She had been the one expecting a Rawls baby and waiting patiently to become the lady of the house. After all, Sharron was gone. Well, she wasn't dead; nevertheless, she was *gone*. Watching that woman die slowly had been excruciating. Catherine vowed to, never again, allow that to happen to anyone she loved.

Then, that same year, it was all taken away from her. Not all—she still had Nathaniel. He taught her how the world worked and showed her that she was loved. Those were gifts she'd never had from her own family. When Nathaniel presented her with the deed to her father's car dealership, it was the greatest gift—the most anyone had ever done for her. He showed her that his love was limitless; he'd do anything to make her happy. Catherine felt the same way. There were no lengths she wouldn't go to for Nathaniel—even today. Catherine would never allow a *Nichols* to live in Nathaniel's home and produce a child. It didn't matter that Nathaniel's home was in New Jersey. The estate where she sat was a worthy facsimile. Catherine was truthful when she encouraged Anton's construction of the estate and told him how proud Nathaniel would be— he wouldn't have been disappointed.

As the tips of Catherine's fingers ran across the top of the private files in the desk drawer, she contemplated the one thing she hadn't done for Nathaniel. Now that she truly was *where* he wanted her to be, Catherine Marie owed it to him to do *what* he wanted. He'd wanted her to contact her daughter. He wanted Marie to raise the girl—but that ship had already sailed.

She eyed the scribed names. There were so many. *How could she figure out which one was her daughter?* Catherine saw her own name. Maybe there was a clue in her file. When she opened it, she feared her heart would stop pumping. The writing wasn't Anton's. Catherine knew his writing well enough to duplicate it, with ease. This writing was Nathaniel's.

Scribbled in the margin of a contract was the name *Sophia Rossi*. Catherine went through the drawer again. The only Sophia was Sophia *Burke*. Suddenly, she no longer remembered her husband's love—she remembered his vendetta. Burke? *Burke?* There was no way *her* daughter could be connected to *Jonathon Burke*.

Catherine removed the *Sophia Burke* file and opened the folder. Above the typed name, *Sophia Rossi,* was the scribbled name *Sophia Rossi Burke*...Catherine searched the pages. There was a plethora of outdated information; nonetheless, written above the text on the second page was a telephone number. Catherine couldn't resist; she used the blocked house phone.

∞∞∞∞∞∞

Derek answered his wife's cell phone. The past few weeks had been too much, and Sophia wasn't up for solicitors or blocked numbers. "Hello?"

Initially, there was silence. Derek was about to hang up when he heard a voice. "I'm sorry; I'm looking for the beautiful baby girl I was forced to give away thirty-three years ago."

Derek listened. He remembered that after Sophia's parents' funeral, she said she didn't want to know her birth parents, yet this moment in time may be their only chance to learn the truth. "I'm sorry; my wife is indisposed right now. She's had a difficult few weeks."

"Yes, that's the reason I'm calling. I never wanted to interfere with her and her adoptive parents, but now—"

Derek interjected, "Tell me the date you gave birth."

Sophia's eyes widened as she heard her husband's question.

"July 19, 1980."

Derek turned to Sophia. Her beautiful gray eyes, which had finally stopped crying over her parents, were now moist once again.

"What did she say?" Sophia whispered.

With his hand over the phone, Derek nodded. "She said your birth date. I think it might be your mother."

"My mother died in a car accident." Sophia straightened her neck and took the phone. "Please, don't call again. My parents are dead. I don't know you."

The woman on the other end of the line spoke, "I'm sorry, I won't call you again."

Derek watched his wife's countenance melt. He knew it was the first time Sophia had heard her birth mother's voice, and he couldn't imagine the questions that were rapidly firing through her beautiful head. *Why did she give her up? Has she ever regretted her decision? What kind of person was she? What did she look like? Did they look alike?*

Sophia swallowed the tears threatening her speech and said, "Wait—if you could give me your number, I'll think about it. Then—when I'm ready—*I* can call *you*."

The woman exhaled and replied, "Yes, of course."

Sophia's strength was spent. It broke Derek's heart to see her fighting this new upheaval of emotion. Wrapping her in his arms, he took the phone from her hand. His voice was neither welcoming nor rejecting, "You may give me the number. When my wife is ready—*if* she's ready—*she* will call you. Please, do *not* call her phone again."

The woman hesitated only a second and then rattled off ten numbers. Derek repeated the numbers. Not offering a closing salutation, he disconnected the line. His concern wasn't the woman on the phone; it was the distraught woman in his arms.

∞∞∞∞∞∞

Catherine grinned. She'd done what Nathaniel had wanted her to do—she'd contacted her daughter. From the information in the file, Catherine could tell that Anton had been watching Sophia. She wondered what, if anything, he'd done for her. Catherine needed more information.

Anton had a list of private detectives and others who'd proven themselves helpful in the past. Briefly, Catherine thought of Roach, Phillip Roach. He'd done an excellent job with Catherine's directives. Of course, it helped that he'd been unhappy about losing his job with Anton. Catherine wasn't sure she'd be able to reach him. If she did, *did Catherine want to know Claire's location?*

Oh, she had so many things to consider. Truthfully, Claire could wait—she wasn't going anywhere. Right now, Catherine wanted to know more about *Sophia*. It was a pretty name—not one she would have chosen, but it was pretty. There were no pictures in the file, well other than a few of a very young girl. Catherine wondered what her daughter looked like. *Did she look like her?* or *perhaps she looked like...* Truthfully, that was why she didn't want to do this in the first place.

Catherine Marie London was *no longer* that scared, lonely, and abused teenager at the mercy of her drugged out uncle. No—she was a strong fighter and a go-getter! She'd loved Nathaniel Rawls and outlasted Anton Rawls—both were impressive accomplishments.

Thanks to both, Catherine now had time and resources. She also had a plethora of questions. *What did her daughter do for a living? Did she go to college? Were her adoptive parents good to her?* Catherine told herself they were. *If not, Nathaniel or Anton would've known, but what about Sophia's husband? Could it be possible? Could Sophia really be married to someone associated with Jonathon Burke? And who did he think he was, talking to her the way he did, demanding her telephone number? Catherine sure as hell wasn't intimidated. If a Rawls didn't intimidate her—a Burke never could.*

She, once again, searched the drawer of private files. As she fingered the tabs, Catherine remembered the saying, *no sense reinventing the wheel.* Knowing Anton better than anyone, Catherine was quite sure of his attention to meticulous detail. Surely he'd already researched Sophia's husband. It was true, she could glean more information, but why not start with whatever Anton had already accumulated. When she passed the B's without a Burke, her hopes began to fade. Then she saw the D's—*Derek Burke.* Removing the folder, she laid it across the desk and began to read. The first page was a series of emails:

To: Anthony Rawlings
From: Cameron Andrews
Re: Ms. Rossi
Date: January 12, 2011

As I wrote in my previous email, Ms. Rossi took an unscheduled trip to Europe. I have since learned the reason for the trip was to wed. I'll remind you, I first mentioned Derek Burke in a December 18, 2010 email. They met at a Christmas party.
I apologize for not relaying the information of their nuptials sooner. I did not expect that to be the reason for her trip; however, a red flag came up when I received notice of her application for marriage license.
Please inform me how to proceed.
CA

To: Cameron Andrews
From: Anthony Rawlings
Re: Ms. Rossi—Burke???
Date: January 14, 2011

It's nearly midnight here, and I just saw your message. I want information and I want it yesterday! How could this have happened so quickly?
Information, pictures, details... now!
AR

To: Anthony Rawlings
From: Cameron Andrews
Re: Ms. Burke
Date: January 26, 2011

Although Ms. Burke is now living in Boston in her husband's apartment, I've just confirmed that they've made an offer on a small cottage in Provincetown, Mass. I'll notify you immediately if their offer is accepted.

Derek Burke's employment record is straight forward. I've attached his dossier. I'll continue to monitor. Please inform me if you would like my activities to change in any way.
CA

To: Cameron Andrews
From: Anthony Rawlings
Re: Ms. Rossi-Burke
Date: January 27, 2011

Let me know the value of the cottage and their offer.
AR

It was reassuring to Catherine—she *did* know Anton, probably better than he knew himself. She could only imagine how upset he was to have Sophia elope without his knowledge! Catherine felt a sudden affection for her estranged daughter—if it wasn't for the name of the man she chose to marry!

Leafing through the pages, Catherine found Derek's lineage:

Father: William Burke—Grandfather: Randall Burke—Great-grandfather: Truman Burke.

It was the notation under Truman's name, the one scribbled in Anton's writing that caught Catherine's attention: *two sons: Randall and Jonathon. There was the connection!*

Catherine's daughter was married to the great-nephew of Jonathon Burke!
Catherine continued to read:

Derek Burke hired in 2013—Shedis-tics Corporation, Palo Alto, California (Rawlings subsidiary).

When there was nothing else for her to learn, she turned on Anton's computer and accessed his private list of contacts. This list was how she'd found Phillip Roach, in the first place. When she last spoke to Anton, he quipped something about Catherine knowing everything *that went on in the house.* Smiling at her access to his private information, Catherine doubted Anton had any idea how truly right he'd been.

Although she may know everything within these walls—Catherine wanted to know more. One of the names on this list would be just the person to help her accomplish that goal.

∞∞∞∞∞∞

Sophia wiped her eyes. "Thank you. You'd think I'd be all cried out."

"I don't think there's anything wrong with being emotional about this. I mean, you were just saying a few weeks ago that you didn't want to get to know any parents other than the great people who raised you, and if you still feel that way, then you have my support. If you've changed your mind, then I'll support that too."

Sophia shrugged. "I don't know what I want."

Derek's grinned. "Then don't decide right now—there's no rush."

Leaning into her husband's embrace, Sophia crooned, "Whatever I did to deserve you is beyond me. Thank you—for everything."

With her head under his chin, Derek sighed. His only desire was for Sophia to be happy. Lingering in the pit of his stomach was the feeling of trepidation. He worried that by engaging in that conversation, he'd set her up for more disappointment. The last thing he desired for his wife was heartache. She'd already had too much.

The Rossi's were wonderful, loving parents, and there was a part of Derek that wished he'd hung up on Sophia's birth mother before the conversation even started.

Perhaps all the dragons in our lives are princes
who are only waiting to see us act, just once, with beauty and courage.
Perhaps everything that frightens us is,
in its deepest essence, something helpless that wants our love.
—Rainer Maria Rilke

CHAPTER 18

During dinner, Francis offered Tony and Phil clothes. It seemed that over the years, a large accumulation of items had been left and stored away on the island; these clothes would suffice until ones more to their liking could be ordered and sent into town. Mumbling under her breath, Claire mentioned, "I was planning on ordering some, but a call changed my mind."

The only person who heard her comment was the man at her side. Truthfully, he was the only one she wanted to hear. With a table of onlookers, Tony didn't verbally respond; however, he did reach over and squeeze her hand.

After dinner, Francis and Madeline left Tony, Claire, and Phil alone, and Tony explained his current status. He told Claire about the questioning and the FBI's ultimatum. He explained how he'd been instructed to stay in contact with the bureau otherwise he'd be considered a fugitive—based on charges of domestic battery.

Claire shook her head vehemently. "No! That's *not* what I said to Evergreen. I told him I was running, but *not* from you! I never said anything about pressing charges."

"I know." Tony didn't sound upset. This wasn't new territory to any of them; they all knew Claire and Tony's history. "Roach told me what you said to Evergreen. It's some ploy of theirs—Brent said it was to get more information."

"Brent?" Claire asked. "Do Brent and Courtney know the truth? Do they know we're all right?"

Tony shook his head. "No. It's safer for them that way."

Claire lowered her eyes and looked at her lap. She understood; however, it didn't lessen the pain of knowing she'd lied to her closest friends—again.

Tony described how Eric helped him leave the United States, and how he traveled around Europe. When he talked about specific stops along his journey, they were shocked to learn how close their paths had been. Tony also asked questions. *How did Claire find the island? Where exactly were they? Had Claire been in contact with anyone since arriving?*

Claire deferred some of his questions to Phil, while she responded to others. "I haven't been in contact with anyone. I do have a non-traceable phone Phil left here, and I have Har...a number for an FBI contact."

Tony sat straighter and looked at Phil. Speaking to no one in particular, Phil asked, "Is that my cue to leave this discussion?"

Claire answered first, "No, you know the answers to more of his questions than I do, but before you two discuss the coordinates of our location, I should tell you, Tony, I saw Harry in Italy."

"So did I"—his voice lowered a pitch—"He told me he'd been with you. Actually, he showed me a picture."

"A picture!?"—Claire stood—"What sort of picture did he show you? And what are you, or was he, implying—*with* him? I saw him—I *wasn't* with him!"

Tony reached out and took her hand. The hardness she'd heard seconds before disappeared as his thumb rubbed the top of her hand. "It wasn't anything—just confirmation he'd seen you."

"Well, did he tell you that he's a FBI agent? I didn't get the impression it was a recent change in profession."

Tony nodded. "He did. Apparently, he's supposed to be my contact." Grinning again, he added, "I'm not supposed to leave Switzerland without contacting him first."

Phil interjected, "Damn"—also with a smile—"I knew we forgot to do something."

"Do you think he'll trace you here?" Claire couldn't hide the panic from her voice.

Phil answered, "As many twists and turns and name changes as we've had? I'll be lucky if I can explain where we are."

Claire exhaled. "Good, I'm so glad you're here—both of you, but the last thing I want are unexpected visitors."

It was Madeline who interrupted their conversation, "Excuse me, Messieurs, Francis has clothes for each of you. They are now in your suites." After they both thanked her, she continued, "Madame el, if there's nothing else, we'll also retire."

"That's fine, Madeline, thank you."

A few moments later, Tony and Phil went into the house to clean up. They'd both been wearing their current clothes for over twenty-four hours and couldn't wait to change.

Sitting alone on the lanai, Claire closed her eyes and listened to the sea. The surge of emotions over the last few hours combined with raging hormones intensified the familiar pounding in her temples. She knew her headaches bothered Tony, and she didn't want anything to upset tonight's reunion. There was a part of her that felt like a newlywed about to join her husband for the first time. It was a silly thought—one that couldn't be further from the truth; nevertheless, the butterflies in her stomach and the tightened anticipation added to her stretched nerves.

She didn't hear Madeline's footsteps or even know she was still present until she spoke, "Madame el, are you all right?"

Claire jumped. "Oh! You scared me. I thought you were gone."

"We were, but I came to check on you. Is it your head again? Does it bother you?"

Claire reached out and touched Madeline's hand. "Please don't mention my headaches around Mr. Rawlings."

"I'm sure he knows. He looks at you with so much adoration, like he knows your thoughts. I knew right away that he was who you've been waiting for."

Claire grinned. "I never said I was waiting for anyone."

"No, Madame el, you didn't." Madeline noticed the diamond on Claire's hand. "Are you to be wed?"

Twisting the diamond, Claire sighed. Her smile tried to disguise the sadness in her eyes. "Oh, it's a very long story."

"You are too young to have a long story."

"You're right, I am—but I do. In a nutshell, Mr. Rawlings and I were married, we divorced, and he asked me to marry him again, and I said yes. Madeline, I've made a lot of mistakes—especially in the last few years. I don't want to make another one."

The whites of Madeline's eyes shone like beacons in the darkness. "Madame el, I don't know your *long story*. I can see you are blessed with people who love you, and in the short time I've known you, I understand why. When Monsieur Rawlings arrived, I saw the love and joy in your eyes. Why are you now reconsidering?"

"Oh, I'm not—I love him—I do." Claire hoped Madeline wouldn't notice the tears quietly descending her cheeks. She worked to keep her voice steady. "Before we marry—again—I need to know some things. I need some answers."

"It isn't my place, so if you don't want my advice, I will leave."

Claire shook her head. "I didn't grow up with *places*. This way of living is part of my long story. So, Madeline, I'd be honored to hear your advice."

"Madame el, things happen for a reason. If your long story is all happy, that's wonderful; however, I believe there's more to it. Some of the answers you seek—you are afraid of what you may learn, oui?"

Claire nodded.

"You love him, despite that long story, oui?"

Claire nodded again. "I do."

"And, Madame el, he loves you. Does he know your story?"

"Yes—he knows my story."

"What we fear is what we do not know. When something is cloaked by the darkness of uncertainty, it's a mystery. Allowing light to penetrate that darkness makes everything clear"—she pointed out to the dark sea—"Look at the ocean. In the darkness, all you can do is listen to the wind and the waves. You ask yourself, are there creatures, boats, or untold dangers lurking? We don't know, and then, in our minds we create perils that do not truly exist. In the morning when the sun shines and you see into the depths of the crystal blue water, or all the way out to the horizon, you know you are safe"— Squeezing Claire's hand, she added—"In the light of day, I see your love. Please don't allow the dark of night to hide what is right in front of you. Even if those answers are not what you want to hear, do you think they can be as bad as you imagine?"

Claire shrugged. "I really don't know. I know I want to not think about them right now and worry about them later."

Madeline's voice slowed. "If that will make you feel best; however, I've found that the longer I put off turning on the light, the bigger the monster under my bed becomes." Once again, she squeezed Claire's hand and then reached into her pocket and handed Claire a tissue. "May I get you anything else?"

Claire wiped her eyes and cheeks. Miraculously, the tears served as a vent, releasing some of the pressure from her temples. Her headache wasn't as intense. With a sad smile, she replied, "You've given me a lot, thank you. Have a good night."

"Good night, Madame el."

Enjoying the calm of the darkness, Claire reflected on Madeline's words. If only Madeline knew the truth—at one time—that monster in the dark was actually the man in the other room. Now the monster was a woman Claire trusted. *Could she ever trust her own instincts?* A faint smile came to her lips as she remembered Phil's words. He told her to do just that—listen and trust her instincts.

When Claire stood to move to their room, she saw the shadow near the end of the lanai move; instead of going through the house, Claire followed her intuition and walked toward the darkness. Just outside of their suite, Tony stepped from the shadow and gently took Claire into his arms.

His freshly showered scent overpowered the salty sea breeze and penetrated her senses. Claire loved the scent of his cologne. In the morning, she'd order some.

Tony looked down into her eyes. "I like that smile. After what I heard, I wasn't expecting to see it."

"How much did you hear?"

He led her to a lounge chair, sat first, and tugged Claire down in front of him. It was their talking position—where their bodies touched—their worlds connected—yet their eyes remained private. Claire felt his chest rise and fall. While she waited for him to answer, he wrapped his arms around her, hugged her chest, and splayed his large hands across her midsection. Settling against his chest, Claire felt the warmth of his toothpaste scented breath blow against her neck. Their bond held a sense of intimacy she'd never shared with anyone else. His hands on her body didn't feel foreign—they felt right. By the time he spoke, she'd almost forgotten her question. His Anthony Rawlings—CEO tone told her that he'd contemplated his answer. "Enough—I heard that you love me and that, before we marry again, you have questions that you want answered."

Claire nodded. "I do." However, at this moment in time, her heart wasn't in the asking mood. It wasn't that she wanted the monster Madeline mentioned to grow bigger. It was that, for the first time in over a month, she felt secure. His embrace completed the release of pressure her small cry had begun. Closing her eyes, she leaned her head against his shoulder and enjoyed the internal peace—never had anything felt so right.

"Do you want to ask anything?"

"I do, but not tonight."

Tony turned her shoulders so that they were facing one another. "You aren't concerned about that monster growing?"

Claire shook her head as their lips touched. "No, it's not going anywhere, but I'm pretty sure it can't get any bigger. Remember, I said I wanted tonight to be just about us."

In the faint moonlight, Claire saw Tony's grin. His tone was lighter, with a hit of seduction. "I do remember that"—his finger traced her lips—"I also remember something about that beautiful mouth."

She stood with her emerald eyes shimmering and the butterflies of desire stirring deep within her. Offering her hand, she grinned. "Come and remind me."

Tony didn't need to be invited twice. As they disappeared into the master suite, the cares and concerns remained outside. There were cards to be revealed, and in time, they would. Theirs was a long, complicated story with a monster and a knight. What made their story unique was that these two players were the same person.

At that moment, Tony was her knight in shining armor. She'd been alone in paradise, imprisoned by the evil witch. Her future had seemed uncertain; then, out of the blue, he arrived. Just like in the fairytales, he came to her rescue, freeing her from her prison of isolation.

The rest of the world disappeared as his lips suckled the sensitive skin between her neck and shoulder. Despite the tropical heat, her arms and legs prickled with goose bumps. A familiar moan escaped her lips. With skilled hands, he eased her sundress over her head and dropped it into a pink puddle. Taking a half of a step back, Tony's eyes scanned her exposed body. His approving smile radiated to his eyes, as dark desire swirled with the chocolate shades of love.

Seconds later, Tony fell to his knees and tenderly kissed her enlarged stomach. Fighting to remain standing, Claire exhaled and wove her fingers through his hair. Instead of enjoying the sensation of his caresses and kisses, she was momentarily overwhelmed with relief. In the last six weeks, their baby had grown, and her body had changed. "I was so afraid..." she mumbled.

Still kneeling, he looked up. "Of what?"

Though Claire didn't want to admit her insecurity, she couldn't look away. She couldn't lie. "That you wouldn't want me—that you wouldn't think I was sexy enoug—"

The fire behind the brown raged. Her legs buckled. Suddenly, on her knees, wearing only lace panties, they were eye to eye. Still fully dressed, he framed her face with his hands. She heard a combination of pain and adoration in his voice. "How could you ever think that? My God, you are the most beautiful woman in the world. You always have been"—bending to kiss her stomach, he regained eye contact—"I didn't think it was possible, but now, with my child inside of you, you're even more beautiful"—Grinning, Tony directed Claire's hand—"It should be very obvious; I think you're incredibly sexy."

He was right; it was obvious. She smiled and smirked. "If that's the case—which I admit it does seem to be—why am I the only one undressed?"

"Because, you are *mighty* sexy, and I want to see you."

Unbuttoning his shirt, Claire suckled his freshly shaven neck. "That doesn't seem fair," she purred. Her kisses moved down his chest until she couldn't bend any lower. Sitting straight, she inhaled. "This does have its disadvantages."

"One person's disadvantages are another person's advantage," Tony said with his devilish grin melting her world. No longer did she feel large and awkward. Claire saw herself as Tony saw her. With her hand in his, he led her to the big bed, where his clothes and her panties disappeared into the pink puddle of the sundress.

Before she could consider or question, their world became one. It didn't matter that her body and shape were changing. They belonged together.

Metaphorically—the wolf was at the door. Realistically—their life was upside down; however, in that moment, in their room, in their home, on their island, and in their paradise they had one another—it was a victory. Catherine had tried to keep them apart, and they had overcome her ploy. They didn't know if they'd won a battle or the war. At that moment, celebration was their only goal.

"Tony?" Claire said as she nestled against his chest with the sound of his heart beating in her ear.

"Hmmm?"

"Tell me something."

His arm wrapped around her bare shoulder. "I thought tonight was a no question night—a just about us night."

She lifted her head, to see his face. "It is. I'm not asking about anything. I want you to tell me something."

"Oh, you do? What do you want me to tell you?"

"I want you to tell me that we're safe, that Catherine, the FBI, that no one can take this away from us."

The amusement of her demand faded. She watched as Anthony Rawlings CEO emerged from the man she'd just held tight. She immediately recognized his voice; it was the one he used with business, the one that left no room for debate, the one she used to hate—it was the tone she needed. "We're safe. No one—and I repeat *no one*—will ever take my family away from me."

Claire kissed his cheek and settled back into the crook of his arm. She knew what he'd just said was beyond his control; however, she could pretend. The illusion filled her with the momentary peace she needed. Within minutes, she was sound asleep on Tony's hard shoulder.

Be more concerned with your character than your reputation,

because your character is what you really are,

while your reputation is merely what others think you are.

—John Wooden

CHAPTER 19

For the hundredth time, Agent Harrison Baldwin read the screen of his phone and wondered if he could avoid the multitude of text messages any longer. *If he didn't respond, would SAC Williams suddenly forget the tirade and possible demotion that was undoubtedly coming his way? There was no question, he deserved it. Harry had done exactly what SAC Williams told him not to do—he'd allowed the case to become personal.* Harry knew that wasn't true. The Nichols/Rawlings case hadn't *become* personal—it had *been* personal from before he saw Claire Nichols in Italy.

Harry decided that his inability to keep his assignment professional was in part due to his own screwed up personal life. Unfortunately, he'd allowed both lives to intertwine—when it came to an FBI agent—that was *never* a good thing.

The best part of his personal life had been his more recent reconnection to his sister. Without a doubt, Amber was his closest family, and after his divorce, that was what he truly needed.

Throughout the history of time, Harry had been too quick to fall in love. Ilona was no exception, and when they were young and living the dream in southern California, there had been love—or so they both thought; then life happened.

Harry's fascination with law enforcement started in childhood. He wasn't sure how or why, yet from a young age, he knew that was the path he intended to pursue. It began with a degree in Criminology, which led him to the California Bureau of Investigation. Ilona knew she'd married a police officer and was all right with that; however, she hadn't signed up to be the wife of an FBI agent.

Harry's initial enquiry into the FBI was actually on a dare—a late night out with police buddies and booze; nevertheless, before he knew it, things started happening—he passed phase one and two of the testing—passed the skills tests—and received the conditional letter of appointment.

Although he and Ilona had discussed his aspirations, neither one of them fathomed the consequences or the repercussions on their recent marriage. After passing the physical test—background check—and medical exam—the goal he never expected to obtain was right in front of him.

The bureau had five career paths. Based on Harry's education and experience within the California Bureau, he was selected for the Criminal Investigative Division (CID). This division coordinates, manages, and directs investigative programs focused on financial crime, violent crime, organized crime, public corruption, violation of individual civil rights, drug related crime, and informant matters associated with these investigative areas. Coincidentally, Agent Nichols was also in the CID.

The most daunting consequence of Harry's dream job was the time away from his new bride. It wasn't a gradual process—not something they eased themselves into. No—one moment, they were together every day—the next, he was gone. That first separation they endured was when Harry went to attend the FBI Academy in Virginia. He should say that, during that time, he missed his wife; however, the training was intense. During those twenty-one weeks, he lived and breathed FBI—and loved every minute of it. At least, during his training, he and Ilona could occasionally talk.

Following the academy, it's customary for new agents to rank their desired locations for their first assignment. Ilona wanted to stay in California, so Harry made that his choice. With four field offices in the state, he used every one of his selections to accommodate his wife. Placement wasn't solely based on preference; it was also based on need and budget. The Baldwins were both shocked when Harry was assigned to Seattle, Washington. Ilona didn't like Seattle. The weather was too cool and rainy, and she missed her friends in California and family out East.

During Harry's second year out of the academy, while still within his probationary period, he was selected for an undercover assignment. It was quite an honor; however, the assignment left Ilona alone again. This time, she was stuck in an area she detested and her husband was gone—totally unreachable for an undisclosed amount of time. To make matters worse, during his absence, she learned she was pregnant. Reflectively, Harry understood her isolation and depression. At the time, he was oblivious. He was too busy concentrating on the job. An undercover assignment for a junior agent was a monumental boost to his career; the experience was exhilarating, and his evaluations were stellar. Agent Baldwin loved the covert world.

When he returned to Seattle, Ilona's pregnancy was visible. They'd had no communication during his assignment, so the pregnancy revelation was—to say the least—shocking. Harry's initial reaction was less than positive. It wasn't that he didn't want kids—he'd never given them any thought. Ilona presented him with an ultimatum—his job or his family. Harry should've chosen his family.

He didn't.

Before their child was born, Ilona moved back East to live near her parents, and Harry asked for reassignment to San Francisco. This time, they granted his request. Since that time, Ilona has remarried. The assignment in San Francisco made sense to Harry. It was the one place he could have his job and some family—Amber McCoy, his half-sister, lived there.

Although the two of them grew up in the same home, they weren't close. Amber was younger, and the one with both parents. Her dad tried to fill the gap for Harry; however, until the FBI, he always felt something was lacking. Sadly, he recognized that he was no better than the man who contributed to his gene pool. Someday, the daughter he only saw in pictures would be faced with the same unmet need.

When Harry moved to San Francisco, Amber was living the dream. She had it all—except the ring. Simon Johnson and Amber were living and working together. He was a great guy, very intelligent, a wonderful entrepreneur, and excellent to Harry's sister. Harry and Simon became instant friends. It might be safe to say Harry enjoyed Simon's company more than he did Amber's; nevertheless, during that time, they all became close.

Harry worked out of the San Francisco field office and occasionally left for undercover fieldwork. When SiJo started having issues with security, Harry offered his resources. Since he was employed by the federal government, he could only do contract work for SiJo. His friend, Lee, from the California Bureau of Investigation took over as head of SiJo's security. Although Harry wasn't officially with SiJo, he felt a connection to the company that his friend and sister were working so hard to grow.

After his divorce from Ilona, Harry wasn't interested in a relationship with anyone else. He promised himself that his days of falling fast and hard for a beautiful face or cheeky personality were over. The FBI was his life.

It's true—sometimes it felt as though life stacked the deck. Harry wasn't always sure if it was in his favor or against him.

The more Harry worked with SiJo Security and spent time with Simon and Amber, the more he questioned his vow of remaining unattached. Honestly, when he first met Amber's assistant, they were just friends; however, the more their paths continually crossed, the more their relationship blossomed. Over time, they started seeing one another—meeting Simon and Amber for dinner—going to a movie—long weekends—cohabitating.

This time, Harry entered the relationship with full disclosure. They both agreed—they were consenting adults with no intentions of a long-term commitment. Harry explained from the beginning that his work could call him at any moment, and he'd need to leave. He told Liz that their relationship could end suddenly if he needed to go undercover. Harry didn't intend to leave another woman waiting for his return as he'd done to Ilona.

When Simon finally proposed to Amber, Harry was equally as happy. Unfortunately, Harry was on an assignment when Simon's plane crashed. As soon as he heard and received clearance, he traveled back to California. Following Simon's death, Harry and Liz moved into Amber's building. Perhaps it was the loss of Ilona and Jillian from his life, but Harry had finally recognized the importance of family, and he couldn't leave Amber alone in her time of need.

When Claire Nichols first contacted Amber, Harry remembered that his sister was upset—both by the content of the email *and* by the sender. Probably more out of curiosity, Amber chose to continue the correspondence. After they exchanged more emails, both Amber and Harry saw the logic behind Claire's allegations.

The investigation surrounding Simon's plane crash had never fully been closed. Harry knew that uncertainty added to his sister's angst and hoped Claire's insight into Anthony Rawlings would help his sister have final closure.

The preliminary results of the National Transportation Safety Board's, NTSB, investigation regarding Simon's crash centered on operator error. The agency painstakingly reconstructed the plane and looked into the flight plans. Simon Johnson was an accomplished pilot—weather conditions were ideal for flight—and there were no signs of malfunctioning equipment or tampering. The numbers didn't add up.

As Claire's suspicions mounted, Harry decided to take this new evidence to his superiors at the San Francisco field office. He not only took the allegations regarding Simon, but the entire recalled contents of Claire's prison delivery. Harry had no idea that he was presenting the FBI with information on one of *their* cold cases. In light of the new allegations, the San Francisco field office assigned a new team to revisit the bureau's old evidence regarding Agent Nichols' death.

When Claire's attorney unexpectedly contacted Amber and requested her help with relocating Claire to Palo Alto, Amber called Harry—Harry called the bureau. Since Harry wasn't undercover at the time, SAC Williams decided—Claire would be Agent Harrison Baldwin's new assignment. It was the FBI who recommended changing Claire's reservations and having her travel via private plane. The bureau had multiple reasons for this change in plans—the intricacy of the case, assurance of Claire's location, and time needed by the bureau to have their cover stories ready.

The morning Harry walked into Amber's condominium, he wasn't sure who he'd meet. There was the woman Simon remembered fondly—and there was the gold-digging, ex-bartender, who tried to kill her rich husband, got lucky with a pardon, and was stupid enough to burn the real evidence woman. Without question, this was an unusual assignment.

Harry understood the FBI's interest in Claire Nichols and their hope that she could bring new information to the cold case involving her grandfather. He also knew that his assignment was one of—right time—right place. By all accounts, Harry should *not* have been assigned to any case that potentially involved Simon Johnson's death—truly, the case was personal from the beginning. There was no question—even before meeting Claire—Harry wanted to prove Anthony Rawlings' guilt.

When Liz and Harry started dating, she promised she understood his commitment to his career. Truthfully, she demonstrated that on numerous occasions. Each time Harry was called away, she'd go on with her life. She didn't ask questions about what he did while he was gone, and if she had—he wouldn't have been able to answer. It wasn't that he had sexual exploits on each assignment—Claire was his first; nevertheless, Liz had shown Harry the support Ilona didn't or couldn't.

Understandably, neither Liz nor Harry ever anticipated his undercover assignment occurring right under Liz's nose. The evening the SiJo plane arrived with Claire Nichols on board, Harry relocated Liz from their condominium to an apartment of her own. He told her what he'd said a million times—when faced with the ultimatum—he'd always choose his job. He also told her that Claire Nichols was just another assignment—a job. It was what he believed at the time. Initially, Liz remained supportive.

As Harry got to know Claire, her definition changed. With that change, came a change in Liz's understanding. From Harry's perspective he was never unfaithful. He'd told her that—while on assignment—they were no longer a couple. It wasn't Harry's fault that when faced with seeing him every day she didn't understand.

For a brief moment in time—when Harry believed that he could be a father once again —Harry told Amber something he never thought he'd say. He told his sister that he wanted the job at SiJo; instead of pretending, he wanted to be the President of Security Operations and planned to resign from the FBI. Harry wanted to give this child the father he hadn't provided for his own daughter. At that moment, sitting with his sister alone in the hospital cafeteria, Harry decided the only part of the undercover case he cared about was keeping Claire and their child safe from Anthony Rawlings.

Again, life happened. This time, the damn cards were definitely against him. Claire informed him that he wasn't the father of her baby. In retrospect, Harry didn't know for sure if his decisions that afternoon in the hospital cafeteria were based on Claire or the baby. Now that he and Liz were reconciling, he leaned more toward the later; nonetheless, he still wanted to keep Claire and her child safe.

SAC Williams reviewed the case and Harry's actions. He decided Agent Harrison Baldwin needed a break from the bureau; he wasn't fired or demoted; instead, the FBI put him on temporary medical leave and required him to attend counseling sessions. These sessions with a bureau psychologist were supposed to determine why he overstepped his professional bounds with Claire Nichols. While he did as they said, it made Harry laugh. This was the first time he'd ever gotten personally involved with an informant; however, he'd been around the bureau long enough to know that it wasn't a unique situation.

In addition to personal counseling sessions, he was required to attend sexual harassment seminars. Apparently, if Claire Nichols were so inclined, she could press charges against Harry. In actuality, six months ago, he'd jeopardized the case and sullied the bureau. Now, by showing Rawlings the picture of Claire and him holding hands, Harry had done it again.

He'd located *and* lost both of his assignments—Claire Nichols and Anthony Rawlings were *missing in action*. If Harry ignored the FBI's text messages any longer, they would consider *him* MIA!

Pacing around his hotel room, Harry contemplated the case. He didn't want to be taken off of it again. He knew he shouldn't have shown Rawlings the picture of him holding Claire's hand—he knew that before he did it. It was unprofessional. Harry could argue that his intentions were honorable. He'd hoped that by creating a rouse—making Rawlings believe that he and Claire were together—it would keep Rawlings away from her. The bureau would never approve of his actions or even his motivation. They'd remind Harry that Claire never pressed charges against Rawlings—in fact, she explicitly said that Rawlings *wasn't* the one she feared.

It wasn't just the connection with Claire. Harry didn't want to be relieved of the case because even before he'd been officially assigned, he'd been researching it. With each passing day and new nugget of evidence, Harry knew that Rawlings was exactly the person Claire Nichols should fear. It was his goal to make the powers that be realize that Anthony Rawlings was connected—not only to the death of Agent Nichols—but multiple others. Some of the deaths, like Claire's parents and Simon Johnson's, had been classified *accidents*—car crashes—airplane crashes...

That didn't matter. Claire had told Harry about Rawlings and *accidents*— Harry had a gut feeling that there was more to this case. He was on the hunt for hard evidence, but in the meantime, he had his gut feeling. To an FBI agent, that was significant. At one time, even Claire had told *Harry* that she believed Tony may have been involved with these accidents. Harry figured that if he could prove to her that her previous suspicions were correct—then maybe she'd see the light.

Not only had Harry messed up the case, he'd messed up any possible reconciliation with Claire as well. No longer could he or the bureau rely on her feelings of familiarity with him for insight. In Harry's opinion, the only feelings

Claire currently had for Harry were anger and betrayal. The way Harry saw it—he hadn't betrayed Claire. In fact, the truth was the exact opposite. He'd been placed with her to protect her and learn from her. Without a doubt, in Harry's mind, the protecting was paramount. Besides, he reasoned that if Claire could forgive Rawlings for his plethora of recognized sins, once she learned the whole truth of Rawlings' doings, then Harry's considerably shorter list of transgressions could also be forgiven.

Above all, Agent Baldwin didn't want Claire Nichols in danger. Even if she refused to believe it, Harry knew Rawlings jeopardized her safety. Closing his eyes, he remembered the look on Rawlings' face when he showed him the picture of him and Claire. Reading people was part of Baldwin's training. The wrath he saw in Rawlings' eyes was palpable. It didn't frighten Baldwin—as a matter of fact—he would've loved for the man to attempt an assault. The rage Harry saw in the man's eyes made Harry's blood boil. Claire's stories came rushing to the forefront of his mind. More than anything, at that moment—in that pub in Geneva—Harry wanted to give Rawlings some of what Rawlings had given to Claire years before. In his mind, Rawlings was a ticking time bomb, and he didn't want him exploding around Claire or her child.

Harry's motivation that evening in Geneva was to keep the two of them apart. He believed he could accomplish that personal goal as well as the FBI directives. Harrison figured he could keep Rawlings in Italy, disinterested in pursuing Claire while locating Claire and keeping her safe. It was a great plan. Unfortunately, the results didn't provide the intended consequence.

Agent Baldwin's phone vibrated again. This time, it wasn't a text, it was a direct call. When he read the screen, Harry expected to see SAC Williams' direct line. His heartbeat accelerated as he read the name: *Deputy Director*. Straightening his stance, Agent Baldwin knew that ignoring *this* call wasn't an option.

Clearing his throat, he hit the *RECEIVE* button and said, "Agent Baldwin here."

"Baldwin—we need to talk."

The use of his name without the title wasn't a good sign.

∞∞∞∞∞∞

In the shadow of the vegetation intertwined through the trellis, Claire rested on the lanai, reading her iPad. The scent of the fragrant flowers and soft breeze from the sea combined to bring her peace. While listening to the waves, Claire read the news from around the world. According to her window to the world, she and Anthony Rawlings were still missing. Rawlings Industries was floundering as temporary CEO Timothy Benson reached out to the stock holders, asking them to have faith in their founder as well as the companies he brought under the Rawlings' umbrella. Claire wondered about Sue and worried how Tim's stress would affect his family.

Every such thought directed Claire back to Catherine. Ripples of vengeance continued to expand in all directions. It was like throwing a rock into Claire's lake. The resulting circles of water went out and out until they faded away. Momentarily closing her eyes, Claire relished the thought of Catherine fading away. Never could she remember feeling such vengeance for one person. When she hated Tony, it was for what he'd done to her. This was different. Catherine's ripples were reaching people who never deserved this vendetta.

Claire knew Catherine wouldn't be stopped until she told the FBI the truth. She looked at the table and read Harry's card for the millionth time—he was her contact—he was Tony's contact. In the three days since Tony arrived, neither of them had bothered to connect their *contact*. Before she made a decision one way or the other about her impending call, Phil's voice refocused her thoughts.

"Claire, do you have a few minutes?"

She grinned. "Well, you know, I'm super busy." He pulled out a chair at the umbrella table beside her. Although it was still morning, the intense sun warranted shade whenever possible. Phil's shorts and shirt amused Claire. It was a much more casual look than he normally wore. "I thought you were going into town with Tony and Francis?" she asked.

"I changed my mind. I'd like to talk to you privately for a minute."

Immediately, she bristled. She and Tony hadn't breeched major topics in the last few days—no specifics; however, they had talked about trust—giving and receiving it. "Phil, I won't lie to Tony."

"I'm not asking you to. I want to discuss something with you alone. I've no doubt he'll give his opinion, but nevertheless, I'd like yours first."

Claire pulled herself up and sat taller as her legs remained outstretched on the soft chaise lounge. "What do you want to discuss?"

"You know I have a few different phones?"

Claire nodded.

"By using a remote server with multiple redirections"—Phil paused, as if knowing Claire didn't need the technical reasons—"never mind the *how*—anyway, I'm positive the phones aren't traceable, nor are the ones you and Rawlings have. Earlier today, I turned on my old phone."

Claire wasn't sure if it was his voice or his tentative cadence, but something about Phil's speech brought concern to her consciousness. "I don't know if you're trying to or not, but you're making me nervous. Please just say whatever it is. Do you want to leave?"

"Do I want to? Not really. Security on this island isn't a bad gig. Many would agree that I have the ideal job. The thing is that, when I turned on my phone, I had multiple messages from Ms. London."

Claire's heart stopped, and she felt the blood drain from her face. "Why did you want to talk to me privately about this?"

"I'm assuming that I still work for *you*?"

The way he emphasized the last word, Claire knew he wasn't referring to her as part of a couple. "Theoretically, yes, you work for me."

He cleared his throat. "In my previous experience, it's usually the person with the bankroll who tells me what I should be doing. Like when I was trailing you, Rawlings told me what he wanted. I don't mind watching the sky for planes or the horizon for boats, but I think I could be more useful to you—to both of you—back in Iowa."

"Why?" Claire asked with increased volume and pitch coming through her one word.

"None of her messages asked specifically about you. She asked if I'd completed my job. If so, she has another one for me. If I go, I could keep an eye on her and report back to you."

Claire knew it was selfish to want Phil to stay on the island; however, she couldn't help it. She never would have predicted that having both Tony and Phil nearby would give her such an overwhelming sense of comfort. After the last few months, she didn't know she'd ever experience this sense of peace again; she didn't want to lose it so soon. Claire responded, "I don't know what to think. I think we should discuss it with Tony." Claire saw Phil's grin and imagined his green eyes with golden flecks smirking behind the dark glasses. "Why are you looking at me like that?"

"Three days—don't you dare let the woman I spent a month with in Europe disappear in *three days*."

She looked down at her lap and exhaled. "I haven't disappeared." Looking back up, she went on, "It's called *team work*. Part of that is refraining from making unilateral decisions."

Phil nodded. "All right, I'll buy that. Now, how about that instinct we talked about? What's your instinct saying about this idea?"

Claire considered and replied, "It's saying this *is* a good idea. If we don't have someone back there keeping us informed, we'll have no idea what she's doing." Before Phil could respond, Claire added, "That's my *instinct*. My *heart* is telling me, not to let you leave. Everyone is safe here. If I could, I'd give you a list of people and tell you to have them all brought here. I'd even authorize kidnapping—I know from experience that it's an effective means of relocation."

Phil lowered his voice. "Speaking of which, is that the only reason you don't want me to leave?"—he hesitated—"Are you and Rawlings...all right? I mean, if I leave, are you safe?"

Claire's shoulders relaxed. She hadn't been sure where he was going with his question. "Yes, Phil, we're good. I'll be fine. I worry about you out there—especially with her."

"I've handled worse adversaries."

"I'm curious to know what she wants."

"So am I," Phil admitted. "She wanted you gone from Iowa. She wanted you to get the money and disappear. I accomplished both of her goals. Maybe I've proven myself worthy. If that's the case, I could possibly learn more valuable information."

Claire smiled. "You've proven yourself *very* worthy. If you go, will you do one thing?"

"I don't know."

"Will you stay working for me? I don't care if she's paying you too. I want to know you have our best interest at heart."

"Claire, it doesn't take a financial obligation to verify that commitment."

She reached over and squeezed his hand. "Thank you...I don't say that enough."

"You say it too much. Now, how are we bringing this up to Rawlings?"

Laying back with her hands on her midsection, Claire sighed. "I'll do it. I'll tell him that you told me about the messages and that my *instincts* tell me that you should go to Iowa and infiltrate the wicked witch's castle"—Removing her sunglasses, Claire peered at Phil—"Just promise me that you'll watch out for those flying monkeys! They've always given me the creeps."

Later that day, after lunch, Claire and Tony were alone in the living room when Claire approached the subject of Phil's departure.

"Whose idea was this?"

Claire stood taller. "It was his, but I like it."

"You like it? Claire, you don't seem to understand how this employer/employee relationship works."

She didn't like his tone. "Excuse me?"

"I'm not sure I trust him"—Tony's dark eyes drank her in—"If you think you're going to retain control of my money and the staff that my money bought, you need to start acting like the employer—not like a friend who sits to listen to everyone's ideas."

"Why? I personally think it's working for me."

His volume rose. "It isn't working for you. Don't you see how easily you can be manipulated?"

"I'm not being manipulated."

Tony turned toward the open doors; she watched as the muscles in his neck flexed. Finally, his words came out louder than before, "Everyone can be manipulated. It's most successful by people who're closest to you. Claire, you let everyone get too close!"

Claire tried to reign in the fire she felt growing in her eyes. "Tony, I trust Phil explicitly. I trusted him with my life and our child's life." She exhaled, softened her tone, and stepped toward her ex-husband. Taking his hands in hers, she said, "He brought you to me. I didn't ask for that. It was *his* idea to go get you. Personally, I'm glad he has his own initiative."

"Initiative is fine. What about agenda?"

"What would you like to know about my agenda?"

They both turned to the sound of Phil's voice. Tony's neck straightened as his business tone emerged. "Excuse us; we're having a private discussion."

Phil shrugged. "There are only five people on this island. I can guarantee all five could hear your *discussion*. I'd say—all things considered—it wasn't private."

In the heat of the moment, Claire wasn't sure if she wanted to laugh or hide. Most members of a staff would be smart enough, or respectful enough, to feign ignorance. Whether it was not hearing discussions or not noticing bruises, Tony was more accustom to a different type of employee. It was at that moment that Claire realized the difference. This staff wasn't *his*—they were *hers*.

Her mind went back to San Diego. Just now, when Phil entered the room, he did so, to do what he'd done that night at the hotel with his note—he'd entered to verify Claire's safety. She knew Tony wasn't accustomed to this behavior. She chuckled, thinking, *poor Tony—his world is upside down,* and said, "Despite the volume, we *are* having a discussion. Since it's about you, I'd like you to join us."

Though Tony didn't respond or rebuff her statement, she felt his stare penetrate before he said through clenched jaws, "Yes, please, since privacy doesn't seem to be an issue, join us. I was just asking about your agenda regarding this job offer in Iowa."

"My agenda is to learn Ms. London's plans."

"And to what means are you willing to go?"

Phil shrugged. "I don't have many limits."

Tony stepped forward. "That's my concern. What if she offers you more money than we're paying you? Would you give up our location?"

Claire interjected, "I told you, Tony, I trust Phil. I believe he has our best interest at heart. I believe that where *we're* concerned, there *is* a limit." She looked to Phil.

He grinned. "When it comes to my current employer—I do have limits. Your location won't be shared by me."

Claire reached for Tony's hand once again. "See, he wants to go—he wants to help us."

Tony's dark eyes went from Phil to Claire and back again. He exhaled. "I think of you as the man I hired to watch Claire. I have to keep reminding myself that you're the reason she's here and safe. Don't disappoint me—us."

Phil extended his hand, and the two men shook. "I wouldn't."

They discussed the plan, including how Phil would stay in touch. They also discussed contacting the FBI. Although Phil didn't believe their calls from the island could be traced, he recommended that if Claire or Tony felt the need to contact Baldwin or anyone else, they keep the calls relatively short.

With time, they all agreed. The island was a safe retreat and the best place for Claire. She wanted Tony to be with her—so, he'd stay. Being safe wasn't enough; they needed to know what was happening outside of their bubble. Phil would do his best to learn what they couldn't.

Maybe all one can hope
is to end up with the right regrets.
——Tom Miller

CHAPTER 20

-AUGUST 2016-

C laire didn't feel the soft restraints keeping her body pinned to the moving gurney or hear the loud noises from the echoing machine. During another time, in another life, the solitude of the Diffusion Tensor Imaging machine (DTI) would have frightened her. Perhaps it would today, if she was aware—but she wasn't.

Yes, her body lay prone in a cold room, covered with a blanket, but the soft cotton sheet wasn't providing the pleasurable warmth radiating through her. No—Claire was somewhere else. The heat emanating through every fiber of her being came from a strong, yet gentle touch and circulated to places where that touch had yet to explore.

Closing her eyes, Claire enjoyed the basking rays of sunshine on her skin and the scent of surf in the humid air. Though her recently applied sunscreen filled her senses, the lingering aroma of cologne comforted her thoughts and lulled her away to a peaceful, dreamless state; then, without warning, the sensation of large hands caressing her ankles and moving toward her thighs reignited her world. Claire's lips turned upward as goose bumps materialized. Often times, people associated those small bumps to cold—on the contrary, at that moment—Claire wasn't cold.

Opening her resting eyes behind her sunglasses and focusing on the handsome face before her, Claire saw his devilish grin. It was a smirk of lust and pleasure, which with only a glance could melt not only her insides, but her world. With the intense tropical sun, his eyes were also covered by dark glass, yet as his smiling lips neared hers and her smile morphed to a willing pucker, she knew there was an unseen intensity waiting for her behind those dark glasses.

Reaching up, she lifted the dark barrier and saw what she expected to be present. Just because she anticipated it, didn't mean the dark reality didn't affect her. Claire's insides quivered as he removed her sunglasses and their eyes met. There was a moment when she thought to speak, but it was short-lived. So much more could be said without words.

When she woke earlier that day, he was gone. Madeline had said he'd gone out early. Claire hadn't worried, she knew he'd return, but after only a few hours apart, she now realized their reunion would be more than a simple, Hi, how are you today?

It was true, her body had been thoroughly fulfilled and used the night before; nevertheless, it now yearned for what was being silently offered. When his full, soft lips engaged hers, the passion of the night before returned with a vengeance. Only moments earlier, her lungs had inhaled without instruction, yet as acquiescing moans escaped her lips, breathing required thought. Maybe it wasn't thought as much as it was timing. Inhaling needed to occur in unison. If it didn't, his unrelenting approach would rob her body of the oxygen necessary to go on. As her bathing suit covered breasts ached for the friction of his chest, Claire decided breathing was overrated. She wanted what was slowly overtaking her—to be consumed by the fire smoldering in the dark penetrating eyes. If in the process she forgot to breathe—did it really matter?

With the open doors looking out to the crystal blue sea, their room was only slightly more private than the lanai; however, it was their room. Madeline and Francis respected their privacy. As Claire's bathing suit fell to the floor, she realized they'd yet to speak, and still, they'd conversed more than some couples did in a lifetime. They'd greeted one another, discussed the pleasantries of the tropical morning, and assessed that each was doing well.

Laying on the soft comforter with her arms above her head, the man she loved gazing down at only her, and the large ceiling fan methodically moving the humid air, Claire's world was right. Had she planned on her morning taking this turn? No. Was she willing? Without a doubt.

The large, talented hands claiming her body also had her soul. While his approach could at times be forceful—it was always gentle. Yes, her mind held memories of contrary times, but those memories were so long ago that they were difficult to resurrect. At this moment, she willingly surrendered, as she'd done a thousand times, to the whims and desires of the man above her. Without any words, he could manipulate and dominate—move her from a state of sleeping bliss to the throes of erotic desire. Similar to years ago, his dark eyes held the passion and emotion that allowed her world to spin. Because he willed it so—the world was right. Without him, the entire planet would spin out of control, lost forever in the darkest depths of the universe.

It didn't seem to matter that her body was changing. The tips of his fingers lingered as he taunted her sensitive breasts. So little was needed to entice her yearnings—a simple puff of air on a taunt, wet nipple made Claire's back arch and her insides liquefy. Teasing her to the point of begging, yet satisfying every desire was his specialty. Despite the way she'd changed—the way her body had changed—she felt wanted and sexy as he skillfully caressed and suckled, moving south over her enlarged...

Claire shook her head and tried to reason.

Enlarged—baby—no—gone—everything gone—

She fought the thought—the idea—no!

Dr. Fairfield watched in horror as the patient, who only moments earlier had been experiencing something which none of them could see or hear, was suddenly flailing against the restraints. The machine wasn't meant for movement.

"I told you to sedate her!" Dr. Fairfield yelled into the microphone.

Trying to remain calm, the nurse beside him replied, "We did, Doctor. She shouldn't be waking."

It didn't matter if she *shouldn't be*—Claire was fighting the restraints with all she had. Her mouth opened, yet with the roar of the machine, the feverish attempt of the medical staff to halt the DTI, and the doctor's angry shouts, Claire's pleas for her unborn child went unheard and unnoticed. By the time the others entered the lead lined room, Claire's flushed cheeks were covered with tears and only wordless whimpers escaped her lips.

Dr. Fairfield slammed his fist against the counter as the staff sedated and moved the patient from the gurney. Speaking to everyone—and no one—he said, "This is her fifteenth day on medication. Do you know how much time and money was spent on that scan?! Now it's useless! She's barely a one-hundred-and-ten-pound woman. How damn hard is it to get her sedation right?"

Though he asked questions—he didn't want verbal answers. Flinging the door to the windowed room so hard that it rebounded off the wall, he called over his shoulder, "When the results we *did* get from this scan are available, bring them to me."

Dr. Fairfield's recently prescribed treatment was both proven and new. There were documented results with these medications; however, Dr. Fairfield was taking it a step further, combining medications and requiring more intensive therapy. It was more than had been tried in the published literature. This scan was supposed to show the first marker. Obviously, even without the DTI, the patient was experiencing a hallucination; however, observation wasn't measurable. The DTI was meant to document increased brain activity. This sedation screw-up would postpone the next DTI for at least a couple of days. Frustrated, the doctor stormed back to his office.

∞∞∞∞∞∞

Driving toward Everwood, Meredith reconsidered her objective. She'd been at this *research* for two and a half months. Soon, her children would be home for a small break before the next boarding school session. The hours she spent at Everwood would seriously detract from time she could spend with them. *Was this story really worth the effort?*

The tightness in Meredith's chest told her what she already knew—she wasn't a detached investigative reporter, like she'd always wanted to be. She was a friend, one who, for lack of a better word, was *compensating* for the pain she'd brought her friend years ago. This wasn't about a story—it was about saving Claire and preventatively restoring pride to a little girl who one day would learn terrible things about her father. Meredith wanted Nichol to know there was more to the story—a *page two* as Paul Harvey used to say. It wasn't that Meredith didn't trust Emily to one day enlighten Nichol to Anthony Rawlings' attributes, although she wasn't sure she did. It was that, even though Claire came to her with the story of her and Anthony's introduction, Meredith was the one who wrote it and made it common knowledge. *If* Claire never recovered and *the rest of the story* never came out, how would the book that's made Meredith millions affect the beautiful, innocent little girl whose last name was *Rawlings*.

Meredith parked her car in the employee parking lot, smoothed her ugly, white uniform, and stood tall; she knew this assignment was more about guilt and obligation than investigation. Until she was convinced Claire was beyond hope—Meredith couldn't stop. Thank God her husband understood. He'd make their children's two week break memorable. Maybe one day, not only would Nichol be proud to carry the name *Rawlings*, but Meredith's children would be proud to share their parents' name—not only because their father was a wonderful, loving person—but because even when it was difficult—their mother had learned to do the right thing. It wasn't an easy lesson. Although Claire carried the scars, Meredith would never forget that she'd been the one to start the wheels of that *lesson* in motion.

Ms. Bali informed Meredith of Claire's change in protocol a few weeks ago. As a member of Claire's *food care staff*, Meredith had been included in meetings centered on Ms. Nichols. It was during one of those meetings that she'd met Claire's new lead doctor, Dr. Fairfield. They weren't introduced. Meredith sat attentively and listened to his directives. Being on Claire's *direct food care team*, she also had access to Claire's records—including the recently prescribed medications. Meredith researched each drug thoroughly—most fell under the class *controlled* and categorized as *antipsychotic*.

Since the induction of the new drug regime, Meredith assessed—Claire had become *more* depressed and agitated. Getting her to eat—anything—of late—was difficult. She now became irritated at any change in routine. Even the suggestion of going outdoors, the activity she enjoyed most, provoked angst. It wasn't that Claire spoke, but non-verbally, she fought; her body tensed and her glare intensified. The compliant patient of two months ago no longer existed. Meredith reasoned *any* change was positive, yet her heart told her otherwise. She truly wondered how much Emily knew, and how much longer she'd allow it to continue. *Was it better to have Claire content in her own world or upset in the real one?*

Today, Meredith's shift began at 4:00 PM, which meant she'd deliver dinner. After a few days into the new protocol, Ms. Bali rearranged assignments, making Claire Meredith's only responsibility. Although Dr. Fairfield wanted Claire responsible for her own feeding, nutrition was important, and any hope of her feeding herself was currently gone. Her sister wouldn't allow her to go without meals. Without a doubt, Claire required more consistent care. It wasn't Meredith's qualifications that landed her this opportunity; it was Claire's positive response to her. The people in charge were willing to do anything to avoid conflicts. Ms. Nichols didn't like change; therefore, anything the doctor didn't demand changed wasn't—that included Meredith.

The more time Meredith spent with Claire, the more she feared Emily would discover her interaction. That's why Meredith requested the later shift: 4:00 PM to 11:00 PM. On the days Emily visited, it was usually earlier in the day.

As Meredith approached the bank of employee lockers behind the kitchen, she saw Ms. Bali. It was obvious that she was waiting for her. Cautiously, Meredith asked, "Hi, Ms. Bali, is there a problem?" Looking at her watch, she saw that there were still ten minutes before the beginning of her shift. "I wasn't scheduled until 4:00 PM, was I?"

Ms. Bali didn't answer; instead, she tilted her head toward the offices and said, "I need to speak with you—privately."

Meredith's heart raced; perhaps her concerns about her children's impending break were unwarranted. If Emily discovered her presence—or Everwood discovered her fake credentials—her investigative—or guilt-filled endeavor was over. Trying to contain her concerns, Meredith asked, "Do you want me to come right now, or can I put my things in my locker?"

Ms. Bali's strained expression mellowed. Forcing a smile, she replied, "Oh, you can put your things in your locker. We've had a rough day, and I need to fill you in."

Remembering to breathe, Meredith nodded, placed her purse and *lunch* in her locker, and fell quietly in step with her supervisor, walking toward her private office. Once inside, Ms. Bali shut the door and asked Meredith to sit.

The truth that makes men free is for the most part
the truth which men prefer not to hear.
—Herbert Agar

CHAPTER 21

They watched as Phil's plane rose above the crystal blue sea and became smaller and smaller as it neared the horizon—eventually fading away. Watching him leave the island—this time—wasn't as difficult for Claire as it had been the first time. Claire knew it was because now she wasn't alone. She had the strength of Tony's arm tenderly wrapped around her waist. Sighing, she tipped her head back to his shoulder and closed her eyes. The diesel fumes from the small propeller plane had faded as the combination of sea breeze and cologne dominated her senses.

Since Madeline wanted to be sure Phil ate before his trip, they all had eaten an early dinner. Now, with Madeline and Francis at their own house, for the first time in months, Tony and Claire were truly alone.

"Do you want to take a walk along the beach?" His baritone voice created the lyrics sung perfectly in tune with the melody of the waves.

"Hmm, that would be nice."

With their fingers entwined, Tony stepped forward, leading Claire along the shoreline. Since their sandals were waiting near the path to the house, their bare feet sunk with each step. Claire glanced back and noticed how the reoccurring waves erased their footprints. For quite a while, they walked in silence. The birds sang and the sea whispered, yet neither spoke. When they finally did, it was at the same time, "Do you think it's time..." Claire said, and simultaneously, Tony asked, "Are you ready to..."

Their walking stopped. Looking up to his handsome face, Claire reached toward his cheek. The slightest stubble abraded the tips of her fingers, and she momentarily imagined the sensation on other parts of her body. "I'm scared," she admitted.

He didn't answer; instead, he dropped her hand and encircled her body with his powerful arms.

"Tony, I'm so afraid that if I ask what I want to ask, that what we have right here—right now—will end. You know the saying—ignorance is bliss?"

He nodded.

"I'm enjoying my bliss."

"We don't have to discuss anything you don't want to discuss."

She nestled her cheek against the soft cotton shirt. "Do you know what questions I need to ask?"

As he replied, his chest vibrated against her cheek, "I have some idea, but I don't want to go anywhere you aren't ready to go. You deserve to know the whole truth. The thing is—I never imagined telling anyone the whole story—the whole truth. The only person who knew it all—well, we never needed to discuss it." Looking directly into her eyes, he continued, "It's as if—if I say any part of it—or all of it—out loud—it makes it real."

Claire shook her head and spoke into his shirt, "No, Tony, whether you say it aloud or not—it's real."

He gently lifted her chin, creating the connection that over the years glued them together. "Do you remember me telling you that sometimes the whole truth is too much to handle?"

"I do. I also remember you saying many other things and doing many other things. I need to know why. I need to know what *you* did, and what was done by someone else. If I don't know the truth, my imagination takes me places I don't want to go." Tony looked away and gazed over her head toward the setting sun; Claire reached up and redirected his eyes back to hers. "We have a child coming—sooner rather than later. I love you. You're the father of my baby. I want a family; however, if we don't have complete honesty—we have nothing."

His chest rose and fell. The eyes looking down at Claire were, once again, filled with remorse. There was a part of her that longed for the black voids of the past—those she could change and pacify. The pain she was witnessing behind the intense brown was his doing—she couldn't take it away. All she could do was share the burden.

Tony sighed. "If after you hear it all, you want me gone—from your life— and from our child's life—I wouldn't blame you."

Claire smirked. "I've wanted you gone before, but you're still here."

He grinned. For a split second, she saw the gleam she loved emerge from the sadness. "I believe I've told you what I think about that smart mouth."

Her lips grazed his exposed neck. "Yes, I believe you've said you like it."

Tony reclaimed her petite hand, and they continued walking. "How far have you walked? Can you circle the entire island?"

"I haven't tried. I've only been as far as the orchards. I did leave the island once, when I went to town with Francis. I went to see the doctor. Other than that, I haven't wanted to leave the grounds around the house."

Tony's cadence slowed. "I don't say it enough. Even though it's deserved, it's difficult for me to say—but Claire, I'm sorry. You're living in fear—on an island—and it's entirely my fault."

Her tone hardened. "No, Tony, it isn't. At least, I don't believe it is—completely. I know some of it's *your* doing, but I need to know how much."

After a prolonged silence, he replied, "I don't doubt you can handle it; you've handled so much. You've always been so strong. It's what—"

"I know—it's what infuriated you about me."

He squeezed her hand. "Yes—and it's what made me fall in love with you." He seemed lost in thought until he went on, "I fell in love with you while you were with me in Iowa. Like I said before, it wasn't supposed to be like that, yet every day, you'd do something, or say something, that would stay with me. I'd be at work or in the gym, and I'd remember it. Sometimes it made me angry, but most of the time, it made me smile." He stopped their progress and peered into her eyes. "Do you have any idea what that's like? To suddenly be thinking about another person when you least expect it?"

She looked up and smiled a closed lip smile. The emerald of her green eyes shone with the spark of the setting sun as she answered, "I do."

Tony shook his head. "I didn't. I never had—never in forty plus years, but then, when you were in prison, I reflected back and I realized—I had. There was someone who appeared in my thoughts, over and over, for years. Someone whose life interested me—someone I watched—and someone who I paid to have followed. It was a different obsession—different than the other people on our list. Without me realizing it, that person consumed my thoughts, and though I didn't think it possible—she took my heart."

Claire's heartbeat quickened. *Did she want to know who dominated his thoughts and took his heart?*

He grasped her shoulders. "It was you—I *fell in love* with you while you were supposed to be my prisoner; however, I've loved you since before I knew love existed." He touched her cheek and bathed it in his warm breath. "Claire, you've been the captor of my heart since you were a freshman in college."

His eyes were wide with need. He'd just confessed something monumental. Claire knew he needed affirmation; nevertheless, she felt the blood drain from her face as her knees gave way. Suddenly, she was sitting in the sand at his feet. Despite—or perhaps because of—his honesty, Claire felt nauseous. Lifting her knees as high as she could, she rested her head against them. Tony immediately knelt beside her. When his arm encircled her shoulder, her body tensed.

Of course he felt it. He had an uncanny way of sensing her thoughts and moods. It was what had always made lying so difficult, even when she was his *prisoner.* She recognized his tone—guarded and aloof. "You said you wanted to know, so I'm trying to start at the beginning."

She shook her head, unsure if she could speak without vomiting. After a few more minutes of silence, his embrace disappeared. Though her eyes remained closed, she felt him move away. When she opened them, she was alone. Claire saw his figure rounding the bend of the beach, going the direction they'd been walking.

Tears coated her cheeks and the gasps of ragged breaths replaced the sound of the surf. This was much more difficult than she ever imagined. Claire wanted to know, yet the thought of being watched—since the age of eighteen or nineteen—made her literally ill. *If it were true, if he had truly been watching since that time, then her other suspicions were probably true. He was probably responsible for Simon's internship and job offer. He was probably responsible for her parents' death, her scholarship, her job loss at WKZP...He'd orchestrated her entire life!* The possible confirmation was too much to bear.

By the time she stood, the sun had set and a blanket of black velvet peppered with stars covered the island. The moon's rays glistened on the now calm lagoon. Each step took effort. Lost in thought, she didn't see her surroundings or hear the sounds of the night. In time, she reached the path. Lying on the sand, all alone, were her sandals. She didn't know how Tony could've gotten back to the house without her seeing him. Then again, she didn't know how long she'd been on the beach. The aching in her head that came with the sudden onslaught of nausea, increased. She wondered *if he'd left. Had her reaction been so hurtful that he'd forget her and their child?* Claire's thoughts went to the boat. If he'd taken it, surely she would have heard the motor; then she remembered Francis' warning the day they went into town. He told her to always schedule morning appointments. *The seas—they are unpredictable after the sun sets.*

While her temples throbbed at the idea of Tony out in a boat alone, her thoughts were dominated by the words and meaning of his revelation. Claire berated her reaction as she passed the threshold of their dark home. She'd asked for truth—he'd given it, yet instead of facing it with strength, as he said she would, she crumbled at his feet. Damp sand fell from her dress and bare feet as she mindlessly walked through the unlit rooms to their bedroom. Once at her destination, she gazed about their room. The doors to the lanai were open wide with moonlight as the only source of illumination. The room and beyond was filled with shadows. As she was about to turn on a light, she heard something—or someone—on the lanai.

∞∞∞∞∞∞∞

-EARLIER-

Tony didn't know where to go—*he was on a damn island!* Each step away from Claire became more and more determined as his feet pushed deeper and deeper into the sand. He trudged forward with his mind a whirlwind of thoughts. *She said she wanted truth; he gave her the damn truth. Was that some kind of sick joke? Ask for something—no, demand it—and then when you get it—throw it back!* When he stopped and looked back, all he could see was beach. He wasn't sure if she'd gone back to the house, or if he'd rounded too many bends.

As he continued walking, the beautiful scenery around him went unnoticed. Before he realized, sunlight was waning. Straight ahead, through the twilight, near the shore, he saw a structure. Curiosity propelled him forward until he recognized the building. It was the boathouse he'd been to the day before with Francis. Tony followed the path through the vegetation until he reached the door. It wasn't locked. Watercrafts weren't his normal means for transportation; then again, he'd never lived on an island before. Yesterday, he'd watched Francis maneuver the boat, and he reasoned it wasn't that much different than a car.

Turning on the light, Tony walked through the garage-like area onto the floating docks and around to the other side of the boat. Francis explained how changing tides made the docks rise and fall. He also mentioned that, occasionally, there were storms which caused the calm seas to rage. A motorized lift hung the boat and kept it suspended above the water. In the case of rough seas, this device protected the watercraft from striking the docks. As Tony neared the controls of the lift, he heard the door to the boathouse open.

Francis entered and asked, "Monsieur, you want to go for a boat ride, oui?"

Tony didn't know what he wanted. Taking the boat out on the open sea, pushing the throttle all the way down, and feeling the wind against his skin seemed like a good release. "I was thinking about it."

"Madame el, she'll go with you?"

"No, she's...tired."

Francis nodded. "Oui, bébés, they do that"—he chuckled—"God has not given Madeline and me bébés of our own, but I've watched many families multiply here on this island, and the mères—oui—the bébés make them tired."

Tony nodded; his mind was busy analyzing the control panel of the boatlift.

Francis continued, "And sometimes—sometimes the bébés also make the mères very emotional. Ladies who usually are quiet—having the little bébé inside of them—it makes them loud—and the tears!" He laughed.

Francis's deep laugh caused Tony to look away from the levers and focus on the man near the doorway.

Francis went on, "The tears, oui! For no reason at all!"—smiling approvingly, he added—"It's a wonder the pères don't all go crazy."

Tony nodded.

"Monsieur, may I help you with the boat? You need to go somewhere? If it is something Madame el needs, perhaps Madeline or I have it at our house?"

"No," Tony said tentatively—his mind no longer on the boat but on the woman he left on the beach. "It isn't anything she needs. I was thinking about going for a ride."

"Oui, of course, you are right." Francis' jovial tone lightened the dim boathouse. "Since you've arrived, Madame el, she doesn't need anything. You can see it—the two of you." Francis walked to the control panel. "Monsieur, this lever here"—he pointed—"it is how we bring her down." As he depressed the lever, the boat began to descend.

Tony placed his hand over Francis', stopping the movement of the boat. "No," Tony said. "I don't think I need to go for a boat ride right now, but perhaps in the morning?"

"Oui, in the morning! In the morning, I'll show you the channels and markers. They're very difficult to see at night if you aren't used to them."

Tony patted Francis' shoulder. "Thank you." As Tony left the boathouse, they both knew Tony's gratitude wasn't for the lesson on the boatlift or the promise of tomorrow's boat ride.

Following the path during the night wasn't difficult. Through the years, Francis had done a superb job of controlling the vegetation and creating clear, well-traveled trails. With the addition of the silver rays of moonlight, which occasionally penetrated the lush canopy, Tony's steps remained confident.

When the path opened to a clearing, Tony saw the warm glow of light coming from Madeline and Francis' home. As he neared the light, the faint sound of music filled the otherwise quiet air, and the aroma of something delicious taunted his non-existent hunger. Thinking about how early they ate, Tony figured Madeline was making Francis dinner. Looking up the hill, Tony saw the big house. There wasn't a light glowing from any of the many windows or doors. It looked empty. He wondered if Claire were there or still on the beach. Though he could've accessed the house from that side, Tony walked out to the beach to retrieve his sandals. Under the cover of the vegetation, he found them lying in the sand beside Claire's and picked them up. Looking out toward the beach, he worried. If she were still out there, he needed to go find her. As he scanned the dark shore, he saw her figure coming toward him. Quietly, he slipped up the path.

You have power over your mind—not outside events.

Realize this, and you will find strength.

—Marcus Aurelius

CHAPTER 22

Claire's eyes were accustomed to the darkness. Turning towards the sound, towards the open doors to the lanai, she saw Tony's silhouette. Again, their words came in unison, "I'm sorry."

They both stepped forward, and when their bodies touched, the pressure which had been building evaporated into a sweet release. The tension he sensed on the beach was gone; Claire's body was liquid in his hands—molding and conforming to his. Their lips united as a different tightness began to build deep within.

Claire was his—he was hers. It had been that way since before she even knew him—or knew of him. She could fight that revelation, *but why? It wasn't debatable; she couldn't rewrite history. She didn't want to—it all worked to put them where they were right now.* Besides, every fiber of her being ached for his touch. Her body wanted him—that was undeniable. Each one of his caresses was but a tease, arousing sparks that only he could ignite into flames. The desire was obviously mutual as he pulled her closer. They didn't say words, yet they both understood the meaning of their sounds. Heavy breaths and moans echoed through their cavernous room out to the sea.

With their sandy clothes lost somewhere on their bedroom floor, their fervent passion led them to the large bed. Though the soft hum of the ceiling fan whirled above their naked bodies, the heat they felt couldn't be cooled. Claire's lips suckled his broad shoulder as his skillful hands roamed the familiar and new curves of her figure. His touch stirred her desires, making her plead for more.

Though faint moonlight cloaked the room in shadows, Tony could see Claire's sleeping mask on her bedside stand. It was black satin, and helped to keep the morning sunlight away while she slept. Reaching for the mask, Tony held it in Claire's line of vision and asked, "Do you trust me?"

Seeing the mask and his devilish grin, Claire's heart began to beat erratically. Yes, she put the mask on herself before she fell asleep; however, it was never something they'd done for fun. Her mind raced back to a room with a lock that beeped. There was a time—long ago, in the beginning—when there were blindfolds and restraints, but she never considered any of that fun. "No," her small hands pushed against his chest. "No!" She wasn't seeing the man on top of her—she was seeing the man from those memories. "I don't want to wear that—please—please don't make me."

Perhaps he made a sound; Claire wasn't sure. Something made her eyes open, and suddenly, she saw the man who was truly there. In his eyes she again saw pain. "Oh, Tony"—her arms surrounded his neck—"I do trust you. I just don't want to wear that." Her heart broke as he nodded and rolled off of her, onto his pillow. Lifting her head to look at him, Claire started to apologize, but before she could speak, he placed his finger on her lips.

Never could she have predicted her ex-husband's next move. Claire Nichols would never have imagined Anthony Rawlings placing such a high bet as to wager himself, yet that's what he did. Lifting his head to gently kiss her lips, he whispered, "I trust you." Then he covered his own eyes with her satin mask. As absurd as he looked with the black satin ruffles around the sides, she'd never been so honored. *He was hers!* That was what he'd tried to tell her on the beach. Yes, the whole idea of him watching her over the years was creepy, but that wasn't what he'd tried to convey. Seeing him lay still with his eyes blinded to her every move, Claire understood—she had him—his heart—his soul—and his body. They were hers to do with what she wanted.

Easing herself to her knees, she allowed her lips to brush his neck. His growls encouraged and the stubbles abraded. Claire loved every sensation and every minute. Next, she moved to his chest where her hands caressed his muscles as her fingers wove through his chest hair. When she licked and sucked a nipple, his arms encircled her.

Within this new paradigm, Claire was empowered. Sitting up, she pushed his arms back to the mattress and said, "No." His grin from below the satin melted her. She was afraid she wouldn't be able to do all the things she imagined; her body was on a precipice, and at any moment, she'd be lost in earthshaking bliss.

It wasn't like anything they'd ever experienced, nor was it how Claire always wanted it to be; nevertheless, on this one night—it was perfect. After Claire's world exploded and Tony's did too, she collapsed against his chest and fought to breathe. Finally, she lifted her head and removed the satin blindfold. The spark within the chocolate bliss made her reconsider her desire for sleep.

Tony's grin infiltrated his words, "Since you removed the blindfold, does that mean I can now hold you?"

"Oh yes, Mr. Rawlings, please do."

Although nothing about their recent history seemed wrong, it didn't take him long to right their world. Turning Claire, he gently laid her upon the bed and fanned her hair on her pillow. "Just so you know"—he whispered in a deep raspy voice—"your hair sweeping over my face and chest when I couldn't see it—was incredibly erotic."

Claire giggled. "Well, that's good to know. I'll remember that for next time."

His brow cocked upward. "Next time?"

She nodded.

Tony shrugged. "Well, my dear, they do say variety is the spice of life."

Claire ran her finger over his pink lips. Before she could remove it, Tony sucked the tip into his mouth. Pressing her breasts upward, her eyes fluttered shut and she purred, "As long as that variety is with me, I think I might be willing."

Nearing his lips to her ear, Tony whispered, "Only you—it's only been you for a very long time."

Before going to sleep, they decided to go for a late night swim. Although they wore robes to the pool, they didn't bother with bathing suits. With the water near the same temperature as the humid air, the only difference was the degree of moisture as they became submerged. Tony disappeared under the water and swam the length of the infinity pool and back. Claire giggled as he came out of the water right in front of her. Taking her hands, he led her out to the deeper end. Holding his shoulders, she wrapped her legs around his torso and gazed up at the stars.

Tony kissed her neck. "What are you thinking about?"

Claire shrugged. "A lot of things—our baby, our friends, and my family."

"It's all right to miss them."

"I've been away from them before, but this time, it's different. This time, I feel like I've betrayed them. I'm the one who left without telling anyone."

"What do you think would happen if they knew the truth?"

Claire contemplated. "They might be in danger? At this point, I wouldn't put anything past Catherine."

Tony nodded. "By keeping them ignorant, we're protecting them."

Laying her head against his shoulder, Claire ran her hand over his arm.

Tony reached for her left hand and looked at the diamond on her finger. "You know that this ring gave me hope and broke my heart at the same time?"

Claire raised her eyebrows.

"When the police found your belongings in that motel in Illinois and this ring wasn't with them, I wanted to believe you were all right, that you were making your own decisions, and you weren't in the hands of some crazy stalker, but then I realized, if that were true, then it meant you'd left me. It meant you didn't want to be with me and you'd never return."

She freed her hand and wrapped her arms tighter around his neck. "I'm so sorry. I was scared and misled." She kissed his cheek while her fingers ran through his hair. "I should've spoken with you." She buried her face in the crook of his neck. "I couldn't leave the ring. I'd promised to keep it. I just couldn't leave it." Tears teetered on her lids.

He gently pushed her away and gazed into her eyes. "Claire, what's the matter?"

She smiled behind the tears. "I think it's the hormones—sometimes I just cry."

Tony smiled and hugged her tightly. "Just today, someone mentioned something about that."

"Today? Who?"

"It was Francis. I know I've only been here a few days, but I think he and Madeline are great people. This island wouldn't be the same without them."

Claire nodded into his shoulder as she tried to suppress a yawn. "I agree."

Carrying Claire, Tony walked slowly toward the steps. "I think you need to get some sleep."

When they reached the steps, Claire let go of his neck. "I'm getting too fat for you to carry me out of the water."

"No, Ms. Nichols—you're not fat; however, I agree. I'd never forgive myself if my wet feet slipped and I hurt you or our son."

Claire looked back to Tony. "Son?"

He shrugged. "Or daughter—I really don't care."

Taking his hand, Claire said, "While we were apart, I prayed for a boy. I wanted him to be just like you."

"Like me?"—he shook his head—"I know you're smarter than that."

As they reentered their suite, Claire said, "Well, the Nichols had only girls—at least, the last generation, and it seems the Rawls had only boys...so soon, we'll learn which family dominates."

Tony kissed her neck. "Sweetheart, the man determines the sex."

Her eyes twinkled. "Not tonight—he didn't."

"If you're up for round two, I'm pretty sure we could even the score."

"I think I'm going to wash the chlorine out of my hair. If it's not too dominating of a suggestion, as you already know the shower is quite large, you may join me?"

Tony smirked. "Are you suggesting water conservation? I mean, I'm all for conserving resources."

Later that night with the score one to one, Claire fell sound to sleep, listening to the soothing rhythm of Tony's heartbeat. Fleetingly, she thought about Tony's revelation. It was only the beginning, and they both knew there was much more to discuss. Their conversations in the past and in the future always had one rule—honesty. Tony had followed that rule—and in essence, so had Claire. If she'd pretended his statement didn't bother her, then she wouldn't have been honest. Her last thought as she drifted away was of Tony's warning. Claire decided he was right—the truth could be better handled in small manageable pieces. It was like her old way of dealing—compartmentalization. The difference was—instead of hiding the secrets in the compartments—this time, they were bringing them out.

When Claire woke in the morning, her world was still dark. As her eyelids fluttered and her lashes grazed the satin, she realized the darkness was her sleeping mask. Claire removed it from her eyes and reached toward Tony's empty place in bed. It was already after 9:00 AM, and he was gone, probably off somewhere exploring the island or with Francis. Thankful for the extra sleep the mask brought, Claire thought pensively about the night before, and warm memories filled her thoughts. When she thought about falling asleep, she realized that she hadn't been wearing the sleep mask. Shaking her head ever so slightly, a smile came to her lips. *That's another point for Tony!* Perhaps soon she could even that score.

∞∞∞∞∞∞∞

"I understand, sir," Agent Baldwin said into his phone.

"Yes, Deputy Director, I'll be back in San Francisco tomorrow evening."

"Thank you, goodbye."

Harry hit the *DISCONNECT* button and collapsed into the hotel chair. The conversation wasn't as bad as he'd imagined. Although *he'd* lost track of both Claire and Rawlings, through the use of digital face recognition, they'd been identified at different times at airports in Papau, New Guinea. Claire was identified at the Baimuru Airport, whereas Rawlings was identified at the Daru Airport.

It's believed they are staying somewhere in the South Pacific—recognizably, this was a broad generalization. The area in question contained thousands of islands of varying sizes. Many of the island nations in this region rely heavily on tourism and have been known to be very welcoming and accommodating to wealthy residents. As a rule—questions were rarely asked.

Since they were no longer in Europe, Agent Baldwin was ordered to return to the field office in San Francisco. Although he didn't mention it on the phone call, Harry vowed to share his research with SAC Williams or anyone who'd listen. He needed FBI resources to request blood samples from Simon Johnson and Jordon Nichols. Harry wasn't even sure whether the samples would be available. If nothing else, he wanted to access the toxicology reports that were available.

If he couldn't locate Claire and Rawlings, then his research would be his number one priority. Writing a note, Harry pondered, *does the presence of actaea pachypodac create any unusual markers visible during toxicology screenings?* Since most agencies don't routinely test for it, maybe there was something else that could identify its presence. The fact it affected the heart—creating heart attack-like symptoms was too broad.

Harry had a few hours before he needed to get to the airport. While he waited, he reviewed medical histories. First, he looked at the known victims:

Nathaniel Rawls—died in 1989, at the age sixty-four. Interestingly, he died with only two months remaining on his reduced sentence. He had a history of high blood pressure, depression, vitamin deficiency, recreational alcohol usage, and nicotine dependence. He was being medicated for the high blood pressure and depression. According to the records, when he died, he still smoked a half of a pack a day. It was fair to assume his death was heart related until actaea pachypodac was positively identified in his blood.

Agent Sherman Nichols—died in 1997, at the age of seventy-three. He also had a history of high blood pressure. In 1995 he had a heart catherization resulting in the placement of two coronary stents. He was medicated for high blood pressure and high cholesterol—past history nicotine dependence. Again, it would be fair to assume cause of death to include heart disease—again actaea pachypodac was positively identified in his blood.

Anthony Rawlings / Anton Rawls—survived poisoning, January 2012, at the age of forty-six. Wife, Claire Nichols Rawlings, pled no contest to charge of attempted murder. Governor Bosley extended a pardon which absolved Claire (Rawlings) Nichols of guilt. The state of Iowa hasn't revisited the case due to Mr. Rawlings' insistence. Also at the time of his poisoning, Mr. Rawlings had a clear medical history. His only medication was vitamins, recreational use of alcohol, and no history of smoking—family history would be the only connection to heart-related problems leading to his possible death. Upon arrival at the hospital actaea pachypodac was positively identified in his blood.

Harry also reviewed his list of other possible victims:

Samuel and Amanda Rawls—COD gunshot wounds. The ballistics reports contradicted the released hypothesis of murder/suicide. The gunshot wounds were quite obviously not self-inflicted on either victim. They died in 1989 at the age of forty-five and forty-four. As much as Harry wanted to pin this on Rawlings—since they had his statement and the

police reports verified his presence at the home the night of the murder—
he couldn't forget his discussion with Patrick Chester. It was clear that,
during that discussion, Chester was being paid by someone to keep quiet
about a woman—a woman in a blue Honda.

Jordon and Shirley Nichols—COD head trauma related to
automobile crash. They died in 2004 at the age of fifty and forty-nine.
Indiana State Police reports indicated the Nichols' car was structurally
sound. The crash was ruled *accidental*.

Simon Johnson—COD combustion, related to the crash and fire of a
Cessna aircraft. He died in 2011 at the age of twenty-eight. NTSB reports
indicated plane was structurally sound. To Harry—that confirmed that
poison was indeed the cause of death, but he needed proof.

Although he couldn't be sure about Tony's parents, Harry's gut told
him the other deaths could all be traced to Rawlings. As he was about to
leave for the airport, Harry scribbled another note, *Check New Jersey,
1989, car registrations for blue Hondas*. He stuffed the note into his
laptop bag and headed to the airport.

The greatest happiness of life is the conviction that we are loved;
loved for ourselves, or rather, loved in spite of ourselves.
—Victor Hugo

CHAPTER 23

Claire loved lunch time. Despite Tony's request for her to *better understand the whole employer/employee relationship*, she refused to give up eating with Madeline and Francis. Breakfast was a free for all—Madeline and Francis had things they wanted to accomplish early in the day. The intense sun and heat made early morning and late evening the best times of the day to do labor. Tony had always been a person to wake early. The fact he no longer had work to attend, or thousands of jobs under his reign of responsibility, didn't change his internal clock. Claire, on the other hand, enjoyed her sleep. While everyone else on the island could be up and going at the break of dawn, 8:00 AM or 9:00 AM was a much more acceptable waking hour for her. It was true that years ago, on Tony's estate, she constantly woke about 8:00 AM. In her opinion, the difference was the seventeen extra pounds resting on her bladder. These days, she woke every two to three hours. Sleeping until 9:00 AM gave her the same total sum of sleep. It made perfect sense, and besides, no one complained.

The midday meal was a great time for everyone to connect. Claire knew it was a whole new world for Tony. In private, while he voiced his approval of Madeline and Francis, he still maintained his concerns regarding Claire's ability to preserve the appropriate employer status. Claire didn't care. She explained how instrumental Madeline and Francis had been to her initial adjustment, and they all knew—it was her decision. As long as she wanted it—they would all continue to eat their midday meal together.

The day after Tony's revelation, as their lunch was about to conclude, Claire asked Francis a question, "I remember you telling me you're ordained. Does that mean you can legally marry two people?"

Claire ignored Tony's wide-eyed micro expression as Francis answered, "Oui, Madame el, here in this island nation I am, as you say—licensed."

She clarified, "What does that mean in the United States? Would we still be married?"

"Oui, after you file for your license."

Tony couldn't remain silent any longer. "Claire, my offer still stands, but you had things you wanted to discuss, so perhaps we should..."

Claire reached into the pocket of the lace cover up. Her fingers found an offering that only he would recognize. She gathered it into her fist, and extended her closed fist to Tony. "I have something for you."

His eyebrows knit together in question as he trepidatiously opened his hand. Although there were very few secrets on a private island, as Claire released the offering with one hand, she closed his fingers around it with her other. In a low voice and with a smile that radiated to her emerald green eyes, she whispered, "I trust you."

Tony nonchalantly glanced into his hand. Claire wasn't the only one to see the spark in his dark chocolate eyes.

"Monsieur, this is your wish?" Madeline's question pulled Tony's gaze away from Claire's.

"Oui, Madeline—it is my wish. I wanted to be sure it was Claire's."

Straightening her neck, Claire said, "Well, just so we're all clear—I'm not the one who filed for divorce." Tony momentarily bowed his head. *What could he say?* Before he returned his gaze to Claire, she worried that she'd said something she shouldn't.

Her concern melted with his upturned lips and evaporated into nothingness with his words. "I admit it wasn't the first mistake I've ever made; however, it is the one I regret the most."

"Tonight?" Madeline asked as her volume increased. "May we have the wedding tonight?"

Claire giggled. "Tonight is very fast. I don't have a dress—"

Madeline interjected, "Madame el, a wedding isn't about a dress. A wedding is about the unification of two souls"—she paused—"In your case—the reunification."

Tony corrected, "Reconciliation."

Claire reached for his hand. "I believe that began a while ago—at a gala—in a faraway land."

"I believe it happened before that," Tony said. "Perhaps in a dream?"

Claire couldn't help but smile. She knew from experience it radiated to her green eyes.

It was Francis who brought the two of them back from their personal memories. "I'll go into town right away. Your marriage will be legal here, once you sign. As for legalizing it in the U.S., I'll help you."

It was enough for Claire. She scooted her chair by Tony's and laid her head against his shoulder. Soon after, they were alone as Madeline and Francis had much to accomplish to fulfill Claire's request. It was then that Tony handed Claire back her sleeping mask and asked, "What happened? Why are you suddenly in a rush?"

"Are you complaining?"

He placed his hand on her leg. "No—concerned."

Claire lifted her eyebrows. Tony sighed and took her hand. "Come with me."

She didn't question; instead, she willingly followed Tony out to a lounge chair in a shady, yet breezy part of the lanai. "First," he said, "you need to put your feet up. Second, we need to talk."

Claire obediently sat, laying her legs out in front of her. When Tony perched himself on the edge of her chair, Claire reached forward, framed his face with her petite hands, and brought his lips to hers. So many things can be said through a kiss. Some people kiss *hello* or *goodbye*. A kiss can be happy, sad, passionate, or regretful. The emotion Claire tried to convey was *forgiveness*. When their lips parted and their eyes met, Claire replied, "I love you. There are probably millions of reasons why I shouldn't—but I do. I've been without you"—she blushed—"since my dream, and I don't like it. I've felt every possible emotion while with you. You asked me to be Mrs. Rawlings—again—you said our child isn't a Nichols or a Rawls—but a Rawlings"—she straightened her neck and squared her shoulders—"I want that."

"I want that too." Taking her hands in his, Tony continued, "However, you need to know what you're signing."

"What I'm *signing*?"

He smirked. "Do you think Madeline has any paper napkins?"

"I doubt it—is cloth more legally binding?"

He quickly kissed her lips. "There it is again."

"Oh, you love it!"

"I do. I love your smart mouth, and more importantly, I love you. Just think about how upset you were last night. My dear, our discussion is an iceberg. That was only the tip."

"Don't you understand why I handed you my sleep mask?"

The corners of his mouth twitched. "Because you wanted to have kinky-sex."

Claire shook her head, trying to hide her blushed cheeks. "No, last night you asked me if I trusted you. Again, there are probably millions of reasons to say no—"

Tony sat straighter as his tone deepened. "I believe there are reasons, but my dear, I'd appreciate it if you discontinue the use of the modifier—one million. You have misjudged the size of the iceberg."

"Actually, I don't recall using the modifier—one."

His finger traced her lips as they formed a smug smile. "So many better uses of that beautiful mouth than to continually spurt out smart comments."

"Tony, last night I felt like too much was riding on our conversation." When he started to speak, she touched his lips so that he wouldn't interrupt. "What you tell me—and I do need to know—won't change the fact I want my family together. I want to be your wife again"—Claire felt the tears begin to build—"I want it more than I wanted it in December of 2010."

Tony gently wiped a tear from her cheek. "In 2010, I didn't realize what a truly amazing wife I was getting. I never appreciated her for who she truly was." He lifted Claire's left hand and touched his lips to it. "This time—I know that I'm the luckiest man in the world. That's why I want you to enter this marriage with your eyes open."

"Tony, will you do anything for me?"

"Anything within my power."

"Today, for lunch, I had water to drink, but I really wanted iced tea. Can you get me iced tea for today's lunch?"

He looked at her quizzically. "For today's lunch? No, but I can get you some tea now, if you'd like."

"Why can't you get it for me for today's lunch?"

"Claire, you aren't making any sense, lunch is over..." A smile of recognition came to his face. Claire saw it in the depth of his deep brown eyes.

"Yes—yes it is," she said. "All you can do is try to fulfill my desires for the future. We can't change the past, and even if we could, I'm not sure it should be changed—it brought us here now. I'm confident that I won't like all the answers I get from you. That doesn't change that I want them and deserve them, but to say that our entire future is riding on them—was too much pressure. That's why I was so upset last night. It freaked me out so much that you'd been watching me for so long that I missed the part about you saying that I've had possession of your heart since before I knew you."

"You have, and as a man of my word, when you're ready to know the answers to your questions—I'll be honest with you. Most importantly, you and our child will always be my number one concern. You've changed me in ways I didn't know I could be changed. Your happiness and well-being are my top priorities. If you're sure of what you're getting yourself into, I will spend the rest of my life atoning for my sins against you and against others. I want my name to be something you're proud to carry."

Claire couldn't control the tears any more than she could change the past. From the man with the dark eyes, in the suite, on his estate, to the man with his head resting on their child was undoubtedly a change. *Was she responsible, or was it life?* After all, she wasn't the same woman who stood in the blue dress and blue heels trembling in fear. *Was that Tony's doing, or was it life?* The man with the eyes devoid of color and emotion wouldn't have wanted the woman Claire was today, and the woman in the blue dress wouldn't have wanted anything to do with the man caressing his unborn child. So, to say they changed each other may be incorrect, yet to say they had changed—was an understatement.

Standing in the glow of the setting sun with her toes in the sand, Claire gazed lovingly into the deepest, darkest eyes. The dark no longer proclaimed anger. The darkness from years ago was different—void, or more accurately—devoid—without. At that time, his eyes were windows to a tormented core whose only outlet was rage and cruelty, but the dark brown that returned her gaze today wasn't empty. It reeled with emotions that the void eyes wouldn't have understood. The new darkness swirled with an all-consuming passion that could ignite Claire in impossible ways with a single glance. They churned with love and adoration, pride and understanding, sorrow and regret. These eyes drank her in, claimed her, and fulfilled her every desire. They were the windows to a man—who once upon a time, signed a napkin that he knew was a contract. As an esteemed businessman, he forgot one very important rule—he forgot to read the fine print. It wasn't an acquisition to own another person as he'd previously assumed. It was an agreement to acquire a soul.

The acquisition was long and painful. There were contract disputes and labor issues, but in the end, the soul found residence—within the businessman. No longer were the rules clear or was the world black and white. Now, color prevailed—especially shades of green.

Francis' rich, deep voice echoed into the breeze. Claire remembered the day in 2010 when she was asked the same question: *do you take this man to be your lawfully wedded husband, to have and to hold, for richer, for poorer, in sickness and in health, to love and to cherish until death do you part?* Her answer hadn't changed. Despite the traumas and her desire to forfeit that promise made three years ago, Claire suspected that in her heart, she never did. This ceremony was a reaffirmation of that prior commitment and a promise of a better relationship. With her long white sundress blowing around her legs—perhaps she was subconsciously planning this when she ordered her clothes—Claire inhaled without effort. The salty breeze penetrated deep into her lungs as the sensation of suffocation was gone.

While Francis prayed, Claire did too. It was a prayer of praise and gratitude. She admitted to disliking parts of the journey, but the destination was true paradise. As Francis announced their union, Claire and Tony kissed. When he backed away, she saw his devilish grin and heard him whisper, "Mrs. Rawlings, you are mine once again."

Her retort teetered on the tip of her tongue. Finally, she swallowed the words and smiled at her handsome husband, deciding that a smart mouthed response wasn't appropriate in the middle of her wedding. It didn't matter. The gleam in Tony's eyes told her he knew—he knew what she wanted to say and loved her as much for her restraint as for her cheekiness.

Madeline somehow had found time to bake a cake. Since Claire couldn't drink alcohol, it wasn't even discussed. The four of them celebrated their wedding, with cake and lemonade. Claire wondered if October 27th was now their anniversary, and whether it meant that December 18th no longer was. Perhaps they could find reason to celebrate both dates. After the *reception*, Francis and Madeline excused themselves to leave the newlyweds alone.

Within their suite, they found chilled fruit and sparkling grape juice. That, however, wasn't the discovery that made Claire giggle and Tony's devilish grin emerge. It was when he pulled the black satin mask from the pocket of his linen shorts and lifted a brow. That was when she couldn't hold back her snicker. He'd kept it with him throughout the entire ceremony.

"I thought you wanted me to go into this marriage with my eyes wide open?"

Each one of his graceful steps lessened the distance between them and pulled an invisible cord, tightening Claire's insides. Her sensitive nipples ached as their chests touched and he pulled her close. Slowly widening his grin, Tony answered, "That, Mrs. Rawlings, was meant metaphorically."

Looking up to his handsome face, Claire opened her eyes wide and replied, "Oh, see, I thought you meant it literally."

Bending down, he neared his lips to hers, and when she closed her eyes, she felt the sweet connection of their kiss. Before she could inhale, Tony's teeth caught her lower lip, and Claire gasped.

He gently tugged and released. His lips moved to the nape of her neck and up to her ear. After he gently nipped at her lobe, his raspy voice sent shivers down her spine. "I knew it couldn't stay hidden for too long."

She opened her eyes wide, displaying her most innocent expression. It was too late—Tony's seductive tone resonated through the suite. "No, my dear, no look of innocence, no deer in the headlights, you know exactly what I'm saying." Once again tracing her lips with his finger, he added, "I believe it's time we find something better for that smart mouth to do."

Nothing can prevent you from learning the truth
so much as the belief that you already know it.

—Jon K. Hart

CHAPTER 24

Sophia walked through their Santa Clara condominium one last time and took inventory of the moving boxes. Calling over her shoulder, she asked for the umpteenth time, "You're sure Rawlings Industries will get all of this to Iowa for us?"

Derek came from the bedroom, magic marker in hand. "They said they would. We only need to have everything packed and labeled. They'll even put the boxes in the appropriate rooms in our new house."

Sophia contemplated his words: *House—it sounded wonderful!* Iowa didn't. There wasn't an ocean near Iowa City—no beaches—well, unless you included the rivers. Sophia had never imagined herself living in the middle of the country, surrounded by corn. Her husband's embrace refocused Sophia's thoughts. He whispered in her ear, "Tonight, they're putting us up in an amazing hotel in San Francisco. Tomorrow, we're flying by private jet to Rawlings Industries Corporate Headquarters. Timothy Bronson, the acting CEO, wants to meet both of us." He nibbled her ear. "Baby, you can paint from anywhere; you've told me that before. This is a big break—Corporate Headquarters!"

"I'm happy for you, I am. I just don't understand how this happened so fast. You said *Anthony Rawlings* wanted you there? Honey, that's great, but he's been missing since September. What happened?"

Exhaling, Derek peered deep into his wife's beautiful gray eyes. "I've told you all I know, all that HR told me. When they scanned Mr. Rawlings' home computer, they found a file about me. He even had a job proposal started. Timothy Bronson was made aware of the file, so he took it to the board of directors. They felt it was something Mr. Rawlings wanted, and together they reviewed my dossier and called. Mr. Bronson believes I can help in the effort to pull Rawlings Industries from its downward spiral."

Sophia's mind whirled. "Who scanned his home computers? Why would they do that?"

"Baby, I don't know. This is a huge promotion; not just the money, or the title, but the responsibility. I'm going from a junior peon in a small subsidiary to a junior peon at corporate!"

Sophia sighed. "Honey, I'm proud of you. I'm just not used to living so far inland. I've always lived near a coast, and the whole thing seems strange. I mean, after Mr. Rawlings was at my studio...I'm sorry—I just have a strange feeling."

His arms tightened around her small waist, allowing his hands to linger on her firm, round behind. "Mrs. Burke, we'll be busy! I learned one of the corporate lawyers—Miller, I think his name is—his wife has a design firm in Bettendorf, and"—his volume increased—"Timothy Bronson, who I keep mentioning. His wife used to work at an art museum in Davenport. They're a little younger than us. Sue's pregnant with their second child, but I'd bet you two would get along very well!"

Sophia closed her eyes and dropped her head to Derek's shoulder.

He grasped her shoulders and pushed her back, trying to see her face. "Baby, what's the matter? You weren't happy about California at first, but now look at you."

Sophia nodded. "You're right. I wasn't. I guess, since my parents died, this has been home." She feigned a smile. "No—home is with you. You're right; I can paint from anywhere, but please do me a favor?"

"Anything."

Sophia squared her shoulders. "Let me develop my own relationships. I'll paint and I'll move, but don't pair me off like a preschooler looking for friends."

Derek embraced her once again. "I'm sorry. That's not what I'm trying to do. I know how hard the move to Santa Clara was for you, so I was trying to make it better."

She kissed his lips. "Don't—it'll be alright as long as I have you." Quickly, Sophia added, "I know you'll be busy and that there will be late nights. I'm more than willing to do the wife thing at events." Under her breath, she added, "I'm not sure what kind of events occur in Iowa." Once again louder, "Nevertheless, I will—because I love you, but you have to let me adjust at my own speed."

"Mrs. Burke, you're amazing. You do whatever it is you need to do. Just know that I love you, and when you're on my arm at the *Iowa City Corn Husker's Convention*, I'll be the proudest husband in the room!"

Sophia smirked. "Oh, jeeze! Please tell me you just made that up."

His lips brushed hers. "I did. Now, if everything is packed then I believe I have reservations in San Francisco with the most amazing woman!"

She kissed his cheek. "You do? Well, don't let me interrupt your plans."

Derek's lips lingered near her ear, purposely exhaling on her exposed neck, creating goose bumps up and down her arms. "I may have even called ahead and asked for a few things to be delivered to our room. You can come too; maybe you'd like to watch?"

Sophia giggled. "I think you know me better than that. Watching has never been my thing." Grasping his hand, she offered, "I'm much more of a participant!"

Derek smiled. "Then let's go participate."

∞∞∞∞∞∞

As Harry's plane taxied toward the small airport outside of San Francisco, he removed his phone from airplane mode. His thoughts volleyed between his research and Deputy Director Stevenson. Although the Deputy Director didn't sound upset on the phone and even offered information about Claire and Rawlings' possible destination, Harry worried about his future. He wasn't ready to lose his badge. *He'd worked too damn hard for it!*

His phone began to vibrate as messages appeared on the screen. The small plane still hadn't reached its destination on the tarmac when Harry looked down to see calls from unidentified numbers. For a split second, he thought about the new practice of solicitation on cellular phones—*it was a travesty. He didn't have time for that!* Then he saw that he had messages. Tapping his voicemail icon, Harry accessed his messages.

"You have three unheard messages..." Harry entered his numerical code and waited. Just as the plane came to a stop, he heard Claire's voice. "Hello, Harry, or Agent Baldwin, I wish I knew your real name." The sound of her voice took his breath away. The pilot was looking at him. Harry hit 7 and saved Claire's message.

He couldn't get out of the plane fast enough. As he walked toward the waiting car, he replayed Claire's message. It seemed to take forever to get through the preliminary crap. All at once the FBI terminal—the people—the waiting car—everything disappeared. Harry was hearing Claire's voice. At the very least, hearing her voice confirmed that she was safe. He covered his other ear and listened. "Hello, Harry, or Agent Baldwin, I wish I knew your real name. I'm sorry I didn't reach you. I won't leave a number, but I wanted you to know—I'm fine and I'm safe. I would appreciate the assistance of the FBI, and I don't have a lot of time. Harry...the woman in the blue Honda wasn't Samuel Rawls' sister—it was Catherine. The woman I've trusted. The woman at Tony's estate I told you about. She's who I'm hiding from. She killed Amanda and Samuel Rawls and maybe even others. She isn't just after me, but she wants Tony and our child. Please have the FBI stop her." Silence filled his ears. Momentarily, Harry wondered if Claire had hung up, but then her voice came back. "Please, Harry. I want my child to have a normal life. Where I am...it's great...but it's not where a child should live. Please help us and make a case against her—Catherine Marie Rawls London. Harry, she was married to Nathaniel. I need to go—bye."

Harry stood motionless with the phone to his ear. The voice was asking if he wanted to save or erase. What a dumb question *he wanted to save!* Save the message—save Claire—save her child—and save—Rawli—Harry wasn't ready to go that far; nevertheless, he had heard the desperation in Claire's voice. *How could he have been researching this for over a year and not realize Nathaniel had a second wife?*

"Agent Baldwin?"

Harry's blue eyes focused on the world around him. He saw the man in the dark suit and heard him say his name. "Yes, I'm Agent Baldwin."

"Please follow me, sir."

Harry didn't question as he followed the driver and sat in the back seat of a large black SUV. While they pulled away from the curb, Harry considered his other missed calls and hit the *VOICEMAIL* icon, once again.

Message two—"Baldwin—Anthony Rawlings. I intend to fully cooperate with the FBI. I know that picture was bullshit, but I'm calling. I don't intend to make my whereabouts known until my child is born, or after. I will—I can't now. If...if Claire ever meant more to you than a damn assignment then just let us have this. We'll call back."

When the line disconnected, Harry let out the breath he'd been holding. *How the hell did Anthony Rawlings believe he—Harrison Baldwin—had that kind of power? Yeah, right? Like Harry could suddenly say, "Hey, let's leave Anthony Rawlings and Claire Nichols alone before their big day—for the birth of their child."*

As the large SUV neared the San Francisco field office, Harry pulled up his third voice message—"Agent Baldwin, our car will be late; please be advised."

We must accept finite disappointment,
but never lose infinite hope.
—Martin Luther King, Jr.

CHAPTER 25

-AUGUST 2016-

Wheeling Claire's dinner down the long, quiet corridor, Meredith contemplated Ms. Bali's concerns and directives—Ms. Nichols underwent tests earlier in the day. Due to an unforeseen glitch, additional sedation was required. As Ms. Bali uttered the word *glitch*, the hairs on the back of Meredith's neck prickled. The supervisor once said that she'd read Meredith's book. *Could she possibly understand the significance of that word?* Fighting to remain stoic, Meredith continued listening. Ms. Bali explained that the tests were scheduled for the entire morning and the additional sedation resulted in prolonged hours of unresponsiveness. Ms. Nichols hadn't eaten all day. Actually, she'd just recently awakened. Her sister had been here most of the afternoon and had only recently left, waiting until Claire was fully awake. The staff, who assisted with daily showers and hygiene, should be just about done. Mrs. Vandersol wasn't happy with the day's mishaps, including an entire day without nutrition. Ms. Bali couldn't emphasize enough—*Claire must eat!* She also praised Meredith's past interactions and offered her confidence in Meredith's ability to accomplish their goal.

With each step toward Claire's room, Meredith questioned that ability. She assumed that, with Claire's new uncooperative state and today's excessive use of sedation, tonight's dinner could go less than smooth. Taking a deep breath, Meredith knocked respectfully and slowly opened Claire's door. It wasn't as though she expected a greeting.

Claire was alone. The people who helped her bathe and dress were gone; however, she wasn't sitting in her normal seat by the window. She was pacing near her bed. Despite Meredith's knock and greeting, Claire didn't turn or acknowledge her entrance.

Something about Claire looked different—determined—purposeful. Meredith saw the straightness of her posture and clenching of her jaw. Each time she changed direction on her invisible track—back and forth—Meredith saw an intensity in her eyes. Meredith hadn't seen that look for a long time; however, she *had* seen it before. It was the expression Claire wore during the hours recalling difficult times in her and Anthony's relationship. Even then, when she'd repeat a particularly bad time, Meredith remembered Claire's expression—it was as if she were seeing the scene before her, which wasn't visible to anyone else. That was the exact expression Meredith saw now. Years ago, Meredith assumed it to be Claire's internal debate. She'd agreed to share her story, knew it was accurate, but she felt conflicted, especially later in their interview process as her and Mr. Rawlings' relationship began its reconciliation.

During those interviews, Meredith waited patiently and allowed Claire the necessary time to sort her thoughts. When she did, Claire would recall the scenarios with eloquence. On some occasions Meredith had to remind herself to type rather than simply listening. Later, when she'd review Claire's dictation, rarely was there need to change or modify—everything was obviously well deliberated. Watching her now, Meredith wondered what she was thinking.

Meredith placed Claire's food on her table and called to her, "Claire, it's me, Meredith. I brought your dinner." Not surprising, neither Claire's stance nor pace wavered. If anything, her internal debate intensified—Claire's step quickened.

Walking slowly toward her friend, Meredith spoke again, "Claire, can you hear me?—You haven't eaten all day—Aren't you hungry?" The pacing continued.

As Meredith reached for Claire's arm, Claire pulled away and momentarily glared. Instinctively, Meredith stepped back to apologize; however, as she did, she realized—*Claire had just acknowledged her presence. It wasn't verbal, but she deliberately pulled away and looked right at her!*

Meredith wasn't sure where the words came from—she didn't want to hurt her friend; nonetheless, after eight to nine weeks of interaction—or no interaction—Meredith chose to break another rule. "You're thinking about him, aren't you?"—no response—"I've seen you like this before. I know you're thinking about Ant"—She started to say *Anthony*, but remembered Claire referred to him as *Tony*. During the book interviews, she recalled how that familiar title was a gift, a positive consequence he bestowed upon her while she was still his captive—"I mean, Tony. Claire, it's all right. You can think about him. Why shouldn't you think about Tony?"

Each time Meredith uttered his name, Claire's pace slowed. By the fourth or fifth time, her neck, shoulders, and jaw relaxed. Finally, Meredith tried one more plea, "Claire, Tony would want you to eat. He loved you very much. You don't want"—she stuttered, wondering if she should say what she was thinking. Swallowing her hesitation, Meredith continued—"You don't want to *disappoint* him, do you?"

Claire didn't speak; however, stepping around Meredith, she walked to the table with the food and sat. When she didn't feed herself, Meredith went to the table, sat opposite her, and lifted the lid on Claire's plate. "Well, it looks like you have salmon. That's one of your favorites, isn't it?" Her eyes didn't register, and the earlier intensity was gone, but each time Meredith lifted the fork, Claire obediently opened her mouth and ate. The exercise continued slowly— food—food—and then drink. By the time Claire finished, her plate was mostly empty. She didn't stand and move to the window as she usually did. Instead, her head dropped, and she looked down with her hands demurely resting on her lap, compliant and obedient.

Meredith praised Claire for her cooperation; nevertheless, it wasn't until she whispered, "I know Tony would be proud of you. Thank you for helping me," that Claire raised her chin and looked toward the still light sky.

August 10, 2016

...Claire didn't speak, but she acknowledged...she cooperated! I want to tell someone what happened today, but if I do, they'll probably fire me. I mean—I'm not supposed to mention Anthony's name or have as much knowledge about Claire as I do.

I can't believe how she responded! She ate! Ms. Bali said she hadn't eaten all day. That wasn't all. When she looked out at the sky, I asked her if she wanted to go outside. For the last two weeks, she hasn't wanted to do anything—but sit in that damn chair. When I asked if she wanted to go outside—she walked toward the door! I don't think that's ever happened. Usually, she'll stand, but wait for someone to lead her to the door. I barely had time to call and request permission to take her out.

I know what did it—it was the mention of Tony's name. Emily will never listen to me, but she's wrong to keep the truth from Claire. How can Claire deal with everything if she isn't allowed to face it? I wonder how much she remembers. I mean, I don't know what happened for sure—just the information I read and saw on the news. There was the information released from the trial, but despite it being such a high profile case, the courtroom was closed to the public, and very little information was made available. I've tapped every resource I know. Everything is sealed. I guess it goes with the money—that can keep everything quiet.

That's why I started this—to learn what happened, but now I wish I knew so that I could help her face it. Emily probably knows. I'm sure she does. She and her husband were at the courthouse every day of testimony. I remember seeing images of them coming and going from the courtroom on the news. Who else was there? What about Claire's friend—Courtney? I don't know if she'll talk to me. If I contact her and she calls Emily, then I'm screwed.

I guess this needs more thought. Maybe I should just wait and see if this behavior continues or if it ends as fast as it began. I'm not scheduled again for two days. I sure hope the progress we made today isn't lost in that amount of time.

Oh! Did I mention when we went outside, Claire lifted her face up to the sun and closed her eyes? I think we need to find her sunglasses. She's never needed them before. She never raised her face or opened her eyes enough. I know I have an extra pair somewhere—I need to remember to take them in Friday! I don't think I've ever been so excited to get back to Everwood!

∞∞∞∞∞∞

For an accomplished attorney, who at one time specialized in courtroom tactics, John Vandersol's voice revealed more emotion than he intended. "Dr. Brown, I'm directing this inquiry to you, because after three hours of trying, I've been unable to reach Dr. Fairfield!" "I understand you're no longer in charge of Claire's care, but my wife and I want answers." "So, are you saying you weren't briefed on yesterday's mishaps?" "I see." "Yes, I'm well aware of confidentiality regulations. I'm also confident you're well aware that Emily and I are Claire's documented next of kin and as such are named under her HIPPA clause to be privy to any pertinent information." "Yes, Emily was with Claire until she woke yesterday, which I'll add wasn't until after 3:00 PM." "I understand." "I hope I'm being perfectly clear, if I don't hear from Dr. Fairfield by noon, then my wife and I will be at Everwood by 1:00 PM. When we arrive, make no mistake, we *will* put an end to this new protocol. It seems that…"

Emily sat wide-eyed, listening to John's side of the conversation while nursing her third cup of coffee. Though she tried to decipher what Dr. Brown was saying on the other end, she wouldn't know for sure until John hung up the phone. It had been a long night. Neither of them had slept much. When Emily got home, the nanny, Becca, was still there. Usually, her day was done after dinner. Luckily, they had a few trusted people they could call at the last minute if there were evening emergencies. Having help was especially nice on occasions like yesterday, when calls came demanding Emily's immediate attention at Everwood. Last night, instead of taking the risk of the children overhearing their conversation, she and John left the house so that she could fill him in on the problems at Everwood. With each word, each description, John's anger grew. Ever since the new protocol began, Claire's response has been negative instead of positive, add to that the recent sedation incident, and Emily was ready to call it quits.

Yesterday, the nurse tried to explain—*too much* sedation would reduce the necessary brain activity keeping Claire from her visions—hallucinations—whatever they wanted to call them; nevertheless, it was obvious, *too little* resulted in a traumatic episode for Claire—and for Emily. It was almost 4:00 PM before she left Everwood, and Claire still hadn't eaten. Emily refocused on John's words.

His tone was more inquisitive. "...do you have any more specifics?" "Has this aide worked with Claire in the past?"

Emily tapped his arm and raised her eyebrows in question. When he didn't respond, Emily whispered, "Does she know if Claire ate anything yesterday?"

John nodded as he continued, "All right, thank you, Dr. Brown, but we still need to hear from Dr. Fairfield. I have questions about yesterday's DTI—questions which apparently only he can answer." "I will, thank you." "Goodbye."

Emily sat her coffee cup down, as sleep deprivation overtook her tone. "Why didn't you ask her about eating?"

For the first time since he came home last night, John smiled. "I didn't ask, because she volunteered. Claire not only ate last night—compliantly—she went outside. According to the aide who works with her"—John's eyes widened—"Claire *wanted* to go outside."

"Really"—sarcasm prevailed—"and how did this aide know that? Did she say that Claire spoke?"

Shrugging his shoulders, John replied, "I didn't ask. I'm just happy she ate and moved from that chair where she always sits. Maybe you should be too?"

Emily stood to leave John's home office. "You know that if I believed them—I would be, but come on—she was incoherent all day—couldn't sit—much less stand—for hours after the last dose of sedative. Now they want me to believe she ate and *wanted* to go outside. Fine—I'll play their game; however, if she's not greeting me with a *Hi, Em* today, I'll know they're lying to pacify us."

As she reached the doorway, Emily turned around. "Are you going into Rawlings today?"

"No, I'm waiting for Dr. Fairfield's call. If it doesn't come, then you and I are going to Everwood. Be sure Becca isn't planning on going home anytime soon."

"Thanks, John. I know things have been difficult at work since Patricia *left*."

Shifting in his chair, John replied, "It was at first. Her knowledge was invaluable; however, the new assistant is catching on fast."

"You never told me, *why* was she let go?"

Smiling, he said, "You know the old saying—I could tell you, but then I'd have to kill you—and well, I like having you around"—smiling wider, he added—"most of the time."

Emily shook her head. "Yes, sorry. Sometimes I forget that Rawlings Industries is as top secret as the government."

"Even more so..." she heard John say as she walked away.

Strength does not come from winning. Your struggles develop your strengths.

When you go through hardships and decide not to surrender,

that is strength.

—Arnold Schwarzenegger

CHAPTER 26

Harry's head throbbed, his face ached, and breathing was more comfortable with shallow breaths. Pushing through the dark veil of unconsciousness, he tried to make sense of his condition. Momentarily, the memories wouldn't come. There were sounds that Harry didn't recognize as he tried to focus on his surroundings. Through blurred vision, he realized he was in a hospital room, and for some reason, his left eye refused to open. An IV ran from his left arm to someplace behind him. Looking beyond his bed, Harry saw SAC Williams in a chair near the window. Fighting to find his voice, Harry whispered, "What happened?"

As if propelled by an electric shock, Williams was instantly at Harry's bedside. "Baldwin, nice of you to finally join the party."

Harry winced as he reached for the controls to raise the bed, so Williams pushed the button for him. As the bed began to move, Harry held his breath—the pain in his side was excruciating.

"Hey, son," Williams said. "You have a few broken ribs—you might want to take it easy for a while."

At that moment, Harry's last memories returned with a vengeance. Suddenly, the pain was forgotten—panic flooded his system, causing his heart to accelerate and his voice to come too loud. "Jillian! SAC? Jillian, someone needs to make sure she's all right."

SAC placed his hand on Harry's arm. "She is, son. Your daughter and ex-wife have been moved to a safe house."

Relief replaced the panic as the pain from his ribs came back. Exhaling, Harry winced and said, "Good—but I bet Ilona's pissed!"

"Her daughter is safe, but you're right, Ilona isn't happy about the situation, but she understands the threat. We need to know what happened." Before he could respond, SAC William's phone rang. He held up a finger and walked toward the window to talk.

Harry closed his eyes, laid his head against his pillow, and remembered the whole terrible episode. Behind his closed lids, he saw the driver of the SUV, the one who picked him up at the airport. When he'd first entered the dark vehicle, Harry hadn't paid the man much attention. He was a driver—the FBI had plenty. It wasn't until he'd saved Claire's message and was listening to Rawlings' that he began to notice the driver's eyes in the rear-view mirror, periodically watching him; then Harry heard the voicemail from the bureau. Before he asked the driver why they were no longer headed toward the field office, Harry casually removed his gun from his holster.

"Give that to me." The man's voice held the slightest of a Lebanese accent. Harry couldn't remember if he hadn't noticed the accent before, or if the man hadn't spoken until that moment.

Harry pointed the gun to the side of the driver's head and calmly commanded, "Pull the car over, asshole."

Laughter filled the otherwise silent vehicle. Seemingly undeterred by the threat, the driver tilted his head to the right. Harry glanced toward the passenger seat, half expecting to see someone materialize. No one did. Instead, the driver reached over and pulled down the sun visor. Taped, where the mirror should've been, was a picture. Staring at Harry, with big, beautiful, blue eyes and light, blonde hair was Jillian. The picture could've come from Facebook or been taken in person. Either way, it didn't matter—Harry was living his worst nightmare—his Achilles heel—his vulnerability. This asshole was threatening Harry's four-year-old daughter. Panic erupted in his gut as adrenaline flooded his system.

"Where is she?" Harry growled.

"She's still with that pretty little ex-wife of yours."

"How do I know she's safe?"

"You don't." The driver lifted a well-worn stuffed bunny—pink and thread bore. Harry had only seen the bunny once—in person—when he purchased it. At the time, he wasn't even sure Ilona would give it to their daughter; however, through the years it'd been a reoccurring item in many of Jillian's pictures. Harry knew, without a doubt, it belonged to her.

Turning the barrel around, Harry willingly handed his gun to the driver. Through the windows, Harry saw that the neighborhood was becoming seedier by the second. He pushed his fear inward and summoned his negotiating voice. "There, you've got my gun. Now, tell me what the hell you want?"

The driver didn't answer. Instead, he spoke into his phone, "Yes, we're almost there." "No idea." "Fuck'n FBI and clueless!"

While the driver was talking, Harry eased his own phone out of his pocket and began to text the bureau while simultaneously turning on his GPS finder.

"No way, asshole! Give me your phone—now!"

When Harry hesitated, the driver tilted his head toward Jillian's picture.

Harry had the training, and he knew the protocol; none of it mattered. He'd activated the GPS but hadn't had time to complete the text. His life no longer counted; protecting his daughter was Harry's only thought.

Jillian's safety and well-being was why Harry had signed away his parental rights, and why he'd only corresponded with Ilona in secret. Jillian had a father—in reality, he was her step-father, but she considered him her *dad*. One evening, about three years ago, Harry had flown East and met with Ilona and her fiancé. It wasn't an easy meeting, but Harry knew, without a doubt, the man across the table from him would add more to Jillian's life than he could. Seeing the gleam in Ilona's eyes and feeling the ache in the pit of his stomach, Harry knew the man had already done more for his ex-wife than Harry ever had.

The legal arrangement didn't stop Harry's interest. He watched his daughter's childhood from a distance. Each birthday and Christmas, each recital and soccer game—social media was a wonderful thing, and thankfully, Ilona allowed Harry's voyeurism. After Harry signed the documents surrendering his rights, Jillian's last name changed. Today it was George, the same as her mother's and her father's.

Harry believed his own happiness was inconsequential to Jillian's safety. Now, the man slowing the SUV near a seemingly abandoned building made all of Harry's sacrifices worthless. For some reason—Jillian was in danger. In Harry's opinion, during their short conversation, the driver had even made veiled threats against Ilona.

Damn, Harry wasn't prepared. Usually, he wore an extra revolver in a leg holster; however, since part of his trip was on a commercial flight, the gun was packed away in a sealed container. Easing the shoestring from his boot, Harry gripped it firmly in each fist and quickly brought it down over the man's head. With all his strength, he pulled it tight against his throat. As garbled sounds came from the driver, the SUV spun wildly. Gasping for air, the driver simultaneously slammed his feet against the brake and gas pedals and released the steering wheel. His hands fought Harry's grip as he clawed backwards.

When the SUV finally came to a stop, the driver's head fell to one side and his hands quit the fight. Harry's relief was short-lived. The doors to the vehicle flew open, and he was pulled to the ground. The concrete was wet as he assessed his situation. Three large men were shouting things he couldn't understand. Harry's linguistics training told him the language was Middle-Eastern, but he didn't recognize the dialect. His heart raced even faster when the sound of a woman's crying came into range. Harry didn't need to see the woman to recognize the voice calling out to him between sobs.

SAC Williams touched Agent Baldwin's arm, bringing him back to present. "Agent, what can you tell us?"

Harry's right eye opened wide with concern. "Liz"—his voice cracked—"is she—all right?"

"Yes, son, she wasn't harmed. Apparently, Ms. Matherly's presence was meant only as a witness. She's filled us in on her story and is anxious to see you, but first, we need your version."

Harry inhaled, taking the throbbing in his ribs as penitence for the pain he'd caused those he loved and cared about. After he explained the pick-up and ride, Harry went on, "I got up off the concrete and asked what they wanted, what *it* was all about. Instead of answering, they taunted, punched me, and yelled. I fought back, more than once, I connected." Harry looked down at his hands. The right one was covered in bandages. "They said I needed to *stop*. I asked stop—*what?* They kept saying—*Leave the past alone. It won't change anything now. Just stop digging around where you don't belong.* When I asked who they were working for, they laughed and said I mustn't be a very good FBI agent if I couldn't figure that out."

Harry's voice lowered with determination. "SAC, I know it was Rawlings— I know it was! I saw his face in Geneva. When he left that pub, he was mad! He's the one who's responsible for this. I'm getting too close to something in my research."

Williams pulled the chair beside Harry's bed. "Did you tell Rawlings about your research?"

With his head and ribs throbbing, Harry reached up and touched his left cheekbone and confirmed his suspicions. The skin was tender and felt swollen.

Williams nodded. "You have quite a shiner. Ms. Matherly said you put up a good fight, but once the driver came to, you were outnumbered four to one."

Harry remembered. He was thrown to the ground, and the driver started to kick him. Finally, one of the other guys pulled the driver off. Liz was crying. The men all got back into the SUV and left. "Did Liz get help?"

"Yes, the men took your phone, but Ms. Matherly still had hers. She called 911. Once the police arrived, she called the bureau. Son, do you remember any more details? Did you tell Rawlings about your research?"

Harry shook his head. "No, I didn't have the chance to tell him, but somehow, he found out. It's the only thing that makes sense"—he paused—"My phone—did you say they took my phone?"

"Yes, the bureau tracked it, and it was found with your other belongings in an ally dumpster about a half of a mile from where you were attacked. Your phone was destroyed."

Harry exhaled. "Good." He knew the saved information was backed up on the bureau's servers. Suddenly, he had a thought. "Was the SD card still in the phone?"

"I don't remember seeing it, but the phone was pretty mangled. Besides, everything should be on the server." Harry tried not to reveal too much emotion in his voice. "Not everything, sir. There's a picture of Claire Nichols with me on that card."

SAC Williams sat straighter. "With you?"

"No, not like that—just sitting together in a booth in Venice."

"We received that picture."

"There were two. The one I sent and another one." He swallowed. "Now I'm concerned about her safety too."

"We haven't located her yet, but according to the messages we accessed from your phone, it sounds like she's with Rawlings. If you think he's responsible, and he sees that picture, then she may be in danger."

Harry nodded. He wasn't ready to tell his supervisor that Rawlings had already seen the picture. "I need my phone back. It's the number Clai—Ms. Nichols called. It's her only way to get in touch with me or the FBI."

"We have your number being monitored. If she or Rawlings calls, it'll be answered."

"Yes, sir." Harry wanted to be the one to answer either one of those calls; however, he understood. Right now, he wasn't in the best condition to do that. "Can I see Liz now?"

SAC Williams smiled. "We have more to discuss, but I don't see any harm in that. First, I believe you need to be checked out by the doctor. They made me promise I'd alert them when you woke." As he began to leave the room, he paused and said, "Oh, Agent, your sister's here too."

Harry grinned. "Good, I'd like to see both of them as soon as the doctor's done."

By the time the nurses were done checking Harry out from every angle—yes, he knew that wasn't their intent, but he sure felt like it was—he was exhausted. He wondered how he could be tired after being unconscious for over ten hours. Next, the doctor came in and probed and prodded; then he asked Harry questions. The doctor didn't ask how Harry received his injuries—Harry couldn't have answered if he did; however, he asked questions like, does this hurt? How many fingers am I holding up? Do you know who the president is? All in all, Harry believed he passed.

He was just about to doze off when his door opened again. Each time someone passed the threshold, Harry saw the uniformed officers posted outside of his door. Their presence gave him comfort. If Rawlings was bold enough to have him attacked in broad daylight—anything was possible.

The expressions on Liz and Amber's faces told him more about his appearance than SAC Williams or any of the nurses or doctors. *He must really look like shit!* "So, do I really look that bad?" His attempt at levity was lost as both women began to cry.

It was Amber who reached his bedside first. She started to hug him and stopped. "Oh my God, will I hurt you if I hug you?"

Harry lifted his arms and Amber leaned in. When she backed away, she asked, "Why Harry? Why would someone do this?"

He heard her question, but it was Liz standing near the wall with her arms crossed over her chest who had his attention. She was looking his direction with her lower lip sucked into her mouth as she tried to control the sobs she muffled. His heart broke—he couldn't imagine how scared she must have been when those men took her. He reached out his hand. It seemed like she was moving in slow motion; however, after an eternity her hand finally touched his. "I'm so sorry they involved you in this. You must have been petrified!"

Liz nodded. "I didn't know what they were going to do to me..." She allowed the ragged breaths to overtake her words. Amber got up from the side of Harry's bed and Liz sat down. He pulled her close. As she collapsed across his chest, Harry's ribs screamed out in pain; however, he didn't wince. He wrapped his arm over her shoulder.

"Shhh, you're all right. Williams said they didn't hurt you." His voice changed—hardened—slowed—deepened. "They didn't hurt you...did they?"

Liz looked up. Her eyes were red and puffy. "No, but I couldn't help you. I wanted to save you...they made me watch..." Her voice trailed away as she buried her head into his chest.

"Hey, I'm fine. No saving necessary."

Amber laughed sarcastically. "Yeah bro, you look great! Maybe now you'll decide to take that SiJo job for real?"

He looked at his sister like she had three heads. "What are you talking about?"

"If being in the FBI is going to do this to you and Liz, you need to have a safer job."

"No freak'n way! This wasn't about the FBI—it's about my research. Rawlings wants me to stop, but I'm not doing it."

Liz lifted her head. "Please, Harry, think about this. He didn't stop at anything when he wanted Claire back. You already know he's capable of murder. Think about Jillian. You have to end this madness—now!"

"Jillian is safe and so is Ilona"—he took a deep, painful breath—"and so are we. All three of us will have around the clock surveillance until Rawlings is found."

"Three?" Amber asked. "I don't need to be watched by the FBI. I'll have SiJo take care of me."

Harry shrugged. "I don't think it's my call, sis. It's pretty standard procedure in cases like this. Why do you think I have those nice greeters at my door?"

Amber asked, "How do you know Jillian is safe?"

"I really can't say. I just do."

"Well, I'm going to call Ilona."

"No, you're not."

Amber's eyes narrowed. "The FBI has them, don't they?"

"I can't say." Of course, that was all he needed to say.

It takes two to speak the truth: one to speak, and another to hear.

—Henry David Thoreau

CHAPTER 27

Claire woke up to darkness. She wasn't wearing her mask; the darkness was the time of day—or more accurately—night. This was her new routine; waking two to three times a night to accommodate their growing baby. Sometimes, when she looked in the mirror, Claire wondered if her skin could possibly stretch any farther. The changes to her body only confirmed the miracle living within her—well that, and the reaffirming movements of their child. She enjoyed the sensation of their baby's movements. Claire told herself, if she were still alone, she'd feel the same way about her growing midsection; however, Tony's constant reassurance made each pound and stretch mark easier to bear. It amazed her how he could sit for hours with his hands on their child. Often, she'd be in front of him on a lounge chair with her back against his chest. Sometimes they talked; often she napped; at times they read, but they were always connected.

When Claire returned to bed, it was empty. Looking to the clock, she saw it was only 3:18 A.M. "Tony?" she called to the open air—No answer. "Tony?" she called again as she stepped onto the lanai.

He was standing near the railing, looking out to the lagoon. In the distant sky, lightening flashed, and seconds later, the low rumble of thunder rolled through the night air. Wrapping her arms around his back, Claire laid her cheek against his warm bare back.

"Hmmmm," he said as he seized her arms and pulled her in front of him. "You need your sleep." His lips brushed her lips. "You should go back to bed."

"I don't like being alone."

Placing a quick kiss on her stomach, Tony smiled. "You're not."

"Why are you out here?"

With his arm around her waist, he caressed the satin of her nightgown as his palm dipped down over her round behind. "I heard the thunder. Do you think the storm will make it here?"

Claire shrugged. "I don't know. Francis talked about the storms and rough seas, but so far, all I've experienced have been afternoon showers. They seem to pop up, out of nowhere and disappear just as fast."

"Come now, Mrs. Rawlings, you're a meteorologist; will that storm make it to our Island?"

"Well, you see, if I had a computer with the right programs where I could assess wind speed, direction, and see the different fronts—"

His lips seized hers—stopping her words. When he spoke again, it wasn't about weather, "You really do need to go back to bed."

There was something in his voice. Claire couldn't determine the meaning or decipher its origin. "What's the matter?"

"Nothing." He smiled and stood taller. "Good night, Mrs. Rawlings."

Claire took his hand and led him back to their room. When they were both under the soft, satin sheet, Claire cuddled close and asked, "Please tell me what woke you, and I know it wasn't a low distant rumble of thunder."

"You woke me when you got out of bed."

She lifted her head to her elbow and looked down at her husband. His skin was darker from only a few weeks on the island. It was his eyes that held her attention. They contained the multi-tasking look she knew too well. "Fine, I woke you. Sorry. What made you go outside?"

The tips of his lips moved upward. "Will you take the answer—thunder?"

Claire shook her head. "No, I won't. Remember our promise?"

"I have a lot on my mind."

"A lot that you don't want to share?"

Tony exhaled. "I don't want to tell you anything you're not ready to hear; however, talking about everything has brought back memories I'd forgotten. Sometimes I feel like I'm talking about another person"—he paused—"a person I'm no longer proud to have been."

Claire rested her head on his shoulder and gently wove her fingers through his chest hair. Tony's eyes stared up to the dark ceiling as his voice resonated distantly, overflowing with pain. Although there were times Tony's confessions upset her, Claire knew in her heart that there was nothing she could say that would punish him more than he was already punishing himself.

He spoke slowly, revisiting the subject of him watching her through the years. He explained how, at first, it was done as a means of identification. He and Catherine had a list—the children of the children. In the early years, Tony was busy creating CSR with his business partner Jonas Smithers. Later, his energies were used creating and building Rawlings Industries. He supported his grandfather's vendetta, but Catherine did, or had, most of the research done. He emphasized that he wasn't blaming her. "I never tried to stop her. It never occurred to me—I mean—it's what my grandfather wanted. He mentioned it to me—Catherine knew more of his plans, so I went along." He stressed, "Claire, I more than went along. She would never have been able to afford to have the people, like you, watched, or have things occur, if I hadn't bankrolled everything. I knew what I was supporting."

Claire nodded into his chest. It was her way of encouraging his words, without interrupting his thoughts.

"You were different." His arm tightened around her shoulder, pulling her closer. "You were the first person who personally interested me. You were so young. I was curious if I could actually influence someone's life without them knowing it. The first thing I did—well, it wasn't really to you. It was—"

The warmth radiating from within Claire suddenly increased; she couldn't stay silent any longer. The subject he was approaching was one of her greatest worries. *Simon!* She lifted her head to see Tony's eyes. "It was Simon, wasn't it?" She tried to keep her voice and breathing calm. "His internship with Rawlings Industries wasn't a coincidence, was it?"

Tony closed his eyes and didn't respond.

As the silence prevailed, Claire exhaled, lay her head back on her pillow and stared at the ceiling. The fan in the darkness hummed while the blades created a hazy blur. In the time it took her to blink, Tony's face was over hers. She'd wanted to see his eyes and understand his emotion, and now, she had him right on top of her. His palpable rage filled their room, the humid air no longer moved, and it was suddenly difficult to breathe. Claire's training told her to walk the fine line; however, somewhere in the three years since that training began, she'd taught herself to disobey. Defiantly, she asked, "Are you going to answer my question?"

"No." His warm breath bathed her face, adding to the still, humid air.

She waited for more clarification. When he didn't continue, she asked, "No? You aren't going to answer?"

"No"—each syllable was strained—"it wasn't a coincidence."

The fury, which had saturated their conversation, evaporated as Claire's muscles relaxed and the air re-entered her lungs. With his confession, she realized the anger she felt wasn't directed at her or her questioning, it was directed back to Tony—he was upset with himself.

The rumble of thunder loomed louder and closer. With their noses almost touching, Claire smiled. "Thank you. I know this is hard on you. I also know that revelation should upset me." She lifted her lips to his. "Honestly, it was more of a confirmation than a revelation. Somehow, I think I feel better knowing the truth, no matter what it is."

Tony sighed. "I hope so, because my dear, there's more."

Claire closed her eyes, unsure how much more she was ready to hear.

"Open your eyes"—Tony demanded—"I need to see what you're thinking." Obediently, she did as he said. His next confession came with more emotion than she was accustomed to hearing from him. "My life hasn't been perfect, yet I've never wasted my time envying anyone else. If something wasn't the best it could be—I made it better. Never did I want to be someone else. That's still true; however, there's one person of whom I was jealous."

"Simon? Why?"

"He was the only man I knew of that you loved. I did what I do—I made it better—for me. I separated the two of you." Tony shook his head. "So you can imagine how shocked I was when he showed up at the symposium in Chicago. When he approached us, I didn't know who he was until he asked to speak with you privately. Suddenly, I recognized him"—he paused—"Then...it was *you* I didn't recognize."

Claire couldn't process fast enough to respond. There were so many thoughts, yet all she could do was listen.

"You were usually so perfect in public—flawless."

She remembered what could happen if she wasn't; nevertheless, she stayed silent; her thoughts monopolized by this conversation's destination.

"Your expression and then..." Tony's words trailed away as he privately relived the encounter. "You could hardly speak. Even the introduction was difficult for you." Tony's sudden restraint became visible as the muscles in his neck tensed and his tone hardened. "For maybe only a split second, because Mrs. Rawlings, you quickly remembered to play your part, I saw something in your eyes I'd never seen. When you recognized him, before you remembered who you were, who I was, for only a moment, you were that eighteen-year-old girl I'd seen in pictures."

She tried to speak, although she didn't know what to say. The Claire from 2011 would have known the exact appropriate response—she wasn't that Claire anymore. "Tony," she steadied her voice. "If you saw that—I'm not denying it was there. Honestly, I don't remember feeling anything except panic. I guarantee, I was more afraid of you being upset than I was happy to see Simon." The warmth from his body covered hers. She continued, "If you expect me to apologize for that split second, then I'm sorry—not for that split second—but that you're not getting that apology."

Tony shook his head. "No, I wasn't expecting an apology. *I'm* trying to give one."

Claire lifted a brow.

"Don't you see? Instead of having confidence in our marriage, I was jealous. You were the woman I manipulated into marrying me, and Simon was the man you loved"—he paused—"To say I behaved badly would be a gross understatement"—Tony inhaled and exhaled, and continued—"to Simon and to you."

"I do love you."

"Now"—he kissed her—"it's all right. Remember, we promised honesty?" His rage, which moments earlier filled their bedroom, faded into the stormy skies. "That look, the one I saw for only a short time, I see it now—every day—every time your beautiful, green eyes look my way. I think perhaps it's a look that one must earn. When we saw Simon in Chicago, I hadn't earned it—I'd demanded it." He closed his eyes. "It isn't the same thing."

She reached up and caressed his cheek. Her touch opened his eyes, revealing the storm of brown behind his lids.

"Claire, I don't want to lose that look. I promise, I'll never demand it again...I don't want that. I want what I have today. I'm concerned that, when all my confessions are out—it'll be gone. "

"I've told you, my love won't change, but you started this story, so are you going to finish it?" Her stomach twisted with each word. Her accelerated heartbeat throbbed behind her temples.

"I apologize for how I reacted in Chicago."

"Tony, you opened this door; I need the rest of the story. Do you know how Simon died?"

She felt his body tense as he said, "I do." His words came quickly as if speed could take away their sting. "His plane was tampered with, but I don't know who did it or how they did it. It's a very complicated network of connections to allow the person paying the fee to stay anonymous."

The air left her lungs. "Oh, God..." She pushed against his shoulders. "Please get up, I can't breathe."

"Open your eyes."

Claire shook her head.

"Claire"—his tone now softer—"Please open your eyes." Slowly, emerald green met sad brown, as Tony offered, "I can call Roach. I can be gone before noon."

She shook her head against the pillow. "Stop that! Stop threatening to leave every time I'm upset. I deserve to be upset!"

Tony lay back onto his pillow. "I'm not threatening—I'm offering."

For a while, they lay in silence, both staring up at the ceiling. Only the sound of their breathing and the rumble of thunder getting louder and louder filled her ears. Finally, Claire said, "I wanted so badly for that not to be true. I wanted you to be totally innocent. I tried to blame Catherine for everything, but"—Claire reached for his hand, their fingers intertwined—"I think I've known it for a long time."

"When the FBI questioned me, they insinuated other crimes. I believe they know about this. I'm not sure if they can truly trace it back to me, but I think they at least suspect. Claire, I'm going to confess."

Her eyes sprang wide. Her sadness for Simon dwarfed in comparison to her sudden panic for Tony. "No, you can't! They'll arrest you—I need you."

"Maybe I can make a deal. I'll tell them about everything with Catherine."

Claire's eyes filled with tears. When she wrapped her arms around the man she loved, the moisture spilled onto his chest. It had taken them a long time to reach this destination—not the island—the place of complete honesty. Claire didn't want to lose it.

His voice resonated through their room, dominating the impending storm and echoing thunder. "You deserve to be with a man who's faced his past. I can't live with the threat that any day the FBI could come and arrest me in front of you or our child."

"Tony, don't do anything rash. Let's work *us* out first, please.'"

Tony smirked. "Now, I bet you wish we'd have talked about this *before* we were married. Then you could still say no."

Claire shook her head from side to side. "No, you're wrong. That's a bet you'd lose. You're laying your cards on the table, and I still think I'm the one coming out a winner. When I said I'd love you—no matter what you told me—I wasn't bluffing."

The morning sky lit with intense lightening. As the thunder roared, the skies opened and large raindrops fell, splattering the inside of their room. Tony and Claire jumped from their bed, their bare feet rushing from open door to open door throughout the house. By the time everything was secured against the storm, they were both drenched. Claire made her way to the bathroom, her nightgown plastered against her skin and droplets falling from her soaked hair. When she was about to take off the wet gown, Claire turned toward the doorway. He hadn't made a sound. If he had, then it had been covered by the raging storm; nevertheless, she felt his stare and knew he was there.

"I *am* sorry." Tony's expression matched his apologetic words. Stepping into the bathroom, he straightened his stance. Claire expected more words of regret; instead, she heard. "I wasn't—not even when we were at the funeral. I felt bad for you—I didn't expect you to take it that hard, and though I tried to be supportive, I'll admit—your grief upset me."

She stared and tried desperately to register each of his words. "*My* grief?" She asked in disbelief. "What about his mother's?"

"What about her?"

"You shook her hand—you talked to her—she told you that Simon admired you!" Each phrase was a little louder.

"I didn't think about it. To me, the deed was justified. I made a business deal. Deals happen all the time."

She stood silently and contemplated her husband. "Then why do you feel sorry now?"

He moved closer. "I don't know if I can explain this, especially to you."

Claire glanced to the mirror. In the opulent bathroom, in the middle of paradise, they both looked like drowned rats. Near their feet the puddle grew. "Try," she said.

"I didn't feel *anything* before—not just about Simon—about everything. It was why business was second nature to me. It'd always been about numbers and formulas." He wrapped his arms around her lower back. "I'm not making excuses. You want the truth—that's it. From the time my parents died until you

206

were with me in Iowa—I didn't *feel*. Sometimes I wonder why anyone wants to. Not feeling was a hell of a lot easier."

Claire stepped forward, leaning her chest and midsection against him. "It can also feel *good* to feel."

Tony wrapped his arms around her. "You're cold. You need to get out of this wet nightgown."

"I probably do, but I want to know more." She buried her face in his chest. "There was a time I did what you're saying, a time when I didn't feel—I just remember it being very dark."

He tilted her chin upward. "I probably don't need to ask what or who caused that time."

"It's over. I can tell you who brought me out of it."

His eyebrow cocked in question.

Her lips touched his and she asked, "So, does that make us even?"

Tony's shoulder's shrugged. "I doubt it. That dark time was a lot longer for me; you had more work to accomplish—to rescue me." His lips grazed the top of her forehead and his eyes shimmered. "Your influence went beyond my personal life."

"Oh?"

"You probably don't remember, but one time you asked me about something, and I told you about a company. It was one I was considering buying. You asked me how I could buy a business and close it without thinking about the people."

Claire nodded. She had recollections of such a conversation.

"Until that moment, I'd never considered—the people."

"What happened to that company? It was in Pennsylvania, right?"

Tony grinned. "That's right—good memory. The company's CEO and shareholders accepted my low-ball offer. Their major competitor, a company where I'm a major stockholder, took over their company. All forty-six employees were given the option to retain their jobs if they stayed and worked for the new company."

"Really?" It wasn't the answer she'd expected. She recalled him talking about closing the doors.

"Really." He moved a strand of wet hair from her face. "Some of the employees declined and they received a severance package. The last time I looked into the data regarding that company, over seventy people were employed, and my profits were higher than projected with the original proposal."

"What made you change your mind? Why didn't you go with your original plan and just close the company?"

"My dear, there has only been one person who has ever made me do anything or question my beliefs, and since she has become a real, true part of my life—my world has never been the same."

Despite their wet clothes and skin, Claire filled with pride and warmth. "So, I helped save those peoples' jobs?"

"You didn't help. Not one of my employees—or anyone—had ever had the nerve to question my motivation or decisions. You were the first." His eyes shone with pride. "Claire, you didn't *help* save their jobs—you *saved them*."

Her smile beamed upward. "I told you some of your confessions would upset me. That doesn't mean I love you any less."

Tony pulled her closer. "You need a warm shower. It sounds like the storm is slowing down. When you're done, you can get a few more hours sleep."

She lifted her arms. "Only if you'll help me get out of this wet nightgown."

Pulling her gown upward, Tony replied, "I told you before, you made a great business negotiator." Once it was completely over her head, he kissed her lips. "You still do."

The family you come from isn't as important

as the family you're going to have.

——Ring Lardner

CHAPTER 28

Amber entered Harry's condominium. Sitting in the living room, surrounded by stacks of papers, open file boxes, and multiple computers, she found her brother. Glancing around the cluttered room, she sighed.

∞∞∞∞∞

Harry hadn't heard her enter, but he heard the sigh. Looking up, he asked, "Hey, have you heard of knocking?"

"I've heard of it. I didn't know you understood the concept. It's not like you use it when you enter my place."

Harry laughed. "Yeah, sorry. I didn't know Keaton was over the other day."

Her cheeks blushed. "Well, since Liz's at the office, I figured it was safe to enter. What are you doing? I thought you were on medical leave."

"I am, but Williams had some evidence shipped over here. I was going nuts with nothing to do."

Amber reached out and gently touched her brother's left cheekbone. The bruise was no longer red and puffy. His left eye now opened as well as his right; nevertheless, the skin around the eye and down his cheek was still discolored. A greenish-yellow tint replaced the dark blue that followed the red.

Harry groaned.

"I guess that modeling career you've had on the back burner is out of the question."

Though Harry tried to appear offended, the corners of his lips rose revealing his amusement. Smugly, he replied, "That's not nice. I've been told I'm still *very* handsome."

209

"Well, Liz is biased." Amber picked up a stack of papers from the sofa, relocated them to his coffee table, and sat down. "Seriously, Harry, what are you doing?"

"You know I can't give you the details."

"Fine, no details, but you're still working the case against Rawlings, aren't you?"

"No details, Amber."

Her shoulders sagged. "Harry, look at you. Think about Ilona and Jillian. Think about Liz—she's still traumatized. It's not worth it!"

His blue eyes bore towards her. "How can you say that? What about Simon? Don't you care that Rawlings hasn't been punished for what he did?"

"Can you prove he did it?"

"Not yet, but my unexpected meeting in a back alley confirmed he's involved."

Amber leaned forward. "No, Harry—that meeting confirmed what you know, what you already knew. Remember what you told me when you thought Claire was pregnant with your child? That attack confirmed that you should leave the FBI and come to SiJo. Simon would want you safe. He wouldn't want you risking your life or the life of your child or anyone else to prove something that can't be changed. I mean—so what if it *is* Rawlings? It won't bring Simon back. What if you're wrong? What if Simon's crash was what the NTSB said in the first place? What if it was an accident? Either way, Simon won't be coming back."

"You don't get it. People can't go around changing other peoples' lives without consequences. We know for certain that he kidnapped Claire."

"So what? I may have felt sorry for her when I first heard her story, but seriously, if she's stupid enough to go back to him—she deserves whatever has or will happen to her!"

Harry stood ready to defend Claire's decisions, even though he hated most of the ones she'd made. When he did, a wince escaped his lips as his back straightened and his ribs ached.

"See, that's her fault too! You're obsessed with this because of *her*. Don't tell me it's Simon's memory—it's because of Claire."

"No! It's not her fault—any more than it's yours."

Amber's eyes widened. "Excuse me? My fault—what the hell?"

"I met Simon through you. Yes, I want to prove that prick is responsible for his death. Would I care as much if Simon wasn't a friend? Probably not—does that make you responsible? No! You're losing focus—Rawlings *is* responsible, and I'm going to prove it."

"The position of President of Security Operations at SiJo is yours. All you need to do is say the word. Walk away from this. Don't let Rawlings ruin any more lives."

Harry didn't answer. He sat back down to his makeshift desk with multiple computer screens and concentrated on his research. He knew there was nothing more he could add to the conversation—nothing productive. Amber must have realized he wasn't turning back around. He heard her huff and get up before the door to his condominium slammed shut sending aftershocks back to the living room.

With no one around, Harry read the screens. SAC Williams had gotten him access to the bureau's server. The databases of information were a wealth of knowledge. Unfortunately, in real life, results for searches didn't materialize as fast as they did on television shows. That was all right. Currently, Harry's only commodity was time. That was one of the reasons the Deputy Director allowed him to remain on the case. That—and Harry's acceptance of beefed up security.

He hated having an agent posted outside his door. It was even worse having one accompany him everywhere he went; nevertheless, in his current state, Harry agreed. He wouldn't be much of threat if he were to be attacked again.

As he read the screens and entered more data, Harry thought about his sister's words. He understood her concern and appreciated her offer of a job. Harry liked the time he'd spent at SiJo. For anyone else, it would be a great career. Amber had even offered him a real position on the board of directors.

When he considered how far their relationship had grown since his divorce, he felt an unfamiliar sense of contentment. Maybe he did have the family he'd always wanted. The fact that he'd had it since he was a young boy, but hadn't realized it, almost made it better. He wasn't as alone as he sometimes thought. Harry hoped that one day Amber would understand his determination to nail Rawlings to the wall was for her—too. She needed closure on Simon's death. No *beat down* in an alley would change that.

He reached for his phone and texted Amber.

"THANKS FOR THE OFFER. I'M SORRY FOR BEING AN ASS. DINNER?"

∞∞∞∞∞∞∞

Claire held tight to Tony's hand while Francis maneuvered the boat through the crystal waters. The trip from the island to town took anywhere from thirty to forty minutes, depending on wind and the roughness of the sea. Since this was only Claire's second excursion off the island, she was surprised by the number of other islands they passed. The first time Francis took her into town, she was too nervous to truly register the world outside of the boat.

Today, through sunglass covered eyes, she took in the beauty around her. The bright, tropical sun danced off the waves and glistened both near and far. The sea was neither calm nor rough. In more open water the waves were

211

bigger. As they traveled between the islands in narrower straights, the seas calmed, reminding Claire of their lagoon. The islands they passed en route varied immensely. Some were small, like hers. Others were large with multiple homes. Many were uninhabitable with cliffs and ragged stone mountains. Claire understood how under the cover of darkness, maneuvering around the channels between the islands could be dangerous. If the seas were too rough, a boat the size of theirs could easily find itself thrown against the large rocks and cliffs.

Despite having been born elsewhere, Francis knew the language and the culture of the area well. He was also known by many of the town's people. Once they were ashore, Claire watched Francis' interaction with the natives. Over the years, he'd obviously earned their respect.

Claire didn't see any motorized vehicles other than water craft. She whispered to Francis, "Does anyone drive cars here?"

"Oui, Madame el"—he pointed toward a large mountain in the distance— "There's one road that comes around the mountain, but driving it takes much time. Most traveling and shipments, they come by plane or helicopter. The airport is not far."

Claire remembered Phil telling her that by air she could be at a state of the art medical facility in less than two hours.

Tony asked, "Are there always planes at the ready and pilots? Or do they need to be reserved in advance?"

"Reserved is better," Francis answered. "However, most requests can be accommodated quickly."

Tony decided, since they had time, he wanted to see the airport. Claire wasn't interested. She decided to spend her time walking around the town until her doctor's appointment. First, she entered what she considered to be the equivalent of a grocery store. Many of the town's people spoke enough English to help Claire if she had any questions. There were also stands or booths along the side of the road with items for sale. It appeared many of the natives did more bartering than buying and selling. The road was defined and hard, but not paved—well-tried dirt. On her way to the doctor's office, Claire passed two taverns and decided alcohol was a universal language.

The waiting area of the doctor's office was full of people, yet when Claire entered, the nurse immediately led her back to one of the examination rooms. "My husband will be here in a few minutes. I'd like to wait for him."

"Your husband?" the nurse beamed. "But of course. Will you learn your baby's gender today?"

Claire smiled. "I sure hope so. Can we please do another ultrasound?"

"Let me check with the doctor. It's his decision."

After a few minutes of being alone, the door opened. When Tony entered, Claire knew why she hadn't heard the customary pre-enter knock. Grinning toward his handsome face, Claire thought how knocking had never been his forte. Tony's deep voice and sparkling eyes revealed his excitement. "I thought your appointment wasn't for another half an hour. I didn't miss anything, did I?"

"No," she reached out to hold his hand. "They brought me back as soon as I arrived. I have a little habit of being early for appointments."

Tony snickered. "I like that habit."

"I know you do."

As their lips united, there was a knock on the door. Claire's eyes twinkled as she called, "Come in."

The nurse entered, "Oh, hello, you must be Mr. Nichols?"

Claire watched as Tony's lips twitched. Suppressing her giggle, she replied, "This *is* my husband. Rawlings is our last name. Nichols was my maiden name."

The nurse apologized and explained that, after Claire's exam, the doctor would allow another ultrasound. When they were alone again, Tony asked, "Are you sure there isn't a problem using our real names?"

"Francis assured me and so did Phil, this place as well as others like it, are known for their discretion. Apparently, we aren't the only people here, or in the world, willing to pay big money to hide. It's a great source of income for areas where resources are limited. They're paid very well to keep our information private."

Tony nodded. "If they're paid that well, then I'd think we could have an ultrasound whenever we wanted"—he squeezed her hand—"And I want one!"

She grinned. "Me too!"—her smiled faded—"Tony, I hope you aren't disappointed, I mean I know you keep saying you don't care if our baby is a boy or a girl, but I think you do."

"I really don't. I promise I won't be disappointed. Healthy is what I want. I also want you healthy and safe. The only things that we'll accomplish today will be learning whether we need to order blue or pink baby things and narrow our name discussion to one gender."

Claire smiled. They'd discussed names a little bit—mostly, they seemed to discuss boy's names. When they Googled the most popular names for the last year, Sophia came up for girls and Aiden for boys. Tony immediately nixed Sophia. When he explained his reasoning, Claire was shocked. She had no idea Catherine had a daughter. The story was especially wild when he explained that Sophia was the artist who painted Claire's wedding portrait. Apparently, he'd been watching her since Nathaniel died. It wasn't done for vengeance—Tony's voyeurism of Sophia was the fulfillment of a promise to Nathaniel—to watch over Catherine's daughter. Tony didn't know why Catherine didn't want to see her, but the night he was taken into FBI custody, Tony was about to tell Sophia the truth about her mother. Obviously, he never got the chance.

Claire agreed. The name Sophia wasn't in the running.

Neither one had a reason for not liking Aiden—they just didn't. Tony didn't want to use family names. As much as he had admired Nathaniel, he now realized that perhaps his grandfather wasn't as good of an influence as he had once thought. Claire contemplated names from her family. She knew, without asking Emily, was a no. Her mother's name—Shirley was very close to Tony's grandmother Sharron. Claire's grandmother Elizabeth was close to Emily. None of them seemed worth arguing for. So far—the only girl's name that they were both receptive to—was Courtney.

When it came to boy names, for every suggestion Claire made—Tony had a counter. He liked names that could be shortened. He said, from experience, he believed it made a nice separation between business and personal. Claire didn't ask if Tony assumed his son would follow him into business. After all, if—and that was a very big *if*—their public issues could be resolved, Anthony Rawlings was a man worthy of having a son follow in his footsteps; however, late at night, when Claire would wake and stare up to the ceiling while Tony slept soundly, she worried. Anthony Rawlings, businessman, had so many worries and concerns. *Did she want that for her son or daughter?* The larger looming concern was Tony's predilection for perfection. Claire had no way of knowing the personality of the child within her, yet if he were anything like his father, *would the combination in a professional setting be potentially combustible? Would it be different with a daughter?* Claire didn't know.

When the doctor entered, Tony stood near Claire's head, kept his hand on her shoulder and listened. She loved his presence—just knowing he was near gave her more confidence. The doctor reassured Claire, her weight gain was within normal limits and expectations. When she complained about filling so fast, he recommended multiple small meals as opposed to three larger ones. She looked up to Tony's knowing eyes and realized he wasn't only filling the role of father and offering emotional support, but also acting as informant. Madeline would know the new meal requirements before Claire made it home.

After the exam, the nurse led them to a different room for the ultrasound. The doctor used the same machine he'd used during Claire's last visit. She and Tony watched silently as the grainy image came to the screen. Again, he used lines and made measurements. They both breathed a sigh of relief to learn their baby was right on target for thirty weeks, measuring fifteen and a half inches long and weighing about three pounds.

"Three pounds"—Claire repeated—"Then why have I gained almost twenty?"

The doctor laughed and said, "Because, Claire, you aren't just carrying a baby; there's a whole lot more in there."

She knew he was right.

"And"—the doctor continued—"your baby will continue to gain, about a half a pound a week from now until you deliver, so eating those small meals is important."

Before Claire could respond, Tony answered, "Don't worry, she will."

The doctor moved the large wand around Claire's abdomen. The coolness of the gel didn't register as she watched the screen. Ever present in the background was the steady heartbeat of their child. As usual, it brought back memories of her lake. They watched in amazement as the doctor pointed out the baby's nose in a profile. When he repositioned the wand, they were able to count fingers and toes—they weren't able to see the gender.

"I'm sorry. Your baby's being modest. I'd hoped if we continued, he or she'd move and reveal their secret. So far, that hasn't happened."

Though they were both disappointed, Tony and Claire understood. Tony replied, "That's fine, doctor. The most important thing is that everything is going as it should."

"Yes, Mr. Rawlings, everything is perfect."

Claire smiled—she knew that *perfect* was exactly the way Tony liked it!

Let us not be content to wait and see what will happen,
but give us the determination to make the right things happen.

——Horace Mann

CHAPTER 29

Phil created a VPN, virtual private network, for both Tony and Claire. This allowed them access to websites and emails while virtually untraceable. When connected through a proxy and the multiple shell accounts he'd established, Phil believed their transactions were completely untraceable.

To communicate with one another, Phil, Tony, and Claire utilized email as well as occasional instant messaging. They could call; however, Phil still emphasized that calls needed to remain short. During the first week of November, Phil sent the Rawlings his second email:

To: Nouveau Alexanders
From: PR
Re: Current assignment
Date: November 7, 2013

Our initial meeting went well. I reminded Ms. L of her original directive—Ms. N's location wasn't to be divulged. She hasn't pursued the subject. My assignment is to watch a woman named Sophia Burke. Her husband, Derek, is employed by Rawlings Industries and was recently transferred to corporate headquarters in Iowa City.

They recently moved to Iowa from California, and I'm gathering background information. Though this seems benign, I have a feeling there's more to it. The name *Burke* concerns me. I don't remember reading about a Derek in Ms. N's research. Is there a connection to Jonathon? I'll learn, but your assistance may speed my research.

◌◌◌◌◌◌◌◌◌

Simultaneously, their iPads notified them of the email. Claire saw the icon and looked across the room. "It has to be from Phil. I'm nervous."

"His last message wasn't very enlightening"—Tony opened the message—"Tell me again why he's addressing us as the *New Alexanders*?"

Claire shrugged. "I think he's avoiding using our real names." *Was it wrong to have a private joke?* She hoped not. There was no way to explain her and Phil's relationship without inciting unwarranted concerns from Tony, and there was no reason for him to be concerned. There was nothing between her and Phil but trust and friendship. It was the kind of friendship that comes when trust has been tested by fire and survived.

She and Tony both read the email. The last time she'd heard the name Derek Burke, it was Brent who brought it to her attention. Although she and Tony pledged honesty and full disclosure, Claire didn't believe their promise included harming his relationship with his closest friends. He was unaware of their support; it seemed best.

Claire had recently learned the story of Sophia. She looked up from her screen. "Tony, is this the same Sophia? Catherine's daughter?"

She saw the darkness return to his eyes as they moved from the screen toward her. "Yes. How in the hell did she manipulate moving them to Iowa? Executor of my estate has no control at Rawlings Industries."

Claire put down her tablet, walked to her husband, and touched his shoulder. "Why would she do that? Why, after all these years of not wanting to know her daughter, would she suddenly move her to Iowa?"

He covered her hand with his. "I don't know, but I don't like it."

"What are you worried about?"

"Accidents."

The word still caused the hair on the back of Claire's neck to stand to attention. "What kind of accidents? You don't think Catherine would harm her own daughter, do you?"

"I'm not sure she has boundaries. Look at what she's done to us."

Claire saw the restraint in his expression, exposed through the bulging veins of his neck. His jaws were clenched as he modulated his voice to its most accommodating tone. "It's the middle of the afternoon and too hot for you to be out in the sun. You should rest and keep your feet up. I need to go for a walk."

Claire wanted answers to her questions. *How did Tony's promise to Nathaniel influence his clandestine protectiveness of Sophia? What exactly were Catherine's capabilities? Where were Tony's boundaries?* However, sensing his distress, she didn't ask. They'd been down too many difficult roads lately. This situation wasn't her battle, her family, or her promise. Tony needed to work it out for himself. She exhaled. "All right, I'll rest in our room. Please come wake me when you get back."

As he kissed her cheek, she saw something in his eyes, something that made her pulse race. "Tony, please don't leave the island."

Her plea pulled him from his thoughts. "What? How did you know I was thinking that?"

She held his hands. "I won't be able to rest if I'm thinking about you out in the boat. I know Francis showed you how to drive it and has taken you out, but I can't bear to lose you again."

"Claire, I hate this feeling of helplessness." He let go of her hands and paced near the open doors to the lanai. "This place is amazing, you're amazing. I *want* to be here with you and our child; however, when I read about Rawlings Industries and now this—I feel like a caged animal. There are so many things I could be doing—if I were back home."

"I hoped you'd consider yourself home."

She saw his shoulders slump. His expression of amusement was short-lived. "How many times am I to hear my own words and phrases repeated to me?"

Claire shrugged. "I don't have a definitive number. What can I say?" She stepped toward him and reached for his cheek. Brushing it gently, she allowed the afternoon stubble to abrade the tips of her fingers. "You're a wise man, and I've learned a lot from you. You should consider it an honor—imitation is the sincerest form of flattery."

"I think there are others who you'd be better to imitate."

Kissing his lips, she lingered on her tip toes and whispered, "Right now, I'm going to lay down. When I wake, I'll trust that you haven't disappointed me."

As she turned toward the bedroom, Tony seized her arm and pulled her back into his embrace. His sudden surge of power would've frightened her in the past. Today, she found it more than mildly erotic. "Tell me"— his dark stare intensified with each second—"why it took an electronic lock to hold you captive and mere words are doing it to me? Because I'll be honest, I want to get in that boat and talk to a pilot. I promised to look after Sophia. She has no idea what kind of a woman her birth mother is capable of being. I'm the only one who can explain, yet with a few words from these beautiful lips"—his finger gently traced her lips—"I'm again helpless."

"Because you love me, and as committed as you are to Sophia, which is honorable, you're more committed to me and our child."

Tony nodded. "I do love you—more than life itself; nevertheless, I'm going for that walk. I feel trapped, and at this moment, I need to remind myself Catherine is the one responsible—not you. As much as I love you"—he seized her shoulders—"and never forget that I do; right now, I'm not fond of the control you seem to have."

Claire nodded. She wanted honesty. *That didn't mean she liked everything she heard—she didn't; however, wasn't that the risk with honesty—accepting the truth no matter how it made you feel?*

Besides, deep down, Claire completely understood his position—she'd been there herself.

∞∞∞∞∞∞

Phil eased into the art gallery behind a twenty-something couple. It was the third one he'd visited in Davenport this afternoon. It looked similar to the others—art work highlighted by spot lights and three dimensional art showcased on stands. It wasn't his thing. He wasn't even sure how to pretend he liked any of it. Most of it didn't look like art to him anyway. Who decided what constituted art, Phil wanted to know.

As he walked slowly, pretending to appreciate the paintings which looked like something a five-year-old child could create, he saw Sophia out of the corner of his eye. She was moving from painting to painting, taking a painstaking amount of time to devour each piece. This was the third Friday in a row she'd gone to Davenport to visit the galleries. Once he found her, his directive was clear; text Ms. London and let her know Sophia's location.

Stepping into a side hallway, Phil did as he'd been told. He texted his employer:

"MRS BURKE IS AT THE JOHN BLOOM GALLERY ON 12TH STREET."

Next, he stood back and waited. As he stared at the canvas before him, he listened to two women discuss the use of color and shadowing. There were many things Phil knew. He could probably teach a course on surveillance—technology was his passion—he loved learning about new devices to make his job easier and more precise. When it came to computers, he could talk programming and hardware with the best of them; however, when it came to colors and shadowing, he didn't have a clue!

His phone vibrated. The text was simple. His job for the day was done. Phil couldn't have been happier. Trailing Claire had been a cake walk. Following Sophia was brain numbing. She spent most of her time at home. When she did venture out, it was either with her husband or to places like this. The gallery was filling with patrons—apparently, his lack of interest wasn't shared by others. As he made his way toward the door, a waiter stopped him with a tray of champagne in tall glasses. He asked if Phil would like a glass. With the refusal on the tip of his tongue, he saw Catherine enter the gallery. She looked different than she had at any of their meetings. Her hair was shorter, her clothes stylish, and her face made-up.

Curiosity was his new downfall. It's what had pulled him into Claire's world. Many times, when Rawlings told him to end surveillance for the day, Phil would continue. Now, nodding and smiling at the waiter, he lifted a flute from the tray, worked his way into a crowd, and watched. It wasn't the art that interested him—it was the woman who had been so determined to rid herself of Claire. Phil was anxious to learn more about the woman who thought she employed him.

Through the next few hours, Catherine mingled in Sophia's vicinity. In time, they began discussing the pieces of art. He couldn't hear their discussion; he could watch their body language. It was alarmingly similar—little mannerisms—the way they tilted their heads or crossed their arms. Phil wondered if they noticed the similarities or if it was more obvious from afar.

The two women were becoming friendly, laughing and talking, until a tall dark-haired man arrived. Phil recognized him from his research—it was Derek, Sophia's husband. It appeared as though Sophia introduced Catherine to her husband, and then shortly thereafter, Catherine excused herself and left.

One last glass of champagne with a side of brie and Phil was done for the evening.

∞∞∞∞∞∞

Claire was asleep on their bed when she felt Tony sit on the side of the mattress. His soft touch gently rubbing her back eased her concern. He wasn't gone—he hadn't disappointed her. Turning toward her husband, Claire smiled a sleepy smile. "Hi, Honey, how long have I been asleep?"

"A couple of hours."

"And where did you go?"

"For a walk around the island. I also made a call."

That last sentence held Claire's attention. "A call—to whom?"

"I thought I was calling Baldwin."

Claire sat up and scooted to the headboard. "Tony, why would you call Harry?"

"He's our only FBI contact. The only one we know how to contact."

Although the air had cooled over the last few hours, it still sat warm and heavy; nevertheless, as goose bumps cloaked her skin, Claire wrapped her arms around her chest. "Why did you need to speak with the FBI?"

"I told you the other night that I'm willing to make a deal."

The sea was still blue, the sky was still clear, and the colorful flowers still filled the air with beautiful scents, yet Claire's paradise disappeared—peace and contentment were gone. Tears filled her eyes as she fought the sudden pounding in her temples. She'd been asking questions for weeks. During that time, she'd also been getting answers—many she didn't want. Before she could ask the question on the tip of her tongue, Claire pushed herself off the bed. The sudden movement made the room sway. She reached for the bedside stand, closed her eyes, and waited for it to stop.

Before the room ceased spinning, Tony was at her side. His distant tone was replaced with concern. "The doctor said you need to be careful; the bigger the baby gets, the harder it is for your blood to flow. He said that sudden standing can cause fainting spells. You need to move slower." His strong arms encircled her body and stabilized her world during each word of his lecture.

Instead of leaning into him, Claire stood straight. "I'm fine. I stood fast because I couldn't breathe. I needed to stand and have more room in my lungs—and I heard the doctor—I was there."

"Laying down would accomplish the same thing."

She wanted to argue, but the swaying room and headache had her stomach in knots, or perhaps it was the thought of Tony's deal. No matter the cause, she chose to press her lips together and stare up into her husband's eyes.

"You need to sit back down."

Her tongue remembered to speak. "I *need* to use the bathroom," she retorted, followed by a decline for Tony's help. When she returned to the bedroom, he was leaning against the wall with his arms crossed over his chest. Before he could speak, she volunteered, "I don't think I want to know about your call."

"Baldwin isn't our contact any longer."

Claire exhaled. She didn't have a choice—he was going to tell her anyway. Claire sat at the small table. The straight backed chairs helped her lower back. "He never should've been. It seems like an obvious conflict of interest."

Tony nodded. "Are you feeling better?"

"Not really. Why would you make that call without talking to me about it first?"

"I had to do something."

"Please, Tony, tell me what was said."

"I thought you just said you didn't want—"

"I don't, all right?" her volume increased. "I don't want you to make a deal—I don't want you to confess anything to anyone—except to me"—Her voice cracked as tears rushed down her cheeks—"I don't want to be without you—I don't even care if it's the right thing to do—I—I—we—need you!"

His resolve melted before her eyes as his defiant stance eased and his voice mellowed. "Claire, my God—this isn't to hurt you or our baby—it's to help you. Since I left Venice without contacting Baldwin, I'm officially a fugitive. In essence, you're harboring a fugitive."

"I—don't care."

Tony pulled Claire into his embrace. "I'm not leaving. I spoke to Agent Jackson. He's the one I talked with in Boston. I told him that I'd make him a deal; I'd tell him about someone who I've helped over the years and confess my wrong doings—if the bureau would agree to allow me to turn myself in—in January of 2015."

Claire pulled back and looked into Tony's eyes. "2015—why?"

"We have a child coming in January. I asked for one year."

"Did he agree?"

"He said it wasn't in his power, but that he wanted to know what I knew."

"Did you tell him?"

"Only the tip of the iceberg—I told him about Simon's plane and that I knew for sure who killed my parents. I told him there was more, but I needed my deal first."

Claire lifted her brow.

"I'm supposed to call back on Monday"—Tony added—"Today's Saturday, but it's still Friday in Boston."

Claire grinned; it was difficult to keep track of days. She leaned into his chest and listened to the strong steady rhythm of his heart. "One year?"—She felt him nod—"I hope it goes very slowly."

There is no greater misery

than to recall a time when you were happy.

——Danté

CHAPTER 30

-SEPTEMBER 2016-

September 12, 2016

    Shit! It's the only word that keeps coming to mind! I have a meeting in two days with the Vandersols! I've done everything to avoid this—minus quitting my job. I've had sick children, dead grandparents—none of it real. I think I've finally run out of personal tragedies. Ever since Claire started making progress, they've wanted to meet the "aide" who works "so well" with her. That's according to Ms. Bali.

    I'm about to go in for my shift, and Ms. Bali will be there. I'm sure she'll ask if I'll be there Thursday. The truth is—I've run out of ways to avoid it. I don't want this to end. Lately, I've gone beyond mentioning Tony's name. I've done homework; at night I've read—my book and my notes. I tried listening to audio recordings of Claire's recollections. Hearing her voice, full of emotion, was too difficult; however, reading has helped refresh my memory of Claire's life.

    Then over the past month, whenever we've been alone, I've shared my research. I've recounted the stories she told me. I started with good memories, talking about her wedding and honeymoon. Over time, as I talked, I watched the stress leave her body. She's even started eating by herself—as long as I talk. If I stop—so does she. I have no idea what results the doctors are getting.

    After not liking Claire's initial reaction to this new regime, I was afraid the Vandersol's were going to stop the new protocol. Ms. Bali said they almost did. Apparently, there was some big blow-up between them and Dr. Fairfield.

*She said that Claire's "wanting" to go outside with me was the small sliver of
hope which persuaded them to allow the treatment to continue.*

*I don't know if they're seeing the same positive results as I am. She goes
to therapy four days a week, and I have no idea what they do there. Whatever
it is, when she returns, she's tired. I've tried to learn what it entails; however,
the answer I continually receive is, it's a "need to know" thing. I've suggested
her fatigue affects her eating; therefore, knowing would help me. Sometimes I
forget my job description—aides aren't supposed to question policy. Long
story—short, I still don't know what they do.*

After Thursday—it won't matter.

*I don't know if I should go to the meeting and let Emily call me out, or if I
should jump ship. It's no secret—I don't want to quit. Well, I need to go. As the
weather has continued to stay nice, I'm hoping for a little walk outside and
time to tell Claire more stories.*

Meredith told Ms. Bali she'd be in Thursday morning to meet with Ms.
Nichols' family. The woman looked like she was about to burst with relief. For
the last month, at the end of each shift, Meredith has been required to
complete a patient assessment. It's a simple computer form asking what she
did and what the patient did. Ms. Bali said the Vandersols and Dr. Fairfield
wanted to discuss some of her entries.

Meredith suddenly wished she'd kept copies for herself. She knew she
hadn't been completely forthcoming. She also hadn't padded her reports with
false hopes. Everything she'd reported was true, minus the preceding stimuli.

Trying to keep the impending meeting out of her thoughts, Meredith went
on with her daily duties. After Claire finished dinner, she helped her with a
light jacket, and they went for an evening walk. Although each night seemed
cooler than last, Claire didn't seem to mind. As they traveled the paths of the
facility, Meredith talked about the changing leaves. They were just beginning to
turn with the start of golden and red hues infiltrating the normally green
landscape. The air held the slightest scent of autumn filling Meredith with
memories of Claire's story. It was fall of 2010 when they had ran into each
other in Chicago.

The meeting had been planned. The other reporters had posted pictures of
Claire and Mr. Rawlings in Chicago. Even though Meredith lived in California
at the time, she couldn't pass the opportunity to get the story everyone wanted.
At the time, she was so proud of using someone else's story to further her
quest. Another article had said Mr. Rawlings was spotted at Trump Tower with
the mystery woman—Claire Nichols. It was sheer luck Claire decided to get
coffee that evening. Meredith had been lurking with her photographer when
they saw Claire enter—the rest was history.

Perhaps it was Meredith's concern about the impending meeting that
caused her to speak without a filter; whatever the cause, she did. Soaking in the

impending autumn and feeling Claire's hand on her arm, Meredith felt the unrelenting need to repeat the apology she'd voiced to Claire years ago in California. Of course, that time it was combined with shock at the consequences of her actions. Today, it was more heartfelt and thought out. After all, it'd been festering for years. "Claire, I know I've told you before, but I hope you know how sorry I am about your *accident*. I know you loved Tony, but what happened to you—because of me—I can never apologize for enough"—She didn't expect a response. It felt good to say this out loud, and honestly, saying it to someone who may or may not understand, but wouldn't interrupt, was comforting—"As a reporter I wanted nothing more than to get the big story. It's no secret—you and Tony were big news. I hoped to use our familiarity to learn what you'd been so careful not to reveal"—Tears came to Meredith's eyes as she realized her time with Claire was about to end—"I had no idea why you'd been so careful, and you didn't say anything to me, but having you there—a picture of us—I could use the clues to infer what you wouldn't say"—Sobs erupted from somewhere deep, somewhere that doesn't exist in a truly hardened reporter—"How could anyone have suspected what you were living through? I mean, never could anyone know what was happening. Claire, he did such terrible things. I don't know *how* you survived. I don't know *why* you survived; most people couldn't. I don't think I could."

They were deep into the wooded path, and the setting sun caused shadows to loom in every direction. Removing her sunglasses, Meredith wiped her eyes with her sleeve and pleaded, "I hope someday you can forgive me, as you forgave him. You may not realize it"—she snickered at herself—"I'm sure you don't, but your ability to love him after all of that—well, it has been inspirational. I mean, my God Claire, the man almost killed you!"

"Stop."

Meredith's feet stopped moving by command. As if on cue, so did Claire's. Inhaling her emotion, Meredith stood still, wondering if she'd imagined the one word. When she heard only the sound of leaves rustling in the gentle twilight breeze, Meredith questioned, "Did you just talk?"

Still wearing Meredith's sunglasses, Claire's face was downcast. Meredith couldn't resist. She removed the sunglasses and lifted her friends chin, revealing tears streaming down Claire's cheeks, overflowing her unfocused eyes. "You spoke," Meredith whispered. "I heard it. Oh God! Claire, tell me I didn't just imagine that!"

The silence grew. With each second, each minute, Meredith's excitement diminished. She was so upset about the meeting and losing this connection to Claire, she must have imagined the whole thing. Finally, she reached in her pocket, produced a tissue, and wiped Claire's tears. The sky was now closer to dark than light. Surely, someone would reprimand Meredith for having a patient out past dark. She smirked again, *it won't matter—I'm getting fired in two days anyway.*

Lightening her voice, Meredith continued her monologue. The apology was done—she'd talk—because, until they fired her—that was her job. "Let's get you back to your room. I'm sure they won't be very happy that I kept you out so late." Waiting for Claire to turn around, she continued, "I'm sure I'll hear about it."

Securing Claire's elbow, Meredith felt her tremble. "Claire, are you cold? I'm sorry. Let's get you back." While Claire stayed steadfast, Meredith remembered the night of Claire's *accident*. She'd been out at the lake, and it got dark. "Oh shit, I'm making this worse. You're fine—no one will be upset with you. Don't worry—there won't be any problems—no *accidents*."

"Stop." Claire's whisper was so low that Meredith had to strain to hear her above the sounds of the country night. Keeping her eyes downcast, Claire continued, "I lived it." "I don't want to hear it." "I want to hear the good times."

It was against protocol, but what the hell—*at this point, what harm was there in breaking another facility rule?* Throwing caution to the wind, Meredith wrapped her arms around her long-time friend and cried. The sobs of earlier, the anguish over the last six years, the fear of losing her job—everything came out.

Slowly, Claire's arms encircled Meredith, and she whispered, "Shhh, I'm sorry." "Please don't cry."

The absurdity of Claire consoling her hit hard. Meredith's tears turned to laughter.

∞∞∞∞∞∞

At first, Claire thought she was imagining it. Then again, she wasn't sure what was real. Tony's visits were becoming less frequent. The bland room with one window was becoming more real, and she didn't want it to be. With Tony, life was filled with colors of varying intensities. This reality was not only colorless, it was lifeless. She yearned for more time with him and longed for his touch; however, day in and day out, the drab room and the people who talked about nothing filled more and more of her hours.

Sometimes she'd focus and see her sister. It was Emily—although, she looked much older. Then again, so did Claire. The people with plain faces and colorless eyes often combed her hair into a ponytail. It was the hairstyle of a young girl—Claire didn't feel young. The reflection she saw—if she focused in the mirror—didn't look young. As a matter of fact, her hair was wrong. There was a time it was blonde—because, he wanted it to be. Now the highlights weren't blonde, they were white. *How could she possibly have graying hair?* The last thing she remembered was...

That was so difficult. She tried to remember. In that room they took her to, they asked her to look at pictures. Sometimes those pictures would trigger something. When that happened, she tried with all her might to keep the emptiness out. Sometimes she'd cover her eyes or her ears.

There were other times where they asked her to do simple tasks like picking up things and putting them in the right places. They didn't tell her what was right. She didn't know if it was acceptable to ask, so she avoided their tasks until they insisted. Claire didn't like to hear people tell her what to do, especially if they sounded upset. Finally, one day, she picked up the miscellaneous items and put them in the small little compartments. Instead of releasing her from the room, they came up with more things for her to do.

The constant that Claire began to anticipate was Meredith's visits. It was only recently she realized who the woman was. After all, even with saying her name, the context was wrong. *Why would Meredith Banks be feeding her?* Then Claire realized—it wasn't meant to make sense—it just was, and Meredith did what no one else would do—she talked about Tony.

Since his visits had lessened, when Claire tried to think of him, she felt waves of sadness. *He was gone. He had to be gone. Why else wouldn't he visit any longer?* Meredith's stories of happy times brought him back. The memories were difficult for her to recall on her own. Meredith's recollections gave her sustenance that no food could. She'd replay the words over in her head and remember. She couldn't feel his touch as she once had, but she could picture the scenes as Meredith spoke.

It recently became obvious that the stories flowed more freely outside. When they walked and were alone, Meredith's stories took on a life of their own. As she went on about dinners or engagements, Claire pictured her dress and Tony's tuxedo. When she talked about trips, Claire's mind saw the snow of Tahoe or the crystal blue waters of Fiji.

There were some memories Claire didn't want to remember. When Meredith mentioned the bad times or the bad Tony, she tried to stop the visions in her mind. She didn't want to feel the fear resurrected by those stories.

She questioned the reality of everything, yet in life or fantasy, Claire had promised Tony she'd keep their private life private. That's what made Meredith safe—she already knew their private life. Claire had disobeyed Tony a long time ago, she wasn't telling Meredith anything—no, Meredith was telling Claire, so she reasoned, telling her to stop was acceptable. After all, Tony wouldn't want Meredith telling someone else these stories. That was why Claire had to stop her.

She didn't mean to make Meredith cry. Claire didn't want her sad. She was the only person willing to help her remember. "Shhh...I'm sorry"—"Please don't cry."

Suddenly, Meredith laughed.

Claire was sure she was having another delusion—people didn't cry then laugh. Maybe Claire wasn't really on a walk with her old friend. Maybe she'd soon feel that too familiar sharp pain in her arm. Settling to the ground, Claire waited. The people would come and then she'd wake up somewhere else. Closing her eyes, she hoped when the sharpness came, Tony would be waiting...

"Claire, you need to stand. You'll get cold out here on the ground." Meredith's voice had regained the composure it momentarily lost.

Claire looked up, then side to side. *Where were the people?*

"I know you heard me. You spoke to me. Don't worry, you won't be in trouble, but we need to get back." Meredith put out her hand. "Please, let's go back."

Claire reached up—the sensation of her hand in Meredith's was real. At least, Claire believed it was.

You must stick to your conviction,
but be ready to abandon your assumptions.
——Denis Waitley

CHAPTER 31

Harry stared at his notes and relived his recent conversation with Agent Jackson from the Boston field office. Jackson was very specific—Anthony Rawlings *was* cooperating with the FBI and would *not* be apprehended at this time. When Harry questioned the attempt on his own life and the threat to his family, Jackson reminded him that there was no proof of a connection to Rawlings.

He was right—there was no proven connection. *Could Harry's gut be telling him he wanted Rawlings guilty, instead that the man was guilty?* Maybe the whole beat down in the back alley accomplished the exact opposite of its intention. Since it occurred, Harry was more focused and determined to close the case. He needed assurance that everyone he cared about was safe. Surprisingly, that list of people—people whom he cared about—really cared about—was more static than he'd previously realized. Harry had family who'd been there for him and friends he could count on. Those people deserved his attention.

Everything became clearer the other day when the deputy director allowed Harry to speak with Ilona. Although he wanted to be assured of her safety, he was prepared for her tirade. The call progressed much differently than he'd anticipated.

"Ilona, are you all right?"

"Harry?"

"Ilona, I'm so sorry. I never imagined there'd be a connection from me to you. I thought you were safe."

"I know...Ron knows."

Harry couldn't believe Ilona's resolve. If only she'd been that strong when they were married; then again, maybe strength came with the love and support of a devoted spouse, something she now had in Ron. "Is Jillian all right?" he asked.

"She is." Ilona chuckled. "She thinks we're on vacation."

Harry smiled.

"Do whatever you need to do, Harry. I have no idea who you're after or what this is about—but if there's a connection to us—please take care of it."

"The threat was meant as a warning for me to back off."

Ilona's voice rang through the field office's telephone. "I think I know you better than that—at least, I hope I do. You nail this person, whoever it is who's threatening us. I know you can!"

"Thanks, Ilona. I expected you to chew me out for getting you into this."

"You're a few days late. I would've, but I've had time to think. Someone feels very threatened. If they didn't, they wouldn't resort to this. I'm fine and Jillian will forget this vacation as soon as it's over."

When they hung up, the indecision that had been looming like clouds around Harry since he'd re-entered the case evaporated. Claire was where she wanted to be—her message said so. There was a time he'd let his personal feelings get in the way. Now, it was strictly business. Claire Nichols was an informant and the granddaughter of an agent who'd been murdered. If the Boston office was confident in her safety then Harry would concentrate his talents where they were better utilized—interrogation and research. Currently, with his ability to communicate with Rawlings severed, research was his mode of operation.

Harry looked over his recent findings. An inspection of the bureau of motor vehicles for the state of New Jersey found twenty-two thousand plus blue Hondas registered in 1989. The search could be considerably refined if Harry could enter a year or model for the Honda—he couldn't; however, thanks to Claire's phone call, he had a name: *Catherine Marie London.* When he ran her name, he hit the jackpot—*1987 Honda Prelude registered to Catherine Marie London.* Further scrutiny of the registration revealed the color: *blue.*

To further follow up on Claire's information, Harry searched marriage records for New Jersey. His search came up blank. Thinking of the Rawlings' somewhere in the South Pacific, he realized that people can go anywhere and get married. The FBI's databases weren't restricted by state or country. Utilizing the bureau's database, Harry tried again. This time, he hit pay dirt— *marriage license issued by the state of New York, February 25, 1988, to Nathaniel Rawls and Catherine Marie London.*

Harry referred to his timeline—Nathaniel Rawls was convicted on charges of multiple counts of insider trading, misappropriation of funds, price fixing, and securities fraud in 1987 and sentenced to three years in Camp Gabriels, a minimum security prison in upstate New York. Nathaniel's sentence was reduced to twenty-four months due to prison overcrowding. It made sense that he and Catherine Marie London were married in New York, at the prison where Nathaniel was incarcerated. Harry wondered why Catherine hadn't kept the name Rawls. *Was she hiding from Nathaniel's crimes as Rawlings had done with his change of name?*

The search he'd started on Nathaniel Rawls continued to generate information. The screen of his computer sustained a non-stop scroll listing a plethora of civil suits. Scanning the generalities, most cases named *Nathaniel Rawls* as *defendant* and asked for financial restitution. *Perhaps that was Catherine's reasoning, distance herself from the financial ramifications of Nathaniel's crimes.*

Out of curiosity, Harry scrolled the list of plaintiffs. The name Rawls caught his attention. He clicked: *Samuel Rawls seeks to void marriage of Nathaniel and Catherine Marie Rawls.* Harry's head spun. The complaint was initially filed with the New York state court in March of 1988. Harry rubbed his temples. *Damn—Samuel didn't waste much time voicing his disapproval of Daddy Dearest's new wife.*

It appeared the complaint met substantial roadblocks until June of 1989—less than a month after Nathaniel's death, when the case went from summons to disposition in record time. Based on *mental incompetence* and *undue influence*, Samuel Rawls's complaint was granted, and the marriage of Nathaniel and Catherine Marie Rawls was voided by the state of New York.

Harry knew without checking that three months later Samuel and Amanda Rawls were found dead in their rented California bungalow. He also knew that Patrick Chester was the only witness to a commotion the same day at the Rawls's home. In the initial interrogation, Chester mentioned a woman— Samuel's sister and a blue Honda. *No wonder Amanda Rawls wasn't anxious to introduce Chester to her step-mother-in-law—her husband had just had the woman's marriage voided. Wow, and Harry thought his family life was screwed up!*

Harry shoved his chair backward and paced about the living room of his condominium. *How in the hell did the police in Santa Monica not put these pieces together? The ballistics evidence alone should've sent up red flags— damn, flares! A rookie cop should've seen that it wasn't a murder/suicide!*

Harry's questions continued—*What did Rawlings do, besides payoff Chester, to cover it all up? Why? Why would he help the woman who killed his parents—unless he was involved in their murder? This may be circumstantial, but it created a connection and a reason why Catherine would want Amanda and Samuel dead. Was there a reason Rawlings would want them dead?*

Picking up his phone, Harry called Agent Jackson. After a string of button pushes and requests, his call was finally answered.

"Agent Jackson, this is Agent Baldwin from San Francisco."

"Baldwin?"

"I believe I have significant information in the Rawlings case."

"Are you well enough to travel Agent?"

"Yes, sir, I am."

"We'll see you in Boston, tomorrow."

Harry exhaled. "Thank you, sir. I'll be there."

His blue eyes sparkled with excitement. Traveling cross country was a hell-of-a-lot better than sitting in his damn condominium. *Maybe, just maybe, there was more to all of this. Harry couldn't shake the thought that somehow Rawlings was still involved; nevertheless, Catherine London was the reason Claire ran—the person who scared Claire into leaving the country, her family, friends, even at the risk of sullying Rawlings' reputation and company in the process. Claire wouldn't have done that if the threat wasn't real. Now, Rawlings was cooperating with the bureau. How deep did this go? Did Rawlings have information on Sherman Nichols or Nathaniel's murder? Harry wanted to know what Rawlings had told Agent Jackson.*

He'd share his information—then Jackson could share his; *quid pro quo.*

Gathering his research, Harry made a mental list. He needed to call SAC Williams and let him know he was going to Boston, and since he'd been forbidden to travel, he needed to be sure to emphasize—this trip was at the request of Agent Jackson. While Harry waited for the computer to finish running a backup, he pulled out his phone and sent a text.

"FYI—LEAVING 1ST THING IN THE MORNING—BUSINESS."

He entered Amber and Liz's names and hit *SEND.*

One last computer search—Harry entered Catherine's current full name— *Catherine Marie London.* Very little information surfaced, not even a reference to her one time husband or his last name. As he was about to exit the search, something caught his attention:

Executor of Anthony Rawlings estate, effective: September 18, 2013— fourteen days after the disappearance of...

The short article described the efficient and unaffected running of the Rawlings' estate, due in essence to Ms. London's ability to oversee day to day operations. It was a small counter article to one about the ramifications of Anthony Rawlings' disappearance in relation to Rawlings Industries.

Hmmm...maybe Harry should visit Iowa City? Did he want to see Rawlings' estate—the place Claire lived—was held captive—and returned to? He shrugged—the past was what it was. Closing this case was his number one priority. First, he'd see how things went in Boston; then, he'd consider Iowa— a definite possibility.

His phone vibrated. Looking to the screen, he saw he had two text messages. The first one was from Amber:

"NEW INFORMATION? WHAT? WHERE ARE YOU GOING?"

Harry shook his head and replied.

"LOVE YA SIS. I'LL LET YOU KNOW WHEN I'M BACK."

The second text message was from Liz:

"TOMORROW MORNING? DOES THAT MEAN YOU'RE STILL IN TOWN TONIGHT? COINCIDENCE, SO AM I!?"

He smiled—they'd been through a lot, but finally, Liz seemed to understand the whole work and personal life separation, and maybe, just maybe, he was starting to understand what it meant to have that special someone in his life—someone who supported you, no matter what. Harry replied.

"YOUR PLACE? I'M SICK OF THESE FOUR WALLS!"

∞∞∞∞∞∞

Phil was thankful Rawlings had projects for him to research. Sophia Burke continued to be uneventful. Honestly, Phil sensed his assignment would soon be over. Ms. London hadn't shared her reasoning for his reconnaissance; nevertheless, with the information from Rawlings, it wasn't difficult to put the pieces of the puzzle together.

Ms. London requested to know Sophia's habits and schedules. Once she did, she purposely intertwined their lives. Suddenly, Ms. London's routine included lunch at a deli near the University of Iowa, visits to art galleries in the Quad Cities, and frequenting art museums in Cedar Rapids. At each encounter, the women appeared more at ease.

Phil had no reason to believe Ms. London had revealed her true identity to Sophia. She hadn't shared it with him either; nonetheless, his job was to help arrange their *coincidental* meetings.

Although the Rawlings had internet, the jumping through servers, private networks, and shell accounts slowed things down considerably. It was much easier for Phil to do the internet surfing for him. Phil's current project was *Nathaniel Rawls*. He knew Rawls' basic information from Claire's research, and from Rawlings, he learned Nathaniel was married to Ms. London when he died in prison. Numerous news articles discussed Nathaniel's demise from natural causes—a heart attack—only two months prior to his release. Rawlings wanted to learn more about Nathaniel's medical records—especially while in prison. His inquiry was in relation to the civil case awarded to Samuel Rawls. The case claimed *mental incompetence* and *undue influence* and resulted in the successful voidance of Nathaniel's marriage to Catherine London.

Rawlings admitted he never saw his grandfather as being mentally incompetent. He wanted to know if there was any evidence which aided the court in its decision. To Phil it seemed irrelevant—the man was dead—the marriage was voided. *What good would it do now to learn if he were or weren't off his rocker?*

Then, Phil would walk into another gallery, see tin cans glued together with paint splashed over it, and remember—*research!* Infiltrating the records of a state penitentiary as well as the state and federal court systems was much more fun than deciphering art.

Phil sent his latest findings:

To: ARA
From: PR
Re: Research
Date: November 25, 2013

Nathaniel Rawls medical records are indicative of person with heart condition: history of high blood pressure, high cholesterol, depression, vitamin B12 deficiency, and nicotine addiction. Nathaniel took several high blood pressure medications, a cholesterol medication, and an anti-anxiety medication. According to the records, he smoked a half of a pack of cigarettes a day until he died. I'm not well-versed on medicines, but I can send the list if you want.

Records indicate that Samuel Rawls was listed as medical power of attorney. It doesn't appear that this changed after Nathaniel and Catherine were married. That's strange?

There were no specific instances of mental instability listed in the records that I've accessed thus far. I will continue to dig as well as access the court's records for the justification of their verdict.

Surveillance—nothing new, Ms. Burke and Ms. London appear to be becoming friendlier. They have now started to meet for lunch once a week.

PR

Phil reread the email. He couldn't help but smile at the *ARA*. It was his secret way of saying *Anthony Rawlings Alexander*. Having something— anything—private with Claire, made Phil smile. He wondered how she was doing, if she and the baby were well. He didn't feel right asking, but if Ms. London ended this ridiculous assignment, Phil knew he was taking a long flight back to paradise.

Time passes by so quickly...change happens all around us every day
whether we like it or not. Enjoy the moment while you can,
one day it will just be another memory.

—Unknown

CHAPTER 32

D ays passed. The sun rose bright and yellow in the East and set like a ball of orange fire in the West. As their candidness grew, so did the strength of their bond. The world was present, they could see it or read about it, yet they were separate and safe. Tony's offer to cooperate with the FBI in exchange for an one year reprieve received Agent Jackson's approval, as well as whoever needed to sign-off from above. The bureau's stipulations were clear—Tony must remain outside of the United States—stay in contact with the bureau—and not contact anyone from his past life. There were very few people who knew Anthony Rawlings was actually in a strange state of witness protection/fugitive status. To the world, he was simply—missing.

Agent Jackson promised Tony leniency regarding possible sentencing and preferential treatment regarding the court system as long as he fully cooperated; he agreed. Before Tony would allow the FBI to speak with Claire and receive her assistance, he secured their promise of full immunity. Tony didn't want any possibility of his wife being charged with aiding and abetting a fugitive. They agreed. During the course of multiple short, untraceable calls, Claire disclosed all she knew first hand and through Tony. When the FBI requested her testimony against Catherine, if the case were to go to court, Claire replied, "There's nothing that can keep me away from her trial. I want to see her face when she's sentenced. When she's in prison—like I was—I want her to remember that I helped put her there!"

They both exposed their cards and revealed all they could—except one. They still had an ace in the hole—they had Phil. His emails came daily, as well as pictures, and an occasional call. He was fully aware of Tony's deal, Claire's immunity, *and* that his communication and assistance was under the FBI's radar. Their contact could be considered a breach of the FBI agreement.

The newly remarried Rawlings knew their time together was limited. In the grand scheme of life, a year was such a short time. Each day, each hour, they vowed to make better than the one before. Revelations came and discussions ensued. Claire no longer feared that Tony would leave each time he took the boat away from their island. She reasoned that his expeditions were like her walks in his woods during their past life. At that time, she needed time away from the estate; it soothed, healed, and strengthened her. Claire said once that she survived the early times on Tony's estate because of Catherine. No longer did she feel that way; however, when she reminisced about her walks and her lake, Claire knew those times were invaluable. Tony went to town, explored other islands, snorkeled at nearby reefs, and always returned. He may not have recognized the importance of his excursions, but each time he returned with his eyes soft as suede and a spring in his step—Claire did.

She, on the other hand, had no desire to leave the island. Unless she had an appointment with the doctor, Claire preferred to stay near the house. Being in the southern hemisphere, the hottest time of year was approaching. If Claire didn't keep her feet elevated, her ankles and feet swelled. The infinity pool allowed her to float and stay cool. Madeline doted on her constantly, encouraging her to eat small meals and get plenty of liquids. Home was Claire's cocoon. She knew if they stayed there, they'd remain safe.

In her third trimester, sleeping at night had its problems, so often times, daytime activities morphed into napping. She'd be sunbathing or reading, and the next thing she knew, she was waking. The early day was her favorite time for sun before it became too intense. With her iPad at hand, she'd begin each day reading the news from the other side of the world. Sometimes it held her attention, and other times she'd lay the tablet face down and be lulled into a peaceful, dreamless state where her senses filled with the warm sun on her skin, lingering aroma of cologne mixed with her recently applied sunscreen, and the omnipresent roar of the surf.

Claire was in such a state, when without warning, large hands caressed her ankles and moved sensually toward her thighs. No longer was she on the edge of sleep. Her world was reignited as the tips of her lips turned upward and goose bumps materialized.

Opening her resting eyes, behind her sunglasses, and focusing on the handsome face before her, Claire saw her husband's devilish grin. It was a smirk of lust and pleasure, one which—with only a glance—could melt not only her insides, but her world. His eyes, too, were covered by dark glasses, yet as his smiling lips neared hers and her smile willingly changed to a pucker, she longed for the unseen intensity waiting for her behind that dark glass.

Reaching up, Claire lifted the dark barrier. Tony's eyes were the windows to his soul. She loved reading his emotions, especially when desire was part of the mix. In response, Tony, slowly and deliberately, removed her sunglasses and their eyes met. There was a moment when she thought to speak, but it was short-lived—so much more could be said without words.

Earlier that morning when Claire woke, Tony was gone. Madeline said he'd gone out on the boat. Now, after only hours apart, Claire realized their reunion would be more than a simple, *Hi, how are you today?*

It was true, her body had been thoroughly fulfilled and used the night before; nevertheless, it yearned for what was silently being offered. When his full, soft lips engaged hers, the passion of the night before returned with a vengeance. Only moments earlier, her lungs inhaled without instruction, yet as acquiescing moans escaped her lips, breathing required thought. Maybe it wasn't thought, it was timing. Inhaling needed to occur in unison. If it didn't, his unrelenting approach would rob her body of the oxygen necessary to go on. As her bathing suit covered breasts ached for the friction of his chest, Claire decided breathing was overrated. She wanted the heat that was overtaking her—to be consumed by the fire smoldering in the dark penetrating eyes. *If in the process she forgot to breathe, did it really matter?*

With the doors to their suite open to the crystal blue sea, their room was only slightly more private than the lanai; however, it was their room. Madeline and Francis respected their privacy. As Claire's bathing suit fell to the floor, she realized they'd yet to speak, and still they'd conversed more than some couples did in a lifetime. They'd greeted one another, discussed the pleasantries of the tropical morning, and assessed that each was doing well.

Laying on the soft comforter with her arms above her head, the man she loved gazing down at only her, and the large ceiling fan methodically moving the humid air, Claire's world was right. *Had she planned on her morning taking this turn? No. Was she willing? Without a doubt.*

The large talented hands claiming her body also had her soul. While his approach could at times be forceful—it was always gentle. Claire willingly surrendered, as she'd done a thousand times, to the whims and desires of the man above her. With no words, he could manipulate and dominate—move her from a state of sleeping bliss to the throes of erotic desire. Similar to years ago, his dark eyes held the passion and emotion which allowed her world to spin. Because he willed it so, the world was right.

Their past was significant, yet—insignificant. Years ago, Tony had told Claire not to talk about the past. He'd said they had a future and they needed to look ahead; nonetheless, at her prompting, the first month of their new marriage had been spent primarily in the past. She hadn't asked to know the truth—she'd demanded it.

When Claire was young, her grandmother told her to be careful what she wished for. Without a doubt, Tony and her grandmother were correct. There were times she wished for ignorance, times she wanted not to know all he'd told her; however, she did know—and in knowing—she wanted to put it all behind them. Claire wanted to look ahead toward a future with the man making love to her, seducing her, and fulfilling her every desire. She knew from experience that life with him could be difficult—but without him—the entire planet would spin out of control, lost forever in the darkest depths of the universe.

Claire closed her eyes and concentrated on his talented fingers as they caressed her skin. Beginning at the nape of her neck, they trailed lightly down her body. Uncontrollably, Claire heard her own voice, truly nothing more than a ragged breath surrounded by a moan as her back arched, pushing her chest toward his touch—wanting—needing more.

He taunted her sensitive breasts, tweaking and suckling. Though she wanted the jubilation to last, it took so little to propel Claire to the edge of ecstasy. Sometimes something as simple as a deliberate puff of air on a taut, wet nipple instantaneously liquefied her insides and removed reasoning from her thoughts. Teasing her to the point of begging, yet satisfying her every desire was her husband's specialty. Despite the way she'd changed—the way her body had changed—she felt wanted and sexy. He skillfully caressed and suckled as he moved south over her enlarged midsection—her baby—his baby—their baby. Its presence only intensified their union.

As their little one grew, creativity became a necessity. *What was it they said? Necessity was the mother of invention.* When they were both satisfied, Claire nestled her cheek against Tony's chest, and he broke their silence. Instead of listening to his words, she enjoyed the reverberation of his raspy voice while mindlessly contemplating his next invention.

A few moments later, Tony tilted Claire's face toward him, lifting her chin with one finger and repeated, "I believe I said, good morning, Mrs. Rawlings."

"Mm mm," she cooed. "It sure is, Mr. Rawlings."

Tony scooted up to the headboard with his arm around Claire's bare shoulder. His voice brimmed with excitement. "I found a nearby island. It isn't large, and it's uninhabited. I've been there a few times. Before I found you at the pool, I asked Madeline to pack us a lunch so that I could take you there."

Claire's satisfied smile faded, and her body stiffened. "I don't know."

"You need to get off this island for more than doctor's appointments."

"Why?" she asked. "I can order anything I want. Francis will pick it up and bring it here." She placed her nose near his neck and inhaled. "I got your cologne." Claire smiled as her lips touched the spot below his ear, and his famous growl filled her ears. "It's not like we can go visit friends. There's no reason to leave."

Stopping her kisses, he said, "I have one."

"Oh, you do? And what would that be?"

"I said so," he answered smugly.

Claire eased herself from bed and shook her head from side to side. "Sorry, sweetheart, that one doesn't work anymore." With the sheet wrapped around her curvaceous body, she stepped toward the bathroom and asked, "Would you like to join me for a cool shower?"

Perhaps it was because she had the sheet or maybe because it wasn't that great of a distance, but as he swiftly got out of their bed and gracefully moved toward her; Claire couldn't look away from his gorgeous body. Totally nude, he reached her in only a few steps. When Claire remembered to focus on his face, she found an expression she didn't expect.

Before it could register, he gripped her shoulders and stared down into her eyes. In his voice, Claire heard the determination and saw the darkness that she felt in his grasp. "I realize our options are limited; however, I won't allow you to be isolated or imprisoned—again—by anyone. For the record, that includes you."

"Tony, that's ridiculous. I'm not imprisoning myself. I'm comfortable and happy. There's a difference."

He exhaled, lifted her chin, and spoke slowly and deliberately. "I'd love to join you for that shower. I'd love to help you reapply your sunscreen, and"—his words were controlled, not loud or harsh—or open for debate—"I know you wouldn't want to disappoint Madeline...or me; therefore, after the shower, you and I are going to the small island that I found, and we're having lunch."

His thumb and finger continued to hold her chin captive. The forced tilt of her head wasn't necessary; Claire wouldn't look away even if she could. She knew his tone and saw his restraint. She also knew he was doing what he did—trying to control a world that was uncontrollable.

While she contemplated her response, he spoke. "Do you want to discuss this more?"

After a prolonged silence, her green eyes began to shimmer. She didn't speak, yet by the softening of his gaze, she knew he was listening. Finally, she said, "Fine, I won't discuss it, but if we're going out without Francis, I want to drive the boat."

Tony released her chin and their room filled with his laughter. Brushing his lips over hers, he replied, "Oh, my dear, over my dead body!"

Claire didn't know why she'd been so hesitant. The water was beautiful, glistening and sparkling in all directions. Every trip she'd taken had been to town. Tony's island was the opposite direction with all new sights. As they passed island after island, Claire wondered how anyone could possibly know which direction they were traveling or where they were.

Tony explained the instruments he'd only recently learned to read. They had a compass, a depth finder, and a virtual map with a grid and coordinates. They also had their cell phones and two-way radios to access help if necessary. When the islands came close together and the straight in between narrowed,

Tony showed Claire how the depth finder indicated the boat's proper position. Running into underwater rocks could be as detrimental as hitting one of the above water cliffs.

While they were still a ways away, Tony pointed toward the West. Claire followed his hand. The view took her breath away. The island he'd discovered was beautiful, the perfect south pacific deserted isle away from the numerous islands they'd just passed. It didn't take a depth finder to tell them that the water became shallower closer to their destination. The sea lightened with rings of turquoise as it surrounded the white sandy beach. Beyond the shore were palm trees and other lush plants. As they neared the island, colorful flowers dotted the terrain. When Tony finally anchored the boat off the shore, Claire was equally as excited to see this new land.

Hand in hand, they walked on the soft sand as Tony showed Claire all he'd already discovered. She loved the sound of his voice. Never could she have imagined Anthony Rawlings so excited about something like a hidden freshwater waterfall. Under the canopy of vegetation, they ate the meal Madeline prepared and listened to the soft breeze through the palm trees. Helping Claire down to the cool shaded sand, Tony insisted she rest.

With her head and back against his chest, she drifted between her reality and a dream world. It was during one of those states where Claire realized they were the same. For a short time, they had the dream. As she lingered between wake and sleep, the sweet aroma of flowers filled her senses and she tentatively opened her eyes. Orange, yellow, and red filled her vision. The most colorful bouquet of flowers she'd ever seen was right in front of her.

"Oh, Tony! They're beautiful!"

The lush shades of green and bright colored flowers didn't right Claire's world as much as the chocolate brown eyes smiling down at her.

"Not as beautiful as you."

"I'm glad you talked me into coming here. It's amazing."

He helped her to her feet and they walked toward the shore. The tide had come in making the beach narrower and the boat farther away.

"How long did I sleep?"

Tony shrugged. "I don't know. You've had so much trouble sleeping at night lately; I wanted to let you rest as long as you could."

"If we wait then the tide will go back out."

"And the sun will set. I don't want to try to get us back in the dark."

Claire smirked. "You could let me drive. I've had a nap."

"My dear, you could sleep for hours, and I'm not giving up the helm."

"So, are we swimming for it?"

Claire saw the wheels turning in Tony's head. He was working out the possible scenarios in his mind. To her, it was simple—they were both good swimmers.

When Claire began to remove her sundress and expose her bathing suit, Tony reached for her hand, stopping her movement. "No, I'll swim for the boat, and bring it back closer."

If she weren't pregnant, Claire would argue; however, she obviously was. Wrapping her arms around his waist, she lifted herself on her toes and kissed his lips. "Be careful."

Tony promised, as he shed his shirt, kissed her one last time, and waded into the sea. Claire watched nervously as he dove under the crystal water. It was then Madeline's words came back to her, reassuring her—darkness verses light. The sun was still bright. Scanning the panoramic scene, Claire was able to see under surface of the clear calm water. "It's safe," she said aloud, to no one in particular, as the familiar pounding in her temples and new tightening in her midsection screamed out their warning.

Lowering herself to the sand, Claire took deep breaths and searched the horizon for her husband. With each passing minute, his figure became smaller and smaller. It was then she realized, not only was the tide coming in, but the boat was drifting out. *Could the rising tide have lifted the anchor?*

The radios and their phones were on the boat. She got back to her feet. The boat was now on the edge of the turquoise circle. Beyond that ring, the waters deepened. Pacing a track in the sand, Claire spoke reassuringly to their child, "It'll be all right. Your father's a good swimmer. He can do this. He can save us."

Were her words meant to comfort the little life within her or to comfort her? Claire didn't know. She wanted to scream his name, call him back, have him beside her, but she knew he'd never hear her. She could yell until she was hoarse, but no one could hear her.

The sun sank lower, and Claire refused to move. Sometimes she'd imagine she saw the boat coming toward her, and then she'd blink and it would be gone. Her mind went all directions: *Would—could she survive? Would anyone find her? Was Tony still swimming? How long had it been?*

We have always held to the hope, the belief, the conviction
that there is a better life, a better world, beyond the horizon.

——Franklin D. Roosevelt

CHAPTER 33

Sophia waited inside the downtown Iowa City Restaurant, shivering inside her thick wool coat. Growing up on the East Coast, she wasn't unaccustomed to cold; however, there was something excessively bitter about the Iowa December wind. As she watched the snowflakes swirl through the air beyond the windows, she buried her hands deeper into the pockets of her coat. The gray skies weren't producing enough snow to cover the drab ground, just enough to exacerbate her spirits. Experience told her that December was only the beginning of the miserable cold. Iowa would get worse before it got better. *I wish we were back in California.* Even Sophia was surprised by the thought. She never would've imagined considering the West Coast home.

Straightening her neck, Sophia encouraged herself, *if I can have those thoughts about Santa Clara, maybe one day I'll be able to consider this home.* It was more wishful thinking, but she was trying. After all, things were going very well for Derek.

He loved his new job, even with the challenges Rawlings Industries faced. Each evening, when he'd return home to their new house, Sophia saw pride in her husband's eyes. She knew he was a hard worker, yet to be singled out by Anthony Rawlings—even under such strange circumstances—Derek considered it his noble duty to help this company stay afloat.

Timothy Benson took a personal interest in Derek. Sophia thought it was funny how Tim and Derek were so close in age, while many of the others she'd met at the Rawlings corporate headquarters were older, probably closer to Mr. Rawlings' age. Tim was forming his personal team of consultants, men and women with fresh ideas ready to take on the challenges of a struggling fortune 500, multibillion dollar conglomerate. He wanted people willing to face cameras, the press, and boards of directors—people who when confronted, would stand firm in the belief that Rawlings Industries *will* survive. It was likely that very soon, the SEC, Securities Exchange Commission, would be investigating Rawlings Industries. Many times, personal wrongdoings by high ranking business people translated to professional wrongdoing. Tim was determined that Rawlings Industries would make it through such an investigation. In the process, he declared that not only would every division be transparent, but without blemish. The founder and CEO may be missing, and there may be continued allegations regarding issues in his personal life; however, the company Anthony Rawlings started from nothing—was steadfast.

Claire Nichols' sister and brother-in-law continued to cause Rawlings Industries headaches. An entire division of the Rawlings' legal team, whom Derek explained *should* be concentrating on company matters, was fully devoted to Anthony Rawlings' personal legal issues. To date, they'd managed to stall production of Claire Nichols' memoirs, but Derek said they probably couldn't be delayed much longer. Apparently, it was a publication tactic from the Rawlings' team. Traditionally, books released near the holidays don't fare well in sales. Knowing they'd eventually lose the war, the legal division's plan was to continue the fight until a time when the release would be theoretically less successful.

In this instance, Sophia questioned their tactics. As an artist, she knew publicity was publicity. The additional exposure the memoirs received from the suits and counter suits would likely propel the book *My Life As It Didn't Appear* to number one in no time.

Thankfully, Iowa wasn't as backwards as Sophia had feared. The Quad Cities and the universities all helped to make it more than a large corn field thousands of miles away from the nearest coast. Sophia had met many of the people in Derek's new circles. Their wives were nice. Sophia especially liked Sue, Tim's wife; however, with one small child and one on the way, their priorities were considerably different. Sophia and Derek discussed children and the possibility was there. Right now, he needed to concentrate on work. Sophia knew that when she had a child, she wanted to do it for the right reason—being lonely in a new state—in her opinion—wasn't the right reason.

Deep down, Sophia knew that before she became a parent, she needed to work through some personal thoughts and feelings regarding her birth parents. Since the phone call back in California, Sophia hadn't heard from the woman claiming to be her mother—of course, she had told her not to call. Sometimes she'd wonder about the woman. *Was she still married to Sophia's father? Was she ever married to him? If they're not together, did she know where he was? What about siblings—did she have any?*

The Rossi's were always open about her adoption; it never bothered Sophia—until they were gone. While they were alive, they did everything to fill her life with all the love and support parents do. Perhaps, now that they're gone, it was a void Sophia subconsciously wanted filled; however, *how did she know if the woman from the phone call was capable of filling that void?*

Sophia wasn't completely without friends. She'd met an acquaintance—repeatedly—at different venues. Although admittedly, Marie was slightly eccentric, Sophia found her presence comforting. There was something familiar about the woman that Sophia couldn't pin-point. With time, when at gallery openings or invitation only showings, Sophia found herself scanning the crowd for the older woman's face. With so many changes, Marie seemed to be a reoccurring constant; therefore, when Marie invited Sophia to lunch at the *Atlas* on Iowa Ave, near the University of Iowa's campus, Sophia gladly accepted. She decided that it was nice to have someone to talk with—someone with similar interests.

"Can you believe how cold that wind is today?" Marie's voice pulled Sophia from her internal thoughts.

Smiling, Sophia shook her head. "No! I know we didn't live out in California for very long, but I miss the climate out there. I liked the more constant temperature."

Marie laughed. "Oh, my dear, this is just the beginning; wait until the snow really starts to fly."

After settling at a table, they chatted about nothing in particular. It was nice to forget the wind outside, the move to a new state, and just talk. Marie's gray eyes gave Sophia a sense of warmth she didn't understand. As an artist, she often dissected people's faces without realizing she was doing it. Sophia saw sadness and loss in Marie's eyes; however, there was also a spark of excitement that tugged at her like a magnet. When Marie would suggest a new exhibit or a museum, the ideas seemed extraordinarily inviting. In some ways, it was like a mirror at a circus. Marie's eyes reminded her of her own—yet they were different—complicated—multi-tasking. Sophia couldn't put her finger on it...nevertheless, she was drawn, like a moth to a flame.

"Did you enjoy your trip out East for Thanksgiving?"

Sophia nodded. "We did. It was short, but it was nice to see my in-laws."

"Since you visited your husband's parents for Thanksgiving, will you be traveling to your parents for Christmas?"

Sophia looked down. "No."

Reassuringly, Marie's hand covered Sophia's. "I'm sorry, did I say something upsetting?"

"It's all right. It's just that...my parents are no longer with us."

"Oh, my dear, I'm so very sorry. I won't pry."

Forcing a smile, Sophia sat straighter. "Really, it's all right. I've—had wonderful parents, but t—they've only recently passed away, late last summer. It was a car accident."

Marie shook her head. "I had no idea. I'm truly sorry."

"Oh, my in-laws have been wonderful. It just takes...time."

"Now, your husband—Derek—is that his name?"

Sophia nodded.

"Does he have siblings?"

Sophia went on to describe Derek's family—he's an only child—his parents were very anxious for them to add a branch or two to the family tree.

"How do you feel about that?" Marie asked.

Shrugging her shoulders, Sophia said, "We've been talking."

Marie grinned. "I'm sure you know—that's not how it happens."

Sophia's cheeks reddened. "Yes, I believe my mother gave me that talk, when I was quite young."

After lunch, they walked through some of the college shops before parting for the afternoon. Later, when Sophia told Derek about her day, she wouldn't remember the exact words of their conversation only that it flowed without effort.

With all Derek had happening with his new responsibilities, Sophia knew that he was pleased that she was getting out of the house and meeting people.

∞∞∞∞∞∞

As the sun set below the horizon, and the lingering shadows cast their last shades of what might have been onto the isolated beach, a hand fell to Claire's shoulder.

At first, she hesitated, unsure if the connection was real or imagined. When she could no longer decipher, Claire turned to see the face—the eyes— the man for whom she'd prayed.

Claire's resolve melted with his touch. The sobs she'd been suppressing erupted as Tony pulled her up to his embrace.

"I didn't think I'd ever see you..." her words were barely audible behind the bellowing cries.

"Shhhh..." If he hadn't been holding her, Claire wasn't sure she'd have been able to stand. As she nestled near, his bare chest quivered with exertion. After a moment, they settled on the soft, warm sand.

"Did you ever reach the boat? Or did you finally swim back?" Claire asked, realizing the boat wasn't in sight.

"It's anchored around the bend." He squeezed her tighter. "Believe me, I considered turning around, but I didn't know which way was shorter the longer I swam; then, as I came back, I couldn't tell which beach was which."

"How long did you swim?"

Tony shook his head as a tired grin emerged across his lips. "A lot longer than I'd planned."

She buried her head into his shoulder. "I kept praying and telling our baby you were safe, but..." the tears came back.

Smoothing her hair, he explained, "I contacted Francis. He knows where we are. He recommended we spend the night on the boat."

"On the boat?" Claire questioned.

"Yes, we don't want to be separated from it again, and there's a small bed in the cabin under the deck."

Claire nodded. She'd been *below* in the boat before—it was a calmer ride if the seas were rough.

"In the morning, when the sun comes up, I'll get you home—I promise."

She looked up to his tired eyes. "I don't care where I am, as long as you're there." She struggled to stand. "Let's go. You must be exhausted."

Taking what was left of Madeline's lunch time feast, they walked the shore around the bend. With the silver glow of moon light, Claire saw the boat only a short way out, bobbing silently in the virtually calm sea.

When they were both on board, Tony lifted the anchors and took them into slightly deeper water. "When the tide goes down, we don't want to be marooned," he explained.

Claire grinned. "I'm impressed. Who would have ever imagined Anthony Rawlings learning the ins and outs of marine navigation?"

Lowering the anchors once again, Tony purposely left slack in the rope. When he looked up and saw Claire's questioning emerald eyes, he added, "See, Francis so nicely mentioned—perhaps I didn't do that the first time." Somewhat sheepishly, he added, "He's right, I didn't."

She reached for Tony's cheek. "I've said it before, and I still believe it's true, you can teach—"

Tony interrupted, "My love, now that the adrenaline is gone, I definitely feel like that old dog. Let's go below and get some sleep before the sun rises."

If the cabin had been truly meant for sleeping—the designers didn't plan for it to be shared by a 6'6" man and a pregnant woman. Regardless, Claire and Tony worked their way into the small space. The rhythmic bobbing of the boat was surprisingly comforting as Claire maneuvered herself in an effort to become comfortable. Once they were settled, Tony said, "Do you know what this reminds me of?"

"Sardines?"

She heard his laugh in the dark cabin. "No, I was thinking of our trip to Europe—the yacht on the Mediterranean."

Her mind went back in time. It seemed like two other people in a different life. "I suppose if I pretend this four inch foam mattress is really a king sized bed and the ceiling is six feet above my head instead of two—"

Tony's lips found hers, stopping her words. "Yes, there are a few differences." Trailing the tips of his fingers along her shoulder and down her midsection as Claire lay on her side facing him, he continued, "Perhaps it's the rocking of the waves, or the sweet sound of your breathing in my ear; regardless, it reminds me of then."

"I suppose I can see a few similarities."

"One day—one day we'll go back, and the yacht we rent will have enough room for all of our children."

Fighting, once again, to relieve the pressure in her lower back, Claire replied, "Children? I'm pretty sure the ultrasounds have only shown one baby."

His voice fought the exhaustion to which his body had already surrendered. "Oh, but think how much fun it will be to create more..."

When his words turned to breathing, Claire kissed his cheek and whispered in his ear, "Good night, Tony."

He may have said it was her breathing that reminded him of the past, but it was his breathing that gave her hope for their future. Only hours earlier, the world turned gray—color was gone—now in the darkness of the boat's cabin, Claire remembered the colors of the flowers Tony had picked. She saw the blue of the sunlit ocean and the greens of the plants. It didn't matter that they weren't in their bed or their room, all that mattered was that he was safe—she was safe—and they were together.

Intuition will tell the thinking mind where to look next.

—Jonas Salk

CHAPTER 34

Harry conferred again with the Boston field office. Since their face-to-face meeting almost a month ago, Agent Baldwin was, again, fully assigned to the Sherman Nichols/Anthony Rawlings case; however, now it had the added dimension of Catherine Marie London Rawls. As much as Harry personally hated to admit that Rawlings' cooperation and confessions fit perfectly into the Harry's timeline, gaps still existed.

During his confessions, Rawlings recalled the death of his parents. He claimed an irrational commitment to his grandfather, as his reason for protecting Catherine London Rawls. His parents were gone; therefore, as a tribute to his grandfather, he did what he could do to save London from a life in prison. At the time, he believed his parents' deaths were the result of an *accident*—a discussion that became heated and grew out of control. He knew at the time, there was a history of bad blood between Catherine and his parents. After his father, Samuel, had successfully voided Nathaniel and Catherine's marriage, she'd been pushed to her limit. Rawlings tried to reach his parents first, hoping to utilize his stellar negotiation skills. He failed—not in the negotiation—in reaching his parents before Catherine.

Rawlings recounted personal knowledge of his grandfather's mission—to make the people responsible for his incarceration *and* their families pay. The first person on their list was *Sherman Nichols*; however, by the time Rawlings had the money to fulfill Nathaniel's vendetta, Sherman and his wife had already passed. The next person was *Jordon Nichols*—Sherman's son. According to Rawlings, there was a network of connections which when utilized, and well compensated, would provide any target with an untraceable deadly accident. He didn't know the details, didn't have time for them, but agreed to supply the money. Rawlings and Catherine discussed the plan ad nauseam. Rawlings willingly admitted a sense of obligation to fulfill his grandfather's agenda. As an entrepreneur and businessman, he would and could affect the lives of others; however, giving the order to take a life was significant—even for him. Rawlings claimed to have procrastinated with that order, making London wait—even though she protested.

According to his confession, Rawlings claimed there were other parts to the plan which he told Catherine needed to be confirmed before he'd authorize the Nichols' demise. One such task was securing the scholarship for Valparaiso University. Before Rawlings finally agreed to the deal, fate stepped in—the Nichols car crashed in a true *accident*.

The other family that was unknowingly involved in the vendetta was that of Jonathon Burke, the securities officer who helped build the FBI case on Nathaniel. During the span of time between Nathaniel's death and Rawlings ability to financially fulfill the vendetta, Burke also died of natural causes. The next in line was Allison Mason, Burke's only child. Certain that fate wouldn't be as kind as to help their cause again—Rawlings agreed to pay the money to ensure her demise—the *network* was utilized. Rawlings claimed that he didn't know the details of the impending accident until after it occurred. Both, Allison and her husband perished.

These were people completely off the FBI's radar. Upon further investigation, Harry learned the Mason's deaths had been officially ruled *accidental*—a tragic fall from a trail, while hiking in the Grand Teton National Park. If Rawlings hadn't admitted to knowledge of this incident, it would never have been found. Each year, about 150 people die in national parks. Most went under reported; some visitors slipped on wet trails or leaned too far over guard rails. Regardless of the incident, they made poor publicity for the nation's national parks and received little attention. Up until that moment, no one suspected that the death of Jonathon Burke's only daughter, Allison, and her husband were anything other than a true *accident*.

Soon, the FBI would contact their niece—their only surviving relative—and seek permission to exhume their graves. Tissue samples were needed to confirm the presence of actaea pachypoda.

The next people on Rawlings' and London's list were Emily and Claire Nichols. This was the next generation—children of children of children. Rawlings admitted to watching Claire off and on for years. He didn't know why he was obsessed—but he was. Although a fatal accident had always been the plan, Rawlings found it unacceptable. He told Catherine that there were some fates worse than death and created the perfect storm of events for what he assumed would be Claire's worse fate. It involved orchestrating circumstances in her life which would lead to Claire's need for money—his one expendable asset. He coordinated her disappearance, with the intent to allow Claire to *work-off* her family's debt while discrediting her credibility at the same time. When he was done, her arrest, humiliation, and incarceration would secure the payment of her debt and allow her to live. He didn't foresee emotions derailing his plan.

Reading Rawlings' account of his *acquisition* nauseated Harry. He couldn't help but compare it to hearing Claire's account—months earlier. The difference was the emotion. Claire recounted a private hell; Rawlings recited a well calculated plan.

Claire also answered FBI questions. Her accounts mirrored Rawlings; he'd confessed everything to her before the questioning. Never once did either one of them mention actaea pachypoda, or any connection to poison. Months ago, Harry petitioned for blood samples from Jordon Nichols and Simon Johnson. His requests finally came through. It took longer than he expected, which didn't matter. Since Claire and Rawlings were playing house somewhere in the South Pacific, time wasn't an issue. The results were irrefutable: Jordon Nichols' retained blood sample tested positive for actaea pachypoda—Simon Johnson's did not.

Interestingly, the transcripts of Rawlings' admissions, which Agent Jackson shared with Harry, also contained information on Simon Johnson. He wasn't associated with the Sherman Nichols' case, yet Rawlings included Johnson in his list of confessions. He stated Johnson's demise was simply a by-product of learning what was possible. Rawlings had learned it was possible to make people disappear. His first choice was by business. If that didn't work, then there was always *plan B*. Rawlings utilized the network he'd discovered years ago. This time, he willingly paid the money to have Simon's plane altered, forcing it to cease functioning in-flight. Rawlings knew Johnson was an accomplished pilot and said he wasn't sure if Johnson would be able to maneuver out of the situation; nonetheless, he paid to have a job done.

When the case began, Harry thought verification would give him peace. He was wrong. It was just as Amber had said, Rawlings was still out there, and Simon was still dead. There was something else; Harry's law enforcement gut wouldn't drop his suspicions. The evidence didn't match. The NTSB's report indisputably claimed Simon's plane was in top notch—inspection worthy— condition. No evidence of tampering was found during their investigation. *Why would Rawlings confess to a crime he didn't commit?*

And Jordon Nichols? Harry had more questions than answers. *Why would Rawlings admit to knowing about the plan, claim it was never fulfilled, yet have him poisoned? Could it be that Rawlings was trying to mislead Claire? But why plan an auto accident if poisoning were already on the agenda? Was Rawlings just that big on overkill—literally, or was there more?* The back alley attack and threat to Harry's family also bothered Harry. *Why would Rawlings want him off the case and threaten Harry's child, if he were planning on confessing everything?*

Of course there was still London. *Perhaps she was the one threatening Harry. Claire said she threatened her child. Did she want him off the case? How did she even know he was on the case?* All of the interaction with London alluded to her being blissfully unaware that she was under suspicion.

According to Marcus Evergreen, London was only cognizant of the case against Rawlings for the possible recent abduction of Claire Nichols.

The entire country was aware of such allegations. After all, John and Emily Vandersol were still pursuing that angle to anyone who'd listen.

∞∞∞∞∞∞∞

Claire rolled on the large bed, relishing the soft sheets against her skin. After their campout, in the cabin of the boat a few weeks ago, their bed was much more comfortable. Smiling, she reached for the man whose warmth filled her days and nights. Instead, her touch met cool satin. Lingering in her cocoon, she enjoyed the ceiling fan's gentle breeze as it moved the humid air around the grand bedroom. When she closed her eyes, the scent of his cologne permeated her senses. Beyond her haven, she heard the sounds of morning— birds singing their morning wake-up songs and the ever present surf.

Forcing herself from the heavenly bubble, she reached for her robe and walked toward the veranda. A veil of tropical vegetation filtered the sun's sultry penetration. Stepping around the fragrant flowers and large lush leaves, she took in the marvelous view. Even after over two months, it still took her breath away. Leaning against the folding wall, she relished the endless blue sky with wisps of white filling the space above the horizon. On most mornings, turquoise dominated. Sometimes, if the sun were just right, the waves sparkled florescent. Farther out, away from the shore and her paradise, the waters darkened. The blue became indigo, purple, or gray, often reminding her of the fog-covered mountains near Palo Alto.

Wearing a white bikini and white lace cover up, she made her way to the front lanai. As her bare feet padded across the smooth bamboo floor, Madeline's friendly rich voice brought her to present. "Madame el, may I bring you tea?"

Claire smiled, "Yes, Madeline, thank you, but please, no food...I'm not hungry."

"No, Madame el, you must eat. I'll bring you muffins and fresh fruit."

Claire shook her head—arguing would be pointless. She settled into the cushioned lounge chair, elevated her feet, turned on her iPad, and waited for the daily news to load. It wasn't the first story to appear on her homepage, but her own picture immediately caught Claire's attention. She clicked and read the title:

Family Files Charges against Iowa City Police Department, Prosecutor, and Anthony Rawlings.

Shaking her head, Claire read:

Associated Press—*John and Emily Vandersol have filed formal charges against the Iowa City Police Department, Marcus Evergreen, I.C. Prosecutor, and Anthony Rawlings(in absentia).*

Mr. and Mrs. Vandersol have requested a hearing based on evidence discovered at the home of Anthony Rawlings. The request states the evidence, currently undisclosed, is sufficient to establish probable cause against Anthony Rawlings. The Vandersols also charge Mr. Rawlings with extortion. "Anyone else would be sitting in jail. It's only because of his wealth and influence that ICPD and Mr. Evergreen have not filed charges. Their delay is corruption." (Another of the many charges listed). The Vandersols claim the prosecutor and police department worked together to protect Anthony Rawlings. In doing so, the ICPD jeopardized the investigation of Ms. Claire Nichols' disappearance. Mrs. Vandersol also charged Mr. Rawlings (in absentia) with the disappearance and possible death of her unborn niece or nephew.

Claire's hand rubbed her very large midsection. Now in her thirty-fifth week, she smiled, knowing that no harm had come to her unborn child. She honestly didn't believe that would be the case if she'd remained at Catherine's disposal. She continued reading:

Ms. Nichols was last seen September 4, 2013. Mr. Anthony Rawlings disappeared after his private plane made an emergency landing in the Appalachian Mountains, September 21, 2013. The FBI will not confirm or deny the survival of Mr. Rawlings following this incident. The FBI refused additional comments claiming an ongoing investigation. Currently, no charges have been filed.

Rawlings Industries is currently operating with a temporary CEO and the same Board of Directors. It has been speculated that the pending charges will force the SEC to investigate Rawlings Industries. Since September the share price has dropped from $142.37 to $86.84 at last call.

Despite her reading material, when Claire realized she'd eaten all of Madeline's food, a smile appeared on her face. Madeline's voice came above the sound of surf. "Madame el, may I get you more tea or perhaps some water?"

"Madeline, I'd love some water. It's getting hotter by the minute."

"Then perhaps you should be in the water?" Her husband's rich, husky voice came from behind. She couldn't see the handsome source, yet instantaneously her neck tensed and goose bumps appeared on her arms and legs. It amazed Claire how something as benign as a voice could continue to incite such a visceral response.

Madeline saw Claire's reaction and laughed, which in turn, made Claire giggle. Claire loved Madeline's laugh, so deep and rich, just like her voice. "Madame el, I will bring you some water, and Monsieur?"

"Madeline, I'd like some coffee, please." Tony bowed toward the woman.

Laughing at his gesture, Madeline replied, "Why, of course. I'll bring it out soon." With that, she disappeared, leaving the lady and gentleman of the house alone.

Tony reached for Claire's shoulders and gently massaged. Closing her eyes, she sighed momentarily lost in his touch. His lips unexpectedly met her exposed neck, causing goose bumps to erupt up and down her arms and legs. His baritone voice brought her back to reality. "My dear, your shoulders are tense. You saw it, didn't you?"

"Yes."

He nuzzled her neck. "I had hoped to make it home before you did."

"Because"—she paused—"you wanted to stop me from seeing it?"

Still massaging her shoulders, he leaned down and whispered in her ear, "No, I wanted to be here, while you read it."

Her shoulders relaxed. "I just wish John and Emily would back off—it's hurting Rawlings Industries."

"We'll be alright."

She inhaled. "I know. I understand their ignorance is best, but I can still wish for Iowa."

He came around in front of her, sat on the lounge chair near her tanned, shapely legs and caressed the silky skin of her thighs. "We'll get there again—I promise. First, we have a little one who needs to join us."

Claire reached for his hand. "It's getting closer every day." She placed his hand on her hard midsection.

"Why is it so hard?"

"I think it's one of those contractions, not the real ones—Braxton hicks. Remember Dr. Gilbert told us about them? They're happening with more regularity."

"Do they hurt?"

Claire loved the concern in his voice. "No. They just feel strange."

"How will you know when they're real?"

She shrugged. "From everything I've read—I'll know when they are real."

His lips engaged hers. It wasn't the fervent passion they were known to share. Instead, Claire felt reassured that Tony would be by her side as they welcomed their child into the world. He removed his shirt, revealing his tanned abs, swim trunks, and a mixture of dark and white chest hair. Finally, he found his voice. "Are you up for a swim?"

She smiled. "I just ate. Aren't I supposed to wait for a half an hour?"

"I promise to keep you from drowning."

His devilish grin captivated her once again, rendering her defenseless to his desires. With a smirk, she replied, "I think I should've learned a long time ago not to trust you."

He raised his eyebrows and cocked his head to the side. His tone held a hint of amusement as he leaned toward her. "I should've learned—I'm helpless to your beautiful emerald eyes." Her fingers threaded through the curls on his chest as her gaze lingered on his chocolate eyes.

In the pool, Claire held tightly to Tony's shoulders relishing the coolness of the water. Her thoughts went back to the article and her sister and brother-in-law. "I'm so sorry about John and Emily—I hate what they're doing to Rawlings Industries."

"I've been watching it too. It seems to me that Tim is doing an excellent job of building confidence in Rawlings Industries from within. He needs that inside support to get the support outside the company. I've always had a good feeling about him."

"I remember you telling me that, a million years ago, when we went to the Simmons' barbeque."

Tony laughed. "That was a million years ago, wasn't it?"

Laying her head against his shoulder, she nodded. "It sure seems like it. Is there any new information from Phil or Agent Jackson?"

"Well," he hesitated, causing Claire to look up. Although she couldn't see his eyes behind his sunglasses, from his secretive smile she knew he was up to something.

"What?"

"Phil said he's been released from his current job. He doesn't believe Sophia's in any danger. Catherine has worked very hard to introduce and include herself into Sophia's life."

"Then I'd say she's in danger." Claire added quickly, "but not enough for you to go protect her. I need you here."

"Yes, you do. You may be pleased to learn who else will be here; let's say for your Christmas present."

Closing her eyes, Claire sighed. "A little Claire or a little Tony would be the best present. I've loved most of this—it's just lately, I'm so tired and uncomfortable."

"We really do need to pin down some names. I'm not comfortable with either a little me or a little you"—He smirked—"You see, I really like the big you, and when I think of the name *Claire*, the feelings that ensue are totally inappropriate for my daughter."

"Big?"

Laughing—"You know what I mean. Now first—back to your Christmas present."

"Yes?"

"Well, it won't be the exact one. Phil can't exactly ask Catherine to go through our bedroom, but he did see your wedding band. After all, he's the one who bought it back and brought it to me."

Claire's voice perked up. "You're getting me a wedding band for Christmas?"

"More than that, Phil will be here in less than a week to deliver it. I thought you might enjoy company, and since he's the only one we can have, my choices were limited."

She wrapped her arms around his neck. "I love it! Thank you." Then she realized. "But wait, what can I get *you* for Christmas?"

Kissing her lips, he said, "I'm not picky. A girl—or a boy—would be fine."

"I'm not due until the second week of January. Will you take your gift late?"

"Only under one stipulation."

"So, now there are stipulations on gifts?"

"Yes, my dear, and before you start with that beautiful, smart mouth of yours, let me say that this one isn't debatable. I must insist upon it."

She shrugged. "Rather demanding, but I guess I'm used to it—what do you want?"

"That nothing happens to you while my gift arrives. I've read a few things too. I thought maybe if Phil were here, if we need anything, well, the man is very resourceful."

"I'll be fine"—she kissed his cheek—"but I love that you're concerned."

"My dear, *you* are my only concern."

Claire felt the tightening sensation once again. "Oh, I think someone else wants to be your concern too."

Truth, like gold, is to be obtained not by its growth,

but by washing away from it all that is not gold.

—Count Leo Tolstoy

CHAPTER 35

-SEPTEMBER 2016-

Septmore* ber 13, 2016

Last night, I was too shocked to write. I had to think about what happened, mull it over, and figure it out. By the time I got Claire back to the facility, she was no longer speaking. I don't understand. She was still hearing me; every now and then her eyes would register and lock onto mine. Then she'd look away.

I've decided she gave me a test. She knows that I know her story. Her recognition of her surroundings is new; it didn't exist last month, week, or even a day ago. If she isn't ready to share this revelation with others, I guess it isn't my place to divulge it. I just hate that I won't be around to help her move beyond this milestone.

I'm off to my last day. I've decided that I owe it to Claire to allow Emily to fire me. My husband reminded me last night that I've been in violation of their restraining order. I'd actually forgotten that—which is in a way comical. This whole exercise has morphed through so many phases—curiosity—investigative reporting—recognition of guilt—and finally, a deep agonizing friendship. No one will believe that I'd given up the reporting, to help Claire. At least, as I sit in jail, I'll know the truth.

∞∞∞∞∞∞

Claire paced the trek she'd created next to her bed. Since she'd found her voice last night, she was anxious to use it. Yes, she considered speaking to some of the other people, but she was afraid. There were so many things she couldn't recall, so many voids, and so many things that didn't make sense. It was painfully obvious; this *facility*—as Meredith called it—was a *mental* facility. She had recollections of discussions about that. Each day, more memories surfaced. Some were clearer than others. She remembered Tony telling her that the offer of a mental facility was to protect her. *Was that why she was here? Was she being protected?*

That's why she needed to talk with Meredith. Claire's speed increased as she walked exactly six steps one way, turned, and stepped six paces the other way. She didn't mean to count, but behind her thoughts, concerns, questions, she heard the numbers: *one, two, three, four, five, six—turn—one, two...*

There wasn't a clock in the drab room. As she truly looked around—there was nothing. No pictures, no personal items, nothing that gave the room her personality. Claire wondered how long she'd been there...*two, three, four, five, six—turn...The only indication of time was the gray in her hair, and what did that tell her?...five, six—turn—one...*

Claire heard the door open. She wanted to look, but what if it wasn't Meredith, she wasn't prepared to speak with anyone else.

"Hi, Claire, it's me, Meredith."

She wanted to turn, but she was only on *two*. Claire waited until it was time to turn. That was a better time to break the cycle; however, by the time the voice behind her thoughts said *turn*, Meredith was talking again, "...when I got here. They told me you were all right after our late night. I think that was their way of reminding me not to do that again. They also said there'd been no changes with you."

Claire turned toward Meredith's voice. She wanted to look up and see her friend's eyes. No, she didn't want to see Meredith's eyes—she wanted to see Tony's. As she forced her glance toward Meredith's face, she saw dark blue irises. Her knees weakened. It wasn't the dark brown she sought, *but it was color!* For so long, there'd been no color. Inhaling deeply, she smelled the food that Meredith had placed on the table. If she ate it fast, they could go outside. If they went outside, she could ask her questions. It was too risky talking in here.

"Why, Claire, why haven't they noticed any changes?"

She didn't answer; instead, she walked to the table, uncovered the dish, found her silverware and began eating. Each bite she took faster and faster.

"Slow down; I can't have you choking on my watch. I'm already on probation for our late night escapades."

It wasn't funny. Claire knew she was supposed to be concerned about appearances. Following rules and behaving was essential for appearances; however, listening to Meredith talk about breaking rules made her smile. It was either that, or the blue in her eyes. All the people around the *facility* wore white scrubs. Well, except for Emily, the doctors, and therapists. Suddenly, more than food, Claire wanted *color. Wasn't that an odd request? Maybe that was what being crazy was all about, seeing things differently and wanting things that others didn't realize were gone.*

When her plate was clean, Claire stood and went to the closet for her jacket. The voice that had been counting told her to look down. She knew to obey; disobeying could have negative consequences; *but hadn't Meredith just been talking about breaking rules?* Shyly, Claire lifted her eyes. There was Meredith watching her. Before she could stop it, her lips morphed into a smile—the rush was intoxicating. The voice would be mad; however, if Tony wasn't going to visit anymore—Claire wanted to talk with her friend.

∞∞∞∞∞∞

Meredith asked, "Do you want to walk by yourself?" The panic in Claire's eyes was enough of an answer. Meredith gently tucked Claire's hand into the crook of her arm and led her toward the outside. As she did, she spoke calmly about the weather and the changing leaves. The entire trip down the corridor, through the multiple doors, along the perimeter of the cafeteria, Claire kept her eyes downcast and walked in step.

Dr. Fairfield had instructed the staff to be less accommodating, to wait and see if Claire would recognize her needs, and then ask to have them fulfilled. In Claire's excitement to go outdoors, Meredith noticed she'd forgotten the sunglasses—that was all right, Meredith had remembered. As they walked toward the outside doors, Meredith wondered if she should've waited for Claire to *ask* to go outside; however, it seemed that when Claire got her own jacket, it was more of a request than she'd previously made. Dr. Fairfield may not agree, but to Meredith it was enough of a request to propel Meredith to walk the ends of the earth—if Claire so desired.

When they stepped into the courtyard, Claire lifted her face and momentarily basked in the sunshine. At that moment, she opened her eyes and immediately closed them. Turning her face toward Meredith, Claire's eyes made the unspoken request. The friend in her wanted to reach in her pocket and hand her the glasses; instead, she contemplated this being her last chance to help Claire and placed her hand over Claire's and walked forward. When Claire's steps stopped, Meredith asked, "What's the matter? I thought you wanted to go for a walk."

∞∞∞∞∞∞

Claire kept her eyes half open and half shut—that action should've been enough to tell Meredith what she needed; however, instead of helping, Meredith continued walking. When Claire didn't move, Meredith said, "If there's something you need, just ask."

Oh, Claire had heard that before—she knew this routine. She also reasoned, if Meredith was using Tony's words, it couldn't be against Tony's rules to ask. Nearing her friend's ear, she whispered, "Sunglasses."

Claire then remembered Tony's requirements from a long time ago. He'd never acquiesce to one word. If Claire wanted something she needed to ask—in the form of a request. Just now, she hadn't asked. Looking from side to side, being sure no one was listening, she cleared her throat and proceeded, "Did you bring them?"—"Can"—"I"—"please"—"wear them?" Her words didn't truly form a sentence, more phrases glued together with silence.

Meredith didn't answer. She reached into the pocket of her white scrubs and removed the sunglasses. Once again, Claire let her smile shine and reached for the glasses. Although Meredith didn't require it, after they'd walked a short distance, Claire said, "Thank you."

It was the most she'd said—or wanted to say—since before she could remember. By the time they reached the far side of the courtyard, Claire was ready to ask the question she knew would take away her happiness.

Although the sun was bright, the breeze blew with cooler gusts than the day before. It didn't bother Claire. She actually appreciated it. The colder weather kept others from going outside; they were alone in this remote area of the grounds. Looking down, Claire summoned the little bit of strength she'd acquired throughout the day. She'd silently practiced her question a hundred different ways. In her mind, it started with an eloquent preamble. Now that the opportunity was present, she blurted the words she could no longer contain, "Is Nichol—dead?"

Before Meredith could respond, the counting voice came back loud and clear. Claire had to obey; it was the only way to make it quiet.

∞∞∞∞∞∞

Meredith momentarily stared. *Why would Claire think Nichol was dead?* Her heart broke. *Hadn't Emily told her anything?*

The focused, smiling woman evaporated before her eyes. Claire began pacing, her eyes seeing something no one else could. Meredith reached for her arm. This time, she didn't back down when the determined expression turned toward her, she answered Claire's question, "No! Claire, your daughter's alive! She's beautiful and healthy."

∞∞∞∞∞∞

Claire collapsed into Meredith's embrace. Burying her face into Meredith's lapel, she willingly accepted her friend's comfort. Trying to quiet the counting, Claire concentrated on Meredith's words. Slowly, they morphed from words to a murmur and back to words. Yes, she'd missed some of what Meredith had said, but now she was listening, "...brown hair and beautiful brown eyes. Emily and John have been taking care of her. Claire you should be so proud."

Timidly, she faced the reality of her insanity. If that wasn't an oxymoron she didn't know what was. Wiping her eyes on the tissue Meredith offered,

Claire asked, "How old? I can't remember"—"how long I've been here"—fighting the tears she added—"I just don't know"—"It's blurry."

Holding Claire's hands, Meredith answered, "She'll be three in December." With a look of concern, she added, "This is September."

It was as if the wind had been knocked from Claire's chest. *Two years!* She'd missed two years of her daughter's life. Her knees buckled, and Claire sunk to the ground. This time, Meredith didn't instruct her to rise. No, she too moved to the cold, hard earth and sat knee to knee.

"I can't imagine what you're thinking. I've only seen her a few times. Emily and John seem to be doing a great job. They've also worked very hard to keep her out of the public eye." Claire feigned a smile as tears coated her cheeks, and she nodded. Meredith continued, "They've done a very good job taking care of you, too."

"Why hasn't"—"anyone mentioned her"—"or To—" Claire couldn't make herself say his name aloud.

"We aren't allowed to say anything about your previous life, which includes names."

"Who's rules?"—"The doctors'?"

"They thought that they were helping you."

Claire sat quietly and thought pensively about her family. That family was now with her sister and brother-in-law. She wouldn't ask about Tony. She couldn't bear to hear the truth of what she'd done. Why else would they lock her up in this place? "Thank you"—"For being honest"—"with me."

Smiling, Meredith answered, "Thank you for talking to me. I'm not sorry that I've broken their rules, if it's helped you."

Claire nodded. "I want to be better—I'm not sure what's real and what's not." She looked back toward the ground. It hadn't rained in some time, and below the blades of grass the earth was cracked. "If I tell you something"—"You'll think I'm crazy"—Claire giggled—"But then, I am"—"aren't I?"

Meredith squeezed Claire's hand, "Sometimes I wonder who's really sane. What do you want to tell me?"

"Up until a short time ago"—"he'd come visit me."

∞∞∞∞∞∞∞

Meredith didn't know what to say. She knew that was impossible—Claire must have imagined his visits. Meredith also believed this confession would be better shared with a doctor or a therapist. Perhaps her departure would be beneficial and force Claire to talk to the appropriate people. Meredith didn't comment. Instead, she nodded.

Claire continued, "He didn't come to *that* room"—"We'd be in other places"—Her voice momentarily hardened—"I don't like that room"—"No color!"

Meredith smiled, "I agree. Why don't you tell Emily you want color?"

Although her eyes were covered with the sunglasses, whose need with the setting of the sun had diminished by each minute, they became terrified at the mention of *telling Emily*.

Meredith soothed, "You don't have to talk to anyone you don't want to. I won't say anything. You decide when you're ready to talk to the others. I know when you do, they'll be thrilled."

Claire's breathing calmed. "Maybe just you, right now?"—"You're the only one who says *his* name."

"What can I say, I'm a bad influence. I've never been good at following rules."

Claire turned away, her voice was only a whisper, "I've been too good."

That night, Meredith returned Claire to her room before the alarms sounded and the reinforcements came. She debated telling Claire about her impending meeting. Her good sense told her to stay quiet; the poor woman had dealt with enough, but as she was about to say good night, Meredith worried what Claire would think that when she didn't return, it was because she didn't want to, and since there was a chance that tomorrow morning, she'd be escorted from Everwood in police custody. Meredith couldn't allow Claire to think she'd abandoned her.

Looking around the colorless room, Meredith made a promise to herself—if—by some miracle—she made it through tomorrow, she'd buy Claire pictures, drapes, and a bedspread with color.

"Claire, what's your favorite color?"

Claire hadn't spoken since they returned to the facility. Meredith wasn't sure why, but it seemed that Claire wasn't as comfortable speaking within the walls of Everwood, as she had been out on the grounds. Meredith watched as Claire walked into the bathroom and reached for her toothbrush. Returning, she handed it to Meredith and smiled a sly smile—the handle was pink. Understanding her unspoken word, Meredith nodded and asked, "Can you please put this back?"

When Claire was within the bathroom, Meredith followed close behind. To reassure her friend, Meredith spoke in more of a whisper, "I don't think your room is monitored. If it were, I think I'd already be in trouble for discussing Tony." Claire's change of expression made Meredith reconsider, finally, she pressed on, "Please let me talk—I don't have much time. They'll wonder where I am."

Claire nodded.

"Tomorrow, I have a meeting with your lead doctor and your sister and brother-in-law."

Claire's eyes widened.

"Don't worry, I won't tell them what you've accomplished. Remember, I told you Emily has done a great job keeping you and Nichol out of the public eye?"

Claire very slightly nodded.

Meredith hurried on, "I know you remember that I'm a reporter." Quickly she added, "I'm not here to do a story. I'm here because I want to help you; but Emily doesn't know that I'm here. I may have lied about a few things to get this job. When Emily and John find out I've been with you for the last few months—"

Claire's eyes widened again.

Meredith seized her hand. "Yes, Claire, it's been *months*. When they learn who I am, and that I lied—I won't be allowed back to see you."

Claire's new expression of terror broke Meredith's heart.

Meredith continued, her words still forming rapidly, "I'm so sorry. Please keep working, and be honest with your family. They love you."

Claire's voice was barely audible as she asked, "When?"—"when's your meeting?"

"Early tomorrow morning." Shrugging her shoulders, Meredith added, "By the time you finish your breakfast, I might be in police custody." Standing tall, she continued, "I'm only telling you so you know that I didn't abandon you. No matter where I am—I'm thinking about you." Placing her hands on her friend's shoulders, she added, "Claire, I know you'll continue to get better and soon you'll be with Nichol."

Before she gave into the emotions demanding her recognition, Meredith turned away. In her most even voice, she called, "Good night, Claire. Please know that I have faith in you."

The tears didn't begin until she was safely down the hall from Claire's room.

Life consists not in holding good cards
but in playing those you hold well.

—Josh Billings

CHAPTER 36

Sea foam green walls with pink, blue, and yellow puffy wall-hangings adorned the small nursery attached to their bedroom. Compared to the nursery they planned back at the estate in Iowa, it was quite small; nonetheless, it was ready for their arrival. The cradle, baby crib, changing table, and rocking chair were all handmade by local craftsmen, giving the nursery a bit of island flare. The linens and colorful wall decorations, as well as most of the clothes, diapers, and necessities were ordered from around the world. Without a doubt, it was a room fit for a little prince or princess.

When their baby decided to play shy and not reveal its sex, Tony and Claire made the decision to wait. Not knowing if they were having a boy or girl added to their anticipation and daily discussions. Sometimes they'd talk about the advantages of a daughter and then later proclaim the advantages of a son. It was entertaining to listen as Tony considered the possibilities of a little girl, one who would grow into a young lady. Claire pitied the young man who one day would show up at their door to take their daughter on a date. Without a doubt, both Claire and Tony knew how men could behave. If memories of his treatment of Claire upset Tony, the idea that someone could do that to his child was beyond his comprehension. Without a doubt, impending fatherhood had changed his perspective. That time of their life—their past—was something Claire didn't want to discuss or remember. Unfortunately, it was the topic of discussion all over the world—despite the best efforts of Rawlings attorneys—Meredith's book had been recently published and was selling like crazy.

Claiming sole access to Claire's firsthand account, the publisher used Tony and Claire's current disappearance to its advantage. Since its release, *My Life As It Didn't Appear* had found permanent residence on both the *New York Times* and *USA Today* bestseller lists. Almost daily, Claire regretted her decision to go public with their past. One day she'd need to explain to their child how she and his father met. She only prayed it wouldn't be until after their child was much older.

Another subject they rarely discussed was Tony's deal with the FBI. With her due date rapidly approaching, Claire upset easily. Sometimes she'd snap, more often than not, she'd cry. No matter her reaction, Claire didn't want to consider the possibility of Tony's incarceration. She admired his strength and resolve and knew that facing his demons wasn't easy for him. On the nights when she'd awaken and he'd be gone, she knew he was wrestling unknown emotion he'd never before faced. Some nights, he sat on the lanai or walked the beach alone. At first, during these times, Claire tried to approach him. Though he never fully explained his state of mind, she believed it was more his inability to verbalize his new rush of feelings, than his unwillingness to share. His confessions were not only earth shattering to her, but in some ways—to him. He'd distanced himself so much from the human aspect of what transpired, that facing it was difficult; nevertheless, when she woke to an empty bed, Claire believed Tony was working through another situation that only he could fully comprehend. She willingly gave him his space.

Without a doubt—despite everything—Claire didn't want to be without Tony, even for a short time. Her mind knew of his sins, but her heart had their future safe and secure. In her imagination, they'd live peacefully on the island for another year while the FBI built an iron clad case against Catherine. When they returned to the states, Tony's testimony and honesty would earn him complete absolution. With his name clear, they'd move back to Iowa and live *happily ever after*. She imagined picnics at her lake, with her on a blanket while the gentle breeze rustled the leaves and Tony taught their son to fish. Claire knew it was a fantasy; but on many occasions it sustained her.

The softness of the baby blanket caressed her fingers as she gently rocked and contemplated their future. Claire truly had no idea what it would be like to be a mother. *Could she do it?* She didn't know. She knew she didn't want to do it alone. In the past, when her life took unforeseen turns, Claire had survived by concentrating on herself and her responses. Now everything was different. Life was about more than her—and more than Tony—it was about their child. As much as she longed for the perfect family, the uncertainty of their future loomed omnipresent. It was like a fog unexpectedly seeping into their daily lives, rolling in from the sea and filling the corners of a room. Perhaps that was why Claire loved sunshine; it dissipated the fog and made everything clear.

"Blaine." Tony's baritone voice permeated the haze and brought sunlight to the small nursery.

Claire freed her hands from the white baby blanket and smiled at her husband's bright grin. "What?" she asked.

"I was looking at names online and found the name Blaine—I like it!"

"For a boy or a girl?"

Tony cocked his head to the side. "Can it be both?"

"I think, but I like it for a boy," Claire murmured. "Blaine Rawlings...Yes, I like that, but I thought you wanted a name that could be shortened?"

"I did, but I think it sounds regal. We could call him B or something for short."

"What about Anthony for a middle name?"

Stifling a chuckle, Tony replied, "His initials would be BAR—I don't think so."

"It would be appropriate if he became a lawyer."

"Or a drunk—yes, to Blaine—no, to Anthony."

"Anton?"

Tony pressed his lips together and shook his head.

Claire shrugged. "Well, at least we're closer."

Tony knelt beside the rocking chair. "Francis made arrangements. After next week's appointment with Dr. Gilbert, we're staying in town."

"I'd rather be here."

"I'd rather have you there, closer to the doctor. As soon as you and our little one are declared healthy, we'll come back."

Claire knew from experience, some arguments would never be won. If Tony's mind were set, rarely did she have a chance at changing it. "I should pack a few things."

"Madeline has already packed a bag for us and for the baby—I mean, Blaine or...?

Claire grinned. "Alyssa?"

"Raquel?"

From a distance, the hum of an airplane infiltrated their consciousness. They both stilled and waited for it to pass. Soon, it became a roar, indicating its increased proximity to their island. Claire's eyes widened. "Oh, do you think it's Phil?"

Standing straight, Tony replied, "It better be."

They made their way to the lanai, joined shortly by Madeline and Francis. When the small propeller plane came to a soft landing on the lagoon, Tony said, "I'll go down to the beach."

Claire's days of excursions were done. Even walking to and from the beach was a struggle. In addition to her increased size, she'd lately been plagued by intermittent lower back pain.

Francis offered, "Monsieur, I'll go with you."

Tony nodded. The men disappeared into the vegetation as they walked the path toward the sea. Madeline commented, "Madame el, you should sit down."

"Not yet. I want to see who gets out of that plane. I want to be sure it's Phil."

"Of course, who else would it be?"

That's what worried Claire. *Supposedly, they were hidden, but would it truly be that difficult for the FBI to find them?* As she and Madeline watched, the door to the plane opened. At the sight of white hair, Claire exhaled.

"Now, Madame el, you can sit. The men will be up shortly."

"I'll sit. Can you please get us all iced tea?"

"Oui, be sure you put your feet up."

It seemed as though Claire never lacked for people willing to tell her what to do. By the time she settled on the lounge chair, the men's voices floated into range. Closing her eyes, she felt her smile grow. She couldn't believe how excited she was to see Phil again. Although he'd only been gone from the island for two months, it seemed much longer; then, without warning, the voices faded as the plane's roar momentarily drowned out all sound. Claire looked up in time to see the small white plane leave the lagoon.

When the three men stepped onto the lanai, Claire awkwardly stood. She couldn't hide her happiness as she wrapped her arms around Phil with a welcoming embrace. "It's so good to see you." Tears glistened as her green eyes shone with sincerity. "Thank you for coming all the way back here."

He leaned back and took in Claire's appearance. "My, Mrs. Alexander, it appears as though you're about to have a baby!"

"Really?" she said, putting pressure in the small of her back and arching her shoulders, "I hadn't noticed. I thought I was just enjoying Madeline's good cooking—a little too much."

Tony laughed. Lowering his voice, he leaned toward Phil. "Be careful, someone—who shall remain nameless—has been increasingly sensitive lately."

Claire eyed her husband. "After you carry around an extra twenty-five pounds in one hundred degree heat for months, then we'll discuss *being sensitive.*"

The men smiled knowingly at one another.

"Fine," Claire said with a feigned pout as she sat back down.

"Monsieur Roach?" Francis interrupted. "Would you like me to show you to your room?"

"Thank you, Francis, but if it's the same one, I know the way." Turning to Tony and Claire, he added, "If you don't mind, I'd like to get cleaned up after that long flight."

Forgetting her *sensitivity*, Claire grinned. "Please make yourself at home. We're so glad you're here." Phil excused himself while Madeline and Francis disappeared into the house. For a brief time, the newlyweds were alone.

Exhaling, Claire lifted her face toward the sea and closed her eyes. Renegade strands of hair stuck to her moist warm skin. She pried the wayward tendrils from her neck and relished the growing, refreshing breeze. When she opened her eyes, the softest hues of chocolate brown filled her vision. Surprised by Tony's closeness, Claire lifted her chin causing their noses to touch, and with a giggle she asked, "What?"

"Don't let Phil fool you; you're beautiful."

She pursed her lips together and reached for his cheek. The slight stubble tickled her fingertips. "I'm glad you think so"—It was then she noticed his position—"Why don't you bring that other chair over here? Why are you on the ground?"

"Because, Mrs. Rawlings, I wanted to be on one knee when I gave this to you." From his pocket, Tony produced a platinum band embedded with diamonds. It was nearly identical to her original ring.

"Oh, Tony! It's beautiful. It looks just like my first one."

"Hopefully, one day, we can get back to Iowa, and you can have both of them."

Her eyes twinkled. "Do you know today's date?"

She watched as recognition overtook her husband's expression. "I hadn't realized," Tony replied. "I'd say Roach's arrival couldn't have been better timed!" He leaned forward and kissed her gently. "Happy *third* anniversary, my love. I seem to acquire more and more regrets, but without a doubt, the fact that we aren't still in our first marriage is one of my greatest."

She framed his face with her petite hands. Before looking into his eyes, she took a moment and admired the sparkling band above her engagement ring. "It's beautiful and somehow—believe it or not—I think this is better. We can have both"—she tried to explain—"Those people—the ones we were when we married three years ago were in a very different place than we are today."

His devilish grin emerged. "I'd say they're about half a world away."

Kissing his lips, she replied, "Literally and figuratively."

Their journey wasn't complete. If their relationship had been a poker tournament, unquestionably, they'd not been dealt the best cards. When faced with the same odds, as Tony and Claire, many players would have folded and walked away. They hadn't—they'd continued to play. In the process they'd grown and changed. At one time, they were opponents, strategizing against one another, now they were teammates, yet their tournament wasn't over. It was too early to declare the winner. They both knew there were more cards to be revealed.

When Phil joined them for dinner, he looked much more relaxed, and told Tony and Claire all about Catherine and her quest to learn more and more about Sophia. "She seems different than when she hired me to send you the packages."

It amazed Claire how casual he was with both her and Tony about what he'd done. Maybe it was true, honesty made even the most absurd circumstances less bizarre.

Phil continued, "I took a few pictures of her with Sophia. Ms. London looks different to me, don't you agree?"

He showed his phone to Tony first. Claire's husband's countenance changed before her eyes. His posture straightened and the veins in his neck became visible. When he continued to stare without speaking, Claire asked, "May I see?"

Phil moved the phone to her line of vision. The golden flecks in Phil's green eyes danced as he murmured something about once seeing a picture on Claire's phone. Her mind immediately went to San Antonio. Thankfully, Tony was too lost in his own thoughts to process what they were saying. She reached out and covered Tony's hand with her own. The diamonds embedded within the bands of her wedding and engagement ring sparkled behind the beacon of the engagement solitaire.

"She does look different," Claire confirmed. "Her hair is shorter and darker, but there's something else—I can't put my finger on it."

"Confidence," Tony replied, his tone restrained. "She looks like she did when my grandfather was alive. I'd say she feels very confident in her future. I'm sure she thinks that I'm hiding out somewhere, and she's safe to sit back and enjoy spending my money."

"Can she do that?" Claire's voice raised an octave.

Phil was the one to answer. "The way Mr. Rawlings' estate is set, Ms. London has access to a very nice trust fund designed to help her manage the estate; however, the provisions are rather non-restrictive. How she chooses to spend the money won't be questioned."

Tony looked skeptically toward Phil. "Did she share this with you?"

"No. I could only spend so much time looking at art. I spent a great deal of time researching different trails—that was one. Your grandfather was another."

Tony nodded as his dark eyes questioned.

Still holding Phil's phone, Claire asked, "Have I met Sophia? She looks very familiar."

"Not to my knowledge," Tony answered. "But then again, you did live close to one another in California."

Claire shrugged and gave Phil back his phone. "I hope she's safe. I no longer trust Catherine—even with her own daughter."

Everyone looked up to the blue sky as a rumble of thunder echoed in the distance. Phil commented, "That's why the pilot rushed to leave the island so fast. The weather predictions had quite a storm coming through this area tonight or tomorrow."

"Typhoon season was officially over the end of October," Claire said, remembering some of her meteorology education.

"Over or not, I saw the weather models and paid extra to get here before the storm hit." Phil grinned. "Okay, *you* paid extra. My other option was to wait until it passed. They told me it could be a one to three day delay—depending on the severity of the storm."

"Most of the weather systems never make it here," Tony offered. "We hear the rumble; however, all we usually get is a steady rain, often in the night, then nothing."

"That sounds encouraging," Phil answered. "I hope you're right. From what little I know about weather, the models looked intense."

Claire sat straighter. "I've read about barometric pressure affecting delivery. I know I'm early, but that would be fine with me."

Tony's eyes screamed alarm, nonetheless his voice remained calm. "Yes, once we're near the doctor—that would be great—not before."

Fighting the resurgence of pain in her lower back, Claire feigned a smile. "There are still a few things you can't control." She stood and reached for his hand. "And, I love that you think you can." Her grip tightened.

∞∞∞∞∞∞

Tony looked up to Claire's expression. He recognized the clouds of pain settling behind her emerald eyes. He'd seen them before, but he didn't want to see them again. Unconsciously, his concern for the child lessened proportionally to his increased worry for his wife. "Claire, it's still early in the day. The sun won't set for hours; let's go into town."

She shook her head from side to side. "I think I just need to lie down for a little bit, dinner isn't sitting too well." Turning toward Phil, she managed, "I'm sorry that I'm not being more hospitable. It seems that eating is more uncomfortable than it is satisfying."

"Let me help you—" Tony interjected, as he began to stand.

Claire stopped him. "Don't be silly. You two talk about whatever Phil's learned about Nathaniel. I need a nap, and by later tonight, I'll be fine. Then you two can fill me in."

Tony's eyes narrowed. "I'll be down to check on you soon."

She released his hand and brushed his shoulder. "All right."

Tony watched as she disappeared through the archway toward the hall. The anticipated delivery was wearing on him as much as it was her. Placing his elbows on the table, he lowered his head to his hands, and ran his fingers through his hair.

He wanted to put Claire on a plane and fly her back to the United States. He wanted the satisfaction of knowing she had the best medical care possible. *He was a fuck'n billionaire! His wife shouldn't be giving birth in the middle of nowhere.* Tony knew he'd put Claire in harm's way in the past—both intentionally and unintentionally—now he'd do anything to keep her safe.

Roach's worried voice caused Tony to look up. "Francis and I can go for the doctor?"

There was a time when having another man so obviously care for his wife would've upset Tony; however, looking across the table, he knew it was right.

269

Tony felt no more threatened by Phillip Roach than he would have by Eric or Brent. He actually welcomed the common bond. Roach was their *ace in the hole*. Tony didn't like admitting that he needed help, and he probably never would verbally; however, having Roach present to go for help or be their eyes and ears back in the states was reassuring.

Tony replied, "Let's give her some time. She goes from one hundred miles an hour to zero a lot lately. One minute, she's going through baby clothes, folding and refolding. The next, she's in the kitchen helping Madeline; then next, she's asleep. I'll check on her soon. If she's still having these pains—I think it'd be a good idea." Looking down at his hands, Tony softly mumbled, "Thank you."

Phil nodded. "In the meantime, do you want to know what I've learned about drug interactions?"

"I have the feeling I do, but mostly, I'm thinking I don't give a damn."

Phil leaned back in his chair, inhaled and exhaled. "You will, I promise."

Crossing his arms over his chest, Tony replied, "Okay, my man, care to enlighten me?"

We all have time machines. Some take us back,

they're called memories. Others take us forward, they're called dreams.

—Unknown

CHAPTER 37

Claire made it to their suite before the nausea hit with a vengeance. Stumbling into the bathroom, she fell to her knees and her trembling hands held her head over the toilet. It was the first time since morning sickness that she'd vomited. Perspiration drenched her skin as she her meal projected into the water below. When she was done, Claire laid her head on her arms and waited. As if awoken by her violent lurches, her temples throbbed and her midsection contracted. Gaining strength, she made her way back out into the bedroom. If she lay down, Claire believed the discomfort would stop. After strategically placing the pillows of the bed around her, she hugged another. The fetal position seemed ironic, yet with another pillow between her legs, it was the only position that gave her solace.

The curtains billowed as a refreshing breeze moved the previously still air about their suite. Claire relished the coolness on her clammy skin and concentrated on her breathing. Officially, she was just a little past thirty-six weeks into her pregnancy. Everything she read said thirty-eight to forty weeks were considered full term. Although she was ready for the pregnancy to be done, Claire didn't want their baby born too early. Unexpectantly, she flinched as thunder rattled the windows. She looked around the suite bathed in the early evening light and listened to the low howl of the growing wind. Suddenly, the room filled with a flash of light.

As she inhaled and exhaled, Claire counted. It was a trick her grandmother taught her as a child. When she saw the lightening, she'd count until she heard the thunder. Grandma said the number between events was the distance in miles from where the lightning struck. Claire knew from meteorology it wasn't accurate; nevertheless, it was a ritual that gave her comfort. Although her head still ached, her midsection had relaxed. Lost in her thoughts, she didn't hear the knock on her door until it was repeated.

She answered, "Come in."

Claire saw the concern in Madeline's eyes. "Madame el, you are in pain?"

"No," she lied and did her best to smile. "I'm having trouble eating. I'm hungry, but I fill too fast, and then I'm uncomfortable." As she spoke, her back suddenly tightened, sending a jolt of pain down her right leg. She didn't mean to wince, but she did.

Madeline sat on the edge of the bed and waited. When Claire's expression softened, Madeline gently took her hand. "Madame el, you are warm. Please tell me about your pain."

Salty tears stung Claire's eyes. "It's in my back. It's been getting worse all day."

"It could be infection. I remember it happens often in late pregnancy. Perhaps Francis could take you to the doctor. If you go now, there'll be enough light. I worry about the storm. They say it is big."

Claire closed her eyes and waited. Another jab tightened her back, stronger than the one before. When she opened them again, she nodded as the tears escaped down her cheeks. "It might be. That makes sense. I read about bladder infections. Besides, I don't think it's labor. First, it's too early."

"Oh"—Madeline chuckled—"babies don't have calendars."

Claire grinned. "Well, second, I'm not feeling it in my stomach. I just feel nauseous. The pain's in my back."

"Although I've helped bring many babies into this world, the doctor is the best place for you. Sometimes things in real life aren't like they are in the books."

Claire considered telling Madeline she'd read it online—not in a book—but the pain returned. *It felt like being stabbed, quick, sharp, and intense!* She bit her lip and squeezed her eyes shut. Through gritted teeth she asked, "Can they bring the doctor here? We can call; maybe they can fly Dr. Gilbert to us?"

"Normally, oui." Madeline walked to the doors to the lanai. Her hair blew away from her face, and her dress flowed backward. "No pilot will fly a plane or a helicopter with this wind."

Regaining her ability to speak, Claire replied, "I don't think I can handle the bouncing of the boat, if the waves are big." The dim room flashed bright then back to dark. Claire watched as Madeline pulled the doors shut. "Oh, the breeze felt so good."

"It's time to turn on the air conditioning. You need to be comfortable."

Despite her affection of the open house, Claire agreed. Droplets of sweat rolled down her back and front. Her breasts were damp with perspiration, and she knew her hair was stuck to her skin. "All right. It might help me sleep." Again the thunder rattled the windows. "It's still far away."

"Madame el?"

"The storm—it's still far away. It took a long time for the thunder to reach the lightening."

Madeline patted her hand. "I'll go turn on the cool air and bring you some water. I have an island remedy that may help—if the pain is infection."

Claire's eyes widened.

"No, Madame el, it's natural. It will not hurt the bébé."

"Okay, thank you."

"Do you want Monsieur Rawlings?"

Closing her eyes to a momentary relief in the pain, Claire answered, "No, I'm feeling better. He and Phil can talk while I sleep."

After Madeline left, darkness prevailed. Their normally open suite was now enclosed; its only source of illumination was the remnants of a clouded twilight penetrating the panes of the windows. Claire rearranged the pillows. With pressure in just the right area of her back, she found relief from the stabbing.

When Madeline returned, Claire drank the remedy she provided, all the while praying it would stay down. When alone again, she settled into her nest of pillows. Another flash of lightening brightened the room and she began to drift away...

Light filled their suite as Claire awoke. The morning noises greeted her as she looked out beyond the open doors to the beautiful blue water. Her arms reached out, stretching to relieve the stiffness of a long sleep. She felt more rested than she had in weeks or months. A full night's sleep and the pain was gone. Lifting the soft sheet, Claire marveled at her own movements. It had been so long since she'd been capable of changing positions without concentration and effort.

On her left hand, the sparkling wedding band caught her eye. It was truly as spectacular as the first. As her bare feet touched the tile of the bathroom floor, Claire looked up to her reflection and the air left her lungs. Her hands immediately moved to her flattened midsection as panic boiled from within.

Unable to refrain, Claire fell to her knees and screamed Tony's name. She yelled until the sobs within her chest wouldn't allow her to articulate any longer. With her cheek against the cool tile, Claire heard the door to their suite open. "What happened? Where's our baby?" The questions formed and started to flow until her eyes met gray.

It wasn't Tony who'd entered the room—it was Catherine. Her gray eyes no longer appeared comforting; instead, Claire saw vengeance. She scrambled to her knees and tried to shut the door between the bedroom and bathroom. Catherine was quicker. Claire pushed the door with all her might, yet she was weak. When Catherine came around the door, Claire asked, "Why? Why are you here?"

Her voice cracked like an old vinyl album. "I own this island. It was bought with my money. Why wouldn't I be here?"

"No! You gave me access to the money. It's mine—a gift."

Catherine laughed. "I wouldn't give a gift to a Nichols."

Claire stood straight. "I'm also a Rawlings! Leave me alone!"

"A Nichols is all you are and will ever be—that's all that stupid baby was too!"

Strength from an unknown source coursed through her veins. Claire lunged forward, her petite hands surrounding Catherine's neck, pushing the front toward the back. Both women fell to the floor. "Where's my baby?" Claire yelled.

Catherine pushed Claire away as Claire held on tightly and continued to squeeze. "With Anton." Catherine spewed as she gasped for air.

"Where?"

Catherine's eyes rolled back and her lids fluttered. Claire couldn't kill her—not yet. She needed to know where Tony and the baby were. Releasing her grip, Claire asked again, "Where? Where are they?"

The gray eyes focused directly on her as her lips curved upward. "Gone. They're all gone—you're all alone! I'd kill you too, but...some fates are worse than death."

The air, once again, left Claire's lungs as Catherine's words immobilized her. Through the haze and fog of disbelief, Claire struggled to stand.

Catherine was gone.

Claire was alone.

In the distance of the attached room, she heard the door close. It was as she opened the bathroom door that she heard the beep.

Looking toward the lanai, the sea was gone and so was their paradise. Instead, Claire's surroundings came into focus. Golden drapes covered large windows. White woodwork and beige plush carpet surrounded her. The vibrant colors of the tropics were gone, replaced by muted, dulled tones. Claire peered beyond the drapes, past the French doors to a stark landscape. Skeletons of leafless trees and thick gray clouds were visible for miles.

Falling to her knees, Claire cried out. Her words were meant for the man who would never again hold her close and for the child she never met. "Gone! No, please God, no! Tony, Tony, Tony..." Eventually, the words faded into nothingness...

Nothingness is worse than gray—it's nothing.

∞∞∞∞∞∞∞

Within the confines of the living room, Phil explained to Tony what he'd learned. "It was the notes from the nurses or aides at Camp Gabriels that made me stop and think."

Tony was interested. He wanted to know more about Nathaniel, his life in prison, and how Samuel was able to void his marriage. Perhaps a portion of

Tony's curiosity was the realization that one day he'd follow after his grandfather in that endeavor, too. Anthony Rawlings wouldn't be incarcerated for business fraud. No, Rawlings Industries was legitimate and so were all of its holdings. Tony demanded that. He surrounded himself with people who also demanded fair business practices, people like Brent, Tom, and Tim. Of course, he made money off of others' misfortunes and poor decisions; nonetheless, each business acquisition or closing was done legally. His sins were more personal and arguably worse. The matter could be debated—the number of victims and the extent of the reach; nevertheless, Tony, too, had sins which required restitution.

"When I accessed the prison's inner files, I found comments about Mr. Rawls' behavior and attitude. Nothing appeared for the first few months of his incarceration. It was after he began taking anti-depressants that there were notations about forgetfulness. Sometimes it was a small rather insignificant entry: *prisoner asked what day it was,* or *prisoner thought it was Friday. When he learned it was only Thursday, he became belligerent.* What I found interesting, were the correspondences between the prison and Samuel Rawls."

Tony tried to concentrate. His mind continually went from Phil's words to Claire. The mention of his father's name snapped him back to the present conversation. "Why were they contacting my father? Shouldn't they have been contacting Marie—I mean Catherine?"

"When Nathaniel was first incarcerated, he and Ms. London weren't yet married. Samuel was the contact—his next of kin and power of attorney. Apparently, to change those titles to a new person required compliance by *all* individuals. Samuel Rawls refused to relinquish his power over his father."

Tony stood and paced as the storm continued to threaten. Torrents of rain blanketed the windows. Seeing his reflection in the glass and unable to see beyond the prematurely dark sky, Tony said, "That's ridiculous. My father never visited the prison. Not one time!"

Phil shook his head. "I saw that too. Ms. London visited every Friday like clockwork. Your visits coincided with long weekends and college breaks."

"Damn!"—Tony looked at Phil with newfound admiration—"Is there anything you can't learn?"

"Me personally"—Phil smirked—"not if I know where to look."

"So, what did you learn in the correspondences?"

Phil explained, as Nathaniel's dementia-like symptoms increased, the prison contacted Samuel. One of the doctors sited a concern regarding drug interaction. He stated that some reports, at that time, claimed a possible connection between anti-depressants and a vitamin deficiency which produced forgetfulness, restlessness, and agitation. The doctor requested Samuel's permission to take Nathaniel off the anti-depressants.

"My father refused, didn't he?"

"He did. He authorized vitamin supplements, but vehemently denied

275

approval to change or alter Nathaniel's anti-depressant regime."

"When was this correspondence?" Tony asked.

"Do you want the date? Or are you more interested to learn if it was after your grandfather married Ms. London?"

"B." Tony replied. *B—the letter propelled his thoughts to Blaine—his son or daughter.* Hearing about the vindictiveness of his father and the deep seeded hatred that flowed through his own family, Tony wondered why the universe was willing to entrust him with a child. The Rawls in him didn't deserve such a monumental blessing. He never thought he deserved any blessings. Everything he'd ever acquired he'd earned, through hard work—except this child—perhaps, the Nichols down the hall, balanced out the Rawls. In a way, it was like Catherine's threats:

Rawls—Nichols

Except, that wasn't the correct equation—it wasn't Rawls *minus* Nichols—it was Rawls *plus* Nichols. It was now clear—Rawls plus Nichols equaled Rawlings.

Before Phil could answer, the sound of Claire's scream echoed through the house, only to be drowned out by the rumbling of thunder. At first, Tony considered he might have imagined his wife's plea, but when he saw the look on Phil's face, Tony knew it was real.

"Did you just hear?" Tony asked as Claire's scream rang from the other side of the house. Both men ran for the master bedroom suite. They reached the door at the same time as Madeline. Tony's heart beat frantically as he reached for the door knob, pushed the door wide, and declared, "I'm going in alone. Then, I'll let you know."

Madeline and Phil both nodded.

Claire lay still near the center of their bed with her back toward the door. The fullness of pillows surrounding her body brought a momentary smile to Tony's worried expression. Lately, she'd brought more and more pillows to bed. He'd teased her, saying a wall of pillows couldn't keep him out, but Tony knew the pillows helped Claire to be more comfortable. He didn't care if she slept in a bed of pillows.

His smile quickly faded when he realized she hadn't turned toward the sound of the opening door. Quickly, he walked to the far side of their bed and stepped closer. Despite her damp hair pressed to her face, Tony thought she looked beautiful. When he spoke, he expected to see her beautiful emerald eyes. "Claire, are you all right?"

She didn't move. In the dimly lit, master bedroom suite, her skin glistened with perspiration and her eyes remained shut. He reached toward her. While only inches away, Claire's head tossed violently from side to side as she whispered, "No...Tony..."

Just as quickly as she called out, her body stilled. He waited. *Was she telling him not to come nearer?* Tony asked in desperation, "Claire, no—

what?"

When she didn't respond, he sat on the edge of their bed and tenderly reached for her shoulder. Shaking her gently, he said, "Claire, I'm right here. Are you dreaming?"

She didn't respond. He shook again—nothing. "Madeline!" he yelled toward the door.

The sky was now dark, with intense flashes of light. The thunder and lightning occurred almost simultaneously. Phil, who'd been joined by Francis, paced silently in the hallway, while Madeline and Tony attended to Claire. Despite his gentle encouragement, Claire wouldn't wake; however, her pleas and the calling of his name ceased.

The temperature of their suite had decreased very nicely. That, combined with the gentle breeze of the ceiling fan, made their room quite comfortable; nevertheless, Tony noticed Claire's blouse stuck to her clammy skin. As he brushed her sun lightened hair away from her face, he felt the warmth radiating from her body. "She's burning up!"

"Monsieur, may I?"

Tony hesitantly stepped away as Madeline approached the edge of the bed where Tony had been perched. She turned her palm upward and moved her hand over Claire's forehead.

"I'm afraid she has an infection. Before she fell asleep, I gave her something to help fight it and help her sleep. She said she didn't want to go to the doctor."

His back straightened. "What did you give her?"

"It's an island remedy. When she wakes, she'll feel better."

"The baby?"

"The bébé will be good, much better than having infection in her mère."

His shoulder's relaxed as he stepped toward his wife. Before he could speak, Madeline pulled the sheet back and revealed Claire's body.

Tony gasped. "What? What happened? Why is she so wet?"

"Her water, it broke. The baby is coming."

Tony fell to his knees and reached for his wife's hand. With his lips near Claire's sleeping face he begged, "Please, please be all right." Holding back tears, he straightened his neck and lowered his voice—the tone he created was one of authority, beyond debate. "You told me you'd be fine. You promised." Lightning and thunder crashed. Softness, once again, took residence in his words, "Claire, please open your eyes. I need to see your beautiful emerald eyes."

His chest tightened with déjà vu. He'd said those words before—almost verbatim. Seeing her on the bed, with her clothes glued to her skin by moisture, Tony cursed under his breath. This—like the *accident*—like Chester—was his fault. *Why did she continually need to suffer because of him?*

I always trust my gut reaction; it's always right.

—Kiana Tom

CHAPTER 38

Harry took one last look at his acquired evidence from the Sherman Nichols' case—all boxed and catalogued. The digital data was secured in the FBI system. Soon, it would be gone from his condominium—gone from his life. He hated to admit the case was done. Well, the case wasn't done, but *he* was done with the case. After all the time, effort, and attachment, Harry had been ordered to move on. Last night, the call came from the deputy director—Agent Baldwin was needed elsewhere. The new assignment required traveling, and he was finally fit to travel. Despite the disappointment of losing the Nichols case, Harry was looking forward to getting away. Even though Christmas was around the corner, he needed a break from Palo Alto, his sister, and even Liz.

Amber's decision to hire John Vandersol at SiJo added to Harry's discomfort in Palo Alto. They had to create a story to explain his abrupt exit from SiJo. One day he was SiJo's President of Security Operations—the next he was gone. Privately, on a personal level, Harry berated Amber for hiring John; however, on a professional level, Vandersol was talented—even gifted; nevertheless, Harry didn't appreciate the added angst. It was increasingly difficult to deal with Rawlings and Claire while simultaneously faced with her *only* family. Harry wondered how Amber and Liz were able to handle the farce on a daily basis.

Since John's law license was reinstated, it seemed as though he itched to make the move from corporate financial investments back to legal. The thing was—John Vandersol had a problem called *loyalty*. He obviously felt indebted to Amber and to SiJo for hiring him at such a difficult time in his career. Many corporations wouldn't have taken a chance on him—despite the fact the charges resulting in his incarceration were later dropped, and his record was expunged. Harry assumed John would remain diligent to SiJo's needs as long as his presence was requested. Amber said she had no intentions of asking him to follow his heart—his assistance with investments and procurements had already helped SiJo immensely. Amber may have initially hired him to solidify her faux friendship with Claire, but as a business decision, it was one of Amber's best.

Sometimes Harry questioned Simon's business sense in naming Amber as vice president of operations of SiJo. Simon's confidence and recommendation undoubtedly secured her future with the board of directors upon Simon's death. As much as Harry liked Simon, the man definitely thought more with his heart, or perhaps other parts of his body, than he did his head when it came to women. The fact he'd spent eight years waiting for Claire was another example of Simon's emotional handicap. It sure-as-hell wasn't a mistake that Harry planned on repeating.

As CEO, Amber McCoy often surprised and delighted her brother. She'd definitely learned from Simon's intuition. Now, with John, the company was, once again, making waves throughout the gaming world. Granted, they were little ripples, but movement—nonetheless.

The knock on his condominium door brought Harry to present. He was expecting someone from the San Francisco field office. They were coming to pick up the boxes of research. When he opened the door, it wasn't a fellow FBI agent, but Liz.

Harry scanned her work clothes. He liked the skirts that got all tight at the waist and stayed tight until her blouse, emphasizing her round breasts. Noticing her black high heels, Harry tried not to think about other times she'd worn those—and not much else. Unable to hide his sly smile, Harry said, "Hi, come on in."

She took a few steps, scanned the stacked boxes and raised her eyebrows. "You're really moving on to other cases."

Harry gently clenched Liz's shoulders, pulled her close, and kissed her cheek. "Between you and Amber, I don't know who has more difficulty remembering—I can't talk about it."

Liz grinned. "I know—or you'd have to kill me; but hey, this case almost cost us—us. So, to say I'm glad you're moving on—is an understatement."

Going into Harry's kitchen, Liz opened the refrigerator and pulled out a bottle of water. Harry was close behind when he asked, "Even if it means that I'm traveling?"

Liz shrugged. "I like it better when you're here. How much of your schedule can I know?"

Leaning against the counter with his faded jeans, tight black t-shirt, bare feet, and messy, blonde hair, Harry grinned. "I can tell you when I'm home."

"But, not when you're coming home."

He stepped toward her, put his arms around her waist, and pinned her against the counter. Inhaling deeply, he took in the sweet smell of her perfume. As he exhaled, his warm breath bathed her neck. Before he spoke, his lips caressed her shoulder and his fingers traced the edge of her scoop cut blouse. Liz tilted her head back, giving him full access and involuntarily moaned. His words were spaced and breathy. "No" "not when I'm coming home" "I promise" "when I'm home" "I'm all yours."

Liz sighed, momentarily allowing her hips to be pulled toward his; however, when his hands lowered to her round behind, Liz pushed away. "Well, I think we need to talk. I mean, what's this relationship anyway? What am I?"

Harry lifted a brow. "What do you mean?"

"Are we dating again, or just having sex?"

Running his fingers through his hair, Harry sighed. "I don't know how long I'll be gone. I don't want you stuck in some holding pattern. It could be a few days—or a few months. That's not fair to you."

Liz set the bottle on the counter with enough force to allow droplets of water to escape onto the granite top. "Fine," she said as she turned toward the door.

Harry grabbed her arm and turned her back toward him, pulling her into his strong embrace. Looking down into her light blue eyes, he softened his tone. "What is this? I thought we'd been through this. You know it's my job."

Liz nodded into his chest. "I do. I just don't know what that means."

Harry lifted her chin. "Why are you suddenly upset?"

"It's not *suddenly*, Harry. It's *still*!"

Exhaling, Harry took Liz by the hand and led her to his sofa. "It was a job. I let it get out of hand. It's over. She's remarried. She's having someone else's kid!"

"You told me it was over with her after you found out about the kid not being yours."

Harry's voice became louder. "It was! We've—you and me—have been back together since then. What is this?"

Liz stood and paced about his living room pretending to have interest in all the things lying around. Finally, she answered, "I want to believe you—I do. I can do the whole *secret-agent girlfriend thing*. Christ, Harry! I was kidnapped and forced to watch some assholes beat the shit out of you!" She inhaled deeply and wiped a tear from her cheek with the back of her hand. "I kept my mouth shut the whole time that stupid slut was here." She turned her eyes to Harry.

He knew she was waiting for a reaction. Luckily, years of training allowed him to remain stoic.

Liz continued, "I did! I smiled and played nice, even after Amber told me you two were sleeping together."

Harry exhaled—*damn his sister! He knew she'd been the one to inform Liz, but hearing it reminded him how Amber needed to learn to keep her mouth shut!* Agent training summoned, Harry stood and walked to Liz. Lifting her chin, he kissed her lips once again—softly and slowly. "I'm sorry. The whole thing put you in a terrible place. Is this something we can ever get past, or will I hear about it every time you're mad at me, for the rest of our lives?"

Her lips curved upward. "The rest of our lives?"

"Or, until you tell me to hit the road."

Her blue eyes closed, and her lashes fluttered on her cheek. "You've never talked about the future, even when we were living together."

Harry shrugged. "The whole kid thing"—he pulled her close—"sorry, but it made me realize I might want that." He felt her breasts against his chest. The tighter he held her, the harder her nipples became under her blouse. "Then, when Jillian was threatened, I thought about her. She's beautiful and happy. She doesn't need me showing up in her life, but another kid..." His lips brushed hers. "Maybe, I'm growing up?"

With her hand in his, he again pulled her toward the sofa. Leaning over her, their lips met. Harry gently pulled her blouse from the confines of her skirt. Within seconds, his hands were under her blouse and bra, caressing the firm, round breast he'd moments earlier been imagining. When his thumb began to trace circles around her nipple, Liz's head fell back and a moan escaped her lips.

"Harry...Harry..."

Later that evening, while they lingered in Harry's bed, Harry watched Liz sleep. With his head on his elbow, he took in her beautiful features. Everything about her said California, from her blonde hair to her tan skin. She grew up in southern California and moved north after college. Working at SiJo wasn't her lifelong dream; she'd shared her desires for her future. That was part of her allure—they had a past. He and Liz had lived together—had good times together—and made mistakes together. It was real, not created by the FBI. She even knew what he did for a living and still wanted to be with him. Damn, hearing her talk about being kidnapped pulled at Harry's heart. As much as he wanted a future with her, he had every right to worry about her safety.

As it was, Ilona and Jillian had only recently been allowed home and still had surveillance. Ilona had been much more understanding than Harry ever expected. Now that Harry was off the Nichols/Rawlings case, the bureau believed the threat to his ex-wife and their child would soon be gone; however, in Harry's mind that attack still didn't make sense.

About a month ago, Harry made a visit to the Rawlings estate. He had to see Ms. London in person. He fully monitored every one of her reactions. The first came when Harry introduced himself as Harry Baldwin—Claire's ex-boyfriend and friend of John and Emily Vandersol. London appeared genuinely surprised to learn Claire had dated anyone else while in California. She offered her condolences regarding Claire's disappearance. She also promised to contact him or the Vandersols if she learned anything. To make the conversation more believable, Harry mentioned Emily and how upset she was about her sister, especially with her emotions running high, due to her recent pregnancy.

Never once during the conversation did Harry get the feeling she knew of Claire's location or that she knew anything about him. That reaction begged the question, *why would Catherine London order an attack on him or threaten his family?* Obviously, the person who did it knew him—knew he was FBI—and knew about Ilona and Jillian. Even though the deputy director had reassigned Harry, he knew that he couldn't let go of this particular piece of the puzzle. One day, he'd learn who threatened his family, his life, and his investigation.

Liz stirred, murmuring as she rubbed her cheek against his pillow. Her blonde hair and soft skin pulled him closer. He wanted to be honest with her, he really did; nonetheless, it wouldn't do either one of them any good for her to know that he still thought about Claire, from time to time. Sometimes when he's alone he remembered what it was like to be with her. It wasn't just the sex. He thought about how scared she was when she first moved to Palo Alto. Every time he remembered her buying her first cell phone, a smile came to his lips. He didn't mean for it to happen, but he felt his cheeks raise. When he first met Claire, she was like a frightened fawn exploring the world on her own. He was drawn in by a need to protect her from all the dangers—including Anthony Rawlings. Even before Harry knew the details, he knew that she'd been hurt. Looking into her emerald eyes, he knew that it was something he didn't want her to experience again.

Harry cared about Liz. He could even see spending the rest of his life with her. She was different than Claire—so strong and independent. *How many women would take him back after what he'd done?* Granted she gave him hell about it—he deserved it. Harry admired her strength and strong will. With an appreciative smile, he knew he also admired her ingenuity. Never once did she blow his cover with Claire or the Vandersols, yet her jealousy played a significant role in his and Claire's first big fight. When Amber received the call—at the last minute—about Rawlings being at the gala, Harry knew Liz had withheld the information on purpose. He even told Amber.

Watching her sleep peacefully, Harry moved her soft blonde hair away from her neck. *Damn, he loved that neck.* Fighting the urge to wake her, he smiled.

There was no doubt that he was pissed during the night of the gala. He was pissed at Liz *and* at Claire; however, now Harry had to give Liz an *A* for effort. She took the cards she'd been dealt and played them—she played them very well.

"Why are you smiling?" Liz asked as her eyes opened.

"I was just thinking about that sexy neck of yours." His fingers went to her collarbone and traced a winding path over her neck and down to her breast.

Liz reached for his hand. Momentarily, their palms touched and their fingers intertwined. "Harry?"

"Hmm?"

"One more question, and then I'll drop it—I promise."

He exhaled and laid his head on his pillow. "Go ahead."

"How do I know that if you run into her in the future that you won't still have feelings?"

"I don't know. Some couples have this thing called *trust*. I realize I'm the one who needs to earn it back"—He lifted his head and allowed his lips to lightly trail over her neck. Breathlessly he whispered—"I will."

"In Venice?"

Harry lifted his head and raised an eyebrow. "In Venice—what?"

"Did you want to be with her again? Did you sleep together—or anything?"

"No!" Harry pulled the covers back and abruptly left the bed. "Why are you on this kick? No! She was planning on meeting up with Rawlings." Pacing nude by the bed, Harry lifted his arms. "I screwed up. All I can say is—I'm sorry."

Liz moved to her knees and crawled to the edge of the bed. With her face lifted, she cooed, "I believe you. I can tell you're upset. I'm sorry. It's just that after I saw that picture of the two of you holding hands—well, I guess I needed to know."

"You saw the picture? How?"

"Amber showed it to me." She lifted herself on her knees, kissed his lips, wrapped her arms around his neck, and pressed her breasts against his hard chest. "I believe you. If you say it's over—it's over." She moved slightly away to look into his eyes. "Oh, please don't tell Amber that you know I saw the picture. She just wanted me to be sure that I knew everything—so that I could make an informed decision."

Her grin widened as she pulled Harry back down on the bed. When his head hit the pillow, she leaned over him. The warmth of her flattened breasts covered his wide chest as their skin united. Liz continued, "She told me not to tell you." Her words came between butterfly kisses to Harry's cheek and neck. "I probably shouldn't have"—"but Agent Baldwin"—"now that I know"—"my decision is informed"—"and"—"I don't want"—"to let you go"—"again!"

Harry flipped Liz onto her back. Before he could speak, she begged, "Please, Agent, can you show me how much you'll miss me? Please?"

Harry couldn't resist her begging—her flushed cheeks—her trusting gaze—or her disheveled hair. It was more than he could take. Any thought unrelated to becoming one, with the woman below him, momentarily slipped away.

Focus on things you can control.

—John Wooden

CHAPTER 39

"**M**onsieur?"

Tony pulled his gaze away from Claire and looked toward Madeline. In her arms, she held a stack of towels and sheets. "We need to clean her and cool her."

Tony nodded and reached for a wash cloth. After going to the bathroom and saturating it with cool water, he folded it in thirds and gently placed it on Claire's forehead. His soft tone resonated through their suddenly cavernous suite, "I know you haven't been sleeping well." Thunder shook the house. Tony continued, unfazed, "If you need to sleep now, it's all right, but pretty soon, our little one will be here. He or she needs their mommy." Tony fought the emotion boiling in his throat. "Claire, *I* need you. With *you* I'm someone I'm proud to be. P—please—don't leave me."

The pressure of someone's hand fell on Tony's shoulder. He was on the edge of a dark abyss. Fear pulled at him, inciting emotions he couldn't control. Anthony Rawlings controlled everything and everyone. The sudden impotence filled his world with red. Other than Claire, he was surrounded by employees. *Didn't these people know anything? They didn't address him without a title, and they didn't touch him!* Tony inhaled and looked toward the touch. His gaze met Madeline's as she smiled a sad smile. Instantaneously, the red faded. Tony covered Madeline's hand and relished her support.

Madeline said, "Monsieur, Madame el, she's not gone—she's resting. The island cure I gave her is helping her. She needs her strength for your baby. We must make her comfortable."

Tony didn't respond. He didn't know what to do. It was an uneasy situation under normal circumstances. With Claire's life on the line, Tony felt completely helpless. Swallowing his pride, he asked, "H—how can we make her comfortable?"

Madeline explained her plan. Once Tony approved, she put it into motion. First, she instructed Francis and Phil to carry a chaise lounge in from the lanai. Rain covered the floor when they opened the door and brought the long lounge into the bedroom. Madeline immediately dried the moisture from the floor and from the lounge cushions; then she proceeded to cover the chair in towels and sheets.

Phil and Francis went back to the hall and kept silent vigil, while Madeline and Tony removed Claire's wet clothes. They cleaned, rinsed, and dried her with cloths and towels from the bathroom. Once she was dry, Tony gently lifted her to the lounge chair where they dressed her in a nightgown and covered her shivering body with a clean sheet. The chase lounge was much lower than a normal bed; however, since the mattress of their bed was saturated, it gave her a clean place to lie.

No longer did station matter. Madeline was no longer house staff or an employee—Tony willingly submitted to her control of the situation. If she told him to jump, it would be he who asked, *how high?* For the first time in his memory, Tony didn't want power. He knew nothing about giving birth. Without a doctor, Madeline was their best bet. She was the dealer—she controlled the deck and had his full respect and attention.

As the sky darkened and night time came, Tony did the only thing he could. He sat by Claire with one hand on their unborn child. When he'd feel the baby move, he'd tell Madeline, "I felt something." His other hand continually touched Claire. It may have been her hand, her cheek, or her forehead. He didn't care where they connected—as long as they did.

Throughout the night, Claire's pulse remained steady, and their baby continued to move. It wasn't until dawn when Claire began to wake. At first, it was the incoherent mutterings of earlier. She pleaded, "Tony....no....gone...Tony...no..." Eventually, the pleadings morphed into tears. With each outburst, another piece of Tony's heart broke. Claire was fighting a battle only she could see. He would've said, paid, or done anything to bring her relief—he couldn't.

All he could do, was offer himself. Never leaving his wife's side, Tony repeatedly wiped her tear coated cheeks with a soft handkerchief, and each time she'd mutter, in his calmest tone, he'd reassure, "I'm right here. I'm not leaving you. No one is gone..." He didn't know if she could hear his words; nevertheless, saying them brought a sense of comfort to their suite.

By the time the sun rose behind the still billowing clouds, Tony's head rested quietly on the side of the chair. There hadn't been a change in hours. He didn't intend to fall asleep, but the rumbling of thunder, rhythm of rain, and constant in Claire's condition allowed him to slip into a false sense of security.

∞∞∞∞∞∞∞

Claire couldn't remember where she was. Her last memory was of the suite in Iowa. The copper colored walls she remembered were gone; instead, the white woodwork and golden drapes of 2010 were back. The fear that infiltrated her thoughts and drained her world of color was the overwhelming sensation of isolation. Claire was, once again, alone. No longer did she wake to the sounds of her paradise. Birds no longer sang and the surf no longer roared. The only reoccurring noise was that of the beep. She didn't need to look, to know why it occurred. Claire knew too well—the beep happened whenever the door to the rest of the world opened.

Alone forever, the beep was a continual reminder of her fate. Claire didn't want to hear the sound or see the person who'd enter. There was a time, somewhere long ago, when Claire yearned to see Catherine, she prayed for that. Now, each time the door opened, she prayed for someone—anyone else, yet each tray of food—each outfit set out—everything necessary for life— came at the hands of the woman who was no longer her comforter—but her tormentor. If Claire turned, she knew she'd see Catherine's sadistic gray eyes.

Though her life was hell—it no longer mattered. Claire's will to continue vanished with her husband and child. She saw the food which arrived three times a day. Never once did she desire to eat. She saw the French doors which opened only upon request. There was nothing beyond the panes she craved. Colors were gone. Showering, dressing, sleeping, and waking were inconsequential. Claire's thoughts and actions were consumed with one desire: to be with her family. If her goal could only be obtained through death, she willed it to occur.

This sense of doom overwhelmed her as she woke. She didn't want to open her eyes. She didn't want to see the golden drapes. Tentatively, more from reflex than want, Claire pried her eyes open. As she tried to focus, the world she feared was gone; instead of white woodwork, a thatched ceiling filled her view. A slow, methodical fan twirled above her bed and cooler than normal air moved through their suite.

Though the angle didn't seem right, she knew she was in paradise. When she attempted to move, stiffness affected each joint. Claire felt as though her body were bruised. With pressure on her stomach, she suddenly remembered their baby. Tears of loss filled her eyes as she reached for her midsection. Before her hand moved that far, her fingers brushed a full head of hair. Raising her face, Claire's lips morphed into a grin as she saw the familiar head of dark hair highlighted with renegade white. It was the most perfect head of hair she'd ever seen.

Reaching below the perfect head of hair, Claire felt her enlarged midsection. The slight pressure she'd felt was Tony's large hand splayed across their unborn child. For a moment, she lay perfectly still relishing her reality. The night of terror was only a dream—a nightmare. As if for confirmation, their child moved. The small, strong life pushed against her skin from within. Every muscle in Claire's body relaxed. Their child was still inside of her, Tony was beside her, and no matter what the future held, she was exactly where she wanted to be.

Weaving her fingers through his hair, Claire whispered his name, "Tony?"

Though his head didn't move, the hand over her midsection shielded protectively, as he murmured, "I'm right here. I'm not leaving you. No one is gone..."

Again, she whispered, "Tony, what happened? Why are you on the floor?"

His tired eyes found hers. Though he looked exhausted, the sparkle behind the soft brown filled Claire with love and hope. He reached up and touched her cheek. "Oh, thank God, you're not hot."

Her lips twitched upward. "Thanks a lot. You don't look all that *hot* yourself."

His lips gently found hers. When he pulled away, Claire watched as his grin emerged, coming from some dark place, and a tear slid down his cheek. *Had she ever seen him cry?* Claire couldn't remember. It was the relief in his voice that overwhelmed her and brought tears to her cheeks. "Mrs. Rawlings, have I ever mentioned how much I love that smart mouth?"

Claire nodded. "A time or two."

He smoothed the hair from her face. "You've had us all very scared."

It was a day of revelations; first a tear and then an admittance of fear. Claire almost asked who this man was, and what he'd done with her husband; however, the sincerity in his voice didn't deserve a quick retort. Instead, she reached for his hand and kissed his palm. "I'm sorry, I scared you. I don't remember. What happened?"

Their voices must have been overheard because before he could answer, the bedroom door opened and Madeline came rushing in. "Oh, Madame el"— her deep dark eyes smiled—"Madame *Claire*, our prayers, they have been answered."

Something as simple as a name shouldn't make her cry, yet hearing Madeline call her by her name, a request Claire had made months ago, ignited warmth. Again, Claire felt movement within her. Smiling, she asked, "At the risk of sounding redundant, would someone please tell me what happened?" At that moment, she noticed the back pain was gone.

"Yes, my dear, we will. We don't want you to have to ask again." She could hear the smirk in her husband's voice.

"Thank you, I don't believe I'm the only one who doesn't like to ask the same question twice." Claire saw the gleam in Tony's eyes and squeezed his hand. It truly amazed her that a simple phrase could possess so much meaning.

"Madame Claire, how do you feel?"

"I think...I feel good..." Claire tried to sit. Tony moved to the back of the lounge chair and repositioned the back. When he did, Claire realized something leaked. With a surge of panic, she confessed, "I think I just..."

Madeline reached for her hand. "Your water broke. Your baby is coming soon."

Claire knew she should be excited, yet looking at her husband and then past him, she saw the gray skies. It was then the drumming of steady rain registered. "Dr. Gilbert?" she asked.

Tony shook his head and grasped her hand. "It's too dangerous. Phil and Francis have both offered to go after him; however, even if they get to town, Dr. Gilbert may not be willing to travel back here."

Claire tried to think. "Madeline, did you say you've delivered babies before?"

"Oui, I've helped."

It was more experience than either of them had. Claire nodded; then she asked, "My water broke? When?"

"Last night," Tony replied.

"Then why am I not in labor?"

"Oh, but Madame you are."

Claire closed her eyes and assessed. She felt more comfortable than she had in weeks. The lower back pain was gone. The tightening was gone. The pressure down low was gone. A tear escaped her eyes.

Tony tenderly wiped it away. "Why are you crying?"

Her words came between ragged breaths. "I don't think this is right." "If I'm in labor, then I should feel something." "My water broke." "It isn't safe for the baby *not* to be born." She looked back to Madeline, "Why am I not contracting?"

Madeline answered truthfully, "I do not know, but you will. Your baby will want to come out."

The lines around Tony's eyes deepened. "I'll go to town. I can't ask someone to do something I'm not willing to do."

Claire grasped his hand. "No! No you won't. I don't want Phil or Francis risking their lives either, but under no circumstance are you allowed to leave me." Not bothering to smile, Claire added, "This is *not* debatable."

His grin twitched, and he whispered close to her ear, "Do you want me to get the satin mask?"

She tried to suppress her smile; however, suppression of any kind was impossible. Her emotions were too raw. The days of figurative masks were gone. With her emerald eyes shining, she replied, "Maybe later, but right now, you're not leaving me!"

"Yes, ma'am." Tony looked up to Madeline. "Do you think she should eat?"

Claire remembered the night before. "I don't want to. Last night, I threw up after dinner."

"Madame el, you can drink? No?"

"Yes, Madeline, I can drink."

"I'll be back."

When Madeline opened the door, Claire saw Phil and Francis standing just through the opening. Suddenly, she remembered modesty. Looking down to her feet, Claire realized she wore a nightgown that she didn't remember putting on and was covered with a sheet. "Please let Phil and Francis come in for a minute. They look worried."

Tony kissed Claire's forehead as he fought to stand. Sitting on the floor all night appeared to have stiffened his muscles as well. "My dear, we were all concerned."

It was nice to have everyone near. Claire wished for the doctor, but the camaraderie was much better than being alone. Francis explained that, although the forecast wasn't promising, if a break occurred in the weather, he'd take the boat to Dr. Gilbert. If he couldn't help Madame el and her bébé in that way, he'd do what he'd been doing all night—he'd pray. When he squeezed Claire's hand, the tension from the storm and impending labor dissipated. The sunshine of faith overpowered the fog of doubt.

After Francis reassured Claire and Tony, he slipped from the room. When Madeline entered with a concoction of fruit juices, Claire noticed Phil. Since he hadn't spoken, she hadn't been aware of his presence. With his arms crossed over his chest, he'd been leaning against the wall, observing. Claire reached out her hand. "Phil, I didn't see you. Please come over here."

His steps were dutiful and painstakingly slow. In all the time she'd known Phil, she'd never seen his current expression. It wasn't anger—she saw that the day he found Harry in their hotel suite. It wasn't concern—she saw that multiple times as they worked to hide. Claire wasn't sure what it was. When he reached her hand, Claire was the one to reassure. Squeezing his, she said, "I'm fine, Phil. The baby's fine. Please don't risk your life to get the doctor. We'll be all right."

He didn't speak—he nodded. Perhaps he was uncomfortable with the whole intimacy of the situation. He'd seen her in a nightgown before; however, this was understandably different.

Claire looked to Tony. When their eyes met, Tony repeated Claire's words, "If anyone's risking their life to get the doctor, it will be me." Tony looked back to Claire, "However, at this point, no one will."

She exhaled.

After Claire drank most of Madeline's fruit juice, Tony helped her stand. She read somewhere that walking could help induce labor. Her first stop was the bathroom; she wanted to be clean. When she turned to close the door, Tony entered. "I'm not leaving you alone. You're stuck with me."

Claire smiled. "Thank you." There were some things that were difficult to ask, but when they were offered or *demanded*, it was comforting. At that moment, Claire was thankful for her demanding husband.

By midafternoon, the rain stopped, the sky began to clear, and patches of blue infiltrated the gray sky. As evening approached the blue dominated, even as the wind continued to howl. The sound of surf filled their ears as the normally calm lagoon produced waves with white tops.

With Claire's arm in Tony's, they walked the length of the lanai and back again. Claire didn't believe anyone else had slept, yet no one complained. It was during their fourth or fifth lap when Phil approached. "Excuse me, Francis believes we have enough time to get to town and back before dark."

Claire looked anxiously toward Tony. The contractions had come back; however, they weren't occurring with any sense of regularity. Thankfully, they also weren't in her back—they were a tightening that encompassed her entire midsection. Claire wouldn't authorize a venture that could harm the people she loved. Reaching out, Claire took Phil's hand. "I don't want anything to happen to you."

His neck straightened, and his tone sounded formal. "Mrs. Rawlings, I can assure you, I've had more difficult assignments than a boat ride in the tropics of the South Pacific."

Tony nodded. When he began to speak, Claire gripped his arm. Both men looked to her as she closed her eyes and repeatedly exhaled.

Perhaps there was an unspoken connection between Phil and Tony. Both men wanted to help, needed to help, yet felt helpless. This was Phil's chance to do something—for Claire. Tony replied, "Be safe—and be fast." Claire didn't argue. When she opened her eyes, she saw Phil's nod before he hurried away.

Moments later, the distant roar of the boat's motor filtered through the reverberating sound of the surf. Claire grasped Tony's arm again—the contractions were getting closer.

Forbidden to remember, terrified to forget;

it was a hard line to walk.

——Stephenie Meyer, New Moon

CHAPTER 40

-SEPTEMBER 2016-

When Meredith left her husband Thursday morning, she couldn't stop the tears. He didn't want her to go, but he didn't argue. He hadn't been married to his college sweetheart for ten years without understanding her desires. Avoiding the scheduled meeting would be the equivalent of the first story Meredith wrote about Claire. It would be lying and cheating—very ironic, considering the stance she was about to support as *truth*—was in fact—a *lie*.

It took Meredith a moment in the parking lot to regain her composure, but summoning all her strength, she pushed the thoughts of her children and husband aside and concentrated on Claire. The meeting would be short-lived; as soon as Emily saw her, it would be over. Her only hope was that she'd be released on bail. Unbeknownst to Meredith, her husband was spending the morning securing their assets in anticipation of such a call.

She wished she could tell everyone the progress Claire had made; however, Meredith wouldn't do that. She'd promised Claire she wouldn't tell anyone, and she wouldn't let her down again.

Making her way to the conference room on the first floor of the doctor's tower, Meredith had a fleeting feeling of pity for Ms. Bali. Yesterday, her supervisor was almost giddy about this meeting. It was unusual for someone as low as a *food aide* to be recognized for contribution to a patient's care. Having the family and lead doctor desiring to speak with someone under Ms. Bali's supervision was the biggest compliment she'd received in over twenty years. Before Meredith went to Claire's room yesterday afternoon, Ms. Bali went on and on about the years of under appreciation. Meredith hypothesized this meeting was why she received a mere verbal reprimand for keeping Claire out so late the other night. Among her other prayers, Meredith hoped Ms. Bali wouldn't be penalized for hiring someone with false credentials.

As Meredith neared the conference room, she fought the urge to make one last trip to Claire's room; instead, she willed her foot forward. She wasn't wearing her uniform. Looking down at her blouse and skirt, Meredith grinned. She'd spent quite a bit of time choosing a blouse she thought would look good in a mug shot.

Stepping through the threshold, Meredith scanned the room. Smiling to those in attendance, she hid her surprise at the empty seats. She'd expected the room to be fuller. The faces smiling back at her were ones of staff members she'd seen periodically in corridors and patients' rooms. The meeting was scheduled for 8:30 AM, and Ms. Bali arrived with minutes to spare. Her normal uniform was replaced with a nice skirt suit. Smiling, she sat beside Meredith. 8:30 AM came and went. The Vandersols weren't present, nor was Dr. Fairfield. By 8:45 AM, the staff present began to fidget. Ms. Bali's expression began to waver, exposing her concerned eyes as she watched the clock on the wall.

At 9:00 AM, a confident, professionally dressed woman came into the room and apologized, "Excuse me, Mrs. Russel and everyone else, my name is Valerie, I'm Dr. Fairfield's assistant. I've been sent to apologize to you for this inconvenience. Mrs. Russel, your help with Ms. Nichols has been noticed and appreciated. Dr. Fairfield apologizes for his inability to attend this meeting, as do the Vandersols. Something unexpected has come up. They wanted you to know that your assistance has been—and is—acknowledged. They hope you'll continue working with Ms. Nichols; she works very well with you. Thank you everyone for coming. This meeting is done."

Meredith stared, trying to comprehend Valerie's speech. When Dr. Fairfield's assistant turned to walk away, Meredith suddenly realized the only possible reason for everyone to miss this meeting. It had something to do with Claire. Meredith asked, "Excuse me, Valerie?"

The assistant turned around. "Yes, Mrs. Russel?"

"Is Claire—I mean, Ms. Nichols, all right?"

"Yes, Mrs. Russel. May I speak with you privately?"

Meredith couldn't resist. Although she'd just received a pardon, she needed to know what kept everyone away and that Claire was well. Meredith followed Valerie into an empty elevator. Valerie pushed the button for the floor of Dr. Fairfield's office and whispered, "Dr. Fairfield said if you asked that I was to bring you up."

"Are you sure she's all right?"

Valerie didn't answer verbally, but her expression morphed from stoic business assistant to a school girl with a secret—one she was dying to share. Meredith decided not to push any further. If she were being included in this gathering, then it was something big.

292

The relief Meredith felt at the conclusion of the non-existent meeting dissipated as she neared Dr. Fairfield's office. She suddenly realized she was seconds away from facing the Vandersols. "Are you sure I'm welcome?" she asked as they entered the quiet hallway.

"You are, but first, let me show you what's happening. Come with me."

Meredith's anxiety grew with each step. Valerie took her to a room. The name plate beside the door read: *Observation*. Inside, there were four chairs all facing a large mirror. Valerie pointed toward the mirror and pushed a switch. The dark glass transformed into a window, giving them visual entry to a well lit room. On the other side of the glass, Meredith saw a surreal scene. Claire was sitting in a chair, maintaining eye contact with her sister. Emily was also sitting, bent at the waist, holding Claire's hands with their knees touching. Claire looked uncomfortable, but it was Emily who appeared visibly shaken. Her eyes were puffy with dark streaks of mascara coating her cheeks.

There was no sound; nevertheless, Emily's lips were moving, Claire was nodding and shaking her head—answering questions that Meredith couldn't hear. John's blotchy face caught Meredith's attention as he knelt next to Emily with his hand on Claire's knee. Dr. Fairfield and Dr. Brown were observing and conversing near the far corner.

"What happened?" Meredith finally asked, choking back the emotion which bubbled in her chest.

"When the staff arrived to Ms. Nichols' room to help her shower, she was already showered and dressed; then *she* told them she didn't want eggs for breakfast—she wanted fruit." As Valerie recounted the scene that sent every member of Claire's care team into overdrive, Valerie couldn't contain her smile.

Meredith, however, was having difficulty holding back her tears. "Do they think this is real? I mean, will it last?"

"Oh, Dr. Fairfield is beside himself. Mrs. Russel, he's invited you to join them. Your care has helped in getting Ms. Nichols to this point."

Meredith knew that was true, but she also knew Claire's public declaration was done for one reason—to save her. If she entered that room, then she'd defeat Claire's efforts. Unable to keep the emotion from her voice, Meredith replied, "I want to, but seeing her with her sister and brother-in-law...I don't want to interrupt this family moment. Besides, I don't want her to see me crying. I don't want to upset her."

Valerie placed her hand comfortingly on Meredith's shoulder. "I understand. This has been very emotional for everyone."

"May I see her later this afternoon? I'm not scheduled to work, but I'd like to bring her dinner to her, if I may?"

"I don't see why not. Does Ms. Bali have your number?"

"Yes, she does."

"If there are any concerns, we'll call you; otherwise, please come back." Valerie patted her shoulder. "Ms. Nichols mentioned you by name. She does appreciate all that you've been doing for her."

Meredith couldn't answer; the soft tears now flowed too freely. She took one last look at the scene through the window, nodded to Valerie, and left the observation room. After retrieving a tissue from her purse, Meredith walked to the kitchen offices. Ms. Bali would want to know what happened and transformed their meeting.

As soon as Meredith reached her car, she called her husband. In retrospect, she understood how he misconstrued her tears. Of course, he thought she'd been arrested. When she explained what Claire did, he promised a celebratory dinner. Meredith agreed, with one stipulation—it needed to be a late one. First, she wanted to come back and see Claire—after the Vandersols left.

∞∞∞∞∞∞

Six steps—that's the length of Claire's trek near her bed. Her mind swirled with the onslaught of new information—it was all she could do to slow thoughts. The repetitive counting, as she methodically paced back and forth, helped to calm her—*One, two, three, four, five, six—turn—one, two...*

She told herself this technique was normal—not crazy.

No matter how much she tried to focus on other issues, Meredith kept coming to Claire's thoughts. *What if she stayed away or didn't know what Claire had done? What if she didn't come back?*

Unfortunately, Claire knew the answer to her own questions—that knowledge propelled her steps—*if* Meredith didn't return—there'd be *no one* to help Claire remember the man she loved—no one to help her remember the man who would *never* return. Meredith was the only person willing to break the rules—*four, five, six—turn—one*—Oh, Claire knew *rules*—but this rule couldn't be maintained—as much as she wanted to show everyone that she could behave, obeying this rule wasn't an option.

Claire knew her memories weren't right. *There were gaps the size of craters!* When Claire tried to remember Tony—real memories mixed with illusions. Meredith's stories helped her remember—they helped to bring color back to the dimming scenes from her past. As Claire tried to recall specific times from her past, panic bubbled up from her chest—*three, four, five, six—turn—one, two*—Sometimes she'd be able to picture a place, but not the faces. Other times she'd imagine the faces, but the scents were gone. Her pacing quickened as she feared her sacrifice—telling everyone she was getting better—was all for not.

Concentrating on *his* face, the color of *his* eyes, and the scent of *his* cologne, the sound of the opening door or moving cart didn't register. Perhaps ignoring the worker was a conscious decision. Claire was tired of talking—*turn—one, two, three*—The day had been so full! There'd been so many different people asking so many questions. She wanted time to process—time to sort things out—time to spend alone with Tony. Yes, she knew that wouldn't truly happen; nevertheless, memories were better than nothing.

Claire didn't notice the woman beside her until she felt the hand on her arm. Turning toward the touch, her friend's voice quieted the numbers and slowed the torrent of thoughts. Although she hadn't heard what Meredith was saying, Claire bowed her head and whispered, "Oh, thank God."—"I was worried about you."

"About me?" Meredith lifted Claire's chin. "What about you? Are you all right?" Hugging her friend, she added, "Thank you!"

Walking toward the table where Meredith had placed Claire's food, Claire replied, "I'm tired"—"That's normal though"—"isn't it?"

Smiling, Meredith nodded. "Yes, Claire, it is, but what you did, oh my God, it was beyond normal. It was amazing!"

"I can't lose you"—"Please don't follow the rules"—Claire spoke in quiet short bursts—"I need you to help me remember"—"You're my only connection to him."

"What you did was a big risk. You told me you weren't ready. Thank you." Reaching for Claire's hand, Meredith squeezed and said, "I'm not your *only* connection. Did you talk to Emily about Nichol?"

Claire's relieved smile disappeared. "I did"—"She doesn't want me to see her"—"Not yet"—"Until they're sure"—"I'm better."

Meredith's heart broke. "What do *you* want?"

"She showed me pictures"—Claire's voice lightened—"She's beautiful!" Lifting her moist green eyes toward Meredith, Claire added, "I want to hold her"—"in my arms." When she closed her eyes, a renegade tear slid down her cheek. "I've missed so much."

"But there's so much more to experience. We'll get you better. You'll be holding Nichol in your arms soon." Meredith questioned, "How did your family reunion go?"

Claire sighed and shrugged her shoulders. She lifted her fork and began to eat. After a few bites, she offered, "There were a lot of questions." "I'm tired of talking."

"It's all right. You don't need to tell me anything."

Hurriedly, Claire offered, "I didn't tell them your last name." "I just said"—"*Meredith*"—"That won't get you in trouble?"—"Will it?"

"No, I'm using Jerry's last name—Russel."

Claire exhaled. "Good"—"can you keep visiting?"—"Will you?"—"Please?"

"Oh, yes!"

Though most of her sentences were incomplete and her words slowed with each sentence, Claire told Meredith she didn't know what to do when

Emily and John walked in. The last memories she could recall of her sister, Emily was mad at her. Thankfully, Emily wasn't mad; instead, she was relieved! During most of the meeting, they talked about Nichol.

It was a much busier day than Claire had experienced in a long time. Although it wasn't late, after Claire stopped eating, Meredith asked it she wanted help getting ready for bed. Claire didn't want to accept Meredith's help, she'd already accepted too much; nevertheless, fatigue prevailed.

∞∞∞∞∞∞

Soon, Claire was in her nightgown and ready for sleep. As Meredith was about to leave, she remembered something else she'd brought Claire. "I almost forgot. I have a present for you."

Meredith went to the food cart and removed a large package, wrapped in pink paper with a brighter pink bow, from the bottom shelf. The colorful box was a stark contrast to the bland room. When she turned back toward Claire, she saw a spark in Claire's eyes she hadn't seen in years.

"Do you want to open it now?" Meredith asked as she set the box next to Claire on the bed.

Claire nodded and whispered, "Yes." Yet, instead of moving, Claire stared at the box.

"Is there a problem?"

"The paper"—"It's so pretty."

Meredith eased the bow off and carefully ran her finger under the tape. With the paper loosely covering the gift, she left it beside Claire on the bed. Apprehensively, Claire removed the paper and took off the lid. Pushing the tissue paper aside, she revealed three bright pink throw pillows. Two were circular and one was a square with ruffles. Hugging one of the pillows close to her chest, Claire smiled and asked, "Can they stay here?" "It would be great to have color."

"Yes, and I'll bring more color! We'll get this room to reflect how much better you're doing!"

"Oh"—"I'd like that." Closing her eyes, Claire added, "I wish..."

Meredith waited for Claire's voice to regain strength. When it didn't, she asked, "What do you wish?"

"You've done too much"—"I can't"—"ask for more."

Meredith lifted Claire's chin until their eyes met. "You saved me from jail today; what do you wish?"

"For the gray"—"to go away."

"It will. Each day, we'll make everything more colorful."

Claire shook her head. "No"—"the gray in my hair"—"I'm not that old"—"What will Nichol think?"

Meredith smiled. "Oh, honey, I'll be back tomorrow, and we'll bring color back to your hair. What color do you want to be?" With a grin, she added, "More pink?"

With her head settled on her pillows, a faint smile came to Claire's lips. "No, I like brown"—"I like brown"—"a lot." Her eyes closed.

Meredith set the box on the floor, placed the pillows next to Claire and covered her with a blanket. Gathering Claire's dinner dishes, she thought about Claire's words. Yes, Meredith remembered the stories of Claire's hair. She also knew the color of Tony's eyes. It went without saying—Claire definitely liked brown.

Tomorrow, Meredith had a new goal—Claire's hair would return to the beautiful shiny chestnut color she had in college. As she turned off the light and closed Claire's door, Meredith giggled. Her job description was ever changing—soon she could add beautician to her résumé.

It's not so important who starts the game but who finishes it.

—John Wooden

CHAPTER 41

The tropical sky darkened; hues of orange and red faded to black. Tony looked out toward the now calm sea as the ball of fire which warmed their world, once again, found its home below the horizon. As evidence of the ravaging the sea had endured at the hands of the tropical storm, seaweed and driftwood littered the normally pristine white sand surrounding the lagoon. The shore wasn't its only victim. Palm trees lay precariously strewn across paths, over one another, all around the island, downed by the strong winds.

Tony paced between the windows and Claire's delivery bed. *Their mattress needed to be replaced, what difference did it make if their baby was born upon it?* Madeline exchanged the cool compress on Claire's forehead for a cooler one and fed Claire ice chips. Tony watched; however, his attention was divided between his wife and the men he'd sent out to sea. Every so often, he'd look out toward the water hoping—praying—for signs of Francis and Phil. Nearly two hours earlier, he'd received a call saying they were on their way back with Dr. Gilbert. The trip usually lasted thirty to forty minutes, so they should've arrived over an hour ago. Occasionally, Tony's gaze would meet Madeline's. Though she didn't say a word, he knew by her furrowed brow that she too was worried. He just didn't know if it were solely because of Francis, who'd warned them hundreds of times about navigating a boat after dark, or if it was also about Claire.

Claire's stifled cries brought Tony away from the reflective glass panes to their brightly lit suite. Every light in their room was on, along with multiple additional lamps that Tony had retrieved from around the house. Claire's contractions were occurring closer and closer together. He knelt beside her bed, kissed her cheek, and waited for her response. One moment, she wanted him near—the next moment, she didn't want to be touched. At one time during the evening, Madeline cornered Tony in the bathroom, while he dampened more cloths for Claire's head. "Monsieur, what Madame el is saying and feeling, it is normal. She needs you to stay strong."

298

Tony nodded. He didn't know what normal was anymore. His whole world was different than he'd ever foreseen. The addition of their child would only further propel it into an oblivion he never before knew existed, and as for strength—he could do that. It was his thing. If he could endure the pain he saw in Claire's eyes in her stead, then he would without hesitation.

"You don't have to be strong," Tony encouraged. "Scream if you need to scream." This time, she took his hand and squeezed. For a moment, he considered screaming. Never before had his petite, gentle wife exhibited so much strength. He worried the bones in his fingers may not survive; and then all at once, her grip lessened and the clouds of pain floated away revealing shiny emerald eyes as tears slipped down her cheeks.

"Where's Dr. Gilbert?"

"He'll be here soon." *Did he sound confident?* Tony hoped he did. He tried multiple times to contact Phil by phone, but Tony knew the phones had poor reception when out to sea. The only way to make contact was the two-way radio. The transmitter and receiver were in the boathouse. Earlier, Tony mentioned going to the boathouse and trying to reach them, but Claire's sudden look of panic stopped him in his tracks. She was determined that he needed to be with her. *Didn't she understand, he was useless, and Dr. Gilbert was the one she needed?*

"Tony? Tony!?"

"I'm right here."

Her face contorted as she made a sound he'd never heard.

"I'm right here. What can I do?" he asked.

Breathing through the pain, she spoke in but a whisper, "There's so much pressure."

Madeline lifted the sheet and felt between Claire's legs. When her hand emerged, it was covered in blood. Tony felt his own blood drain from his face. Mercifully, he was on his knees. If he'd been standing, Tony feared his show of strength would fail as he'd be prone on the floor.

Madeline looked directly into his eyes. "Monsieur, we're going to bring your bébé into this world."

Tony nodded—at least he thought he did.

Madeline emphasized, "Now, Monsieur!"

Claire screamed as Madeline, once again, explored below the sheet.

Although Madeline's voice was calm, her words took the air from Tony's lungs. "I'm not feeling your bébé's head. It's too soft. She's coming bottom first!"

Before he could respond, Claire's hoarse voice pleaded, "Oh, please, please help my baby."

Tony soothed her forehead with his hand, unsure what else to do. "Madeline, tell me what to do."

"Let me see your hands, Monsieur."

He did as she asked and held up his hands.

"Too large—I will help your child come. I worry about the cord. Did the doctor ever mention *breach*?"

Claire shook her head, tears flowing easier than words. "No, but the last ultrasound was almost two months ago."

"She has turned, but it is all right. Many women deliver bébés this way. I worry about pulling if the cord is where it should not be."

Claire's breath was a ragged plea, "Please...I don't care about me, save my baby."

The hair on Tony's neck stood to attention. "I care! We will save both of you!"

Before he finished declaring, Claire screamed again. The sound echoed through the house and over the island. Blood now covered Madeline's hands and arms. Tony saw splashes on the front of her dress.

Madeline instructed, "Go to the kitchen; in the cabinet near the stove there is a case. It is brown. Bring it to me."

Tony looked down into Claire's now clouded eyes. Again, she cried out.

"I'll be right back," he promised as he kissed Claire's damp head and stepped away. Rounding the end of the bed, Tony's shoe slipped on the wooden floor. Looking down, he stopped. On the floor, seeping into the cracks between the bamboo planks, he saw a puddle of blood.

"Go, hurry!" Madeline's command propelled his stilled feet.

Tony wasn't well-versed on anything in a kitchen; however, he knew a stove and a cabinet. Flinging open the doors he found a brown case. When he opened the case, his heart stopped beating. The cutlery was shiny and clean with sharp looking blades. Bile rose in his throat as he imagined one of these knives being used on his wife. Tony couldn't let Claire endure this pain without something. Quickly, he grabbed a bottle of bourbon. He'd make her drink if he had to; or perhaps it could be used to sterilize the knife. Tony didn't know the exact reason; however, as he rushed back toward his bedroom, he held tightly to both the case and the bottle.

When he entered the brightly lit room, Claire's eyes were closed and her chin rested against her chest. "What happened? What did you do?"

"Nothing, Monsieur, it's her body. It knows. Her muscles must relax, and this way, she will not feel the pain. Please open the case."

He did.

"That one, with the shorter blade"—then she saw the bottle—"Pour the bourbon over the blade."

He wasn't sure how he managed to move. Everything was on high alert, yet in slow motion at the same time. The red filling their room wasn't that of anger—it was Claire's blood. Tony wanted it all to stop.

As he handed the knife to Madeline, their eyes met. "Monsieur, I'm doing my best to save your child."

"And my wife, Madeline—save my wife."

She nodded.

At that moment, they heard the voices on the lanai. Turning, the doors to their suite opened and they saw Francis, Phil, and Dr. Gilbert. Francis said something about trees blocking their way as the doctor entered and assessed the scene. Looking to Tony, he said, "Mr. Rawlings, I need to wash my hands. Follow me and tell me everything."

It was the abridged version—they didn't have time for a full length novel. Tony emphasized the main points—Claire's water broke roughly twenty-four hours ago—the contractions returned about six hours ago and had gained in intensity over the last two hours—she'd lost what appeared to be a lot of blood—had recently gone unconscious—and Madeline believed the baby was breach.

Dr. Gilbert nodded as he opened his bag. With a paper gown covering his clothes and surgical gloves over his hands, he took Madeline's place at the end of the bed. When he eyed the knives, he nodded toward Madeline. "You have good instincts. Go wash your hands; I need an assistant."

Tony moved to Claire's head and stayed at her side. He talked in her ear and smoothed her perspiration drenched hair from her face. With all of his might, he tried not to listen to Dr. Gilbert and Madeline's words. This wasn't his personality. He was a take-charge person, a man who demanded all of the facts. Right now, he wanted to pretend everything was all right, especially when Dr. Gilbert asked, "Mr. Rawlings, I hope it won't come to this; however, if you must choose between your wife and your child, what is your decision?"

How can anyone answer such a question? The life of the woman he loved more than life itself or the life of an innocent child who'd never experienced the world. Inhaling deeply, Tony looked Dr. Gilbert directly in the eye, and despite his new feeling of impotence, found his CEO voice, "Doctor, that decision will *not* be necessary. You *will* save them both."

There wasn't time to debate. Claire's body continued to contract. Although she was unconscious, her muscles worked to expel their child. Tony heard the awful pop, sounding much like the puncturing of a piece of plastic. Burying his face in Claire's shoulder he spoke—about what—he didn't know. He talked about walks, lakes, and beaches. In the background, he heard a suctioning sound and the call for a scalpel. It wasn't until he heard the cry of a baby, while still feeling the drum of Claire's pulse under his fingertips, that he had the strength to lift his head.

In Dr. Gilbert's hands, with Madeline gently wiping it clean, was the pinkest, most beautiful baby Tony had ever seen. He'd told himself that, if he needed to decide, it would have been Claire. He knew that was the way he would have gone. Once again, his life was a contradiction. He still would have chosen Claire; however, seeing the round face, tightly shut eyes, and open mouth—his body shuddered with relief, thankful he hadn't been forced to make that decision.

Above the loud and proud wails of his child, Madeline proclaimed, "Monsieur, welcome your daughter."

Before he could move, he squeezed Claire's hand. "Doctor, is Claire..?" His voice trailed away, as he was unable to finish his question.

"She's lost a lot of blood, as you said; but I believe once we deliver the placenta, place some stitches, and get her some fluids; your wife will be okay."

With that reassurance, Tony stepped toward Madeline who now held his perfect baby girl wrapped in a blanket. Her eyes were shut, and she appeared content with the new warmth. The top of her small head had a thin layer of dark brown hair. Leaning near, Tony cooed, "Hello, my princess. I'm your daddy."

The angst of the last few hours dissipated as Tony moved the rocking chair from the nursery and placed it near Claire's head. After he washed his hands, he sat and Madeline placed their bundle of joy in his arms. Never had Tony imagined another woman taking residence in his heart. It belonged to Claire and had for a very long time. Once again, he'd been wrong. It wasn't that the little girl he held replaced her mother—that wasn't possible. No, this little girl expanded his heart, making her own space. It seemed unbelievable that his heart could grow—it wasn't that long ago that Tony didn't even know it existed. Gently, Tony kissed his daughter's forehead and watched her nose crinkle.

"Monsieur, what is her name?" Madeline asked with anticipation.

"We'll wait until Claire awakes. We never pinpointed one girl's name."

Tony saw the exchange of looks between Madeline and Dr. Gilbert. Dr. Gilbert explained their concern, "Mr. Rawlings, it's almost midnight. The people of these islands are strong in their traditions and beliefs. No child should enter the next day without their proper name. It'll bring uncertainty and unhappiness to the rest of its life."

Tony looked at his watch; it was 11:53 PM. His mind went back over all of their naming discussions. They had gone through list after list of names. She'd said *Blaine* could be for a girl too, but that didn't feel right. The conversation that came to Tony's tired mind was one from when he first arrived on the island. This baby, he'd said, won't be a Rawls or a Nichols but a Rawlings. She was a Rawlings; nevertheless, Rawls was part of Rawlings no matter how much Tony tried to run or hide from the fact, and his daughter was also a Nichols, something he wanted her to know with pride. Clearing his throat, Tony looked up at Madeline and Dr. Gilbert's expectant eyes, and said, "May I introduce our daughter, *Nichol Courtney Rawlings*."

Madeline's smile beamed, reaffirming the joy that now filled the suite.

∞∞∞∞∞∞

When Claire awoke, she was lying on a bed in her room. Somehow, she knew it wasn't their bed, but nonetheless, next to her propped against the headboard was her husband. When she turned toward him, her eyes opened wide and her lungs forgot to inhale. In his arms, wrapped in a blanket was a sleeping baby. With tears streaming down her cheeks, Claire lifted her head. Her body ached, yet she could move without effort. "I did it?" she asked as his tired eyes met hers. The soft chocolate color drew her nearer.

"Yes, Mrs. Rawlings, you did." He leaned down and their lips met. Looking lovingly into her eyes, he added, "*You* did a superb job."

Claire righted herself to sit beside her family. In the bend of her right arm was the too familiar pinch of an IV. Choosing to ignore the painful sensation, Claire concentrated on her family. Despite Tony's obvious exhaustion, she saw the pride behind his expression. Once again, Tony brushed his lips against hers before he placed their baby in her arms. "May I introduce our daughter?"

Claire's heart melted. "A girl—M—Madeline was right."

Shaking his head, Tony replied, "I don't think she should ever be doubted again."

"We didn't decide on a girl's name." Claire's words came as she gently unwrapped the blanket, exposing the present she'd been carrying for nine months.

"She has a name."

Claire looked up. "Oh?"

"There's some island wives' tale that forbids the changing to the next day without a name. I hope you don't mind. I didn't want to risk our daughter having any unnecessary ill fortune."

Claire tried to grasp the reality of not only having a daughter, but that she was already named. "Is it Raquel?" It had been his go-to name in all their debates.

"No, I wanted a name that would unite our family; one that said the Rawls vendetta is over."

Claire didn't know what to say. Tony's words were more emotion filled than she could remember hearing. "What is it? What name did you choose?"

"Nichol." Tony's eyes begged for understanding.

Claire's lips parted and her eyes sparkled. The game was done—no more strategizing or manipulating; instead of declaring a winner, they'd called it even. Their daughter's name was Claire's ultimate prize. Claire's heart filled with pride. Immediately, she knew it was Tony's way of telling their daughter she was both a Nichols and a Rawlings. "Oh, Tony, I love it! We never even talked about that."

Tony's chest moved as he exhaled with relief. "Nichol Courtney Rawlings."

It was the most beautiful name she'd ever heard. As Nichol's eyes opened and Claire saw the chocolate brown she loved, she whispered, "I wanted your eyes. You wanted a girl. We've been blessed with both of our wishes." Nichol's mouth rooted toward Claire's breast.

Tony's eyes drifted closed as his head fell back to the wall. It had been a long forty-eight hours. Before he fell asleep, Claire heard him say, "A wish, a dream, a miracle—Whatever it is, it's real."

It has been said, 'time heals all wounds.' I do not agree.
The wounds remain. In time, the mind, protecting its sanity,
covers them with scar tissue and the pain lessens. But it is never gone.
—Rose Kennedy.

CHAPTER 42

Sophia eased her car onto the circular brick drive in front of Marie's massive house. On her cell phone, she heard Derek's voice, "Have a nice lunch, babe. Is the house as nice as you anticipated?"

Her mouth gaped open as she looked up at the Romanesque-style mansion with facades of river stone, limestone, and brick. It was like something out of a 1940's movie. "It's amazing. I can't believe she really lives here. Do people actually live like this?"

Derek laughed. "Well, she worked for Rawlings. That's his house—or it was. No one knows if he's alive or dead, but it's probably not great table-talk for your lunch."

"I'll try to remember that—keep conversation topics away from missing employers. What did you say; she's named the executor of his estate?"

"Yeah, the information I found just named her as a long-time trusted employee—"

Sophia interrupted, "Hey, honey, the front door's opening. I should get out of the car. I'll call you when I'm on my way home."

She heard him say he loved her as she turned off the car and the Bluetooth disconnected. "I love you, too," she said to the warm air within the confines of her car. It was a stark contrast to the cold February chill between her and the mansion she was about to enter. Sophia secured her coat and gloves and bowed her face to the snowflakes as she hurried toward the grand doors.

The gentleman within nodded as her shoes hit the marble floor. Looking down, she saw the traces of snow that had fallen from her shoes and created puddles within the beautiful foyer. "Ms. Sophia?"

"Yes," she said sheepishly. "Hello." Sophia offered her hand.

The gentleman nodded again and said, "Ms. London is expecting you. May I take your coat?"

Sophia tried desperately not to gawk at her surroundings as she removed her coat and gloves and handed them to the butler—um—servant? She didn't know who he was—only that apparently, he didn't shake hands. "Yes, thank you. Where is Mar—Ms. London? Is she here?"

"Yes, miss. She's waiting for you in the sitting room. Please follow me."

Each step reminded Sophia of a fantasy. Growing up in New Jersey and being a fan of the arts, Sophia loved watching old movies, especially those in black and white. If there was singing and dancing, it made it all the better. When she'd go to bed at night she'd think about the movies and the places the characters lived. She dreamt about mansions, servants, and opulence. As she grew up, Sophia learned that a life like she saw in the movies was mostly a world of fantasy. She could glean inspiration from it, but it didn't truly exist. Stepping down into a warm sitting room, Sophia hypothesized—*maybe this world did exist*. She glanced toward a fireplace that was nearly the size of her living room in Provincetown. Within its limestone walls a warm fire roared, filling the room with warmth.

"Welcome, Sophia!" Marie said as she stood, placing the tablet she'd been reading on the nearby table.

Sophia leaned toward her friend and accepted her welcoming hug. "Marie, your house is amazing."

Marie shrugged. "I know it seems that way, but after so many years—it's just home."

Looking through the windows, Sophia saw a sun room. Beyond, there was a large yard where blades of grass showed their heads through the thin layer of snow while more flakes swirled in the frosty air. Trees lined the yard creating a private haven. Refocusing on the room, Sophia concentrated on the heat radiating from the fire. "That fireplace is huge! On a day like today, it feels fantastic."

Marie smiled. "It does feel good. Can I get you some coffee?" Before Sophia could answer, Marie corrected, "No, it's tea you like, isn't it? Would you like some warm Earl Gray?"

"That would be wonderful, thank you."

Within seconds, a woman was in the sitting room taking instructions from Marie. Sophia was sitting on the sofa talking with Marie when the woman returned with Sophia's tea. Apparently, lunch would be ready momentarily. A few minutes later, a young girl rushed into the room with a piece of paper in her hand. Her voice cracked with each word, "Ms. London, I'm sorry to bother you."

"Cindy? Is there a problem?"

The young lady shook her head. "I didn't mean to interrupt. I know you're busy; however, perhaps later, I could speak with you..."

Marie turned her gaze toward Sophia.

Sophia didn't know what to say. It was obvious there was an issue. "Marie, I'm in no hurry. If there's something the two of you need to discuss, then I'll gladly enjoy the fire."

"Thank you, Sophia." Marie turned toward Cindy. "Come with me to my office."

As the two of them walked away, Sophia heard Cindy mention something about a letter, the FBI, and her parents. Before she could truly glean any meaning from the conversation, Marie and Cindy had disappeared down a long corridor. Sophia sighed. This was a strange and different world from anything she'd known. The owner of this house was missing, yet no one seemed concerned as they carried on their daily lives, and the young maid received letters from the FBI...Sophia leaned back against the plush sofa and looked into the flames. The crackle and snap of the wood added to the allure. In Provincetown, she and Derek's home had a real fireplace. Everywhere they've lived since then had gas logs. Supposedly, the two were the same. Inhaling the distinct wood aroma, Sophia knew, they weren't.

"Are you ready for lunch?" Marie asked, pulling Sophia from the hypnotism of the flames.

"Yes, is everything all right?" Sophia saw Marie brush her palms against her thighs. It was the same technique Sophia used when she tried to hide her uneasiness.

"Yes, let me show you to the dining room."

As they walked, Marie mentioned that Cindy had worked for this estate for quite a few years. She was only eighteen when her parents died in a tragic accident. Now, it seemed the FBI was interested in their death and wanted to exhume their bodies."

Sophia gasped. "Oh my! How terrible! I'd never let anyone do that to my parents."

Marie's hands again brushed her thighs as they sat. "Perhaps you'd be better to speak to Cindy than I? I knew her mother—we were friends. I recommended that she deny the FBI access. There's no good to come from digging up the past."

Sophia sat back against the high backed chair and gazed around the lovely dining room. The built-in cabinetry at one end of the table held exquisite china. When her gaze moved upward, Sophia saw the ornate ceiling with reflective gold flecks. "I agree. It's better to move on."

The rest of the afternoon was spent back in front of the fire, discussing art and upcoming events in the Quad Cities. Before Sophia was about to leave, she asked, "Marie, do you mind if I ask you something?"

"Not at all. I can't promise I'll answer, but ask away."

"I really don't have many people to talk to—not here anyway. The thing is"—Sophia hesitated—"before we left California, I received a call from my birth mother."

Marie stared and slowly asked, "You received a call from the woman who recently died?"

Sophia shook her head, the absurdity of Marie's statement made her grin. "No, the people who raised me were wonderful. I loved them and will love them forever; however, I was adopted. My parents were honest about it. I never felt deprived or less loved because my mother didn't give birth to me. Honestly, I never really gave a damn about the woman who gave birth to me, or my biological father, until I got that call."

Marie's hands were again experiencing the sensory input of her slacks. "What happened after you got the call?"

"I started wondering about her and about him."

Marie's head tilted as her brow rose. "Him? You started wondering about your father?"

Sophia's breathe expelled. "Well, yes! I mean, the woman who gave birth to me called, but what about my biological father? Are they still together? Did they love one another or do they still? Do they regret giving me up?"

"Oh, I see. Did you ask any of those questions?"

"No, I have a telephone number, but sometimes I think not knowing is better. I mean, I can make up my own answers."

Marie smiled. "So, what's your question, dear?"

Sophia readjusted her legs, curling one under herself as she leaned back into the plushness of the large chair. "I don't know." Her voice sounded far away. "I guess I just need to talk about it. Derek listens, but he's protective. He doesn't want me to get hurt."

"Do you think you will?"

Sophia's lips pressed together and she feigned a smile. "I've thought about the possibilities from all directions. If I learn I have this great set of biological parents who have a great life, then I'll wonder why they didn't want me to be a part of it. If I learn they didn't stay together or they're not good people, then I'll wonder if dealing with me was part of the cause."

Marie leaned forward and put her hand on Sophia's knee. "That's quite a decision. I've known many people who have done things they regret. Perhaps that's why the woman called, or perhaps she regrets what she did thirty-three years ago; however, I don't believe *you* should feel responsible for anything other than who you've become." Marie's gray eyes shimmered in the firelight. "Sophia, you're an accomplished, lovely woman. The woman you spoke to should be proud."

The scene melted as Sophia fought stoically not to cry. "I miss my mom and pop." With the back of her hand, she brushed a renegade tear away.

"Thank you Marie. I suppose the holidays left me feeling lonely." She reached out and held Marie's hand. "Thanks for listening."

"Anytime."

"You know, we don't seem that different in age, yet look, Cindy came to you when she had a problem, and now, so did I." Sophia chuckled. "You're probably sick of listening to everyone else's troubles."

"Not at all. I'm honored you feel comfortable enough to talk."

"I do, and I think you're right before—no good comes from digging up the past. I don't want to know that woman. I've been blessed with great parents, a fantastic husband, and good friends. Why push my luck?"

∞∞∞∞∞∞

After a delightful afternoon, Marie walked Sophia to the door. Once Marie watched Sophia's car pull away and the barrier to the outside was closed, Catherine murmured, "Eighteen years; that's our age difference, and you *do not* want to learn about the man who donated his DNA to make you—I refuse to consider him any kind of father. He doesn't deserve any credit for the beautiful woman you are today! The way things are now *is* much better than bringing memories of that monster into the equation."

As she walked toward her office, Catherine smiled, her words not audible to anyone, "In time, my dear, I promise, that it'll be even better."

∞∞∞∞∞∞

Harry finished his report. His case in West Virginia was done. Tomorrow, he'd fly back to Palo Alto. He considered calling Liz and warning her, but as a sneaky grin came to his lips, he decided it would be more fun to surprise her. Since he'd been called away before Christmas, they hadn't had a chance to celebrate the holiday. With Valentine's Day just around the corner, he'd try to think of some way for them to enjoy the next one. Harry believed if he gave it a little thought, something would come up.

With a few minutes to spare before leaving the field office, Harry decided to utilize the bureau's database. It didn't take him long to back-door his way into his old case. Within seconds, he'd accessed the Rawlings/Nichols files. When he did, he was rewarded with new information. It appeared Anthony Rawlings had continued to stay in contact, as ordered by the FBI. Claire Nichols Rawlings had given birth to a healthy baby girl. For a split second, Harry wondered if the baby had blue or brown eyes. As fast as the thought entered his mind, he pushed it away. That wasn't his purpose for this walk down memory lane. For the last two months Harry had successfully distanced himself from all things Rawlings/Nichols. He wanted to keep that distance—

forever; however, there were a few things that kept eating at him. If he were to truly ever have closure—he needed to resolve some issues.

He accessed the tissue sample analysis for Simon Johnson. Since Rawlings confessed to paying for Simon's demise, no one had taken the time to verify the Johnson case. Harry wanted to let it go. He wanted Anthony Rawlings to rot in jail for a very long time. Without a doubt, hiring someone to sabotage a plane was a crime, and of that—without a doubt—Rawlings was guilty. Of *actually murdering* Simon Johnson—Harry wanted to say—yes, Rawlings was responsible—but he couldn't. Johnson's body had been so badly burnt, the forensics were difficult.

The toxicology report came back with one hundred percent accuracy that actaea pachypoda was *not* in Simon's system. Over the last few months, Harry had begun to wonder, what *was* in Simon's system. Now, as he accessed the data, he found the answer to his question—the only foreign substance detected in Simon's tissues was diphenhydramine. Harry scrolled to the raw data—diphenhydramine, micrograms/liter 17.5. Saying a silent prayer that his snooping would go undetected, he wrote down the information and backed out of the system. He was finally getting his life and his head where they needed to be. Harry didn't need the powers that be to know he was still obsessing over a closed case.

A quick Google search on his phone confirmed Harry's thoughts—diphenhydramine was more commonly known as Benadryl. He and Simon had been friends for a few years. Harry tried to remember if Simon had allergies—after all, his plane did crash in the late fall. With the dryness and fires often associated with autumn in California, it would make sense that he'd take Benadryl during allergy season. Harry had Simon's medical history on his laptop back at the hotel and made a mental note to check for allergies. One last search, then Harry was done—he wanted to know the *lethal volume of distribution* for diphenhydramine...he waited.

After a few clicks, the answer appeared—lethal volume of distribution for diphenhydramine in adults—19.5 mg/L—children 7.5 mg/L—and infants 1.53 mg/L. Simon's *volume of distribution* didn't fall in the lethal range. Once again, Harry had more questions than answers.

Courage is resistance to fear, mastery of fear, not absence of fear.

—Mark Twain

CHAPTER 43

Claire stared down at their three-month-old daughter. She remembered to breathe, as air fought with pride and love, to fill her chest. Staring at Nichol's big brown eyes, she watched the chocolate come and go as her stubborn little girl fought unsuccessfully to keep her eyes alert. The lids fluttered slower and slower, each blink lasting longer than the last, until sleep overtook her round, angel like face. While her pink lips pursed and her long, dark lashes rested upon her rosy cheeks, Claire swooned helplessly, finding it difficult to look away from the child resting peacefully in her arms. Claire wasn't the only one held captive by Nichol's charm. It reached out to anyone within her sphere, including Madeline.

Claire rocked Nichol gently as Madeline's rich laugh and hearty voice filled the tropical air, "Madame el, she eats well! Your beautiful daughter, she's growing every day. Look at those cheeks!"

Both women peered at Nichol's soft skin nestled against Claire's breast. Answering in a stage whisper, Claire replied, "She *is*—too fast! I want to hold her and rock her forever."

"Enjoy, because soon she'll be crawling all over this floor. Next, she'll be running all over the island."

Claire shook her head. She couldn't imagine her little baby girl crawling, much less running. Enjoying the even pace of the rocking chair, Claire closed her eyes and sighed. "I never imagined it would be so amazing."

"Madame el, do you want me to put the princess in her crib?"

Claire started to say, *no*, when she looked up and saw Tony enter the room. The gleam which normally occupied his soft brown eyes—especially since the birth of their daughter, was gone. In its place, Claire saw darkness. She wasn't sure the cause. *Was it worry or concern?* His stoic expression hid any revealing clues, yet she knew there was something. It wasn't just his eyes; she could feel the tension radiating from his every pore. It'd been so long since she'd seen him this way. Instinctively, she understood he wanted to speak to her alone.

Feigning a smile toward Madeline, Claire relinquished the sleeping bundle. "I'd love to sit here all day; however, I'll admit, Nichol needs a good nap in her crib—if we're going to ever get her on the right schedule."

"Oui, Madame el, we will." Madeline looked toward Tony and back to Claire. Her smile faded as the lines in her forehead deepened. She continued, "If you need anything, or you Monsieur, please call for me. After I put the little angel down, I shall be in the kitchen."

Tony remained silent as Claire acknowledged Madeline's words and watched her walk away. Once they were alone, Claire made her way toward her husband. With each step forward, she analyzed the man before her, standing silently staring out at the beautiful, blue sea. Despite his casual attire, Claire recognized his stance, the tightness in his shoulders and clinched jaw. She knew he was contemplating a thousand things—he was, once again, the CEO of a billion dollar conglomerate—the man with unfathomable responsibilities— the man before paradise. She needed to know why.

Reaching for his arm, Claire looked up into his dark eyes. "Tony, what is it? What's the matter?"

"I need to tell you something"—his tone matched his gaze, strong and demanding—"but first, I want you to promise that you'll do as I say."

Claire stood a little taller. "I love you—I promise that. What I'm going to do has yet to be determined." The muscles under her fingertips tensed. Softening her pitch, she implored, "Tony, please tell me what happened. You're scaring me."

Turning, he clutched her shoulders as his stare bore down from above. Undaunted, she waited for his explanation. Behind his eyes, where she used to see only darkness, Claire now saw fury, indecision, and love. The sound of the surf filled the void while Tony wrestled to organize his words. Finally, his warm breath hit her cheeks and he implored, "Don't you understand? I need to know that you and Nichol are safe."

"We *are* safe. We're all safe. What's this about?"

Squaring his stance, he relayed the information emotionlessly, as if addressing a board of directors, "I just got off the phone with Eric. I'm going back to Iowa."

Claire pulled herself free and took a few steps backward in disbelief. "No! No you're not! We talked about this. Catherine can wait. Nichol needs you." Reaching for his hand, she continued, "I need you."

"Let me finish."

Claire nodded. "Fine, finish, but you know what Agent Jackson said. There are charges and a case against you. You helped hide Catherine's crimes and ran from the FBI. When you step foot on U.S. soil, they'll take you into custody." Tears trickled from her eyes. She'd begged for less. Begging to keep her husband safe, with her in paradise, came without hesitation. "Please, Tony. Please remember, we said *one year*. Let Nichol celebrate her first birthday with us, *all of us*, here—together."

"Damn it, you're killing me," he said as he wiped the tears from his wife's cheeks. Gently taking her hand, he led her out onto the lanai, to a shaded chaise lounge. Sitting, he directed, "Look at this view."

She turned toward the horizon. It was the same view she'd seen each day for months. Some days, she could stare at it for hours, but now she wanted answers.

Tugging softly on her chin, Tony pulled her gaze toward him and kissed her lips. Claire's heart ached at the sadness she saw. He continued, "I need to know you two are here—safe and sound. I won't inform the FBI I'm back in the States." As Claire's rebuttal began, Tony shook his head in an effort to keep her quiet. Obediently swallowing her protest, she nodded and he went on, "Then—then, I'll be back. I've contacted Phil. With his help, we can finish our objective sooner rather than later."

Phil had returned to the States after the first of the year. He stayed in constant contact, and Claire hadn't seen any worrisome emails. "Why?" Her voice quivered as she tried to voice her multitude of concerns all at once. "Why would you take that risk? What's so important that it can't wait a year? And how did you talk to Eric? Both the FBI and Phil told you not to contact anyone who doesn't know our location. What if he told Catherine?"

"He won't. If there's one person in this world I trust explicitly besides you—it's Eric. He's proven himself over and over."

"Yeah, you used to say the same thing about—" Although Claire stopped herself before she completed the sentence, it was too late. In the pools of black staring at her, she saw the pain she'd just inflicted.

Tony's volume rose. "You don't think I know? You don't think I've berated myself over and over for trusting her and putting you and Nichol in harm's way." Claire reached out, but when the tips of her fingers neared his arm, he pulled away. His response was as much a confession as a wish, "I thought the estate was a haven—hell, you were probably safer in California with—"

Claire wouldn't let Tony go there, she interrupted, "I'm sorry. I know you trust Eric. I also know you thought you were protecting us. We can't rewrite history. If we could, our pen would probably run out of ink"—this time, as she touched his hand and intertwined her fingers with his, he didn't stop her— "Please tell me what's happening."

"I have to go back and be sure everyone is safe. It's a responsibility I can't avoid."

"Is this about Sophia—Catherine's daughter? Do you really think Catherine would do anything to her own daughter? Besides, not to sound selfish, but I don't think she's worth you leaving *us* and taking the risk."

"It's not about Catherine's daughter." Tony hesitated.

"Then who is that important?"

"Emily."

Claire's heart stopped. Despite the warm ocean breeze, her body shivered while goose bumps formed. "Emily? What do you mean? Did something happen?"

"Not yet, but Phil called, and he's concerned. Emily and Catherine have been communicating quite a bit recently, via email and phone. His instincts told him something wasn't right."

Claire studied her husband's features. In her heart, she knew she'd misjudged his sincerity involving her family in the past. She reminded herself that things had changed—*they* had changed. Seeing the lines around his eyes and the angst in his expression, she believed that he truly looked worried. She continued to listen.

"Phil didn't know any more, so I decided it was worth the risk to call Eric. Our cell is blocked—Phil's made sure that it can't be traced. When I got a hold of Eric, he agreed—there's something going on with Catherine and Emily. He said your sister and brother-in-law have agreed to come to Iowa next week. Catherine convinced Emily to visit and retrieve some of your things."

Claire stood and paced near the edge of the infinity pool. The beautiful surroundings no longer registered. Her mind was on the other side of the world. "That doesn't make sense. Why would Emily be talking with Catherine? She shouldn't trust anything Catherine says."

"But Emily doesn't know that. All she knows it that *you* trusted Catherine. I'd bet you told Emily multiple times how wonderful Catherine was to you."

The bile rose from Claire's stomach as her mind recalled the glowing endorsements she'd bestowed upon Catherine in her recollections of life on the estate. "I did, but..."

Tony put his hand out, and Claire walked toward him, tears teetering on her lids, as he continued her sentence, "*but* Emily doesn't know the truth."

"Then I'll call her. After all, you just called Eric—I'll call Emily."

"You've been missing for six months. How do you think that conversation will go?"

Claire knelt before Tony and laid her forehead on his knees. "Do you think"—sobs of fear resonated from her chest—"Do you think Catherine would *hurt* Emily?"

Although she looked up to her husband for confirmation, Tony didn't need to answer. Claire knew the truth before she posed the question. Emily *too* was a child of a child.

He stroked her hair reassuringly. "I *will* stop this. It can't go on. We can't live in hiding forever, and John and Emily shouldn't live in fear of a threat they don't even know exists."

Taking a deep breath, Claire said, "You're right."

Standing, she brushed her lips against his. Tony pulled her into his lap, exhaled, and said, "Thank you. It'll be a relief to know you're safe."

Claire leaned away, her voice stronger. "*You're right*—this can't go on, but you're not right about Nichol and me staying here—Phil better get us an extra seat because we're going with you." She saw his finger moving toward her, about to silence her talking, but Claire shook her head and leaned back. Momentarily, their eyes meet. Hers contained a fire she didn't try to subdue—it was a fire with a purpose. The flames masked the growing fear coiling through her thoughts. "Tony, this isn't debatable—I'm not asking. We aren't staying here and worrying. Besides, Emily is my sister—I'm going."

Breaking their stare-off, Claire ended the conversation by surrendering herself to his embrace. She concentrated on the steady beat of his heart as her head rose and fell with his deep exasperated breaths. The sounds resonating from his chest pacified her. She fought the desire to stay this way forever—safe and secure in her husband's arms.

Claire had played this game before. She'd just called his bluff. Now, it was up to Tony. He needed to decide to *call, raise* the stakes, or *fold.* She didn't think folding was an option. Although he wasn't happy with her proclamation, and it jeopardized his sense of control, they both knew the money to pay Phil—keep them hidden—and secure their return—technically, belonged to her. Ultimately, Claire would decide who would travel—and who wouldn't.

As minutes ticked by, Claire lay silently in his embrace. She didn't need to see his eyes—the color didn't matter. If she wanted to go, then she was going. Claire could've yelled or fought to make him understand; instead she waited. Tony needed to justify this reality on his terms. When his arms squeezed her tighter, she knew his decision was made. With a sigh, Tony acquiesced, "I'll call Phil. We'll see what he can do; however, I'm confronting Catherine *alone.* I don't want you or Nichol in her presence—unless she's in police custody"—he kissed the top of her head—"Hell, even then—no, I'd don't want Catherine to *ever* be near Nichol!"

Claire nodded in agreement. He believed he'd made a compromise. Truthfully, she'd won, yet if making his declaration helped Tony accept her company—she didn't care. Claire didn't want Catherine near Nichol either. Her priority was keeping both Nichol *and* Tony safe. After they assured Emily and John's safety, Claire wanted her family back in paradise. Eventually, Tony would need to surrender to the FBI—it was inevitable, but she wanted her nine more months of paradise.

The last five months had been magical. Tony and Claire were finally partners with all the ups and downs accompanying those roles. They didn't always agree; however, after a life with false conformity, they learned disagreeing wasn't negative. It didn't mean disobedience or insubordination; instead, it meant discussion, voicing opinions, perhaps arguing, and then making up. Even this last conversation illustrated their recently established equality. They'd faced the demons of their past and chosen a future.

Parenthood was an excellent induction—it took them both into uncharted waters and evened the playing field—which admittedly had at one time been tilted in Tony's favor. Every day with Nichol was an exciting new adventure. Claire didn't want it to end any sooner than necessary. For the first time, she had her dream. It was the relationship she witnessed with her parents and grandparents. At one time, she believed *happily ever after* was outside of her reach. Now, it was her reality. She wasn't ready for that to end. After all, it wasn't supposed to end. The fairy tales her dad read to her as a child ended with—*they lived happily ever after*.

Claire wanted to believe that was the end of their story, but she feared it wasn't.

That night, Claire lay in bed and listened to the sounds of her paradise. Unless she concentrated—the ever present surf, no longer registered. What brought the smile to her face and peace to her heart were the sounds coming from the attached nursery. The rockers of the chair creaked against the bamboo floor. Claire closed her eyes and pictured Tony holding Nichol.

Tonight, their daughter had made it all the way until 3:00 AM, before waking to eat. Before her cries registered to Claire, Tony was out of bed. Minutes later, he brought a freshly changed, cooing bundle to Claire. The middle of the night feeding was their special time. It was as if their room—their bed—and their family existed in a bubble which no outside force could penetrate; then, as was their routine, when Nichol's belly was full, Tony told Claire to sleep, took their daughter to the attached nursery, and rocked her back to sleep.

Normally, Claire would drift away as his deep baritone voice spoke softly in the other room. Some nights, she'd try to listen to his words; however, sometimes she felt like an intruder on their private talks. Tonight, she gleaned words here and there as he lulled Nichol back to her world of slumber. The words that registered were Tony's affirmations of devotion. She couldn't help but notice that the word *safe* seemed to be tonight's reoccurring theme. Claire twisted on the satin sheets realizing that hearing him repeat that word had the opposite effect on her.

When Tony finally climbed back to bed, Claire nuzzled against his chest. The lingering scent of cologne combined with a faint aroma of baby powder overpowered her senses. Her voice cracked as she tried to sound strong, "I love you." She didn't want him to know how scared she was. After all, she was the one who demanded to accompany him to the States.

Tony stroked her back and whispered, "I love you, too." As if to reassure not only Claire but himself, he pulled her tighter and proclaimed, "It'll all be all right. I won't let anything happen to you or her."

Claire nodded into his chest. She knew, even with his hushed tone, he meant every word, but at this moment, it wasn't hers or Nichol's safety Claire doubted. "What about you? Who's keeping you safe and assuring your return?" Her tears ran onto his chest as she no longer attempted to feign strength. "I'm not just worried about Catherine"—her words came in snippets, interspersed with deep painful sobs—"what about the authorities?" "I don't want to lose you," "I don't want *this* to end."

Tony's head fell against the headboard as he continued to rub circles on the soft exposed skin of her back. "I don't deserve to be kept safe."

She sat up and stared at him through the darkness. "Don't you dare say that!"

"It's true. I've done awful things, and I deserve to pay for them."

"Tony, please stop."

He sat taller, pulling Claire close and tried to explain. "The thing is, if this had all come down years ago—before you—I would've thought it was undeserved—an injustice. Like how I used to see my grandfather's consequences, but now—now I know I deserve it. Back then, I would've gone away concerned only with Rawlings Industries. Now, everything's different. The idea of being away from you and Nichol kills me. That separation—no matter if it starts sooner or later, will be worse than anything they could've done to me, before."

"You're turning state's evidence against Catherine. With Brent, Tom, and all your legal team, maybe you can avoid jail time?"

"Damn it, Claire! You don't deserve any of this. Maybe we shouldn't have remarried; then you wouldn't be married to someone who's discussing jail time, and you sure as hell wouldn't be harboring a fugitive."

Claire smirked. "I don't know. You're married to someone who's been in a federal prison."

His head fell to hers, as if he couldn't allow any part of him to not be in contact with her. "You're so much stronger than I."

"I hardly think that's true."

"I don't know if I could survive what's happened to you." She felt him stiffen as he corrected, "What *I've* done to *you*."

She let her fingers swirl through the soft hair on his broad chest. "It's over, and *you will* survive it—we'll survive it—we've made it this far."

"I've never asked, and you've never said, what was it like?"

"Tony, please—"

He rolled her over to her back. From the faint light of the nursery and the moon over the sea, Claire saw the emotion in his eyes—she saw regret, sadness, and perhaps even fear. Instead of making that pain worse, she wanted to take it away. Swallowing her memories of prison—the memories of loneliness—the desperate need for fresh air—and the ever threatening depression—she answered, "It was very *routine*."

He raised his brow.

Claire reached up and caressed his cheek. The stubble made her smile—she loved the sensation of that stubble on her skin. "Every day is the same. You wake at the same time, eat, go from place to place, shower, sleep—everything is scheduled."

"You'll never know how sorry I am that I've ruined your life. You deserve so much better than me."

She arched her back so that her lips contacted that same stubble. After a lingering suckle, she replied, "Are you saying you wish we weren't here—right now? That you wish we weren't together?"

Tony shook his head. "You know I'm not."

She pressed her breasts upward. The sensation of his hard chest brought her over sensitive nipples to attention. "I'll admit there were parts of the journey I'd prefer to forget; the destination is"—she suckled the rough skin—"worth it—and—amazing."

His eyes closed and tone turned sultry. "Mrs. Rawlings, you're playing with fire. I'm fighting a lot of thoughts and emotions right now. If you aren't careful, then I can't promise I'll be able to control my actions."

Again, she arched upward this time, her teeth playfully nipped the lobe of his ear. She smiled as she received her desired effect—the familiar growl resonated from the back of his throat. His words were gone.

While he pulled the satin gown away from her breasts, she ran her fingers through his hair and whispered, "I've played with fire before—I like it." Feeling his desire against her leg, she murmured, "And sometimes control is overrated."

The sandpaper like stubble scratched the soft skin of her enlarged breasts. With each turn of his cheek, her senses electrified. Currents of yearning coursed through her body. The combination of pain and pleasure melted into ecstasy. Claire hugged Tony's face to her breasts while his hands caressed and encouraged. Nichol wasn't the only one who enjoyed the liquid feast Claire had to offer.

The next few minutes faded into a cloud of passion. Her nightgown lay upon the floor in a puddle of satin, and his gym shorts disappeared. The tropical humidity added to the sultry moisture molding their bodies together. His broad chest weighed heavily upon her breasts as he pinned her petite body to the soft sheets. Skin to skin they were lost in one another. She closed her eyes as she mindlessly responded to his caresses. Endlessly, his fingers probed as he teased and taunted her desires. Claire couldn't stand the anticipation any longer. Her entire being cried out as she begged for relief.

No other man had filled her so completely. No other man had taken her to the pits of hell and the uppermost parts of heaven. Her fingers clutched tightly to his shoulders as they momentarily forgot their troubles. Their world was right here and right now. Her body convulsed as she cried out to the only man who knew her completely. Before she could think coherent thoughts, before her body settled from its intense state, Tony too found relief. It was a brief reprieve from the demons surrounding them; nonetheless—it was a break. With the breeze from the ceiling fan stirring the early morning air, they fell asleep in each other's arms—pretending their safety in paradise would last forever.

Phil secured their new identifications and accompanied them through the multiple TSA check points. Not once was his documentation questioned, as they safely re-entered the United States. Claire's wig was short, and Tony's contacts made his eyes a shade of green. Their travel clothes mimicked those of everyone else, and they traveled economy class. Although Nichol didn't wear a disguise, the four blended well into the anonymous masses.

Before they left their haven, Claire hugged Francis and Madeline and promised their safe return. The couple didn't know the ins and outs of the Rawlings' legal issues. They did know they'd all grown fond of one another, and Nichol was the light of their world. Tony explained that he had created a trust fund that would assure the island retreat's financial solvency. He assured Francis and Madeline everything would remain flush until they returned.

They both promised the couple, that their return would be sooner rather than later. Claire's heart broke as Madeline's large tears dampened her shoulder during their farewell. She knew if it wasn't her sister's life at stake—she'd never have left their island.

It took two full days flying commercial, but finally, they arrived in Cedar Rapids. It was late at night—after midnight, and thankfully, the airport was quiet, calm, and uneventful. After spending six months in the tropics, the cool March Iowa air chilled Claire to her bone. She shivered in the back seat of the van Phil had arranged to have waiting. With each shiver, Claire covered Nichol with another blanket.

While Phil drove, Tony reached over the baby seat and held Claire's hand. "You're trembling. Are you all right?"

"I think I'm just cold."

Rubbing her gloved hand, he moved it to his lips. "No one noticed us, Mrs. Rawlings. You can relax."

She exhaled and watched her breath create a frozen mist. "I can't believe we're going to show up on Courtney and Brent's doorstep. I'm excited to see them, but what will they say? We lied to them."

Tony and Phil's eyes meet in the rear-view mirror. Claire asked, "What? If there's something, tell me—I'm sick and tired of secrets."

Tony squeezed her hand and tried to explain, "Knowledge is leverage for the law. Right now, I'm *wanted* and you've been harboring me. If the Simmons' were caught communicating with either of us, they could be charged with aiding and abetting a fugitive."

"Then let's stay in a hotel. I don't want to put them at risk."

This time, Phil answered, "Claire, *they* want you there."

"But, how? How would they know?"

Tony replied, "They've known since before you and I met up in paradise. Brent's known you're alive since the FBI questioned me. The authorities wouldn't allow him to share. Of course, he told Courtney."

"All these months! Why didn't you tell me? I've been berating myself over lying to my family and friends. Do Emily and John know the truth?"

Tony's tone became businesslike. "If you'd have known—you would have wanted to communicate, and no, it made more sense for the Vandersols to remain in the dark."

Claire stared.

Tony continued, "We'd hoped their pursuit of me and Rawlings Industries would keep them safe—that as long as they were helping to *hurt* me—we hoped that Catherine would leave them alone."

Tears coated Claire's cheeks as she turned toward the dark, dead landscape. Thankfully, there wasn't any snow, but each tree along the way was leafless and the fields were empty and dark. Claire wasn't sure why she was crying. Perhaps it was exhaustion or stress. Maybe it was anticipation at seeing Brent and Courtney and John and Emily again.

Her thoughts evaporated as her husband's hand reached for her chin. With his thumb and forefinger, Tony turned her gaze toward him. Through the darkness of the van she saw his clenched jaw. "Can you please be mad at me later? We've got a lot going on."

Not trying to move away from his determined tone, Claire closed her tired eyelids causing more tears to rush down her cheeks, and explained, "I'm not mad. You're right—I would've thought about calling daily. After Nichol was born, I probably would've done it—even if I knew I shouldn't." Claire used her gloves to wipe her face. "I'm tired and scared."

Tony reassuringly took her gloved hand in his. Phil interjected, "The Simmons know about Nichol, and they can't wait to meet her. Emily and John aren't due to arrive until tomorrow afternoon."

Tony smiled and said, "We'll get some sleep and you'll feel better." His devilish grin reappeared as he whispered, "Or not sleep?"

Claire shook her head. "I'm afraid our princess won't understand the time change. We may spend the night up—in shifts—with her."

Still holding his wife's hand, Tony shrugged, leaned against the vinyl seat, and sighed. "That's not quite the *up* I was imagining."

Claire's eyes darted toward the rear-view mirror. Courteously, Phil appeared lost in his own thoughts, unable to hear the whispers which only moments earlier he'd answered. Claire shook her head and peered under the blankets at a sleeping Nichol. With a weary smile, she placed one hand over their daughter, and enjoyed the sensation of her little chest moving up and down.

For a moment, Claire envied Nichol's ignorance. As long as she was fed, clean, and loved—their daughter didn't know the evils that lurked in the shadows. With her other hand, Claire clung tightly to Tony. Closing her eyes, she said a prayer to keep her family safe.

Friends show their love in times of trouble, not in happiness.
—Euripides

CHAPTER 44

Forty-eight hours of traveling took its toll—Claire must have fallen asleep because, when she opened her eyes, Phil was pulling the van into the Simmons' garage. Even in the dark of night, she recognized the brick drive. Inside the garage directly in the beams of the headlights, Claire saw Courtney and Brent. Her heart leapt. "Oh! I can't believe we're really here." Turning to see Tony's face, she read a hundred emotions. Happiness or even relief didn't seem to be the top contenders. She asked, "Aren't you happy to be here?"

"I am." He squeezed her hand. "I just realized the last time I saw or spoke to Brent we discussed something I'd rather forget. He probably told Courtney—" The van stopped as did Tony's words. Claire watched Brent hit the button to close the door as she and Tony reached for their handles.

Phil stopped them. "Don't open the van doors until the garage is closed. I don't think we were followed—I took a lot of back roads, but you can't be sure their house isn't being watched."

The reality of their situation came rushing back with the familiar pounding behind Claire's temples. She'd taken some acetaminophen during their last layover before Iowa, but that was hours ago and the dull ache was becoming a nonstop pound. Trying to relieve the tension, she rolled her neck right then left. She wasn't thinking, or she wouldn't have done that in front of Tony.

"Do you have a headache?"

Claire smiled and shook her head. Telling him wouldn't make her feel better, and she knew how much he hated her headaches. They reminded him of a time long ago. "I'm fine; what did you two talk about?"

Before he could answer, Phil had his door open and Courtney was rushing toward the van.

Claire's door sprang open, and without warning, she was swallowed in Courtney's hug. "I'm so glad you two came here! Let's get you in the house where it's warm."

Freeing herself from her best friend's embrace, Claire interjected, "Thank you for letting us come...all three of us!" Tony had unbuckled the baby seat. Claire moved it to her lap, pulled back the blankets, and revealed their daughter. The biggest brown eyes stared up toward her mother's voice.

"She's beautiful!" Courtney squealed.

Tony was now to Claire's door. "May we introduce Nichol Courtney Rawlings?"

Courtney put her hand to her lips as tears moistened her eyes. "Nichol *Courtney?*"

Tony nodded as a proud smile emerged.

Courtney hugged Tony and whispered, "We've missed *all* of you."

Brent put out his hand. Though Tony had worked to mask whatever he was feeling, Claire saw a micro expression of relief as the two men shook hands. She wondered again what they'd discussed, many months ago.

Within the warmth of the kitchen, Claire removed Nichol from her seat while Phil casually asked where he could retire. Claire's pulse quickened when Brent said, "Mr. Roach, let me show you to your room. Tony, would you like to join us for a minute?"

Although Tony showed no outward signs of concern, Claire knew from his earlier comment there may be need. As the three men disappeared, she wondered what they needed to discuss. If it was about Emily or Tony, then Claire wanted to know. Courtney's voice brought Claire back to present. "We had no idea you named her after me." Her blue eyes glistened as she asked, "May I hold her?"

"Her name's a long story, but Courtney was a name we both agreed upon. You've always been so good to both of us. Of course you can hold her; let me change her first."

Courtney couldn't pry her eyes away from Nichol. "I don't mind. Oh my, Claire, look at those eyes."

Placing her daughter in her best friend's arms, Claire replied, "Aren't they beautiful? Just like her daddy's."

Claire followed Courtney through the house to one of their guest rooms. The men were nowhere in sight. Hearing Courtney talk on and on loosened the tight muscles in Claire's shoulders and relieved the pain behind her temples.

"I'm so glad Mr. Roach contacted Brent," Courtney said.

"Cort, you do realize this is illegal, right?"

"Honey, I'd break any law to have you here, safe and sound."

Claire added, "And Tony?"

Courtney nodded before she closed the bedroom door, and asked in a hushed tone, "We don't have a lot of time before the men get back. You promised you'd be honest with me."

"I know"—Claire looked down—"I'm sorry about the way I left. Do you know about Catherine?"

"Yes, Mr. Roach filled Brent in on everything. We understand what you did and why you did it. Who would've ever imagined, sweet Catherine? We've been careful to never let on to anyone what we know. Mr. Roach said the FBI's still working to put it all together."

Claire listened as she changed Nichol and settled into a plush chair to feed her.

"I'm sorry," Courtney said. "Do you want me to leave?"

"I don't think I'd invite Brent in"—Claire joked—"but I'm fine with you."

Glancing toward the door, Courtney lowered her tone. "I want you to know, we *really are* glad you're here and safe. I don't want to upset you, but I have to know."

Claire braced herself for something. She didn't know what; perhaps it was about what Tony had said. "What do you need to know?"

"Are you sorry?"

"Am I sorry? That I left without telling anyone?"

Courtney leaned forward. "No, are you sorry you allowed Tony back in your life? Is it truly different? You know, than the first time..."

The trip had been exhausting, yet Courtney's directness continued Claire's relaxation. It felt so good to be talking openly with her friend. There'd been too many secrets—she longed for truth. Claire settled against the soft cushions as Nichol, hidden discretely behind a blanket, suckled her breast. Smiling, she answered, "I don't know what I was afraid you were going to ask, but that wasn't it. Without a doubt, it's different! He's changed. I know some people say that people don't change—but they do. I have too. The life we shared in our first marriage and before is a distant memory. For Nichol's sake, I wish it could remain hidden. She doesn't need to know any of that. Her father *is* a good man."

Courtney replied, "But some new things have come up—things from that box you told me about—allegations and suggestions of other things Tony may have done—or at least, he may have been involved with."

"I promise—I know everything. I'm not saying he was *always* a good man or a good husband. I'm saying he is *now,* and when we were here in Iowa, before I left, he was also. Courtney, he knows what he's done, and he's sorry."

Courtney knelt beside Claire. "I believe you. I can see it in your eyes." She reached out and held Claire's hand. "I hope this can all be worked out. You've been through enough."

"I'm sorry that I've dragged you along."

"Oh goodness, don't be sorry."

Claire sighed. "As always, you're there for me. Hopefully, someday I can repay the favor. I know it's late; do you want to go to bed? We can talk in the morning."

"If you don't mind me being here until the men get back, I want to talk, and maybe when she's done eating, I can hold Nichol *Courtney.*"

Claire smiled, her heavy lids fluttered as she stifled a yawn. "I'd love that." Suddenly, Claire had a thought. "Tony knows that you two know about our past, doesn't he?"

Courtney nodded. "The FBI showed him and Brent your testimony from 2010 when he was being questioned. After keeping his thoughts silent for almost two years, Brent confronted him."

"Tony never told me. Well, not until we were almost here. Even then, he didn't finish."

"Brent didn't tell Tony it wasn't new information, but he did call him out."

Claire smiled. "Tell Brent thank you. I know that must have been very difficult for him."

Courtney shrugged. "It was good for them. Now, with all Brent's done in Tony's absence, I think they too will be better than before."

Claire squeezed her best friend's hand. "I've missed you so much. I only learned in the van that you've known our secret all along."

"Once Tony disappeared, Brent knew he was out looking for you. He never thought he was hurt in the emergency landing. The FBI were too elusive. Eventually, Mr. Roach contacted Brent with a message from Tony. They hoped it would escape the FBI's radar. After all, Brent was the one who hired Mr. Roach to track you last year."

Claire listened in marvel as all the memories of the past twelve months cascaded through her mind. It seemed impossible that she'd been released from prison only a year ago; so much had happened.

Courtney proceeded to fill Claire in on her and Brent's children. Maryn, their daughter, was about to complete her doctoral thesis, and Caleb and Julia were doing well. As Courtney took Nichol from Claire's arms, she added, "No grandchildren—yet."

Claire remembered how Courtney wanted them. "Well, hopefully one day we'll be living back here, and you can be *Aunt Cort* or *Grandma* if you'd prefer."

"Oh no, *Aunt* is just fine, even when I am a grandma we'll need to come up with a younger sounding title." Claire went to their bags to get her things, when Courtney's voice rose in volume. "Oh, my goodness, you probably don't know!"

Startled, Claire turned and asked, "Know what?"

"You're going to be an aunt!"

Staring at Courtney's nodding head, Claire teetered between excited and scared. "Emily's pregnant?"

"Yes, but she isn't due until July. We started talking periodically after you disappeared."

"And, even after you knew we were safe, you didn't tell her?"

"It was difficult, but not telling her was supposed to keep her and John safe. Brent hated what they were doing to Rawlings Industries, but Mr. Roach assured us that Tony thought it was best."

Claire collapsed on the edge of the bed. She was too tired to censor everything she said. Shock and disbelief were evident in each word, "Tony knew? He knew you had information that would convince John and Emily to stop their pursuit of Rawlings Industries, and he told Brent *not* to use it? He chose my family over his company?"

Courtney's blue eyes twinkled. "He did, sweetie. He didn't know about Emily's baby, probably still doesn't, but he knew about the plan to keep them safe. Actually, I think the plan was his idea. That's why I thought you were all right. I hoped and prayed"—she squeezed Claire's knee—"It was just that seeing you—I needed to be sure."

"I am. Now, I'm even more worried about Emily. Oh, my God, she's pregnant! I wonder if that's why Catherine wanted to see her. I mean, now there will be *another* child of a child"—her hands trembled—"Why would Emily agree to visit Catherine?"

"I wanted to tell her not to come. I even tried to dissuade her—I told her I could get things from the house. She said she wanted to see everything herself."

"That's my sister. She probably thinks she'll learn more about me if she goes to the estate." Claire tried to focus on all the issues. "With all the bad publicity she and John generated, how bad is it for Rawlings Industries? I've tried to keep up, but it isn't the—"

Before Claire could finish her question, the ladies turned to see the opening door with Tony's questioning eyes peering toward them. Grinning, he opened it wider and exposed Brent. "I wanted to be sure Nichol was done eating," he explained as both men entered the room.

It was obvious that Tony and Brent's issues were resolved. The four friends had entered a new world. Too much time had been lost to secrets. In the midst of chaos, they'd reached understanding and openness.

Tony large hands massaged Claire's tight shoulders as Brent stepped closer to Nichol. She was sleeping soundly in Courtney's arms. Approvingly, he remarked, "You did great, Claire. She's beautiful!"

Courtney added, "Wait until you see her awake. She has the biggest, most beautiful brown eyes."

Tony laughed. "Evidence that Claire had a little help."

"I hope we can all be together tomorrow evening. I have a meeting in Chicago"—looking at his watch, Brent added—"in less than six hours, so perhaps we should get some sleep."

Courtney asked, "Do you know how long you two will be here?"

Claire looked to Tony. She wanted him to be in control. No—she needed him to be in control. She knew, in order for everything to work, he needed to take charge. Finally, he answered, "We don't. We'll need to see what happens tomorrow."

Courtney kissed Nichol's head as she handed her back to Claire. Before the Simmons' left the room, Brent added, "Claire, I can tell you're scared. I like

Roach—he's good. As long as he and Tony work together, everything will be fine."

They all knew there were no guarantees. Too many things could happen in the next twenty-four hours—Claire refused to consider the possibilities; instead, she nodded and smiled at their best friends as they closed the door. Claire laid their sleeping daughter on the soft sheet of a portable crib near the foot of their bed and covered her with a thin blanket. Envying Nichol's innocence, she knew it was like her glass house from years ago—quietly, she said a prayer, "Please, God, help us all work together and not allow it to shatter."

Before Claire walked to the bathroom to get ready for bed, Tony seized her arm and pulled her toward him. "Brent's right—you were right—Roach is great. His knowledge and expertise has exceeded my expectations, and I'll listen to his advice. Tomorrow, after I get back, *we'll* decide when we're leaving."

Claire nodded. She couldn't respond verbally if she wanted—the lump in her throat was too big to swallow. Burying her head against his chest, she enjoyed the sensation of his arms around her, a shield to keep all the bad away. For the moment, she could pretend everything was all right and forget about the danger. After all, compartmentalization was her specialty.

As they settled into bed, Claire asked, "The thing you remembered in the van, about the last time you talked to Brent, is everything settled?"

Tony wrapped his arm around her and pulled her close. Claire's head rested on his shoulder, she inhaled his musky scent, and listened to his confident tone, "Yes, I believe we've reached an understanding."

"They didn't have to help us like this."

"You're right. Someday, we'll repay them."

Nuzzling against his skin, Claire considered pressing Tony to confess the subject of his and Brent's argument. She wondered if he'd tell her, but then she wondered why she wanted him to confess. After all, that testimony was about another time—another life—a life she had no desire to discuss or remember. Soon, her thoughts faded into nothingness. Traveling had worn her out—sleep would no longer wait.

A friend is one who walks in when others walk out.

—Walter Winchell

CHAPTER 45

-LATE SEPTEMBER 2016-

Meredith desperately tried to scroll the contacts in her phone. Her trembling hands, combined with the emotion coursing through her veins, made the simple task more complex. *Did she want to go to jail? Was that her goal? If it wasn't, why then did she continually find herself in these precarious situations?*

It had been almost two weeks since Claire came *out* to her family. With each passing day, she seemed stronger and more resilient. She now engaged in flowing conversation—her one word or phrased responses were a thing of the past. Meredith surmised it was a testimony to Claire's thoughts. Instead of having fleeting, individual ideas which Claire felt the need to protect, her thoughts now came together in embellished trains—much more conducive for speech.

There were also marked improvements in Claire's appearance. Truthfully, it wouldn't have taken much to enhance the lost vacant expression she'd possessed for so long. Just the addition of recognition to her green eyes made her appear a different person; then add hair color and some light make-up, and Claire Rawlings was back. Of course, no one referred to her that way—she was still Nichols as far as the staff at Everwood was concerned. As long as Emily was in control of her care—that wouldn't change. Emily's control was undeniably the cause of Meredith's trembling hands. Claire was more than capable of making her own decisions, yet Emily's power of attorney hadn't been lifted.

It wasn't that Claire's demands were unreasonable—she wanted access to her daughter—to see her—to touch her—and to love her. The pictures of Nichol, that now decorated Claire's more colorful room, were a blessing upon arrival; however, with each passing day, they served as a reminder of the beautiful young girl who remained two dimensional. Maybe it was too early—that was Emily's continual answer to Claire. *What if Claire relapsed?* It wouldn't be fair to Nichol.

While Claire's desire to see Nichol sparked Meredith's fury, it was Claire's desire to see *anyone* that fueled the vehemence to the point of this impending phone call. Courtney Simmons' number had been programmed into Meredith's phone for a while; however, since the Vandersol's were still unaware of her true identity—calling that number was a risk, perhaps even an invitation to a potential jail sentence.

Closing her eyes, Meredith remembered the tears of her friend only minutes earlier when Meredith exited Claire's room. For two years, Claire had been unaware of her surroundings, yet content. In two weeks, she'd made phenomenal progress and experienced reoccurring disappointment. Although Meredith hadn't left Everwood's parking lot, she decided to throw caution to the wind, yet again. The corner of her phone read—8:57 PM. Swiping the screen, she found Courtney's number and prayed. She couldn't guarantee that her current willpower would be present tomorrow or even in ten minutes; Meredith needed to make the call now.

On the second ring, she heard Courtney's voice, "Hello, this is Courtney."

"Hello, Courtney, please don't hang up. This is about Claire Rawlings."

The momentary silence accelerated Meredith's heartbeat. Finally, she heard, "Who is this?"

"My name is Meredith Rus—Banks."

"Goodbye."

Meredith spoke quickly, "Please, Courtney, I know you know who I am, but this isn't about a story—it's about Claire. She's my friend too—and she needs you." The words came so fast, Meredith hoped they were separated by enough space to make sense. When the line didn't go dead, Meredith continued, "She's doing much better. She's asked for you."

"How do you know this?"

"I'm in Cedar Rapids right now. Will you please meet me? I think it's better if I explain in person."

After what Meredith assumed was cautious deliberation, Courtney replied, "Fine, perhaps I should call John or Emil—"

"I know Emily hasn't allowed you to visit. You don't have any reason to believe me, but I can help you *and* Claire if you'll please meet with me—alone. If you call them, I don't know when you'll be able to—"

This time, Courtney interrupted, "All right. Where can I meet you?"

Meredith remembered to breathe. "Thank you, I can be in Iowa City in..."

Short's Burger and Shine was a popular bar, and although Meredith thought a drink to calm her nerves sounded like a good idea, that wasn't the reason the two women had come to this particular establishment. Basically, it was a matter of convenience; the hour was late, and the small quaint pub on Clinton Street was open. When Meredith arrived, she saw Courtney seated at the last booth. The long, narrow room with the brick walls echoed with the sound of happy patrons; nevertheless, Courtney's expression, as she watched Meredith approach, told Meredith that Courtney didn't share the joyous elation of the others.

"Thank you for meeting with me," Meredith offered as she eased herself up the platform and into the hard booth.

"I'm not usually a rude person, but I hated your book, and I guess I've transferred those feelings to you. Tell me why I'm here and make it quick."

Meredith momentarily looked down and took a deep breath. "I understand. This isn't about my book, or even a new story, although I admit it started that way."

Courtney raised her brow.

"About three months ago, I asked Emily's permission to visit Claire. She denied me."

Courtney nodded in agreement.

Meredith continued, "My goal was to learn *the rest of the story*. I guess I wanted to write something that would make Nichol proud of her parents."

Courtney continued to listen silently.

"Since I couldn't go to Everwood openly, I decided to apply for a job there. I did. I got it. Over time, I worked my way into Claire's room as part of her dietary team."

"I'm pretty sure there's a restraining order—"

The waitress interrupted, "Ladies, what can I get you?"

The thought of that drink was getting better and better. Finally, Meredith asked, "Can I get you something for joining me? Or are you leaving to pursue the violation of that order?"

∞∞∞∞∞∞

Still somewhat stunned by Meredith's open confession, Courtney answered, speaking to the young girl near the end of their table, "I'd like a glass of white Zen, please."

Meredith added, "Make that two." When the girl walked away, Meredith leaned forward. "Thank you, I knew it was a risk to come to you. You could turn me in to the police, to Everwood, or to the Vandersols, but if you don't, maybe I can help you see Claire."

Courtney nodded. "I've been trying to see her since she was first admitted. Each time I ask, I'm met with comments about not having visitors *for her own good.*"

After the wine arrived, Meredith walked Courtney through her three month journey—she shared everything. When she spoke about Claire's original condition, Courtney was unable to suppress the tears. "I'd heard she wasn't talking, but I had no idea it was that bad."

Meredith told her about the recent change. "She wants to see you. I think she's trying to put the pieces back together. She's trying to recall what happened to get her where she is today. She also wants Nichol, but I can't do anything about that. I thought maybe if you spoke with her. Maybe you could help her with some of the details. I mean, you were at the trial, right?"

"I was. What does she remember?"

"I'm not sure. One of her therapists told her to journal. She's supposed to write about her feelings and things that happened. I haven't read them; she hasn't offered. Claire did say she's writing about Tony."

At the mention of his name, Courtney looked into her near empty glass. "I was told that if I were *ever* to get the opportunity to visit then his name couldn't be mentioned."

"As was I—it's a documented means for immediate dismissal, but, well"—Meredith shrugged—"I broke that rule too. He was the topic that I believe brought her back. Oh, it was the medications that helped her hallucinations go away, but it was his name that pulled her back. She said she missed seeing him, and when I started recounting the stories she'd told me, it helped her remember."

"I want to go"—Courtney's blue eyes smiled—"I've been known to break a rule or two myself. Thank you for including me. I'm sorry I was so rude when you first arrived."

"I understand. Despite all that the book has done for me and my family financially, if I could do it again, I wouldn't write it." After Meredith took a drink, she rephrased, "Maybe not. I mean, that knowledge helped me to help Claire, so I understand where you're coming from, but it might have been written for this reason—who are we to know the grander scheme?"

Courtney shrugged. "How can we do this?"

With the animosity gone, the two women worked toward a common goal and brainstormed ideas. During their second or third glass of wine, Courtney and Meredith devised and tweaked their plan. Though it was almost October, the days were staying warm with a sunshine whose rays shone until early evening. Meredith would take Claire on a walk, and Courtney would join them at the far west end of the grounds. It would be a short hike for Courtney to park and meet them undetected, but she didn't mind. As long as it didn't rain, they planned a visit for the next evening. When they left the restaurant, Courtney hugged Meredith. "I can't tell you how excited I am. Thank you for all you've done." Still gripping her shoulders, Courtney's speech slowed and she added, "And, if you use any of this to write another book, I will personally come after you."

∞∞∞∞∞∞

The late afternoon September sun glistened through the trees. Claire didn't know why Meredith rushed her dinner. It wasn't that she minded, but she could tell something was different. It wasn't until they were away from Everwood's immediate grounds and into the paths through the woods that Meredith finally explained, "I have a surprise for you. I hope you're all right with it."

Claire eyed her friend suspiciously. "I trust you; however, I'm just not a fan of surprises."

"I think you will be this one time. I know Emily has made it difficult for you to reconnect with anyone."

Claire exhaled. "*Difficult* is a nice word. I mean, I understand her reasoning with Nichol—I do. That doesn't mean I don't want to see her. I think about her constantly. It's just that I want to see others. It almost feels like—"

The squeeze of Meredith's hands stopped Claire's words. She saw a figure up ahead, through the darkening forest. Unconsciously, her steps slowed. Claire could tell it was a woman. Somewhere in the back of her mind, she heard the numbers—suddenly, she realized she was counting her steps—*twenty-three, twenty-four, twenty-five*—She worked to block out the numbers and concentrate on the person ahead.

Claire continued walking.

Slowly, the figure came into view—the person took shape and her face became clear. Gasping—Claire realized it was Courtney—merely yards in front of her. She dropped Meredith's hand and ran to her friend. By the time they embraced, tears covered both of their cheeks.

Strength does not come from physical capacity.
It comes from an indomitable will.
——Mahatma Gandhi

CHAPTER 46

Claire woke with a start. Blinded by the sunlight streaming through the unblocked window, she tried to focus. The split second of disorientation faded as she remembered they were at the Simmons' home. Reaching for her husband, she found only an empty bed. Claire crawled to the end of the mattress and peered into the empty crib. Her eyes searched for a clock while questions bombarded her thoughts: *How late had she slept? Why hadn't Tony brought Nichol to her to feed? Was he still here or had he and Phil already left?*

Panic boiled through her veins as she wrapped a robe around her nightgown and rushed toward the kitchen. By the time she reached her destination, tears teetered on her lids and breathing required thought; then all at once, the tension severed—her world was right. Tony was seated at the table, coffee in hand with Nichol in his arms. Phil was seated across from them as Courtney stood by the stove. The wonderful aroma of coffee and fried food filled the room as Courtney's voice chatted on about nothing. Despite the worries of the world, Claire had entered the calm in the midst of a storm.

Hearing Claire enter, Tony looked up. Immediately, his expression darkened. "Claire, what's the matter?"

Shaking her head, she exhaled the breath she hadn't realize she'd been holding. "Nothing"—going to him and Nichol, she kissed his cheek and reached for their daughter—"I was afraid you'd already left for the estate."

"I wouldn't do that," he answered. Petting Nichol's head, he straightened the fine strands of brown hair, and his tone lightened. "We were going to need to wake you soon. Someone was becoming impatient."

Claire's breasts ached as she settled into the nearby sun porch with Nichol. The windows offered a bright spring view. The earth had yet to wake from its winter nap, but the blue skies and warm rays of sunshine were promises of a greener world to come. The porch offered Claire modesty while keeping her close enough to hear the men discussing the logistics of the upcoming day.

Emily and John were due to arrive in Iowa around 3:00 PM—Eric filled Phil in on the itinerary, would keep them up-to-date, and promised to get them into the house unnoticed. While they talked options and scenarios, Claire had visions of a bad spy movie. Tony knew every inch of the estate—he explained entrances and exits while discussing security. For the first time, it seemed as though Tony wished he hadn't installed the *finest* in security software.

Phil assured him, he'd check everything first. There wasn't a security system he couldn't disable or manipulate. With Tony's intimate knowledge of the surroundings, Phil promised he could have it figured out in no time. Tony wanted to get to Catherine before the Vandersols arrived. His plan was to talk with her and stop anything from happening—before it even started. He had a valid concern that the Vandersols wouldn't understand his presence, and, therefore, contact the authorities. Early intervention was safer for everyone.

Claire liked their confidence. For a plan that sounded like *James Bond* meets *Inspector Gadget*—they actually made it sound plausible. By the time she joined them at the table, she began to feel more confident herself. *Hadn't Phil once told her about his military career? Hadn't he mentioned his history with the special ops?* Surely, he'd dealt with enemies better trained and more frightening than Catherine London; besides, Tony had the element of surprise on his side. As long as Eric was truly trustworthy, Catherine should be caught unaware.

It was nearly noon when Phil's phone buzzed and everyone stared. "It's Eric, excuse me a second." When he stepped from the room and walked down the hall, the room where they sat was, once again, taut with tension. The earlier calm evaporated with the sound of Phil's fading steps. Even Courtney remained silent as they waited for Phil's return.

From out of nowhere, a forgotten memory returned to Claire. The room where Phil now stood—talking on his phone—was the same room where Marianne and Bonnie stood years ago. She remembered the cattiness in Bonnie's voice as she discussed Claire's clothes and undeserved devotion from Tony. At that time, Claire's world was a lie. Every move she made and every word she said was solely to pacify the man Bonnie deemed as her *sugar daddy*. Looking at Tony now, she recalled the man he'd been and remembered the fear of disappointing him.

Today, her fear wasn't the same—Claire didn't fear disappointing Tony— she feared *losing* him. While they waited for Phil to return with his news, she yearned for the simplicity of a life with one goal—to please one man. The obstacles currently before them seemed insurmountable—Emily and John's safety—Catherine's plan for vengeance—the authorities—and their safe return to paradise. For a moment, she wished for the two of them alone in the beige walled suite with heavy golden draperies. Never had she imagined those memories would be her go-to safe spot.

The sound of Phil's determined steps claimed everyone's attention. He spoke as soon as he entered the room, "Change of plans—it seems that John and Emily caught an earlier flight. Eric said he just dropped them off at the estate. He didn't know about the change of plans until Catherine informed him they were going to the airport. This was his first chance to call." Tony stood, but before he could speak, Phil continued, "There's something else. Sophia Burke is at the estate."

"Why?" Tony asked. "Has Catherine told her the truth?"

"Eric said that Sophia doesn't know who Catherine is. The two of them have become *friends*, and since Derek is out of town with work, Sophia is staying with *her friend* Catherine."

Courtney interjected, "Yes, Derek Burke is with Brent. Remember that meeting in Chicago? Another member of the Rawlings legal team was supposed to go instead of Brent, but she had a conflict, so last night, Brent volunteered to go, but they left early this morning and are coming home this afternoon. Why would Sophia need someplace to stay?"

Phil shrugged. "We can't get you to Catherine before the Vandersols arrive."

Tony stood straighter. "We need to go now. I don't trust her alone with them any longer than necessary. Besides, it's a big house. With the security monitored I should be able to avoid encountering"—he looked toward Claire— "your family. It would be nice if I could get in and out without additional conflict."

Phil answered, "I'll text Eric, and we'll confirm our meeting point."

Claire summoned every mask from her past. She wasn't trying to hide her feelings—she wanted to be strong for Tony. Hoping that her voice didn't reveal her insecurities, she said, "Good."

He raised a questioning eyebrow.

Claire continued, "The sooner you get this done, the sooner we can get back. Once you've secured Emily and John's safety, if there's any threat of them calling the authorities, call me. I'll convince them to give us *our* year as a family."

"No! Claire, you're not getting close to the estate—you're not getting involved. We discussed that." Authority filled every word. He had no intentions of his directive being disobeyed.

"I know that. I still might be able to help." Tony's eyes spoke volumes. It was a look she'd seen too many times. Claire didn't want to distract him from his objective. She softened her voice. "*If* you need me—call. I won't come unless you assure me it's safe."

Gripping her shoulders, he said, "I love you. Your safety isn't debatable. Do *not* disappoint me."

She stared for only a moment, knowing Tony and Phil needed to leave. The vast darkness pulled her in. His tone sounded like the man from years ago; however, behind the darkness—within the black holes—she saw love—possession—and protection. She wouldn't look away—she never could. For a split second, she marveled at how warm and secure his gaze made her feel; such a contrast to the memories of coldness. Lifting her face, she brushed her lips on his and replied, "I won't Tony"—then with a knowing grin, she added—"Don't disappoint me, either."

He hugged her and paused a moment to kiss Nichol, who was laying in Courtney's arms. His lips lingered on her fine hair, as he seemed to be inhaling her fresh baby scent. Claire fought the lump in her throat as she watched him close his eyes, savoring their daughter. Seconds later, he walked away, saying, "We'll call when it's done."

They were gone.

Claire stared at the hallway in silence. Staying strong was no longer necessary. When the empty corridor became blurry, she turned toward Courtney. The tears continued to flow as her anguish came out with each word. Claire wasn't looking for validation. She knew her statement was correct. Instead, she took comfort in the ability to relay her thoughts honestly and audibly. "Our lives are so fucked up!"

Courtney's laughter filled the room. "You certainly do know how to sum it up!"

"Well, you said you wanted honesty."

∞∞∞∞∞∞

Sophia excused herself from the dining room, once again marveling at Marie's home. It didn't matter how many times she visited, she always found something new. Although she rarely watched television, Sophia enjoyed a good movie—especially the classics. Quietly, she made her way to the lower level and the movie room. As she searched the menu of hundreds—if not thousands of titles—she thought about the couple upstairs, the Vandersols. Marie explained that they were Ms. Nichols' family, and since her disappearance was still unsolved, they wanted to retrieve some of her things. Truthfully, they were polite enough during lunch, but Sophia couldn't shake the feeling that there was something happening below the surface. For one thing, they didn't refer to Marie as Marie; instead, they called her *Catherine*. Spending a few hours in the theater would allow the Vandersols and Marie, or Catherine, some privacy. It was the least she could do for Marie after all she'd done for her.

∞∞∞∞∞∞

Tony never thought much about Eric. He just was—he always had been. From Tony's first million, Eric was by his side. In all those years, they'd never sat down and had a heart to heart. He'd never asked Eric about his personal life. *Did he even have one?* Yet Eric knew Tony's deepest darkest secrets. Not only did he know, he'd participated, without question, without hesitation—just like a good trustworthy employee. It was true, Eric was paid exceptionally well for his loyalty; however, as Tony and Phil waited in the shadows of an old country church, with the van safely stashed along a side road, Tony wondered if Eric's devotion had a price—one that could be bought by someone else.

Phil had made his price known from the beginning. Yes, Tony understood Phil changed allegiances from Catherine for more than money. Tony would be an idiot not to see the man's devotion to Claire; however, Tony acknowledged that while Phil was unsuccessful at stopping Patrick Chester in California—for weeks on end, he'd kept Claire safe in Europe. Tony also knew that if this were a trap with the FBI waiting—Phil would continue to devote himself to keeping Claire free from harm. Anyone capable of doing that was worth their weight in gold.

Things with Eric were different. Over the years, his responsibilities morphed and grew with Tony's expectations. Not once, no matter the directive, could Tony remember Eric disappointing him. *Had he ever told Eric he appreciated all he did?* Tony couldn't remember that either. After all, men don't discuss their feelings regarding one another. More than that—Tony had never given gratitude much thought. Eric had a job—he did it. When everything goes down and Tony turns states evidence, he would *not* take Eric with him. *Most of his activities were done without Eric's knowledge, and when he was required to participate—it was coerced and done under duress.* If asked—that was the story Tony planned to maintain.

Now, as he watched the dark limousine come into view, Tony wondered if his devotion was truly reciprocated. *Could Eric have been bought out? Could Tony and Phil be walking into a trap?* They needed to be prepared. Tony leaned toward Phil and whispered, "I've changed my mind."

Phil's normal facade cracked. "You came all this way, and you're not going through with this?"

"No," Tony corrected. "When we get to the estate, I want you to go *with* Eric to the command center of the house. I want *you* to verify what cameras are working and that the house is free of feds. I also want you to stay with Eric to be sure my encounter is being recorded. Maybe I can get Catherine to talk."

The limousine was now rolling to a stop. Tony didn't need to voice his possible concern of insubordination. Phil understood the hidden meaning. No *one* person could be trusted. This new plan would assure them of Eric's honesty.

Watching Eric get out of the car, Tony hoped that he was only being paranoid. After all, he and Eric had been through a lot; nonetheless, when Eric opened the back compartment, Tony glanced at Phil who nodded in return and touched his side. Tony nodded. *Phil had a gun and was willing to use it.*

As Tony stepped passed Eric, he realized how genuinely glad he was to see him. Perhaps life on the run had made him suspicious. Tony patted Eric's shoulder and said, "Good to see you, my man."

With a tip of his head, Eric responded, "And you too, Mr. Rawlings." It was as if Tony had been gone on a business meeting, not hiding on the other side of the world.

Once the car moved, Tony began, "Tell us what's happening at the estate."

"Ms. London is preoccupied with her guests. I'm sure, taking the car out for maintenance wasn't one of her concerns."

Phil interjected, "The limo was a smart move—dark windows."

"Thank you, sir. I figured I can get the two of you in the garages without any issues."

When the gates to the estate opened, the dam on Tony's anger broke. Previously, it had been held back with thoughts and feelings he didn't care to visit. Honestly, there were too many other concerns; however, hiding in the back of *his* limousine, driving through *his* iron gates, and onto *his* property— Tony saw red. He couldn't believe *he'd* become the victim. He hadn't been played by some business associate—no, he'd been victimized by the woman he'd trusted for most of his life. If he'd ever wanted revenge—it was now. The fleeting thought of killing Catherine made the tips of his lips rise. *Not that he'd ever physically murdered anyone before, but with all he'd done—would the addition of justifiable homicide really matter?*

When the car entered the large garage, Tony said, "I'll wait here for your call."

"Sir," Eric answered. "The garage cameras, as well as those in the garage to house corridor, stopped working yesterday. We weren't sure of the issue. Someone is coming to work on them tomorrow."

Phil took the lead. "Smart thinking, that'll help you and me get to the command center. While I get a feel for this fortress's technology, you can scan the security footage and verify Ms. London's location as well as Mrs. Burke and the Vandersols, then we'll call Raw—Mr. Rawlings."

It wasn't their original plan, but Tony was obviously in line with it. Eric had never challenged Tony's orders, and this wasn't going to be the first time. "Very well, Mr. Rawlings, please wait for our call."

Phil and Eric disappeared through the doorway toward the house. The silence in the empty car was deafening. By the time Phil's text came, Tony was ready to confront whoever he saw, but with all his might—he wanted it to be Catherine.

Tony and Eric looked nothing alike, yet they did have a similar build. Wearing Eric's jacket and cap, Tony kept his head low and walked through the corridor toward the house. Once inside, he'd likely encounter other members of the staff. His plan was to walk by—unnoticed. It took all his concentration to keep his posture dutiful—far from his normal confident gait.

When Tony passed through the kitchen, two women stood discussing the evening meal. He recognized them immediately; however, as he kept his head and eyes down, they seemed oblivious to his intrusion.

Each step toward the west corridor became more determined. The dutiful pose forgotten—Anthony Rawlings was on a mission. With his shoulders back and his head high, he advanced toward the grand double doors. This was *his* office—*his* command center. Eric's text a few minutes earlier said that Catherine was in her suite. Tony wondered if in the time it had taken him to get to the office, if by chance he'd find her sitting at *his* desk. *Did she too have rules about entering?* Tony didn't care. He consciously fought the red infiltrating his vision.

Not only had this woman jeopardized Claire and Nichol's lives, she'd blatantly lied to his face. He knew he needed to control the rage—this encounter demanded diplomacy. The fleeting thought of murder was nice, but if he could play nice and save the Vandersols—then the FBI would take care of the rest. His desire for physical retaliation would only result in more time away from his family—Catherine wasn't worth it.

Pushing the door ajar, he scanned the room. Overall, it was the same—the same cherry paneling, trim, and bookcases. His mahogany desk, which mimicked Nathaniel's, stood facing the doorway, yet there were subtle differences—picture frames, light colored draperies, and flowers. His masculine domain had taken on a feminine hue. The door to the attached bath was closed. Slowly, he approached the barrier and laid his head upon the wooden door. The only sound he heard was silence. Tony opened the door to find an empty bathroom—Catherine wasn't here.

As he eased himself into *his* chair, behind *his* desk—he assessed *his* mission. Suddenly, the pictures on the desk caught his attention. There was one of Nathaniel and Marie. He stared at his grandfather's likeness; if someone didn't know better—they'd think it was him. Tony had never seen the photo before, but then again, he couldn't recall ever going into Catherine's suite. There was another picture—one that Tony recognized. It was of Sophia as a young girl. Obviously, Catherine had found all the information he and Nathaniel had accumulated and knew that Sophia was her daughter. *What kind of game was she playing with Sophia? Was it as dangerous as the one she played with Claire and him or with the Vandersols?*

Eric said that the Vandersols had come to get some of Claire's things. *Would they be in the suite he'd shared with Claire or in her old suite upstairs? Had Phil scanned each monitor and found their location?* There were many cameras and each image was relatively short-lived as the monitors rotated their feed—scanning each frame took time.

As these and many more questions raced through his mind, the door to the office suddenly opened. Catherine casually entered, oblivious to her unexpected company. She didn't even notice Tony until she looked up. Her initial expression verified her surprise as an audible gasp escaped her lips. Tony instantly knew that Eric *could* be trusted—he hadn't set a trap. Quickly, she closed the door behind her. Tony remained silent as Catherine Marie straightened her shoulders and appeared to gather her thoughts. After a prolonged silence, she glared in Tony's direction and said, "Anton."

The evil that is in the world almost always comes of ignorance,

and good intentions may do as much harm as malevolence if they lack understanding.

—Albert Camus

CHAPTER 47

Tony incredulously stared, wondering what he'd planned to say. Thoughts formed fast and furiously as he rose from the chair and walked slowly toward her. With each step forward, he watched Catherine analyzing his expression. She wanted to know his thoughts, and if he knew her master plan. Striving to keep his gaze indifferent, he stopped inches in front of her. "Good afternoon, Catherine."

She exhaled and brought her hands to her chest. "Oh, thank God. I was afraid you were dead. Tell me, where have you been! Did you find Claire?" Each statement came a little quicker than the last.

He turned and walked back to his desk, contemplating his plan. Shaking his head, he sat and pointed to one of the chairs next to the desk. Her lips tightened into a flat line as she walked toward the seat he'd just assigned. Tony waited for her compliance. Once she was seated, he answered, "I've searched everywhere—it's like she fell off the face of the earth." Leaning back, he purposely hesitated and furrowed his brow.

Taking the bait, she asked, "What is it?"

"She stole our money."

"What?"

"I went to Geneva, and the money Nathaniel left—for us"—he paused—"for you and for me—the bulk of it was gone. To the best of my calculations, she took somewhere over 200 million dollars!"

"How? How did she know about it? And how have you been able to survive? I mean, when they wouldn't say if you were alive or dead—I assumed you were using that money for your search."

Tony explained how he made it to Geneva and found the almost empty safety deposit box. The only documentation inside was to a savings account, in his name, with merely half of a million and an unsigned note.

"Oh, what did the note say?"

Tony lowered his eyes and cleared his throat. "It said, *this time,* I'm not walking away empty handed."

Catherine gasped. "Oh, Anton, she *did* leave you. So the reconciliation was bogus—nothing but a sham for your money"—she shook her head—"I'm so sorry. Did you keep looking?"

Blood rushed to Tony's cheeks as he fought his emotion—fought to continue the charade—as he fought the red. Although Catherine probably assumed the rage that threatened to erupt was meant towards Claire—the true recipient was a mere few feet away. Pounding his fist against the desk, he replied, "Of course I did! She's alive and took my money!"

Catherine leaned toward him, her voice only a whisper, "Anton, lower your voice."

His tone softened, yet remained equally determined, "I'll scream from the damn rooftops if I want."

"I have guests. You don't want anyone to find you, do you? Last I heard, if you're alive, then you're a wanted man."

Enunciating each word, he asked, "Guests? Who Catherine? Who's here?"

Catherine glanced toward her hands. As she hesitated, he took in the woman before him. When she first entered the room, he'd been preoccupied, now he saw her—really saw her. Just like his office—she too had changed. The transformation wasn't dramatic, not one stark difference; however, it was like the picture Roach showed them months ago. Her hair was shorter, more stylish, and the color was lighter—she wore more make-up than before—and her clothes were nicer than he'd ever seen her wear. Without a doubt, the changes made her appear younger and more confident. She no longer gave the air of house hold staff—Catherine looked like the lady of the manor.

When she finally raised her eyes, he saw a familiar gleam—one he remembered from years before. It was a look she had when she was working on Nathaniel's vendetta. If she'd had it when she entered his office, he'd missed it; however, he recognized it now.

Tony deepened his tone, "Catherine, I'm sure you remember—I don't like to repeat myself."

She pulled her shoulders back. "Well, you see, in your absence there have been some changes. You may remember that you named me executor of your estate."

"I remember."

"As such, I've modified and altered a few things."

Tony looked toward the pictures and flowers. "I see."

Moving to the edge of her chair, she explained, "Not just appearances Anton," Catherine went on to say how she hadn't been sure if he'd return. Even if he were alive, she figured as long as he was suspected in Claire's disappearance, he'd need to stay hidden; therefore, there were matters she decided to deal with herself—the first was Sophia.

Catherine's eyes brightened. "Anton, you were right—when you told me my daughter would need me! She's so beautiful, and I've wasted too many years not knowing her. I should've listened to Nathaniel—and to you." Before breaking their gaze, she added, "It's a shame you'll never have this experience with your child."

The pencil he'd been holding splintered in his grasp. The loud crack caused Catherine to jump back in her chair. He didn't respond to her last comment; instead he confirmed, "So your guest is Sophia? She's here and knows you're her mother?"

Catherine shook her head. "She's here. I haven't told her of our relationship. The time hasn't been right. In time, she'll understand how much she needs me."

Tony contemplated; *if he pressed about additional guests, then she may become suspicious.* "You don't want her to know I'm here—in *my* house?"

"Anton, you can't tell anyone you're here. The FBI will arrest you." Furrowing her brow, she asked, "Why are you here?"

"As I just stated—it's *my* house."

"Yes, of course it is. Do you plan on staying?"

"I plan on ending the Rawls—Nichols—Burke vendetta once and for all."

Catherine's serious expression morphed—her whole guise brightened, from her gray eyes to her round cheeks, as her smile extended from ear to ear. Tony suddenly wondered how Nathaniel had loved her—the smile combined with the coldness behind her expression made the bile in his stomach rise, leaving a foul taste as he worked to swallow.

"I want that too—I want to be done!"—she leaned closer—"and we can— Anton, we can! Our goals are in sight. The end is so close! We must hurry, before there are more. I know we don't know where Claire and the child are, but we can find them. We can finish this once and for all!"

Claire and the child?! Tony sprang to his feet; the poor chair sailed helplessly backwards until it crashed against the cherry bookcase. "No, Catherine!"—He towered over her—"No, I'm stopping it from going any farther. It's over—now!"

"Anton, we can't stop—not now." Her voice mellowed as she reached up and caressed his cheek. "You look so much like your grandfather. He had eyes—"

A cold chill ran down his spine as he recoiled and every muscle in his body tensed. It was as if her touch were from the devil himself. Tony seized Catherine's hand, and by the pained look on her face, he was squeezing too tight—Tony didn't care. His words came slowly, through clenched teeth, "Do— not—touch—me—ever!"

It was then he noticed the white gold cross with the large pearl hanging from a fine chain around Catherine's neck—Claire's grandmother's necklace—Emily's grandmother's necklace! Releasing her hand, he grabbed the pearl and tugged the delicate chain. He'd broken the damn thing before—he could do it again. Once it was free, he shoved the necklace deep into the pocket of his slacks.

Catherine gasped and reflexively touched her neck. "How dare you! It isn't like Claire will ever see it again." Again, her features morphed. Standing defiantly, Catherine brushed invisible debris from her expensive clothes, and walked toward the open room. When she turned, her eyes displayed both hatred and vengeance. Tony remembered that look when she used to talk about his parents. As their proximity decreased the distain in her voice increased. "Are you so *love sick* over the woman who played you for a fool that you want the necklace as a memento?"—She'd never spoken to him in this tone—"That's fine. Who knows, they may even let you keep it in prison. If not"—she sneered—"I could always send it to you. I hear they deliver *boxes* all the time. "

All coherent thought forgot to register—the grand office was a hue of crimson. Though Tony didn't know what he was about to do, he knew, without a doubt, it was about to happen. He took two steps toward her, and Catherine's gaze didn't waver. He took one more step—when suddenly, the phone on the desk rang breaking the deafening silence. They both turned and stared at the source of the ring, as if it were an alien life form infiltrating their private storm. Finally, their eyes met. The phone which was ringing was the estate's *private number*, known only by a few people. On the fourth ring, Catherine asked condescendingly, "Mr. Rawlings, would you like to answer that?"

Clenching his jaw, he took a step back and motioned toward the phone. Although seconds earlier they'd both been visibly upset, as she answered the call, her voice held no indication of unease. Tony stood and listened.

"Yes, this is Ms. London." "I see." "When did this happen?" The menacing smile from earlier reappeared as she replied, "That *is* terrible." Walking around to the other side of his desk, Catherine sat and reached for a paper and pen. "Can you please give me that information one more time?" He couldn't see the words as she scribbled on the blank page. "Thank you, for the information. I'll pass it on to Mrs. Burke. Please, keep me informed." "Goodbye." When she hung up, she leaned back against the soft leather and shook her head. "Tisk, tisk—It's such a shame."

Her words, combined with her expression, sent shivers down his spine; nonetheless, Anthony Rawlings had never backed away from a challenge—today wouldn't be an exception.

"I believe you're in my seat." Ice dripped from his words.

"I believe I am"—she stood and motioned toward it—"Please, enjoy it while you can. I believe it would be better for you to hear this news while seated."

He didn't move forward; instead, he stood taller, towering over her with every bit of his six and a half foot build. "Why? What have you done?"

"Yes, it's always me, isn't it? Mr. Anthony Rawlings never got *his* hands dirty! We all know how important it was to *appear* innocent."

"Catherine?"

She lowered herself once again to his chair and explained, "As executor of your estate, I'm kept abreast of pertinent Rawlings Industries information."

He nodded.

"It seems as though one of Rawlings' private jets has gone down."

Tony's knees buckled as he fought to remain standing. "Down?"

"There was a distress call, and shortly after, the plane disappeared from radar. The FAA is investigating—it's assumed the plane has crashed. There's no information regarding survivors—none are expected."

"Why, Catherine? Who's on that plane?"

Before Catherine could answer, they heard a knock at the door. Turning toward the sound, they both stared in silence. The second knock echoed as they waited. Finally, deliberately, Catherine walked to the door and opened it—at first, only she could see the person on the other side.

Initially, Tony didn't recognize the voice. "I'm sorry, if I'm bothering you, I just finished the movie. If you're still busy, I was thinking I may go for a walk—your gardens are lovely, even this early in the Spring."

Catherine opened the door wider and ushered Sophia into the office. "No, Sophia, you aren't bothering us"—leaning her head toward Tony, she said— "I'm sure you recognize Mr. Rawlings."

Surprised by Catherine's candid introduction, Tony worked to keep his external calm.

Sophia stopped and stared. "But I thought you were—"

Catherine interrupted, "We all did—it's a miracle. He just came back moments ago."

Tony stepped forward and offered his hand in greeting. "Mrs. Burke, I apologize for my abrupt departure a few months ago. I so wish we could've continued our conversation—I believe it would've been very enlightening."

Before Sophia could respond, Catherine interjected, "Sophia, my dear, please have a seat. I'm afraid I have some terrible news to share."

Tony's back straightened, the muscles of his neck twitched, and the hairs stood to attention. Suddenly, he knew exactly what Catherine was about to say.

"My dear"—Catherine sat on the sofa next to Sophia. Taking Sophia's hand in hers, she began—"We just received a call. I don't know any way to say this, except quickly."

Sophia eyed Catherine suspiciously. "What? Did something happen?"

"The Rawlings plane your husband was on—was on its way back to Iowa—and it went down."

Sophia stared in disbelief.

Catherine continued, "The FAA is investigating."

Shaking her head, Sophia found her voice, "Down? No—no—it isn't true. There's been some kind of mistake."

Tony watched in horror as Sophia's world crumbled around her. The display was both heartbreaking and educational—Tony was too late to save Derek. As Sophia's tears fell, he also witnessed the previously unrecognized emotional toll of Nathaniel's vendetta. Obviously, Catherine's plans were in motion; suddenly, Tony's mind swirled with possibilities—ways to stop further tragedies. As the whirlwind of thoughts cascaded, he heard another familiar name. Instantaneously, Tony felt the pain he'd just witnessed.

"...others on board...Rawlings' employees...and...Brent Simmons."

Before he could register his movements, Tony was standing in front of both women and his tone was harsh, "Catherine, we need to speak in private—now!"

Sophia sobbed quietly while Catherine stood and faced Tony. "I'll get her settled, and *then,* I'll return"—she straightened her shoulders—"Your concerns can wait. We both know, *accidents* happen—a few more minutes won't change the past."

Tony stepped backward, displaying restraint, solely for Sophia's benefit. At this moment, he wanted to harm Catherine, more than he'd ever wanted to harm anyone. His reply came through clinched teeth, "Return *quickly,* this *will* end today."

With that, Catherine led Sophia out of the office. Tony heard her say, "My dear, let me get you something to calm your nerves..."

Her voice trailed away, leaving Tony alone to reel with the news. Pacing the length of the office, he contemplated his best friend—the man with whom he'd finally been honest—the man who had a wife and children. Nausea erupted in Tony's stomach as he thought about Courtney, Caleb, and Maryn. *Did Courtney know? Had she received a similar call?* His pocket vibrated.

The text was from Phil:

"*LONDON'S TAKING BURKE TO SECOND FLOOR. VANDERSOLS ARE IN THE ROOM LABELED 'S.E. SUITE'.*"

Tony immediately texted back:

"*CLAIRE'S OLD SUITE. ARE THEY OK?*"

Response:

"*NO SIGN OF DISTRESS*"

Tony:

"*KEEP THE MONITORS ON THEM. TELL ME IF ANY THING CHANGES.*"

Phil:

"CAMERAS IN OFFICE WERE DISABLED—THEY'RE NOW ONLINE."

Tony sat at the desk and accessed the computer. He didn't know if he was more upset that Catherine hadn't changed the passwords or that she knew his. Either way, he now knew exactly how his grandfather felt. Despite Tony's best efforts—he too had trusted the wrong person. Accessing Catherine's email, he found her correspondence with Emily. The Vandersols had come as a result of Catherine's invitation. He wondered what exactly she had planned. Before he could give it more thought, he turned toward the opening door.

By the time she closed the door, he was half way across the room. "You bitch! You arranged for that plane to go down, didn't you?"

Sounding somewhat apologetic, she explained, "I never intended for Brent Simmons to be on board. He wasn't on the original manifest."

"So, you're admitting it?"

"I'm saying that when Claire felt she had no one else—she needed me. I thought it would be the same when she came back, but it wasn't. You let her walk all over you! You were too blind to see how she manipulated you! Now we know why—it was only for your money."

With the mention of his wife's name and each step toward her, the crimson hue of the room darkened.

Catherine continued, "Sophia doesn't need money, you saw to that, but with her husband gone, she'll be alone—now she'll need *me*." Seemingly unaware of Tony's rage, Catherine added, "Besides, her husband was a *Burke*."

"Don't you see how out of hand this has become?"

"Really"—Catherine explained—"Mrs. Simmons should consider it a gift."

Tony stared in disbelief. "Sick! You're not only crazy—you're sick!"

"Mr. Rawlings, you're dead wrong." Smirking, she added, "I've waited a long time to say that." Before he could respond, she continued, "You see, in your absence, your friend has been well—forgetful"—Catherine stepped closer—"You probably don't remember how your grandmother suffered"—she laughed—"Of course, everyone says that. They say it's the patient that suffers, but in reality, it isn't. Oh, don't get me wrong Sharron was a sweet, loving woman; however, the one who really suffered was Nathaniel. Every day, he sat with her, talked to her, held her, even when she couldn't respond. It was tragic." Catherine shook her head, lost in her own thoughts. "No one should ever have to deal with that. So you see, with Brent heading that direction, because *forgetfulness* is how it starts—Courtney has received the gift of not having to witness her husband suffer."

Tony listened in disbelief to Catherine justifying her actions. *Had Brent been forgetful? Or was he just walking an invisible tight rope when with Catherine, keeping his knowledge hidden?* Tony wanted her to stop. He wanted to release the crimson that wouldn't go away. Without thinking, Tony slapped her cheek. "Shut up! There's no justification for what you've done."

The action was supposed to help him; however, instead of making him feel better, memories of slapping Claire came rushing back. The crimson continued to infiltrate. Turning toward the desk, he saw the vase of flowers. In one swift movement, he hurled it against the wall. Shards of crystal, water, and flowers littered the carpet as the vase shattered.

"You will *never* be the man your grandfather was!" Catherine screamed. "He never would've struck someone he loved."

Tony turned maliciously, his eyes meeting hers. "If you're referring to me—at this moment—neither did I! And as for my grandfather—he did. I saw him!"

"You're lying."

Tony's face burned as he remembered the scene. "I watched from the doorway"—he pointed toward the doors—"He slapped my father."

Catherine shrugged. "*He* probably deserved it."

"So do you! You don't get to decide who lives and who dies! Brent had a wife and kids!"

"I loved your grandfather, but even I realized that I couldn't watch him take the same path as Sharron."

Tony tried to process her words. *Same path*?

"With each visit to the prison, he became more and more forgetful. He'd ask me the same questions over and over. Some days, he'd talk about someone, and then tell me the same story again. Mostly, he'd talk about the past."

Tony seized her shoulders. "My grandfather had a vitamin deficiency. That, combined with the anti-depressants the prison prescribed can create *dementia-like* side effects. I found documentation that the prison contacted my father about it. My father refused to allow them to take him off the medication. I assumed it was to help his case—giving him validation to void your marriage."

Catherine's eyes blazed. "No! He *was* losing it. I was there—not you. He trusted me—I had to take care of him."

"Take care of him?"

"It was very simple. My mother believed in herbal cures. When I was a teenager, she thought she could cure my uncle's drug use with herbs and plant extracts. She taught me about plants—those that heal—and those that kill. It's actually very ingenious. The natural extracts don't register on normal toxicology screens. Oh, it can be found, but only with specific tests."

Tony collapsed onto the leather sofa and studied the woman he'd known most of his life. He could scarcely form the words to his question, "You poisoned my grandfather?"

Catherine stood taller and shook her head. "Don't you dare make it sound bad! I did—what I did—to save him, from himself. You know, like how you planned to have Claire take the insanity plea—to save her from you."

His volume rose with each word. Tony suddenly feared the reason the Vandersols hadn't heard their argument or exited the suite. "Who else? Who else have you poisoned?"

She shrugged. "Well, after I knew it worked, I tried it with Sherman Nichols."

Tony couldn't believe his ears. "No! He died of natural causes, years before we started any plans."

"Years before *you* started any plans. I was tired of waiting. His death sustained me until you were man enough to get involved."

"But I paid for *accidents*."

Smiling, she beamed. "And quite a bit too. It's made a wonderful nest egg, thank you very much. The poisoning resembles a heart attack, as you probably remember from Nathaniel's cause of death; therefore, the only difficulty is determining the perfect time of ingestion, for example, before someone gets into their car to drive, or goes on a dangerous hike—it works amazingly well and is rarely questioned. Besides, it doesn't take a genius to administer it, just a little in a drink or on their food. Finding a willing executioner wasn't difficult. It also wasn't as expensive as *accidents*."

"Why are you telling me all of this?"

"Because I deserve recognition—everyone thought you were so wonderful, and I was just the *stupid housekeeper*. None of what I'm saying can be proven. Months ago, I had the cameras in this office turned off, and after I took Sophia upstairs, I called the police. They should be here any minute. I told them that you just arrived and how afraid I was of what you might do. No one will believe your story. I'm just the quiet housekeeper. I wasn't even in California when your parents died"—her eyes lit up—"You know the best part?"—She didn't wait for him to answer—"I poisoned *you* with the same plant extract. Oh, I debated about the amount. I knew our plan was for you to only go unconscious. At first, I planned to use sleeping pills, but the irony was too beautiful to pass up."

Tony walked toward her. "This *is* done. Why are the Vandersols here?"

"H—How—" she stammered. "How do you know about them?"

"Why are they here?"

She smirked. "I couldn't have planned it better myself. The police will think you hurt them after all they've done to ruin your name. Did you know she was pregnant? Of course you did—that's why you came here—to stop another Nichols from entering this world."

His voice lowered as he walked closer. "Tell me if you've hurt them."

"It depends."

Tony glared.

"I don't know," she confessed.

"What the hell do you mean—you don't know?"

Catherine shrugged. "We could check the video. I don't know if they've decided to drink any of the water in the refrigerator. The room is quite warm and packing Claire's things can be thirsty work."

"Fuck'n sick! The police will take you away! You killed my grandfather for having *a reaction to medication*. He could've gotten out of jail and none of this would have ever happened. My father was right—in not trusting you! He was wrong too—my grandfather wasn't crazy—you are!"

This time, Catherine attacked. Tony's face stung as her open palm assaulted his cheek. Before he could form words, she was gone. He rushed after her, seeing her disappear behind a door in the corridor of his and Claire's suite. Reaching for the handle, it didn't move. He pounded on the wooden barrier and screamed her name. Within seconds, members of the shocked staff began to surround him.

"Mr. Rawlings!"

"Mr. Rawlings?"

Their surprised and questioning voices filled his hearing. Tony hoped Eric or Phil heard Catherine's plan and were rescuing Emily and John. He continued screaming. Suddenly, smoke wafted from the opening below Catherine's door.

Tony yelled, "Get out of the house and call the fire department!" At first, the staff didn't move; finally, he yelled, "Now! Get out! Call for help!"

Everyone scattered.

His thoughts went from Catherine—to Sophia—to the Vandersols. He'd saved Catherine's life, on more than one occasion—he wasn't doing it again. As smoke billowed from below the door filling the corridor, Tony raced toward the backstairs.

Running toward the S.E Corridor, he went directly to Claire's old suite. The lever wouldn't budge. Cupping his hands against the door, he yelled, "Emily? John? Are you in there?"

Despite the commotion below, he heard nothing through the door. His heart sank until he heard a faint pounding against the door. He'd forgotten the room was soundproofed. There was a time that had been necessary. Reaching for the electronic release, Tony prayed it still worked. What seemed like an eternity later, he heard the once familiar *beep*. Grasping the lever once again, he pushed the door open to find his brother and sister-in-law laying upon the ground.

John looked up. "How? How are you here? Did you do this? You're sick!"

Tony shook his head. "We don't have time. No, I didn't!" He pointed to Emily with her face down. "Is she all right?"

John shook his head. "You're going to jail for this!"

"We'll argue later—is she all right?"

"Yes—we're trying to avoid the smoke."

John was right; the smoke whirled in gray waves near the ceiling. Tony and John both helped Emily to her feet as water began to rain from the sprinkler system. Within seconds, they were all soaked. Leaving Claire's old suite, Tony looked both directions down the long corridor. As smoke and water limited their visibility, Emily clung to John's arm with her other hand protectively covering her mouth and nose.

"John, listen to me"—Tony screamed above the *whoosh* of sprinklers— "Go right—in about thirty feet, you'll find the backstairs—when you reach the ground floor—go right again. There's a door that opens to the kitchen. From there, you'll be able to get out into the backyard."

John reached for Tony. "You're coming with us. You can't stay up here."

"Just go. There's another person I need to find."

"Oh God! Claire?"

Tony shook his head. "No, Claire's safe. She isn't here." He could tell John was debating their next move. "Go! Get Emily and your baby out of this smoke!"

John didn't argue. Tony stood, momentarily watching his brother and sister-in-law disappear into the gray haze. Wiping the water from his eyes, he headed the other direction toward the grand staircase. Each room he passed, he opened in hopes of finding Sophia.

As he neared the front stairs, he considered the southwest corridor when he stopped dead in his tracks. Straining his ears, Tony listened again. Suddenly, his world crashed in around him. With all his might and his shoes slipping on the wet marble, he ran toward the voices.

∞∞∞∞∞∞

-ONLY MOMENTS EARLIER-

The feeling of foreboding that Claire had experienced ever since she learned they were coming back to Iowa, was too strong to deny. Phil had told her to trust her instincts and her instincts told her that they should've stayed in paradise—but her heart wouldn't allow Tony to travel to the U.S. without her. Now, she knew why.

When Courtney received the call about Brent, Claire knew she needed to get to Tony. He'd told her to stay away from the estate, but she couldn't. It wasn't that she wanted to save Catherine from his wrath—she wanted to save Tony from the consequences of his possible actions. She knew if he learned about the Rawlings plane while with Catherine, he'd blame her—possibly rightfully so; nonetheless, Claire didn't want Tony to do something else that he'd regret. He didn't need another crime added to his list.

As Claire entered the gates of the estate, she glanced in the rear-view mirror. Nichol was peacefully sleeping in the car seat. She should've left her with Courtney; but Courtney was too distraught to watch over their daughter. Besides, Claire's plan was simple—find Tony, Emily, and John and get them out of the house. She could've called, but then she'd have had to tell him about the plane crash. Claire didn't want to do that over the phone. As she parked the car in front of the house, she thought about Phil and Eric, *where were they?*

Looking up at the stately home, she pushed away the onslaught of memories, and straightened her stance. This was *their* home—Nichol's home, and Claire wanted it back. Fury filled her chest as she thought about Catherine. The woman's plan had worked successfully to force both her and Tony into hiding. Suddenly, Claire was tired of running, tired of revenge, and tired of the fight. Lifting Nichol from the car seat, Claire declared, "Look, sweetie, this is *your* house. This is all yours, and your mommy will *not* let that mean woman have it a second longer."

Yes, she wanted to get Tony out, and she wanted to get Emily and John out, yet what Claire wanted more than anything, was to get *Catherine* out—out of the house—and out of their lives. *Damn it! I'm Mrs. Anthony Rawlings, and I've had enough. No one is taking this away from our daughter!*

Her mind focused like never before, making each step toward the grand doors more determined.

To Claire's surprise, when she depressed the lever and pushed forward, the doors opened without hesitation. Looking around the empty foyer, she heard voices coming from the corridor of Tony's office. As she walked quietly down the hallway, the voices grew in volume. She wasn't ready to confront the entire staff, so when she heard footsteps coming her direction, she opened the door to Tony's office and slid inside. Immediately, the smell of smoke filled her senses. Even the room appeared to be dimming with a gray haze.

This wasn't right—this house was a fortress. She had difficulty comprehending that there could possibly be a fire, but the undeniable burning in her lungs confirmed her fear. Claire's mind spun between the need to get Nichol out and the desire to assure Tony's safety. "Oh, my God, where's your daddy?" she said aloud.

"Good afternoon, Claire."

The coolness of Catherine's voice rendered Claire motionless. She hadn't had time to see anything except the room where they stood, and hadn't realized Catherine was in the attached bathroom.

"Catherine, where's Tony? What's happening? Is there a fire?"

Claire's feet stayed planted to the lush carpet, as Catherine approached. Catherine's gray eyes darkened with intensity while the distance between them lessened. She was no longer looking at Claire—her eyes were focused on the baby in her arms. Her hand reached out as she said, "So this is *it*—the Rawls—Nichols baby."

Instinctively, Claire pulled Nichol away. "Don't you dare touch her!"

"Her?! You have a daughter—Anton has a daughter, and you've been together, all this time"—Catherine's gaze locked on Claire's—"Haven't you? You two have been together!"

Claire's eyes blazed, displaying her lack of fear. Never had she felt such hatred. Yes, years ago she hated Tony—that was different, stemming from the anxiety of his actions. This was deep and visceral—a loathing for someone who'd been trusted and loved—to learn that person had lied—forever. *Had anything she'd ever said been real?*

Not only had Catherine lied, but she'd tried to harm both Claire and Tony. She'd sentenced them both to a life alone—a life without the love of the one person who completed their world. She'd sentenced them to her reality.

"Yes! Yes, we've been together. Our daughter is a Rawlings—we're a family. Something we would've, at one time, shared with you! Instead, you gave it all up, for some sick, old vendetta!"

Catherine laughed and turned away. The smoke continued to thicken. "Share with me! Oh, so that I could clean up after you and soothe your hurt feelings when Anton upset you—so that I could be ordered out of a room—by *you!*" As her volume increased, Nichol began to cry.

Claire tried to soothe her daughter as Catherine's tirade continued, "You don't belong here. I sent you away! *You—a Nichols*—don't get to have what I couldn't. I won't allow Nathaniel's home to be run by a *Nichols!* If my daughter didn't get to live within these walls, then neither will yours."

"How can you be so sick? She's an innocent child!" Claire's yelling spurred Nichol's cries to become louder.

"Innocent! No one is innocent. Your grandfather's actions killed the only man who ever loved—"

The door burst open and more smoke flooded the room. Tony's eyes met Claire's as his booming voice stopped Catherine's words. Claire heard and saw his terror, "My God, Claire! Why are you here? Get out, the house is on fire!"

Instead of fear, Claire felt relief. "Oh, you're safe—I was so afraid."

The commotion outside the office became louder with voices and footsteps. Nichol's cries resumed as cold water came raining down from the ceiling. When Claire turned back toward Catherine, she saw the gun. It wasn't big; nevertheless, it was pointed directly at her and Nichol. Tony saw it too.

They say time slows down during life threatening events. Supposedly, your entire life flashes before your eyes. Claire wasn't seeing her entire life, only the part that mattered, only the part that included Tony and Nichol. Voices spoke and chaos erupted on all sides, but Claire didn't notice. Her attention was monopolized by the threat in Catherine's hand, as well as the growing fire crackling and smoldering around them—consuming their home.

Tony's voice rang above the chaos, penetrating the smoke and sprinkler induced rain. "Get out, get Nichol out!"

As Claire moved to obey, she saw Catherine's expression change before her eyes. Emerging from the woman who'd consoled her over the years was the sadistic smile from her nightmare, yet this time, it was real, and she was repeating their daughter's name, "*Nichol?*" Turning the gun toward Tony, she asked incredulously, "*Nichol?* You named a Rawls—Nichol?"

He didn't answer; instead, he hit the gun free of her hand. In the commotion, it fell near Claire's feet. She heard his command, "Claire, get the gun!"

Her wet hands searched for the weapon, and water blurred her vision. Bending down, she didn't see Catherine rush forward until she was right there. Claire expected a fight for the gun; instead, Catherine grabbed Nichol from her arms. The next few seconds melted together in a space and time haze. Tony fought for their daughter as Claire secured the gun in her grip.

Phil's voice yelled above the fray of Tony's loud accusations. Nichol cried and Catherine...

Claire didn't intend to pull the trigger. She was trying to hold the gun steady, but when Phil seized her shoulders, her finger depressed the small lever. The deafening bang drowned out the commotion, removing all other sounds. Through the smoke and water, Claire watched in horror as the three people before her fell to the ground.

Memory is a complicated thing, a relative to truth, but not a twin.

—Barbara Kingsolver

CHAPTER 48

-OCTOBER 2016-

The autumn sun warmed the days, and the darkness cooled the nights. Claire's knuckles blanched as the death-grip on her pen refused to subside. She knew Meredith would arrive soon with her evening meal, and they had plans to go out onto the grounds. Courtney was visiting again; nevertheless, Claire's present confidants and their support couldn't take away her past—no longer could the *consequences* of Claire's *truth* be denied.

Dr. Brown had told Claire to write—just write. No other directives had been given, nor restrictions. Once Claire was confident that her writings were safe from the eyes of others, the good and bad memories of her past came to life on each page. Painstakingly, she filled notebook after notebook. With her heartbeat echoing in her ears, Claire's hand seemed to take on a life of its own. This reflective therapy had been effective. She now knew why her mind had shut down. She understood why she had lost touch with reality. After enduring so much—so many highs—so many lows—she couldn't take anymore.

Perhaps it was the knowledge that Nichol was alive and well or the hope that one day she'd be allowed to hold, care for, and love her daughter. No matter the reason, Claire knew before all else, she needed to face the truth of her conviction...She continued to write—

The office filled with smoke. It'd been a haze, but after Tony opened the door, waves of dense gray saturated the air, filling every void and compartment. As it consumed our history, I worried about our future. I worried about Nichol. I knew I needed to get her out of the fire, yet the aroma of burning wood and crackling of the flames also filled me with an unnatural comforting sense of déjà vu, one which momentarily, replaced the feeling of loss. I know it sounds unreal, but instead of seeing the fire before me—the one that threatened the lives of those I held the dearest— I, for a split second, remembered other fires. I remembered the Iowa state prison incinerator and couldn't help wonder, if only I'd left the past in ashes, then would we all be safe today?

I remember hearing voices and chaos coming from all directions. I couldn't see them, and I really couldn't hear their words. My attention volleyed between the flames and Catherine's gun; however, other scenes filled my memories. Is this what happens when you face death? I've heard your entire life passes before your eyes. Maybe that was what was happening. I knew at that moment death was imminent.

Could that be the answer for the last two years? Was my break with reality—as the doctors call it—my self-imposed death? After what I did, it'd make sense. After all, I've learned actions have consequences.

In those few seconds—that took a lifetime—I remembered scenes of surrender and desperation. All the memories I'd successfully compartmentalized away instantaneously proclaimed their presence, only to fade into the gray smoke. With Nichol still in my arms, I took a step back and rubbed my burning eyes. Still there were other scenes playing out before me. They weren't of oppression or vengeance—no, in those last seconds, I remembered true love and affection. I prayed those scenes would prevail; however, when I closed my eyes they too disappeared into the growing haze and mayhem.

I knew that I couldn't fall down and surrender to the fire or Catherine's gun. I'd surrendered too many times, yet I knew no matter what choice I made, our lives would never be the same. I just didn't realize the magnitude of that realization.

For once, with not only my life at stake, but those of my daughter and husband, I chose to face the reality. With soot covering my face and those around me, I stood tall and saw the horror in Tony's eyes. I couldn't surrender—I couldn't give into emotion, not yet. In my heart, I knew there were cards yet to see—the game wasn't over—I knew the rules—and I wouldn't disappoint.

Claire wiped the tears from her eyes. She hadn't been aware that she was crying until the large droplets of moisture hit the ink on her paper, causing her words to bleed.

She looked at the clock. Meredith would be there in less than ten minutes. She should stop writing, yet the memories were too clear. Claire needed to finish the story—

Nichol's cries cut through the cold water that fell from the ceiling. Tony was yelling—telling me to get her out of the house. If only I'd listened. Of all the times I'd obeyed him, ironically, this was when I chose to exert my independence.

I've asked myself why, and I've seen the answer in my nightmares. It was the look in Catherine's eyes as she was saying Nichol's name. That look haunts me to this day.

Everything happened so fast. Tony knocked the gun away from Catherine. He told me to pick it up, so I did. Catherine rushed toward me and, oh God—I can't keep writing. If I write it—it's real.

Closing the notebook, Claire placed it in a drawer, went to the bathroom, and washed her face. She didn't want Meredith to find her in this state. When she returned to her quiet room, Claire looked around at all the new items: the colorful throw pillows, the new bedspread, and the pictures on her dresser. It broke her heart to see Nichol's big brown eyes. They looked so much like her father's.

Slowly, she walked to the dresser and opened the drawer. The end of their story was quite simple. It could be summed up by writing only a few more sentences—

As I retrieved the gun from the floor, Catherine stole Nichol from my grasp. When she did, Tony was there! He fought for our daughter. I saw the panic in his eyes when he noticed that I had the gun. I don't think I meant to pull the trigger. I remember shaking. I don't know if it was the cold water or fear, but when I heard Phil's voice and felt pressure on my shoulders, I flinched, and I pulled the trigger.

Claire heard the sound of her door opening. Squaring her shoulders, she finished their story—

The sound was deafening. In that moment, I watched them all fall and knew, without a doubt, I'd shot the love of my life—I'd killed Anthony Rawlings.

Stoically, she placed the notebook back in the drawer. If Meredith noticed Claire's red eyes, she didn't acknowledge them. Instead, she did what she'd been doing since before Claire could remember, she chatted as Claire ate her dinner.

Later, when they stepped outside into the early evening, the air was still comfortably warm. Unfortunately, the nights were descending faster by a few minutes each passing day. The setting sun returned the cool crisp chill to the October breeze. Although this was only Courtney's third visit since Meredith had brought them together, Claire constantly feared raising questions if they stayed out too late. She hated that the twilight dictated the length of their visits. It wasn't like she wanted to lie to Emily or to anyone. She'd repeatedly asked Emily to allow more visitors. Emily always had a reason to deny her request—according to her sister the time was never right.

During Courtney's first visit, she and Claire mostly hugged and cried. The emotion was too raw and intense to discuss Claire's condition or the reason for her *break with reality*. On the second visit, they concentrated on Nichol. Courtney told stories, saying that she'd visited and been in contact with Claire's daughter ever since Emily started caring for her. She reminded Claire, "How could Aunt Courtney stay away from Nichol Courtney?"

It wasn't like Claire had forgot Nichol's middle name or the person she and Tony wanted to honor—well, maybe she had momentarily forgotten—but hearing Courtney's pride and seeing the adoration in her bright blue eyes, Claire knew that she and Tony were right to name Nichol after their good friend.

Claire believed this visit would be different. She knew what she wanted to discuss—what she needed to say—aloud. It had taken some time and reflection, but the therapists were right. The journaling helped take her along her own safe, personal journey.

The walk to and from the clearing, as well as the impending nightfall, only allowed Claire and Courtney thirty to forty minutes of together time. It wasn't much, but it was something—*to Claire, that was a lot!*

Claire couldn't thank Meredith enough.

As they approached the small clearing, Claire fell into silent reflection. Her mind swirled; she worked desperately to control her thoughts, wanting to phrase them correctly, in a way her friends would understand. Perhaps Emily wasn't ready to believe Claire was better—maybe the doctors and therapists weren't convinced she was beyond relapse—but Claire wanted her friends to know—she'd come to terms with her past and was ready to move on to her future.

Once their greetings were said and the three ladies sat on the blanket that Courtney brought, Claire began her story, "I want to thank you both for believing in me." Claire reached for Meredith's hand. "So many years ago, when we pledged sisterhood, I don't think either of us had any idea where it would take us. I know that I wouldn't be here without your help."

Meredith smiled.

Claire reached for Courtney. "I can't imagine anyone else standing by me like you've done. Who would've thought, when Tony took me to your house so many years ago, we'd end up here? You've had many opportunities to walk away from me and all the drama, but you never have, thank you!"

Claire sat straighter. "Courtney, I told Meredith I wanted to see you to learn what happened at the estate. Recently, I've been writing things down and working them out. I don't need you to tell me...I remember"—bravely, she fought the emotion and pushed it back down—"I know why there're rules about Tony, mentioning his name, or acknowledging that he existed. The thing is"—she inhaled and wiped the tears from her cheeks with the back of her hand—"I'm tired of people acting like I can't handle the truth...I remember shooting him—I know—I know that I killed him."

Courtney and Meredith looked at one another, their expressions ones of confusion and disbelief. When they started to speak, Claire spoke over them, "You don't have to pretend. I remember the gun, the deafening sound as I pulled the trigger." Claire stammered, "I—I remember him falling, Catherine falling, and Nichol—thank God she wasn't hurt. I don't think I could live with myself if I..." Her voice momentarily trailed away.

Regaining her composure, she said, "I was so happy to hear she was all right. I don't understand where I was for so long, or how I got there. Maybe I *was* crazy? Sometimes I wonder if it's craziness to deal with real life—day after day—or if it's crazy to want to live in the good times"—she smiled through her tears—"I want the two of you to know that there were good times! The man I married—*the second time*"—she added. "We had something I'll never forget. Emily and the doctors may think I should forget and move on, but I'll never forget. The thing is—I'm ready to move on."

Meredith interjected, "Claire, oh my God, if I thought that was what you thought—I'm so sorry."

Courtney squeezed Claire's hand. "Honey, Tony isn't dead! You didn't shoot him. You shot Catherine!"

Happiness erupted throughout her entire being, only to be immediately replaced by a heaviness that filled Claire's chest—she fought the thoughts and memories. Suddenly, the numbers were back—counting dominated her thoughts—*three, four, five, six*—Pushing everything away, stopping the lineation of numbers, she asked, "If he's alive, why hasn't he been here? Doesn't he want to see me? Is it Emily or is it *him*?"

Courtney reached out and grasped Claire's shoulders. "No! He wants to see you. Claire, he's in prison. He can't get here." Giving her a reassuring hug, Courtney softened her voice and added, "I saw him recently, he wants to see you very much—I promise."

Prison—Claire tried desperately to recall their conversations. She pushed forward, "Why?

I thought the FBI was going to make him a deal...is it because of Simon—because Tony hired someone to sabotage his plane?"

This was all new territory for Meredith—she couldn't answer Claire's questions if she wanted; however, Courtney could. She knew what Claire needed to learn.

"No!" Courtney looked to Meredith. "I don't know what to do. Can she handle this?"

Claire's eyes sharpened, the days of treating her with kid-gloves were over, she replied, "Hello, I'm right here. Yes, I can handle this—I need to know. I need to know what happened."

Courtney shrugged. "Tony was upset that Simon approached you in Chicago."

Claire nodded.

"He was so upset that he contacted someone to arrange for an airplane malfunction."

None of this was news. "He told me. That's illegal."

"It is." Courtney continued, "However, that wasn't how Simon died. Tony's connection, the man who was supposed to arrange the malfunction, took his money, but he didn't complete Tony's request."

Claire tried to reason. "But Simon's plane crashed..."

"Simon's plane crashed because Simon fell asleep. His body was so badly burned they had very little evidence. It was your friend Harry. He was the one who put it all together. Ask yourself, who benefited from Simon's death?"

Claire contemplated and finally answered, "I don't know—all I can think of is Amber, but she—"

Courtney interrupted, "Yes! The way I understand it, she was upset. Things had been rocky in their relationship and Simon was obsessed with you. He'd gone to see you on multiple occasions. Apparently, Amber wasn't happy. She knew he'd planned to leave a great deal of money to her, and she hoped she could convince the board of directors to follow through on Simon's lead and allow her to run the company—he also left her the majority of the stock in SiJo, so she arranged for an overdose of antihistamines prior to his flight. Actually, the amount she arranged for him to ingest wasn't too much for most people, but apparently, Simon had sensitivity to that kind of medication. It caused him to fall asleep while flying the plane."

Claire tried to follow. "Amber? No, that can't be true."

"It is," Courtney replied. "When you contacted her from prison and told her your theories, she decided it was a great way to deflect any suspicion away from her. She told her brother, Harry—who happened to be Agent Harrison Baldwin—and the FBI became involved. There were lingering concerns about your grandfather's death and some other cases which led to Anton Rawls. When Amber talked to the FBI, they saw it as the perfect storm. By utilizing Harry—having him get to know you, they assumed they'd learn more about Tony."

Claire shut her eyes and tried to concentrate. Finally, she asked, "So, Tony *didn't* kill Simon? Amber did?"

"That's right, and last I heard, she'd been convicted and is still in prison."

Meredith shook her head and mumbled, "This is unreal! You can't make this shit up!"

Courtney's blue eyes sent piercing stares toward Meredith. "Remember what I said!" Courtney's voice no longer held the reassuring tone she'd used with Claire.

Meredith responded with a simple nod of her head.

After a moment of deliberation, Claire said, "Oh, my God—poor Harry. He had to build a case against his sister?"

"I don't know much about him. I think I heard he retired from the FBI, but honestly, I don't know."

Claire sat silently and contemplated, she couldn't even think about her grandfather. Her thoughts centered on her husband. Finally, she asked, "So why is Tony in prison?"

Courtney exhaled, "I hope to God I'm not telling you anything new. He confessed to everything."

Wide eyed, Claire repeated, "*Everything?*"

"He admitted to hurting you, kidnapping you..." Courtney looked toward Meredith. "He admitted that everything in *her* book was true. He also admitted to having knowledge regarding other incidents—some people who went for a hike and never came back—and John's legal issues." Courtney squeezed Claire's hand, "He admitted publicly to everything. He didn't want it to be dragged out in a lengthy legal battle. He asked to do his time and pay for his sins."

Claire sat silently for a minute and tried to comprehend this new information. After a moment, she asked, "The FBI, they knew most of this before we returned to the states. They said Tony would receive preferential treatment for his help with Catherine. Did he get it?"

Courtney smiled. "His sentence has been served at a minimum security prison which gives him many more rights than you had during your incarceration, and his sentence was significantly reduced. As a matter of fact, Brent thinks he'll be released during his first parole hearing."

Claire's heart momentarily skipped a beat. She stared at her friend. Up until now, Claire hadn't been ready to discuss Brent. The last she'd heard, he was on a plane that went down. "Brent?" Claire's eyes filled with new moisture as she searched the deep blueness of her friend's eyes. "Brent's okay?"

"Yes! He wasn't on that plane—the one he was supposed to have been on. He later said he wanted to get home to you and Tony, but there were extra legal documents requiring modification. He stayed a little longer in Chicago and decided at the last minute to catch a later commercial flight. It wasn't until he landed in Cedar Rapids that he knew anything about the crash."

Claire shook her head—this was all so much. "Parole, when could that happen?"

"I don't know the date—Brent said soon."

Claire smiled, she liked *soon*! Though the sky was darkening, she wasn't ready to leave this conversation. Her thoughts went back to the plane and Catherine. "What happened to Catherine?" Her voice quivered, "D—Did I kill *her*?"—she looked down—"I wish I could remember more specifics. I remember something about an insanity plea. All I could think about was Tony telling me years ago that it was my best option. If I needed a plea, I must have killed her."

Meredith chimed in, "You didn't. You shot her, but her wound wasn't life-threatening. She stood trial—a long and drawn out one—but one that was kept very quiet from the media. She was convicted on multiple counts including multiple murders."

Courtney added, "That day at the estate—Tony baited her into confessing to more crimes than he even knew existed. Eric arranged for the office to be wired, and Phillip Roach made sure it was all recorded. That information was essential in her conviction."

Claire stared in disbelief. "So, there was a reason for him to go to the estate."

Meredith said, "Well that and your sister and brother-in-law. Apparently, they were trapped in an upstairs suite. Tony got them out before the fire or smoke reached them."

Claire rubbed her temples. "There was a time that I trusted Catherine without question."

Patting Claire's leg, Courtney added, "I know Honey—I know you did. We all thought she was so kind and sweet. The saddest part was her daughter."

Wheels turned, Claire stuttered, "H—Her daughter? Oh, yes, I remember Sophie—no Sophia."

Courtney nodded, "She didn't make it out of the house. They said it was smoke inhalation."

"Oh!" Claire's stomach wrenched. She'd never met the woman, but she knew Tony thought highly of her.

Courtney continued, "Her husband was on that airplane. Brent said he had great potential."

Claire contemplated the onslaught of information for a moment. She thought about her grandmother's beliefs and those of Madeline and Francis on the island. Slowly, she wiped the tears and felt her cheeks rise into a seemingly inappropriate smile. "So, Catherine's goal was to keep Sophia and her husband apart?"—she didn't wait for an answer—"I guess God had other plans. Her husband's name was Burke, wasn't it?"—she went on—"I hope Sophia never knew her biological mother was Catherine."

Meredith and Courtney shrugged. Finally, Courtney answered, "I'm not sure what she knew. From the audio of Tony's office, I think we're right to assume she didn't. She died peacefully unaware."

In the days that followed, Claire replayed the conversation over and over in her head. The loss of any life was terrible. Catherine had been directly responsible for so many; however, what kept coming back to Claire was the idea that Sophia and Derek were still together. She had to believe they were. If their love could overcome death, Claire believed her and Tony's could overcome insanity and incarceration.

It was that belief that inspired her to confront her sister again, two weeks after her conversation with Courtney and Meredith. "Emily, seriously, I'm not a child. I'm much better. I want to see Nichol. I want out of here, and I'm ready to address the world."

Emily leaned forward and covered Claire's hand. "You know I love you?"

Claire nodded.

"We're all happy your hallucinations are gone."

"Memories," Claire corrected.

Emily pursed her lips before she continued, "Honey, I worry about delusional thoughts. Your doctors and I believe some of this has been occurring for a long time"—she patted Claire's hand—"You have a history of irrational decisions. I don't want you making decisions now that will later come back to upset you or Nichol."

Claire continued to plead her case as Emily recited her concerns. It was a different version of their same discussion. Unexpectedly and without warning, the door to Claire's room opened behind her. She didn't need to turn, she didn't need to see. His presence overwhelmed her—filled her and the room with electricity that only seconds earlier didn't exist. According to the law of conservation, energy can neither be created nor destroyed, which meant the electricity was already present; nevertheless, when the door opened, she felt unbridled power surging through her veins. There was only one person—one man who held that kind of power. Seeing the astonished look on Emily's face, Claire knew she was right.

Without thought or concern, Claire stood. Closing her eyes, she turned toward the doorway confident of who she'd see when her eyes opened. This wasn't a hallucination or a memory—it was real. Although Emily's voice pleaded for Claire to listen, she didn't hear her sister's words. There was nothing and no one else at that moment other than her husband. The rest of the world ceased to exist, and she was powerless to do anything other than surrender to his gaze.

They were the eyes she'd dreamt about—the eyes she saw in pictures of their daughter. They were the black holes which years ago swallowed and consumed her heart and soul.

Did she move? Did he? There were noises, but the words being spoken weren't coming from either one of them. They didn't need words. Over the course of the years, there'd been *too many* words—words they remembered— and ones they sought to forget. At this moment, none of them mattered.

In merely a split second, Claire took him in—prison had changed him, to a degree. His black mane now held more hints of white—new lines appeared around his eyes—and the hardness in his expression was replaced by something stronger, yet more serene. No matter the differences, he was still her husband—he was still Anthony Rawlings.

Their bodies nearly touched when the scent of his cologne filled the air. She inhaled the intoxicating scent she'd imagined over the years and melted into his embrace. Her face rested against the lapel of his silk suit as her body molded to his. Closing her eyes again, she relished the sensation of his muscular chest and beating heart. They still hadn't spoken, yet the volume of the room around them had increased exponentially. His hand reached for her chin and brought their eyes together. It was the blending of brown and green— light to dark and dark to light—it was their connection—and it surpassed all other obstacles.

"I've dreamt of those eyes." The sound of his deep baritone voice brought a smile to her face.

"As have I." Suddenly, Claire worried and looked away. *Did he know about her break with reality? Did he know people thought she was crazy?*

"Look at me." His commanding tone required obedience. Claire looked back up. "I've missed you so much. Why are you looking away?"

"Do you know? Do you know what they say about me?"

His eyes lightened and his cheeks rose. "I know—I love you."

"They think I'm crazy."

His hands which held her tightly caressed and soothed her back. "I think we're all crazy. That doesn't mean that I'm leaving here today without you. My love, you're coming home."

She caught her breath and tried to comprehend. Slowly, the rest of the room came back into focus. Apparently, they weren't the only two people on earth. Her normally empty room overflowed with people. Emily stood to the side, with tears in her eyes and an anguished expression, as she spoke on her phone. Brent and Courtney were there, and Brent was talking to another man, showing him documents. Courtney was hugging herself, smiling, with tears running down her cheeks.

Finding her voice, Claire sought the reassurance of Tony's gaze, "I'm leaving here? How?"

Brent nodded at the other gentleman and stepped toward Tony and Claire. Claire reached out and squeezed Brent's hand. "I'm so thankful you're..."

Brent smiled and said, "Me too—if I weren't alive, I couldn't be the one to tell you"—he grinned toward Claire. His eyes sparkling with new vitality—"I wouldn't be the one to *help* you."

Claire remembered him telling her one time, how he'd always wanted to help her—not hurt her. While holding tight to Tony's hand, she smiled at his clandestine reference.

Brent continued, "As long as Tony was incarcerated, Emily was your listed next of kin and held your power of attorney. I'm holding the judgment by Judge Wein, your husband is, once again, legally your next of kin. Until you're completely cleared medically, he has the power to make your medical decisions including your release."

"I thought I was here because of an insanity plea?"

Brent shook his head. "Originally, that was true, but you were cleared of all charges by self-defense." He looked to Emily and back. "You've been kept here for your safety; however, I've obtained statements from your doctors substantiating your mental health. Soon, you should legally be able to make your own decisions. In the meantime, with Tony's signature, you can go home. There are some hoops we need to jump through—therapy you must agree to complete—but we're not leaving Everwood without you."

Turning toward Emily, Brent continued, "You can choose to fight—if you want. I'm sure John will be here soon; however, I can assure you—I've left no 'T' uncrossed or 'I' undotted."

The aguish in Emily's expression broke Claire's heart. Barely able to bring herself to let go of Tony's hand, Claire walked to her sister and wrapped her arms around her neck. "I know you've been doing what you thought was best, and Emily, I love you for it, but now it's time for all of us to move forward."

After a moment of obvious internal turmoil, Emily said, "John *is* on his way, but we're not going to fight."

"Emily, there's one more thing," Brent said as he handed her another document. "This is from the Family Court. Anthony and Claire Rawlings have been granted full custody of their daughter, Nichol Rawlings. They will be assuming the roles of custodial parents—soon."

As they listened, Tony's arm tightened around Claire, and she smiled up at him. It was more than she'd ever hoped—more than she'd dared to dream. "We're going to be a family again." Her words were a mere whisper that only Tony could hear. Feeling the warm grasp of his large hand around hers was confirmation enough. The terrible ordeal was over.

Never have plans for the future as you never know how things will turn out.

—Nigella Lawson

CHAPTER 49

Claire clung to Tony's hand, listened to the voices, and responded appropriately. As long as she held on—as long as they touched—she knew he was real. The Everwood administration required them to meet with doctors and administrators before granting Claire's release. With Brent's legal documentation and Emily's concession, these meetings were Claire's last hurdle to freedom.

She watched in awe as the Tony from her memories argued for her release. There was nothing about the man in the Armani suit with the gelled back hair and perfect diction that hinted toward ex-con. Tony personified affluence and business success. He sounded like a CEO. Never once, despite what a doctor or therapist said, did Claire doubt Tony's ability to fulfill his promise—she'd be going home.

Once in a while, Brent would need to remind someone of Tony's legal rights *as her husband*. It warmed her heart to see the two of them working together on a common goal. Occasionally, someone would ask Claire a question—some were simple—the date or name of the president. Others were questions about her feelings or concerns. After each appropriate answer, she'd feel the squeeze of Tony's warm hand or see the reassurance of his smile. It didn't matter that behind the smile she also saw sadness. They had both endured too much. What mattered was that they were together and soon they'd have Nichol. Claire couldn't wait to leave the facility and have her family united. With each second, her anticipation grew. She knew, when they were, again, a family, the sadness would leave Tony's eyes, and she'd see the light chocolate brown they once had in paradise.

After they'd signed the last document and answered the last question, she whispered in his ear, "Let's go get Nichol."

She expected a smile and a nod—some sign of affirmation. Instead, he directed the Everwood staff, "Gather all of Mrs. Rawlings' things. I want everything sent to our home."

Claire offered, "I don't need everything. I can get the things I want."

"No, you can go through it later. We're getting you out of here. You aren't spending another second in this place."

She didn't argue—nor did she want to. Although she detested having the facility's staff direct her movements, she loved Tony's control. It was his way of protecting her. She knew that. Yes, he could be domineering, but she'd missed every part of him, his overprotectiveness included.

John was now waiting with Emily as Tony and Claire exited the administrator's office. When Claire saw her family, her body tensed in anticipation of a confrontation. Before she could speak or devise a mental plan, John held out his hand.

"Anthony."

With his hand extended, Tony replied, "Tony—please, call me Tony. Thank you, John, for all you've done while I was away. Brent tells me you've been quite helpful at Rawlings."

"It was for Nichol and Claire."

Tony nodded. "And for that—for *our* family, I thank you."

"I've been privy to many of your decisions. I want you to know, I respect them."

"Then I hope my return won't cause you to search for another job. Rawlings Industries *and I* can always use someone like you on our side."

John nodded. "Emily and I need to talk, but I think I'd like that."

Claire released Tony's hand and encircled John's neck. Her emotions were all over the place. One minute, she was excited and the next, she was unsure. As she hugged her brother-in-law, tears of joy fell from her eyes. "I had no idea you were working at Rawlings."

Claire released John and immediately hugged her sister. "Thank you, Emily. Thank you for not fighting this."

John explained, "Anth—I mean *Tony's* right, and you're right, we *are* a family—for our children, we need to behave like adults."

Claire stammered, "C—children—I can't wait to see Nichol and meet Michael."

Emily's eyes filled with tears. "She's so little. She won't understand—"

John spoke over Emily, "Your daughter is beautiful and intelligent—she's also young. As long as we do this together, she'll make the transition just fine."

Claire looked up at her husband. Although she wasn't sure what she expected to see, the sadness mixed with gratitude took her by surprise. Taking one of his hands, she said, "We've missed so much. I can't wait to hold her again."

Tony replied, "Thank you again, not just for Rawlings, but for taking care of Nichol. We're anxious to come and see her, but first, I'd like to take Claire somewhere. It won't take long, and then we'll be over to your house. The child psychologist I consulted recommended a gradual transition before we bring her home to stay."

"I thought..." Claire's heart ached.

Emily's moist eyes came to life as she nodded. "Yes—gradual, I think Tony's right." She feigned a smile toward Tony. "Thank you. This'll give us time to talk with her—to try to explain things. Let's make this as easy for Nichol as possible."

When they all walked outside, Claire lifted her face toward the sky. Inhaling, she savored the fresh autumn breeze. Despite the gray sky, the changing leaves added color to an otherwise dark day. An overwhelming sense of freedom momentarily paralyzed her movements.

"What is it?" Tony asked.

"It's beautiful. The trees are colorful and the season is changing. It feels so good to be free."

Tony smiled and wrapped his arm around Claire's shoulder. "I want to show you something."

For most of the drive from Cedar Rapids to Iowa City, Claire watched the landscape through the window, and with her hand in Tony's, she contemplated their family. Of course, it would be hard on Nichol. *Why hadn't she thought of that? But Tony had.* He'd even consulted a child psychologist. Claire rested her head against his shoulder. After everything they'd been through the world was right—Tony would make everything right.

When she recognized their location, she asked a question she hadn't thought to consider, "We're near the estate. What about the fire? Was there a lot of damage?"

His eyes twinkled. "That's what I want to show you."

Nervously, Claire watched as they drove toward the entrance. The front gates opened and they wound up the familiar drive. When the trees parted, Claire gasped. "What happened?"

"You don't like it?"

She heard the disappointment in his voice, but she couldn't lie. "I—I don't know? Did the whole house burn?"

"No. There was a lot of smoke and water damage, but the fire was pretty much contained to the first level southwest corridor."

As soon as Tony stopped the car, Claire opened her door. Silently, she stood trying to comprehend the grand, white, brick structure. Mesmerized, she stared at the tall windows, long porches, black shutters, and lovely columns. The landscaping was perfect, with tall trees and beds of colorful mums. At one end of the house, there appeared to be an enclosed porch, while at the other end, she saw a carport.

Finally, Tony asked, "Do you want to see the inside?"

Claire didn't move—it didn't seem real. Searching for answers, she asked, "What happened to our house?"

"I had it demolished. I built for the wrong reasons"—he took her hand—"it was our house, but it was never a *home*. It contained too many memories."

"So, you got rid of it? Tony, there were good memories there too."

"I built that house for Nathaniel." His brown eyes sparkled. "Claire, I had this home built for you." Standing in front of her, he tugged her hand. The uncertainty behind his eyes pulled her forward; she allowed him to lead her inside.

The entry was beautiful—instead of marble, the flooring was a light polished oak. Immediately, Claire felt the warmth of a home. Yes, the estate had been their *house*, but there were times it felt more like a museum. As Tony took her from room to room, Claire saw the attention to detail—bookcases, cabinetry, custom ceilings and intricate lighting. The back of the house was nothing but windows. In the living room, the windows extended two stories. When they entered the kitchen, her eyes shone. It wasn't the industrial kitchen of the old mansion. This room was designed with a family in mind. The granite countertops, stainless steel appliances, ornate tile work, stone floor, and back wall of glass all added to the casual yet luxurious feel.

"Oh, this looks like a kitchen where I'd love to cook."

Tony smiled. "You have a cook, but it's your kitchen. You can do whatever you'd like."

The lower level contained all the amenities of the old house: a theater room more modern than before, a fun family area, as well as an exercise room and lap pool. When they entered the pool, Tony squeezed Claire's shoulders. "I couldn't build you a house without your favorite room."

Speechless, she shook her head. Finally, she whispered, "It's beautiful, thank you."

Next, Tony took Claire upstairs to Nichol's room—it was a room fit for a princess. Shades of pink and purple dominated the senses as the canopy bed set center stage. Each door or drawer Claire opened was filled. The closets were stocked with clothes and shoes, while the shelves were full of books and dolls. Lastly, he led her to the master bedroom suite.

Compared to the rest of the house, Claire was surprised by the darkness of the room. Letting go of her hand, Tony walked to the far wall and lifted a switch. The draperies moved and the room filled with natural light—more ceiling to floor windows. Claire gasped. In the middle of the windows were two large French doors. He opened the doors, allowing the fresh air to fill their suite and motioned toward the balcony. They stepped through the glass and Claire exclaimed, "Tony, everything is so open and bright."

Reaching for her hands, he stared down into her emerald eyes. Suddenly, the cooling autumn air no longer registered—Claire knew she could stand in his gaze forever. Before the sadness behind the dark registered, his baritone voice replied, "This is your glass house—one that won't shatter. I don't want you to ever feel trapped again. I want you to be able to see the sky and sun—or moon and stars—whenever you desire."

She melted against his chest. "Thank you, I love it! But how—how did you do this? You were in prison."

"I had a lot of help."

Their balcony contained furniture perfect for enjoying the woods behind their home. Standing at the rail, Claire peered below and saw many other amenities—a pool, a basketball court, a play set—bigger than those in most local parks—and the gardens. Sitting on a gliding seat, looking over the tree tops, Claire sighed and laid her head against her husband's shoulder.

Tony spoke, "Of course, you still have your island—if you'd prefer you can move back there. Although this view is beautiful, it's difficult to compete with the view from your lanai. I just thought it might be easier on Nichol if you lived closer to John and Emily for a while."

She looked up. "Why do you keep saying *you*? You mean *we*."

Tony reached into his breast pocket, removed an envelope, and extended it toward her. "You and Nichol, Claire—this house—the entire estate—it's yours."

Her world stopped spinning. There weren't enough masks ever created to hide her emotions. Whatever was in the envelope he offered—she didn't want. Never in the history of time had any documentation he handed her been good. Claire stood and backed away from his hand. "I don't know what's in that envelope, but whatever it is, I don't want it."

Soothingly, he said, "It's for you."

"I don't care. I said *no*."

"You just said you didn't know what it was. How can you say no?"

Her volume decreased. Fighting the sobs, she whispered, "Tell me—tell me why you're saying *you* instead of *we*?" When he hesitated, she straightened her shoulders and spoke louder, "Tell me!"

"Calm down."

"Don't tell me to calm down. I deserve a straight answer."

"If you'll sit down, I'll explain."

Claire eyed him suspiciously and slowly retook the seat beside him. She steadied her voice, closed her eyes momentarily, and said, "I'm sitting—talk."

He looked out at the trees and exhaled. "I tried to contact you. I wanted to be with you, to be there for you. The scene at the estate was crazy. When you pulled the trigger, the police were already here and they immediately arrested both of us. Apparently, the Iowa City Police weren't aware of our cooperation with the FBI. Catherine had called them to say I was there, and that she was afraid. The police assumed that you and I were trying to kill Catherine.

"Eventually, Brent got me out on bail. Of course, that was after he returned from Chicago and learned he was supposed to be dead. He was the only legal counsel who knew about our cooperation with the FBI. By the time I was out—Emily had obtained a restraining order against me. You weren't talking to anyone, and she assumed you were trying to kill *me*—to get away from *me*. Brent, Tom, my whole damn legal staff tried to lift her order. Meredith's book was out—the whole world knew what I'd done to you."

Claire heard the emotion in his voice.

Tony continued, "There were two theories as to your condition. One was traumatic brain injury—Emily argued I was the cause. Even though I was out on bail, the courts wouldn't let me get near you or Nichol. The other theory for your condition was a psychotic break brought on by Catherine, Nichol, the fire—"

Closing her eyes and shaking her head, Claire pleaded, "Tony, stop! I know the past. I don't want to hear it or talk about it. I want to move on. I want what we had in paradise—right here."

He gripped her shoulders. "Don't you understand? You can't keep doing that."

"What?"

"You can't continually push every bad memory away to deal with later."

"Why? I can, and besides, we dealt with our demons in paradise. I remember it all. You're the one who always said—the past is the past—think about the present or the future."

"I was wrong. You need to face it, and so do I. In all those discussions on the island, we never spoke about the things in Meredith's book."

Tears trickled down her cheeks. "Because we were both there. During our discussions in paradise, you told me things I had no way of knowing—I know what happened between us. I also know it was a long time ago and it's over. I don't want to rehash it. I want the future."

"That's what I want—for you too. I want *you* to have a future—free from all of our past. That's why I built you a new, memory-free house and Claire—that's why Brent is ready to file for our divorce."

Claire couldn't think—or speak—or move. She stared blankly as even her tears suspended their decent.

Finally, Tony asked, "Did you hear me? I won't be the one to hurt you anymore, nor will Emily. You deserve fresh air and freedom. No one will ever be able to control you. Besides the money you still have invested overseas, I'm giving you the estate, a handsome settlement, and child support. With your wealth you can do anything you've ever dreamt of doing. You'll be in control of your and Nichol's future—I won't fight you on anything." He looked down and implored sheepishly, "I do hope you'll allow me to see our daughter, but I understand if you don't." Regaining his authoritative tone, he added, "I think we've thought of everything regarding this house, but if there's something else you want or need—it's yours. You can have anything you want."

Her voice cracked. "You don't want m—me?"

Reaching out, Tony lifted her hand and kissed the top. "Don't ever think that. I've never wanted anyone the way I want you."

"I don't understand what you're saying."

"The reason the judge wouldn't lift the restraining order and allow me to see you, was because when the judge asked me if the accounts in Meredith's book were correct, I told him yes. I admitted to everything. He ruled that I was a danger to you and Nichol."

"That's ridiculous. You never would have—nor will you ever—hurt Nichol. Obviously we're together now, so all that legal drama's over." Her voice cracked as she asked, "Why are you throwing me away—now?"

Tony stood and faced the trees—his knuckles blanched as he clenched the railing. "I'm not throwing you away! I'm setting you free."

Claire lowered her face to her chest. "It's because people think I'm crazy— you don't want a crazy wife." Sobs resonated from her chest, separating each statement. "I know I broke your rules." "I know appearances are important." "I'm sorry, I disappointed you."

Though her eyes were closed, she felt his gentle touch as he lifted her chin. When she opened her eyes, Tony was kneeling before her and the darkness memorized her. She couldn't look away. Conversely, there was no darkness or disapproval in his voice. Instead, she heard remorse. "No, Claire. I'm the one who's disappointed you—over and over." He wiped her tears gently with his thumb. "While I was in prison, I learned you were finally getting better. I tried—but Emily still wouldn't allow me to contact you. She wouldn't allow hardly anyone to contact you. Courtney told me she only saw you through Meredith. She also said Emily wouldn't even let you see Nichol"—The intensity of his eyes grew with each word—"I hated your sister! I was powerless to help you, and she was keeping you prisoner. I couldn't even talk to you—hell, I heard that even your time outside was monitored."

He stood once again and paced the length of the balcony. Claire didn't know what to say. Everything he said was true, but she knew that Emily did what she did with good intentions—Emily was afraid if Claire relapsed, it would be devastating to Nichol.

Once he'd calmed, Tony continued, "In order to receive my early release, I agreed to counseling. I didn't want to do it, but if it got me out of there early, I figured *what the hell*." He sat back down. "I spoke to this shrink three times a week. It started with me answering his questions. Over time, it became easier to talk. When I told him how upset I was with Emily and what she was doing to you, he asked me *why I was upset*? I said it was because of what she was doing. He told me to think about it more and figure out *why* I was so upset. I had two days before I saw him again. Throughout those days, I couldn't stop thinking about his question. It seemed obvious, until I realized..."

Claire's mind tried to process, "What? What did you realize?"

"I was so angry with Emily, because she was doing the same thing to you that I'd done. I didn't just hate Emily—I hated me!" He knelt before her and bowed his forehead to her knees. "I will *not* allow anyone to hurt you again—that includes me."

Claire's fingers wove through his hair. "Tony, you were at Everwood—you heard me. I forgave Emily, and many years ago—I forgave you, too. I don't want to be free from you. I lived almost two years believing I'd killed you. I thought that was why no one mentioned your name. During that time, I fantasized about you and cried for you. Now you're here. I can touch you! I want my family back together."

When he didn't respond, she babbled on, "Besides, I'm still an outpatient. If you divorce me, they'll never allow me to have custody of Nichol. If you do this, you're not freeing me, you're abandoning me." The tears were freely flowing once again.

He stood and squared his shoulders. "You're right." His dry and businesslike tone fortified his stance. Nothing she said or could say would change his mind—he'd made his decision. "I don't want you to lose Nichol. We'll start with a separation. I rented an apartment near the office. I'll live there. You and Nichol can have the estate and all the staff you need. With a nanny to help, there shouldn't be any legal concerns."

For an eternity, she sat silently and stared at the man she'd dreamt about. Although their eyes met, there was no connection. No longer did his swirl with emotion. There was no rage or joy—even the sadness had subsided. She couldn't read his thoughts. It was as if he were staring at a document—a car—or anything else inconsequential.

The memory of seeing him the first night of her captivity rushed back. She remembered him standing near the fireplace in her suite. His dark glistening eyes frightened and paralyzed her. Suddenly, she longed for that emotion—it was better than nothing and *nothing* was exactly what she saw.

Claire stood and straightened her shoulders. She knew from experience this conversation was over. She'd already begged—she wouldn't do it again. Without verbally replying to his last comment, Claire nodded and walked past him, back into the bedroom. In the attached bathroom, she found tissues and wiped her eyes. Her crying was done. Looking at her reflection, she saw the plain ugly Everwood clothes, very little make-up, and her hair pulled back into a ponytail. Swallowing the emotions she refused to show, she walked back into the bedroom. Tony was still on the balcony as the autumn sky beyond him darkened. The earlier light had faded. She momentarily wondered if it would ever return.

His current stance reminded her of his rejection of her at the Iowa City jail. She recalled begging him to take her home—pleading for him to make her world right. She couldn't bear it again. If he didn't want her, then she'd move on. Claire was done begging—if someone were to truly make her world right—it would be her.

When she said his name, he turned around. Keeping her voice neutral, she said, "I can't see Nichol looking like this. I'm going to take a shower and clean up. I presume my closets are full, like Nichol's?"

"They are."

"Where's the staff? I'd like something to eat."

"I gave them the night off. I'll go into town and get something. By the time I get back, you should be ready."

Claire nodded. Without another word, she turned and walked away from her future ex-husband.

Birds sing after a storm; why shouldn't people feel as free to delight

in whatever sunlight remains to them?

—Rose Kennedy

CHAPTER 50

When Tony returned with Claire's dinner, she was ready. She hadn't had more than basic cosmetics at Everwood; however, when presented with an excess of the best, she remembered how to use it. She also found a pair of well-fitting jeans and sweater in the well-stocked closet. Her hair was styled and her face painted. If Tony truly meant what he said about still wanting her, then Claire wanted to make his separation declaration as difficult as possible.

She was in the kitchen setting two places at the breakfast bar when he arrived. She didn't hear him enter, but she knew he was there. It was a feeling—a connection—alerting her to his presence. Looking up from the silverware, she saw him in the doorway. She wasn't sure how long he'd been there, but his eyes were as black as the country, moonless night, beyond the glass wall. Helplessly, she stood before him. Time momentarily stood still as his gaze devoured her. It wasn't just her appearance as he scanned her up and down—it was her soul. With each tick of the clock it slipped further and further away. He already owned it—he'd taken it years ago. She waited to see if he planned to keep and treasure it, or discard it—like yesterday's news.

When he didn't speak, she walked toward him, drawn by an invisible pull. Her body ached for his touch. From the look on his face, she believed the feeling was mutual. When she was mere inches away, he said, "I got you a salad. I forgot to ask what you wanted."

Her heart sank. His voice didn't match his gaze. Dejectedly, she replied, "A salad is fine," and turned away.

Claire had thought the years of separation while in Everwood were unbearable. That was nothing compared to the pain of having him in front of her, yet—inaccessible.

During the drive to Emily's, they calmly—too calmly—discussed their separation. After some debate, they both agreed to keep it temporarily concealed. The Vandersols wouldn't understand, and the charade would be easier on Nichol. They planned to ease her into it, after she moved to the estate. Claire's hands began to tremble as they pulled up to the Vandersol's home. Surprisingly, Tony reached over and covered hers with his. It was the first contact since the balcony. His tone was kind and reassuring, "It'll be all right."

She didn't move or attempt reciprocation; instead, she enjoyed the sensation of his warm touch and replied honestly, "I'm scared, what if she doesn't want us?"

"She will."

Turning toward him, she asked, "I haven't even asked, have you seen her?"

He shook his head. "No, pictures are all. I was just released yesterday, and she was never brought to me. It was probably better—a little girl shouldn't be visiting her father in a federal penitentiary."

Claire looked at him in surprise. "Yesterday? And you've accomplished all of this?"

"Like I said—I had help. I've been planning my release for some time."

She looked back down at his hand on her lap as her neck straightened. "And our divorce—how long have you been planning that?"

Pulling his hand away, he rebuked, "Claire, not now. Let's not go back there."

A new thought came to her mind. With it came fire that instantly dried her once moist eyes. She suddenly needed to know the answer to a burning question. "Is there someone else?"

"What?"

"Is—there—someone—else?!"

"No!"—his volume rose—"I told you, I've never wanted anyone the way I want you."

"Well, you obviously don't want me! And you're *Anthony Rawlings*. You were in prison and your wife was crazy; nevertheless, you're still Anthony Rawlings. You would eventually get out of prison, but your wife would always be crazy. I bet there were letters of devotion, propositions, and proposals."

"Claire, our daughter is waiting."

Sudden rage boiled within her. *While she'd been living in a fantasy world, was he communicating with another woman or women?* The intensity of her stare grew as she asked again, "I've already asked this once, don't make me ask again. Is there someone else?"

"Claire, calm down."

Her hand contacted his arrogant expression. Tony stared in disbelief as he seized her fingers. "What the hell was that?"

"You never answer my questions. Tell me, were there letters? Did women write to you promising anything you wanted, all for the chance to take my place?"

"You're getting yourself all worked up. Calm down; Nichol is waiting."

She glared as her voice lowered. "I deserve to know."

"Yes." His eyes glowed in the illumination of the dashboard. "Are you happy?" His growl deepened as he continued to painfully hold her seized hand. "There were letters—I didn't respond. I don't give a damn about anyone—anyone but you. Hell—I even—"

Claire's heart raced. She waited for him to finish his sentence; instead, he released her hand and turned away. She prodded, "You even what?"

"We'll finish this discussion another time." It wasn't debatable. He'd said more than he'd wanted, and he wasn't saying any more. That conversation was done. "Now, do you plan to join me, or do you plan to sit in the car all evening?"

Rubbing the fingers of her right hand, she replied, "I plan to join you."

When Emily met them at the door, they wore the masks of the perfect smiling couple. It was all right—Emily wore a mask too. "We told Nichol she had some special guests coming to see her." Despite Emily's show of strength, Claire heard the sorrow in her sister's voice.

Walking into the living room, they both stopped when Nichol came into view. Without thinking, Claire grasped Tony's hand. Once she realized her action, she quickly let go, thankful that he hadn't pulled away.

The last time they saw their daughter, she had been less than three months old. The little girl before them was nearly three *years* old, and the most beautiful child Claire could ever recall seeing—even prettier than her pictures. Her wavy, brown hair, held back with barrettes, framed her beautiful face. Her thick dark lashes fluttered as big brown eyes peered upward. She'd been sitting on the floor playing with a dollhouse when she turned to see Aunt Em's friends.

Claire knelt to the ground, afraid to get too close, afraid of scaring her daughter away. Mustering her confidence, she said, "Hello, Nichol."

Their daughter stood and stared. Claire marveled at her perfect, petite body. Finally, John stepped forward, and Nichol reached for his hand. "Nichol," John said. "Can you say *hi* to the friends we told you about?"

"Hi."

Tony knelt beside Claire. *Is it possible for a heart to melt and break at the same time?* Claire reached out and Nichol's small fingers shook Claire's hand. Their daughter asked, "Who are you?"

Tony laughed. "Direct, isn't she?"

With a snicker, Emily replied, "Very, I can't imagine where she gets it."

"Nichol, my name is Claire"—she hesitated—"but you can call me Mom."

Nichol's eyes grew wide as she peered from Claire to Tony. Finally, she asked, "Are you my daddy?"

"I am."

They all waited. Dropping John's grasp, she stepped forward and touched a small hand to each of their cheeks. Claire closed her eyes and savored her daughter's touch. Instantly, Claire understood their daughter's actions. It was the same thing she did when Tony arrived at Everwood—touching him—verifying that he was real. Claire reached up and covered Nichol's hand with hers. "We're really here, honey, and we're so sorry we've been gone."

Nichol smiled, her big brown eyes lightening. "I knew one day you'd come. Aunt Em said you were sick, and when you got better, you'd be here. Are you better?"

Fighting back the tears, Claire answered, "Yes, I'm much better. Nichol, can we hug you?"

Lowering her little hands to their shoulders, she nodded. For a few seconds, their family was whole; then without warning, Nichol released her parents and rushed to her cousin. It was the first time Claire had noticed the little blond boy hugging Emily's legs. She was about to say something about Michael when Nichol announced, "Mikey, know what? I have a mommy and daddy too!" Looking up to Emily, Nichol asked, "Does that mean they're Mikey's aunt and uncle, like you and Uncle John?"

Emily and Claire's eyes met. Emily replied, "Yes, honey, it does. Michael, this is Mommy's sister, your Aunt Claire." She hesitated as Tony and Claire stood. "And—your Uncle Tony."

The children couldn't hear the anguish in Emily's voice—at least, Claire prayed they didn't, but she could. They all knew what a long road this had been. Claire put out her hand. "Hello, Michael, I'm so glad to meet you."

Michael took her hand and smiled bashfully. John's voice filled the otherwise quiet room. "Kids, if it wasn't for your Uncle Tony, we wouldn't be here."

The blood rushed from Claire's face as she looked to Tony and back to John. Suddenly, it was six years earlier and Claire feared John's next words. It wasn't that she feared for herself or possible consequences. Claire was tired of conflict. She only wanted for her family to co-exist without confrontations. John continued, "Before you were born, Michael, Uncle Tony saved your mom and me from a fire. If he hadn't done that then you wouldn't be here, either."

Nichol's eyes widened. "Really? You did that?"—she added—"Daddy."

"Wow!" Michael gasped as he looked up at his new uncle.

It was a first step—a baby step—but progress nonetheless. Claire's eyes glistened as she mouthed *thank you* to John. She couldn't recall a more congenial gathering with her family—all of her family. The addition of children not only brought joy to their individual lives, it provided a new bond to hold them together. Pensively, she wished it had done the same for her and Tony.

The first morning that Claire woke in her new home, she lay staring at the ceiling. It had happened again. In a twenty-four hour period, her life had, once again, taken an abrupt turn—new cards and new decisions. She was free—from Everwood—from everyone. Tony made sure of that. He provided her with the means necessary to do anything she ever wanted. She had access to Nichol—it wasn't full access—but that would come with time. As Claire recalled their brief family hug, her heart ached.

From the time she learned that Tony was alive, she'd imagined the perfect reunion. For a couple of hours, it was her reality. The way Tony fought for her release from Everwood fit perfectly into her knight-in-shining-armor fantasy. She wished the few seconds in Emily's living room would have gone on forever. If they had, if their story ended right there, she could've had her *happily ever after*.

Tossing on the soft sheets, Claire looked out to the bright morning sky, through the giant wall of glass. She wondered what happened to those fairy tale couples after the last page. *Was happily ever after even obtainable? Her new life wasn't terrible. She'd take the cards she'd been dealt and try to make the best out of it. After all, that's how she'd survived until now. As a young girl, she'd never dreamt of wealth, yet she had more money than she could ever spend. Fame? She never wanted it and detested having it. What had she wanted out of life? What requests had she made?*

Her mind slipped back through the years to a cold, snowy day. Wrapped in Tony's arms, in his suite, in front of a warm blazing fire, she made requests—access to her own invitations—the ability to contact her sister—to leave the estate whenever she wanted—and for Tony to contact her directly. She had it all. Her new home came with a laptop and tablet. Emily wasn't just reachable—she'd be visiting her each night. In the garage Claire had two vehicles—a car and a SUV, safer for when she drove Nichol. She also had access to a driver whenever she desired. Lastly, the cell phone near her bed was available to anyone who wanted to call. Thinking about the new house, there weren't any requests Claire could recall that Tony hadn't delivered. Even the tall windows and sunlight throughout the house were fulfillments of promises made. He'd provided everything she ever wanted—except him. On that cold, snowy day she didn't realize what she had. Perhaps no one ever does—until it's gone.

Forcing herself to move, Claire got out of bed. She *would* move forward, one step at a time. She'd almost folded once—that wouldn't happen again.

As the days went by, Claire lived for her visits with Nichol. She anxiously anticipated her daughter's move onto the estate. In the meantime, Claire decided if she were to oversee a 6,000 acre estate, then she needed to know her staff. It was much easier than her first move to this property. This time, she was the mistress of the house, not some woman being held prisoner in the upstairs suite. The entire staff was new. The only original remaining member of Tony's staff was Eric, and he worked for Tony—not Claire. Since Tony always drove to see Nichol, Claire rarely saw Eric.

Each evening after dinner, Tony would pick Claire up at the estate and drive to the Vandersols. In the beginning, everyone was present. With time, John, Emily, and Michael made excuses to leave Tony, Claire, and Nichol alone. It was as the child psychologist predicted—day by day—Nichol's comfort level with her parents increased. After their visits, Tony would take Claire back to the estate and go to his apartment. There was no reason to discuss or argue—the decision was made, and the conversation was over.

After a week, the Vandersols brought Nichol to the estate. It didn't take long for her to find the treasure of toys and clothes awaiting her in her new room. The psychologist recommended one more week of visits before the final move. Nichol seemed to be adapting well.

Two staff positions remained open on the estate which Tony asked Claire to fill personally. The first was a nanny. Over the course of many days, Claire interviewed potential caregivers. Finally, she decided on a younger woman named Shannon. Granted, the grandmotherly types were experienced, but each one reminded her of Catherine in some way. She felt much better with Shannon.

The second position Claire needed to fill was the head of the estate's security. At first, Claire protested about the need—Tony reassured her there had always been a security team on the estate. Regardless of a decreased threat level, people in their position were always in need of security. Thinking about Nichol, Claire acquiesced. After the fourth interview, Claire realized who she wanted, and it wasn't one of the names listed on her paper. That night when Tony arrived to take her to Nichol, she told him, "I know who I want as head of my security. I just don't know how to contact him."

"You were supposed to get a list with numbers. Was one missing?"

"No, I don't want anyone from that list. I want Phillip Roach."

Tony's look of surprise quickly morphed into his new constant expression of indifference. "He isn't the type of man to leave a forwarding address. I don't know if he can be reached. Besides, the people on that list have been prescreened. Any one of them will do nicely—"

Claire interrupted, "I don't *want* one of them."

"Why do you want Roach?"

"I know him, and I feel comfortable with him," Claire argued her point with conviction. "With all the new people working around me, I'd like some familiarity."

"Anyone can become familiar after time."

"Tony, you said I could have anything I want. I want *him*."

He didn't offer further protest. This time, Claire had closed the conversation. She wanted Phil, and Tony would find him.

During her days before Nichol's arrival, Claire learned her way around the responsibilities of her new home. She also enjoyed outings with Meredith, Courtney, or Sue. There were even times she'd get in her new car and drive. It wasn't that she wanted to go anyplace in particular. It was more the validation of knowing she could. Years ago, when she'd made her requests, they all came with the same stipulation—each freedom required authorization. Although she remembered hating that domination, the complete opposite didn't make her happy either. Each time she drove through the gates, she realized, no one knew or cared where she was going.

Her only obligation, other than evenings with Nichol and their sessions with the child psychologist, was her outpatient counseling sessions. Twice a week, she drove the thirty plus minutes to Everwood. Although an essential rule of therapy was complete honesty, Claire never mentioned her and Tony's living arrangements. Only Meredith and Courtney knew the truth. Perhaps it was her reluctance to discuss it at length. Her friends heard her brief explanation and mercifully accepted it at face value. The counselor would want to know her *feelings* and *thoughts*. Claire didn't want to admit those to herself much less someone else.

She didn't want to admit that Tony's placid stare hurt not only her pride, but her ever crumbling heart. From their first meeting at the Red Wing there'd been a hunger in his eyes. When he first brought her to the estate, that hunger frightened her and filled her with a sense of vulnerability and defenselessness. It was as if his eyes told of a need that only she could fill. To someone with no knowledge of what that need might include, it was a daunting assignment. With time, the hunger became comforting. No matter how much money or success Tony obtained, there was part of him that sought what only she could give. In a world of opulence, it made her feel needed and desired. That same hunger pulled her back into his arms, bed, and life when their reconciliation was only a charade. While on the island, the ravenous hunger transformed. No longer were his attentions divided, yet at no time did she feel unwanted. Through the years, when she saw him across the room, she'd look into his eyes and know he was thinking of her. Just one look, one glance and her insides would tighten—most of the time, she *knew* before she *saw*. His black eyed gaze could reach out and touch her, even without visual confirmation. Now, the look was gone—his eyes were neutral—void of emotion. Unless they were with Nichol, the color wasn't black and it wasn't light. With each glance into the tranquil pools of brown, another piece of her heart broke.

It's the repetition of affirmations that leads to belief.

And once that belief becomes a deep conviction, things begin to happen.

—Muhammad Ali

CHAPTER 51

Privately, Tony and Claire spoke superficially discussing staff concerns and weather. Their only sincere talks involved Nichol. That was until the night before Nichol's move. Claire decided she wanted to show Tony something. She didn't expect a consequence for her compliance; nevertheless, he'd told her there was something she needed to do—something she needed to face. Claire wanted him to know, she'd done it.

Following their nightly visit with Nichol, driving up the winding estate drive, Claire asked, "Do you need to leave right away?"

"I have some work back at the office."

"It's after 9:00 PM. Can't it wait until tomorrow? I have something I'd like to show you."

"I can't stay long."

It wasn't enthusiastic, but nonetheless, he'd acquiesced. Silently, they entered her home. Claire went from room to room turning on lights. Tony trailed a few steps behind, looking around each open space. It was his first time inside the house since Nichol's visit. While she and the Vandersols were present, he did a stellar performance, pretending it was his home too.

This house wasn't as large as the former dwelling; therefore, most of the members of the staff lived in another building on the estate. The only exception was Shannon who now had a room near Nichol's. Finding each room empty, Tony asked, "Why isn't someone from the staff here?"

"I gave Shannon the night off, since Nichol is moving in tomorrow, and the rest of the staff is done for the day."

Tony shook his head. "What do you mean *done*? They should be here so that you don't come home to an empty house."

"That's ridiculous. Phil's familiarizing himself with the security and obviously there was a guard at the gate. I'm a big girl."

He didn't argue; however, Tony's posture revealed his displeasure with the way she was overseeing the staff. Claire wanted to say, *if you lived here you could do it differently, but since you don't, it's my decision*. Although the sentence was on the tip of her tongue, she reminded herself of the reason for her invitation and swallowed the words. Baiting him into an argument wasn't her goal; nevertheless, she couldn't help the slight bit of sarcasm as she motioned toward the kitchen and said, "Since there's no one here to wait on you, help yourself to something to drink. The thing I want to show you is upstairs. I'll be back down in a minute."

Earlier in the week, her belongings had arrived from Everwood. She'd been through some of it, but she hadn't opened all the boxes. What she wanted to show Tony was still packed away. Honestly, she hadn't been sure she'd be brave enough to ask him to stay and see it, but on the drive home, she decided if she were to do it—it should happen before Nichol's move.

Hurriedly, Claire searched box after box. Aware of her internal time clock, she didn't want to make Tony wait too long. When she reached the bottom of the last box, Claire found what she'd sought. From the surface, they didn't appear to be anything special—your garden variety spiral notebooks; however, both she and Tony had learned years ago that things weren't always as they appeared. As she freed the notebooks from the other items, she *felt* Tony behind her.

He hadn't touched her, but her increased pulse told her he was there. For the first time since the day of his divorce declaration, every fiber of her body surged with electricity. Without turning, she said, "I'm sorry it took so long. I thought I knew where they were."

Trying to remain unaffected by the familiar, yet recently unaccustomed feeling, Claire stood. When their eyes met, she fought to breathe—her lungs momentarily needing direction—inhaling took effort. Determined to stay strong, she looked directly into Tony's black eyes as unbridled hunger consumed her. The intensity of the gaze staring back at her instantly reminded Claire of her captor—not the one who took her body—the one who took her heart. Pretending to remain aloof, she pressed forward and presented her notebooks. "Here they are."

∞∞∞∞∞∞∞

He tried to subdue the hunger boiling within him. As he watched her walk bravely toward him, he felt the intensity behind his eyes grow. Reaching for the notebooks, he asked, "What are these?"

"My compartments."

Tony opened the top notebook. "Your compartments? What do you...?" His words trailed as he began to read—

I suppose I should start in the beginning—March 2010. No, that wasn't when I was born. It was when I began to live. Most people think I'm crazy—maybe I am. You see I began to live, the day my life was taken away. Funny, I don't remember how it happened. I do know now, it never could've been stopped. Anthony Rawlings wanted me. If I've learned one lesson in my life—and believe me, I've learned many—Anthony Rawlings always got what he wanted.

I can't explain how it happened. I can't explain how I fell deeply and madly in love with a man who did what Anthony did—but I did! These feelings have been discounted by multiple people: family, doctors, and counselors to name a few. They've told me, my love wasn't and isn't real. They say I'm a victim of abuse, and as such, I don't understand the difference between love and applied behavior. How can that be true? If I don't know my own feelings, how can anyone else?

These people haven't lived my life. For the sake of my sanity, I need to know my feelings are and were real. I'll always and forever, love and be in love with Anthony Rawlings!

It didn't start that way. There was a time I both hated and feared him. When I say he took my life, I'm not being dramatic. One day I was Claire Nichols, a twenty-six-year-old, out of work meteorologist, working as a bartender to make ends meet, and the next day, I was his. He owned me. He bought my body, a commodity I never intended to sell, and while, with time, he earned my heart and soul, the transaction began with no transition and no introduction—just a brutal initiation.

I'll never condone the things he did to me, nor will I deny them. They are a part of us, building blocks of our foundation. Some would argue that a foundation built on kidnapping, isolation, violence, and yes—even rape—would never stand. I must disagree. We lived through hell and came out the other side. Like the song says, what doesn't kill you makes you stronger. I can't imagine anyone having a stronger foundation than ours. It sustained us when the storms of life and vengeance threatened our very being. Not only did it make "us" stronger, it made each of us stronger. Most importantly—it made Nichol.

I've come to terms with the fact that Tony is gone. No one will say his name, much less discuss his tragic death, and I know why. It's because I killed him. It truly was an accident. An ironic term as you'll learn; however, as I ponder these thoughts, I can't help but find it strangely parallel—he took my life, and I took his.

The people here want me to get better. I don't think I can do that without acknowledging how I got to this place, and how I killed the man I love.

I'm doing this, recalling the worst and best times of my life for one reason: Nichol.

For months, even years, I was content to live in a world that didn't exist. Truthfully, I wasn't cognizant of being anywhere. Day after day, night after night, I lived with memories of the strong, controlling, domineering, loving, tender, romantic man who made my life worth living—who validated my existence. It wasn't until recently that I even realized I'd gone away. Some days, I wish I could go back, but I can't. I now remember I have a daughter who needs me. I won't let her down. I must distance myself from fantasy and focus on reality.

The memories that will sustain me as I face a lonely life are of our few months together as a family. I'll learn to go on alone. Despite the opinions of others, I've faced equally greater challenges and lived to talk about them. I will survive this. While I do, I'll be comforted in knowing that no one else has ever loved as completely or has been as loved, as I have been by Anthony Rawlings.

CONVICTED

Someday, I hope I can explain to our daughter the man her father became; however, until I admit the man he was—the man whose eyes burnt my soul—before those eyes found the light—I can't relish the man I lost.

So here I go. I've lived this story, and I've told this story. Now, I'm going to try to do both, because without reliving it, even in my mind, I can't possibly explain that I'm not crazy...

I met Anthony Rawlings March 15, 2010. That night I worked the 4:00PM to close shift at the Red Wing in Atlanta. He came up to the bar and sat down. I remember thinking...

Tony peeled his eyes away from the page. This was so much different than reading her official typed statement. This contained Claire's raw emotions—in her handwriting. He wasn't reading—he was listening. Fluttering the pages of all four notebooks, he noticed every page of every book was filled with writing. Glancing up, he saw Claire leaning against the wall, her arms folded over her chest watching him. Her stoic expression failed to reveal her thoughts; however, in her eyes—her damn green eyes—he saw the fire he'd missed. The one he'd doused too many times, most recently with his talk of divorce.

He truly thought she'd pushed their past away, glorified him in some unhealthy, undeserving way, yet on these pages, she'd recounted everything, and despite it all, she proclaimed unyielding love. Her words were correct, especially when she wrote, *Anthony Rawlings wanted me.* Tony didn't realize how much at the time, but he did. The shrink at the prison helped him see that the terrible things he did—and he did some awful things—were his way of keeping her away—keeping her at a distance. He never intended to become emotionally attached. Blame it on anything from his past—there was no excuse for his behaviors. Anthony Rawlings never anticipated being emotionally vested in anyone. The psychologist also said, *no one* can come back from that kind of relationship. It can never be healthy. *Is that what her therapist said too? Could they all be wrong? Could they be the one-in-a-million?*

Staring into Claire's eyes, Tony fought the urge to touch her, comfort her, and apologize for ever thinking they should be apart. Once again, his desires overwhelmed him. The self-control he'd elicited for the last two weeks dissipated with each beat of his heart. If he'd truly wanted to maintain their distance, then he never should've walked up the stairs. He wanted her more than he wanted life. *How did he ever think he could let her go?*

∞∞∞∞∞∞

Claire waited. She wondered how he'd react—what he'd say. She hadn't read that notebook in a while, but she knew it was the first one—the one explaining why she wrote everything down. Tony told her she needed to face their past. She wanted him to see—she had. She'd faced every minute. Although he hadn't said a word, his eyes pulled her in. She wouldn't look away—she couldn't. At the sight of the familiar black gleam, her insides tightened to a painful pitch.

The temperature surrounding them warmed as his unrelenting stare bore through her. Claire felt heat radiate from every molecule within the room. While maintaining their unbroken gaze, he laid the notebooks on the dresser. The only reason she wanted to show him the notebooks was to show him that she'd already obeyed his directive. Besides, she reasoned—*she'd told him to stay downstairs. This overwhelming sensation of lust wasn't what she had planned.* Her mind fought her body. He'd already rejected her. She couldn't bear to have him do it again, yet without thinking, her feet moved his direction.

Did he move forward too? She didn't know. Somehow, they were mere inches apart.

Willing herself to stop, Claire broke their gaze and looked down. Seconds later, she felt the warmth of his finger and thumb lifting her chin, forcing her eyes to meet his. Obstinately, she lifted her chin, but kept her eyes shut.

The rich baritone voice commanded, "Open your eyes. Look at me."

Tipping her forehead against his broad chest, she inhaled. His cologne filled her senses as she mumbled, "I can't."

She felt his words rumble from his chest. "Look at me"—it wasn't a request—"I want to see your damn eyes—now!"

"Please, please, Tony—don't. I can't take another rejection—not from you."

Lifting her face, his lips brushed hers just before his words softened and he asked, "Why did you show me that?"

He hadn't released her chin when her eyes finally opened. Looking up, she knew, despite her claims to the contrary, not only did he control her chin—he controlled her heart. "So that you'd know...I *have* faced our past—multiple times. Even knowing that past, I wanted a future."

His words dripped with heat, each one blowing a warm breeze against her cheeks, "*Wanted?* Past tense?"

She wanted to say, no, I *want*, but she'd been hurt too many times. Her indignation rose. "*You* don't want me!"—"You left me in the Iowa jail!"—"You told me two weeks ago you wanted a divorce!"—"I can't live in a fantasy! You don't want me"—"or a future with me!"—with each phrase, her volume grew—"let go of my chin and stop pretending!"

∞∞∞∞∞∞

He obeyed her demand and released her chin; however, relinquishing his hold wasn't even feasible. Forcing her to keep her face tilted toward his, Tony slid his hand to the back of her neck, while his other hand wrapped around her petite frame. He didn't think or reason as his lips captured hers.

For two weeks, he'd tried to let her go. He'd wanted to release her and give her the freedom she deserved—the freedom he'd taken away so many years ago, but—each day, each hour, each minute, each second—was agony. When Tony wasn't near Claire—he thought about her. When he was near her—his energy was devoted to fighting his desire. It was exhausting. With his lips against hers, he no longer wanted to fight. His chest pushed against her, moving them, step by step, until they were flush with the wall. His needs intensified as he felt the sensation of her breasts against him. He told himself to stop—he was no good for her—but he didn't listen—he couldn't. Unapologetically, his tongue penetrated her lips, and his grasp pulled her hips against his.

∞∞∞∞∞∞

Momentarily, Claire's fists pushed in protest. Soon, she realized resistance was futile—mostly because—she didn't want to fight. His actions had her on the verge of forgetting any reasonable arguments. All she wanted was the present, then Tony's voice rumbled like thunder, and his fist pounded the wall above her head, "I told you before, I've *never* pretended to love you! I do love you! That's *present* tense!"

While the wall vibrated, she watched the illuminations of darkness dance through his eyes. *She'd wanted to see emotion and now she had it!* Before she could respond, his body pinned her against the wall. The scent of cologne mixed with musk overpowered her olfactory senses. Her body liquefied at the sensation of his lips and hands. She heard the sound of her own heart beating as the rush of blood pulsated too quickly through her veins. Soon, their ragged breaths filled her ears, and she fought to regain the breath he'd taken. Her body was mindlessly responding to his touch as his desires became more pronounced and her moans echoed through their large suite.

Before long, he led her to the bed, and her world tilted as he followed her onto the mattress. Her body ached for everything he could offer, but her mind couldn't take another disappointment. While his hands found their way under her blouse, she found the strength to speak, "Stop." When he didn't respond, she repeated herself, louder, "I said, stop!"

She saw the pain in his expression as he pushed himself away.

Rolling out from under him, she exclaimed, "You need to go. I can't do this. I won't let you hurt me again."

"Claire, don't you understand?"—The emotion in his voice stilled her movements, as well as her speech—"That's why I wanted a divorce. I don't want to hurt you and—and I can't take it again, either. You talk about me leaving you at the jail and this divorce"—he stammered—"W—what about you?"

387

Claire stood and stared in disbelief as Tony paced beside the bed. His unbuttoned shirt allowed a clear view of his still muscular chest. "Me?" she asked. "What about me?"

"You left *me*. *You* drove away from *me—twice*! You don't think I don't remember that every damn time you drive away from this estate?" His hand ran through his salt and pepper hair as he fought his words. "The other day when you were gone for over three hours and driving around Bettendorf—of all places—I was scared to death that you're considering doing it again."

Claire's knees buckled as she sunk onto the bed and stared incredulously. Her words came slowly, "What do you mean...the other day? How did you know that I was in Bettendorf?"

"Claire, *they* say we're no good for one another, but your notebooks—you said you still loved me after everything—is that still true?"

Now standing, Claire stared up into her husband's face and moved closer. "Answer me. What do you know about my comings and goings?"

He closed his eyes and exhaled. "The reason I didn't want Roach working for you, was"—he hesitated—"he'd been working for me since the day you came home."

Claire's eyes filled with moisture. They weren't angry tears—although perhaps they should've been—they were happy tears. Her voice was barely a whisper, "Why? Tell me why you've had Phil following me."

He gripped her shoulders. "You have every right to be angry. That's fine, but I'm not sorry. I worry—I'll always worry. I don't want anything to happen to you—ever again." His words came fast. "I don't really care *that* you go—I just need to know that you're safe."

Slowly, she turned away and found her seat on the edge of the bed. From somewhere deep, she tried to summon a mask—any mask—but they were all beyond her reach. Her emotions were real and her expression transparent.

Tony knelt beside her. "Please, tell me what you're thinking."

Claire shook her head. "I don't know—there are so many things." Her voice quivered as she searched for the right words. "I—I've been asked over and over, why I didn't try to escape from you in 2010 when I had opportunities." Tony's eyes reflected the pain coming from her words. Claire went on, "When I tell the story about us, and talk about shopping or the symphony—they tell me I *should have* run or told someone. I didn't"—she inhaled—"because I was afraid—I was afraid that if I did, and failed, you'd punish me—hurt me." Claire watched the torment grow in her husband's expression. Framing his face in her hands, she continued, "That physical pain I feared was nothing—nothing compared to the pain of thinking you no longer cared. These last two weeks have been hell. They taught me that pain can be present, despite every physical need being met."

Small pools of moisture teetered on Tony's lower lids. "The divorce wasn't meant to *hurt* you."

She reached out and hugged his neck; her lips brushed his. "Tony, maybe I should be upset that you've had me followed, but I'm not. Honestly, I'm relieved—I didn't think you cared anymore."

His eyes shimmered while the tips of his lips curved into his signature devilish grin. Pushing her back against the mattress, Tony covered her body with his and replied, "Mrs. Rawlings, I will *always* care and *always* love you. I promised you that almost six years ago."

This time, she didn't protest as his weight held her to the soft satin comforter. Removing his shirt from his broad shoulders, Tony added, "I've told you. I am—and despite it all, I continue to be—a man of my word."

Claire watched his chest expand and contract. Unconsciously, her fingers threaded through the soft chest hair, which, too, had lightened with the addition of intermingling gray. As her hands caressed his warm muscles, any thought of age slipped from her mind. Her only thought was of his skin against hers. They were two pieces of a larger puzzle that fit perfectly together. Without their union, the puzzle would be forever incomplete.

The sensation of his lips trailing across her exposed collarbone as his fingers unbuttoned her blouse, incited goose bumps on her arms and her legs. Claire yearned to be closer—to have him inside of her and though every fiber of her body wanted what only he could give, she needed to know more. Finding her voice, she asked, "If we do this—if we reunite—can I trust you not to leave me again?"

"I wanted to protect you. The divorce was only to keep you from being hurt—by me."

"Don't you see?"—her questioning stopped Tony's seduction—"Not being with you—hurt me. Every day hurt more than the one before."

Tony nodded. "It was agony. When I was in prison and we were separated by distance, it sounded good in principle, but seeing you"—he lifted his head and looked down at her now nearly naked body—"and touching you"—the tips of his fingers softly trailed the warm flesh from her collarbone down to the band of her lace panties—"and not being allowed to taste you." His lips seized a now exposed nipple and gently tugged while his tongue swirled the hardening nub, eliciting moans Claire didn't know she'd articulated—"Was agony."

Her breath quickened as the stubble of his beard prickled her skin. Unabashed, Claire wanted the kind of agony that only he could provide. Arching her back, she exposed her breasts for more of his delicious torture. While she still had the ability to speak, she murmured, "First—first, I have a request."

His mischievous grin caused Claire's muscles—the ones deep inside that had yet to be touched—to tighten. With a raised eyebrow, he quipped, "Yes? I think I might like this. Does it involve black satin?"

Fighting the carnal desire, she snickered. "No." Trying to focus, she replied, "I want you to promise that you won't leave me, no more talk of divorce—ever. I want my *happily ever after*. Despite everything, I trust you *and* your word. If you tell me you'll never divorce me or discuss it—I'll believe you."

His baritone pitch resonated throughout their suite and deep into her soul as he spoke between kisses to her exposed skin. "You, my dear, are my drug. I'm so damn addicted"—"I can't quit you"—"I know, because I've tried—not for me—but for you"—"I failed miserably"—"The more I have of you—the more I need"—"I can never get enough"—"If you'll have me back—*after all, this is your estate*"—"If you'll allow me to move back, I'll try every day to give you exactly what you deserve"—"And I promise I will *never* mention divorce again."

Claire pulled his face toward hers. Their kiss lingered as his fingers continued to roam, each move delving lower and lower. His promise returned color to her world—she was his, and he was hers. Her nails bit into his shoulders as he teased and electrified her body with taunting caresses. Breaking the spell, he looked honestly into her eyes. "I want you so badly, but I need to be honest."

Her mind whirled with the possibilities of his confession.

Tony continued, "I can't promise you the *happy ever after*." A lump formed in her throat, fearing his next words. "Not because you don't deserve one—but because I know myself, and I'll probably screw it up; however, I can promise I'll spend the rest of my life trying. Is that enough for you?"

Tears of relief cascaded from the corners of her emerald eyes. She captured him with her expression of acceptance; however, it was her words that secured the lock, "Tony, it's more than enough." Kissing his neck, she offered, "I promise that I'll never drive away to leave you again, and I'll never listen to anyone else without learning the truth from you, but"—she paused to deliver more butterfly kisses—"I *will* drive away, to multiple places." Claire waited. When he didn't argue, she continued with a smile, "And I'll travel easier knowing Phil is there—when you can't be."

Tony's approving smile lit her world—his touch kindled a smoldering passion on the brink of an out of control wildfire.

"I think we have a deal."

With a playful smile, Claire added, "Now, if you don't make love to me right this minute, I'll have you thrown off my property."

"My—Mrs. Rawlings, will my lodging payments continue to be so extreme?"

She shrugged. "I don't know. I have the rest of our lives to come up with new ideas. You know, I'm very creative and let me warn you—the payments will be daunting—I hope you're up for it."

His dark chocolate eyes liquefied into molten pools of brown, glistening above his signature devilish grin, as he said, "I believe that you know that I am—and Mrs. Rawlings, I look forward to your challenges. Apparently, only you can decide whether I make the cut."

Claire's eyes fluttered as her body quaked in anticipation. Gripping his shoulders, she whispered, "Don't disappoint me—there *will* be consequences."

The bond that links your true family is not one of blood,

but of respect and joy in each other's life.

—Richard Bach

EPILOGUE

The aroma of sea filled the air as a gentle breeze brought the sound of the surf into the large living room. Madeline's smile reflected the mood of the occasion. It had been years since she'd had so many people on the island. By the glow in her big brown eyes, her heart was as full as the house. The little baby she'd helped bring into the world was a beautiful little girl with large brown eyes—soft as suede and filled with joy –just like her father's.

Claire held tightly to her sister's hand as they both watched Tony place their grandmother's pearl necklace around Nichol's neck.

"Look, Momma! Look, Aunt Em! Isn't it pretty?" Nichol exclaimed as she spun toward them, exposing her precious gift. Turning back, she wrapped her small arms around Tony's neck. "Thank you, Daddy!"

As Tony swung their daughter into his arms, Claire let go of Emily's hand and walked toward Nichol. Kissing her cheek, Claire replied, "It sure is, honey; this necklace means a lot to Mommy—and Daddy"—Claire's eyes shifted momentarily to Tony's as the emerald glistened with memories only the two of them shared—"So," she continued to Nichol—"it's only for special occasions. A long time ago, it belonged to Aunt Em and Mommy's grandmother—your great-grandmother."

"Is today a special occasion?" Nichol asked.

"It sure is!" Tony exclaimed. "It's your third birthday. I don't think anything is more special than that!"

Claire leaned closer as Tony wrapped one arm around his wife and held tight to their daughter. Their group hug had the attention of everyone in the room—John, Emily, Michael, Brent, Courtney, Maryn, Caleb, Julia, Meredith,

Jerry, their children, Madeline, and Francis. Undoubtedly, it was a *full house* and would be until after Christmas.

Tony and Claire couldn't think of a better way to thank all of the people who'd worked to keep their daughter safe and helped to make their world right. Truly, it was an unlikely assembly—one brought together against all odds. Some might say that, at one time, this assembly would've been considered improbable—maybe even impossible; however, as everyone rejoiced and wished Nichol a happy birthday, they were a family—united with unbreakable bonds.

Their ties had gone through the fires of hell and come out stronger—refined by the flames—not consumed; nevertheless, the safety of their family would never be taken for granted. That was why Eric and Phil where outside, patrolling the shores and watching the skies. Phil had updated the security, both at the estate and on the island. He and Tony both told Claire it was only a precaution. After all, Catherine was in the Iowa State Penitentiary and would be for a long time; however, even Claire realized there would always be threats. The Rawlings were wealthy people, and despite Claire's dislike for fame, their money would forever make them possible targets. There was no measure Tony or Claire wouldn't be willing to endure to insure the safety of their family—*all of them.*

∞∞∞∞∞∞

Phil looked at the text message and shook his head.

"Did something else arrive?" Eric asked.

"Yes, this one's also addressed to *Nichol Rawls.* This time, it came with a birthday gift."

"Has it been opened?"

"Not yet; it has to be scanned to be sure there aren't any explosives."

Eric stiffened his neck. "So far, the only clue we've had was that one of the envelopes was sealed with female DNA—the feds have ruled out Catherine London."

"That isn't enough. Maybe we'll get more on this one." Phil squared his shoulders and looked out toward the crystal blue sea. "I believe it goes without saying—I'd have no problem getting rid of this threat once she's identified, and I think we both know who the most likely candidate is."

Eric nodded. "After Mr. Rawlings had her fired, it was as if she dropped off the face of the earth."

"I still support his decision."

"As do I," Eric said with pride. "You'd think she'd be smarter than to rehash this shit."

"I'd go all-in that she's the sender of these little reminders."

Eric's lips formed a straight line. "Next to me, she worked the closest with Mr. Rawlings—for many years."

"Yeah, she'd certainly know their history. The thing is, I'm not sure if she's a real physical threat or if she's just trying to upset Claire"—Phil squared his shoulders—"Either way, when her identity's confirmed, I promise she won't be around long enough to stand trial. No one will put them through that again. Besides, there isn't a person I can't find."

"Hmm," Eric murmured. There was no reason to confirm Phil's statement; their understanding transcended words. As unlikely as the assembly was up in the big house, so was their intimate family; nevertheless, that was what they were—a family, and Eric and Phil knew the truth. They would do anything within their power to keep their *full house* consequence free.

-THE END-

-NEXT, LEARN THE STORY BEHIND THE STORY—FROM

BEHIND HIS EYES-

-A NOTE FROM ALEATHA-

Dear Readers,

Thank you! Thank you for joining me on this journey.

Tony and Claire's story is complete. I'd like to imagine their life together as one filled with the ups and downs of marriage, parenthood, and life's other challenges. I don't believe that each day was easy or that they didn't face other hurdles. I do believe they overcame. I do believe that they were truly—the one in a million—the ones who, with the support of one another, as well as family and friends, were able to overcome insurmountable odds.

They were the ones who played the games and won!

It brings a smile to my face to imagine the scene where a young man arrives onto the Rawlings estate to take Nichol on her first date. The eyes that meet that young man at the door undoubtedly won't be those of an employee. I foresee a very overprotective father with a warning dark gaze.

There may be more Consequences to tell; however, when it comes to these characters, I'll leave it up to your imagination. Just know, it does end—and as they say—they lived happily ever after!

Aleatha

CONVICTED

BEHIND HIS EYES:

CONSEQUENCES

TRUTH

CONVICTED

THE CONSEQUENCES SERIES READING COMPANIONS

Books #4, 5, and 6 of the CONSEQUENCES Series

You've experienced the CONSEQUENCES, you've learned the TRUTH, now you know who was CONVICTED...the time has come to see it from TONY'S point of view!

Each novella will be a collection of significant scenes, from each book, of the Consequences Series. These will *not* be full length novels and won't retell the entire series—*only* significant scenes, and because you asked for it...Behind His Eyes will also contain timelines and family trees.

It has been said that to truly understand a person, one must walk a mile in their shoes. BEHIND HIS EYES will be the rare opportunity to step into Anthony Rawlings' Gucci loafers and experience the Consequences from his perspective.

BEHIND HIS EYES

The tragic or the humorous is a matter of perspective.
—Arnold Beisser

COMING SOON

-ALEATHA ROMIG-

Aleatha Romig was voted #1 *New Author to Read* on Goodreads in September of 2012 and hit the best seller's list in June of 2013! Writing has always been her dream. She has lived most of her life in Indiana—growing-up in Mishawaka, graduating from Indiana University, and currently living south of Indianapolis. Together with her husband of twenty seven years, they've raised three children. Before becoming a full-time author, she worked days as a dental hygienist and enjoyed spending her nights writing. When she isn't spinning twisted tales—she enjoys spending time with her family, friends, and readers. Her pastimes include: exercising, reading, writing, and wine. (Not in that order!)

Aleatha enjoys traveling—especially when a beach is involved! In 2011, she had the opportunity to visit Sydney, Australia, to visit her daughter studying at the University of Wollongong. Her dream is to travel to places in her novels and around the world.

CONSEQUENCES—her first novel, was released in August of 2011. TRUTH, Book #2 of the CONSEQUENCES Series, was released in October 2012. The final installment, CONVICTED, Book #3 of the CONSEQUENCES Series will be released in October of 2013. Watch for BEHIND HIS EYES *The Consequences Series Reading Companion*, to be released in the future.

-SHARE YOUR THOUGHTS-

Please share your thoughts about Convicted on:
  *Amazon, *CONVICTED by Romig*, Customer Reviews
  *Barnes & Noble, *CONVICTED by Romig*, Customer Reviews
  *Goodreads.com/Aleatha Romig

-STAY CONNECTED WITH ALEATHA-

"Like" Aleatha Romig @ http://www.Facebook.com/AleathaRomig to learn the latest information regarding Truth, Convicted, Behind his Eyes, and other writing endeavors. And, "Follow" @aleatharomig on Twitter!
Email Aleatha: aleatharomig@gmail.com /
Check out her blog: http://aleatharomig.blogspot.com